The E

By
Khalilah Smith

Cover Design and Illustration by Bozee

Penny
Thanks for your
help
Khalilah
OC

This book is a work of fiction. Although events and places may be real, all characters and the storyline are completely fiction. Any similarities to actual people are simply coincidental.

ISBN# 0-9767834-0-1

Printed in the United States by Morris Publishing
3212 East Highway 30
Kearney, NE 68847
1-800-650-7888

Dedication

To my children, Julian, Bobbi, and Robert Jr., you give me the will……..

To all of you reading this book, I want to thank you for the support. I also want to advise you that this creation was truly grass root, from the typesetting to the editing. I did my best to give you the best. However please forgive any errors that may have occurred, this was a learning experience.

Thank You

First and foremost I want to give honor and glory to my lord and savior Jesus Christ. All things are possible through you. Thank you for all my blessings, especially the one's we tend to take for granted, like family.....

To my three angels, my children, thank you for inspiring me. Thanks for having patience with me when I was in the zone (writing), and you needed my attention. You are truly my greatest accomplishment.

To my husband, thanks for being you. You were the driving force behind making this happen in more ways than you know. I hope you realize now that, although art imitates life, it doesn't mean it's our life. Pick up the pom-poms baby!

To my mom and dad, you are the best example of Black love, hard work and survival. Thanks for always supporting my dreams. Please don't pull out any old letters and poems I wrote you if I blow up. I love you ...

To my sister, do you believe this? Who would have thought it when I was writing break-up poems for you for old boyfriends back in the day? On the real, I have always looked up to you, you were one of the few women from our neighborhood that stayed above our environment. Thanks for introducing me to the Essence Festival.

To my brothers:

-My oldest brother, thank you for sharing in the love of writing and for all the information on self publishing. It's your time too, so let's do it!

-My other older brother, my twin although you are two years older than I, thanks for all the trouble you got me into and out of growing up. We were just some hood kids trying to do it big. All experiences bring wisdom and I am so wise now!

-My little brother, you are probably one of the smartest people I know but life is all about the chances we take and the choices we make. You are still young enough to take this world by storm.

To my cousin, my road dog, my crib mate, thank you for asking me everyday, "how's the book going" even when you knew I hadn't wrote in weeks. Thank you for keeping me supplied with every Black book that comes out. A special thanks for typing this entire manuscript (reading my chicken scratch), for editing, and for listening to my ideas in the middle of the night. You are the queen of M.S.H.! You know the deal, this book would not be, without you. I am forever in debt.

Writing this book was a journey filled with good and bad days. I am most thankful for the blue days, they really pushed me through this project.

To the city of Oakland, you helped raise me and you will always be home. To all of my family and friends, thanks for all the love and support. To all the people I've told over the years that I would hook them up when my ship comes in, get ready to head to the port. It's our time!

Extra shot out to Bozee for the cover design.

I'll blame it on the heat, the alcohol, the vibe of Essence that had me all fucked up in this individual's presence

I'm talking high school giggles, bubble guts butterflies scared to look you in the face because the truth is in the eyes.
Ready to tell you my life story straight up no lies. It wasn't nothing about your physical that had me mesmerized
Maybe some Louisiana voodoo had me hypnotized but I believe it was your being...

(And) Since you're a man, I know you you would have jumped at the chance for a little less talk and a little more romance since conversation didn't attract you, it was me in 'dem' white pants but as we sat on separate couches you were a perfect gentleman.

We sat up and exchanged our hood stories
All of our bad & good stories
Only those who been through somethings could understood stories
Then night became day

So it's time to depart, and here's the case
Do I give you a pound, or hug and embrace
Wondering if you read the awkwardness written on my face
So I give a dry goodbye

So now do I chalk this up as something that woulda, could've, should have never been
Someone with a kind heart and an ear to lend

Someone that 7 years ago could have been
a good friend
Or is my heavenly father testing me.

Weekend over, back to reality, seems so
easy to do
But every song that reminds me of Essence
reminds me of you
"To the window to the Wall" is on all the
time

It's crazy how something that feels so right
just can't be
My husbands a good man, and my children
need me
And how I know that things happen without
reason or rhyme
So I look forward to meeting you in my next
lifetime

"Bitch, this fucking car can't go any faster! Where's your car?"

"Well when I rented it, I didn't plan on using it as a getaway car. I got the $9.99 Enterprise special. Ray's crazy sister put sugar in my tank because she saw me on a date."

"You went on a date? Well anyway, bitch I need to get to Alameda County Jail-Santa Rita quick. Can you turn that damn music down, I'm trying to figure some shit out."

"Firstly, call me one more bitch and I'm taking you back to the Highland hospital. Matter of fact, I'll take you right to the police station. Secondly, visiting days are on Thursday and Sunday, so we are wasting our time. And, last of all, this is my theme music so, no I can't turn it down. Mary J. Blige be trying to school you sisters, so figure that shit out!"

"Nigga, is 'firstly' a word?"

"Oh, now the sinning, hospital fugitive want to be educated."

"Why is it so much traffic on 580 on a Saturday"

"I think the A's have a game, something called the Bay Battle."

"It's called the 'Battle of the Bay,' it's when the A's play the Giants. I completely forgot due to being sleep for a week."

"I knew you would know about that sports shit, it seems like that's what got you into trouble. Do you have a baseball player too?"

"That's fucked up Kim." I responded.

"Well since we're stuck in traffic, how in the hell did you get yourself into this mess?"

"Kim, girl it's a long story but it all started at the Essence Festival………..

Quarter 1
Chapter 1

"Mya, I am not about to stand in that long ass cab line I'm just about to get us a limo."

"Oh Sonya, baller, baller, all of us ain't blessed to have the NFL as our husband." Mya replied.

"Well Bitch, you just as well, because it ain't like you paying for this shit either." I was getting a bit irritated by the constant hating from my older sister. Many had told me she was envious of how my life had turned out, a husband who was a prominent running back in the NFL, four beautiful children, body still banging, a master's degree and I was four years Mya's junior. I was always the hoody of the family, hung in the hood, dated hood niggas, basically soaked up the environment we were raised in. Mya on the other hand never really experienced the lows of living in West Oakland, she disassociated herself, so how did her sister end up living the good life.

"Anyway, Mya, you know Alisha's flight came in earlier than ours and the room is in my name, she may be waiting for us in the lobby of the hotel."

"You know that girl is up under that nigga that was picking her up, I'm sure she is cool."

"You right."

"Well, regardless, I need to get some rest before tonight, I need to look good for Magic Johnson's All White Party, by the way do you have the tickets?" I asked.

"Well, I don't have to worry about that beauty rest, I look good already and no, I don't have the tickets, Alisha has them."

We shared a look of concern by the fact that Alisha had the tickets.

"Well, whatever Sonya, it's your money to spend, let's ride."

We headed to the limo stand where only one couple was ahead of them.

Before you knew it, we were pulling up at the Wyndham at Canal Place.

"You ready to take over the Big Easy, Big Sis?" I said to Mya

"Let's do it." She responded.

After generously tipping the over accommodating driver we headed up to the 11th floor of the Wyndham to the Lobby to register. In the elevator we talked about how you could feel the Southern hospitality out here from the time you exit the airplane way different from the fast living in California and Arizona where Sonya had relocated after getting married. On the elevator with us was a Black couple that look like they were in the late sixties (probably older because we age so gracefully) there was a couple of sisters that look a like they were around 21 straight out of Atlanta with burgundy hair. That was the beauty of the Essence, it's something for everyone, all ages, single, married, whatever. The one thing that was consistent everything always seemed friendly.

Essence Festival had become an annual vacation for Mya and I. This was my get away because all through football season she was alone with her children while her husband worked. Over the years different people accompanied us but the sisters always represented.

"Hey Mya, while I check-in, try to call and find out where Alisha is, let her know we're here and that we're trying to leave for the party at 10:00 so she has five hours to fall out of love and get here."

"What?" Mya replied. "Why can't you call her?"

"Whatever, Mya I'll call her."

"Alright, I'll be in the bar, get me before you go up, I'm trying to see who's in here. Oh and watch my bag okay."

"You are too much." I laughed as Mya put on her best look at my ass walk and headed towards the bar.

"Excuse me, my sista, looks like you can use some help. Damn how long are you here, a month?" The guy joked, referring to all the luggage.

"Ha ha," I laughed, "this is my sister's luggage as well as mine and yes I can use some help to the bar, my brotha." Before we could get any further, here comes Mya.

"Were you coming for me? Thank you, what was your name?" She said to the guy.

He replied, "Sorry, I'm Sam, I take it you're the sister."

"Oh I see you met my baby sister Mrs. Jackson." Mya stated making sure to let him know I was a Mrs.

"Actually," I jumped in, "we hadn't exchanged names, however he was gracious enough to assist me with your luggage. Thank you, was it Sam?"

"Yes, my name is Sam, Samuel Walters from Jackson, Mississippi."

"Bye, thank you again and oh, by the way, my name is Sonya."

Mya and I headed up in the elevator and although she was talking I couldn't hear her, I was just deep in thought, was she looking out for her brother-in-law or hating – my thoughts were interrupted by Mya calling my name.

"Sonya, Sonya, so what floor are we on?" In the midst of thought I forgot to push a button, "Oh push sixteen."

"So anyway, lil sis, that nigga was hella bamma that was trying to holla at you."

I laughed. "He wasn't trying to holla but he was bamma." We both laughed.

I thought, yeah that's my sis, she's just looking out for me! As we got off the elevator, I remembered I needed to call Alisha. I dialed her number twice, no answer. So I decided to leave a message.

"Alisha, get off your back and call me. No, don't call just be here by 10pm dressed. I'll holla," and then I hung up.

11

"Alright Mya, I'm about to get that beauty sleep for a couple, you going out?"

"Naw, though I don't need it, I'll get some beauty rest as well."

"You are stupid – good night sis.

Ring, ring, ring…..

"Mya, answer your cell phone, shit she is in the shower, damn they must really want to talk."

Ring, ring, ring….

"Hello," I answered Mya's phone.

"Hey Sonya, ya'll out here, where's your sis, wuz you sleeping?" It was our cousin Keisha, she always ran several questions together before getting an answer.

"Yes, we are here, Mya's in the shower, yes I was sleeping but I need to get up and get myself together. It's loud in the background, where ya'll at?"

"We're at the Superdome, I was trying to see if ya'll was coming to the concert tonight, you know Stevie Wonder is headlining."

"Girl, I know, but naw we ain't going, I know he's gonna turn it out. Are ya'll going to the White party?"

"You know it, we have our tickets already. I just hope I don't get nothing on this white, while I'm at the concert."

"Okay, well I'll tell Mya you called. Tell Miko I said what's up, I'll see you later. Alright, bye."

Since I was up and had some spare time since Mya was holding a monopoly on the bathroom, I needed to call and check on my babies. (It was eight here, which meant it was six in California).

~I called my mom~

Ring, ring, ring…

"Hey Mom, what ya'll up to, how's my babies?"

12

"Child, you know your kids spoiled. We just finished eating dinner, chicken, French fries and salad." As she was mentioning food, I realized I was kind of hungry. "You know Desean is stuck in front of that video game, Lamar is right up under him begging for a turn, E.J. is laying on the bed with Papa. I think he might be getting some more teeth coming in, he's a little cranky and the princess Kayla Renee' is being my super helper."

I know my mom meant too helpful because Kayla was the only girl in the family. She tended to get up under women and try to help in any way, especially being mama to E.J. who she was only four years older than.

"So Mom, are you cool, they're not too much trouble?'

"Girl, I raised six of ya'll and you turned out alright. Have you some fun, you deserve it."

"Okay, let me talk to them really quick."

"Kids, your mom is on the phone."

"Hi Mama"

"Hey Princess, you miss me?"

"Yes, I miss you, I'm helping grandma with the baby and with doing the dishes, where's aunty Mya."

"She's in the bathroom, Okay you be good. I love you."

"I love you too Mommy"

"Okay give the phone to one of your brothers"

"E.J. just went to sleep with Papa, so I'll give it to Lamar, Sean is playing Madden."

"What's up Mama?" Lamar got on the phone sounding seventeen not seven.

"Hey Tank, (he got this name as a baby because he was so big) what you doing?"

"Mama, Sean won't let me play the Playstation 2 and I've been waiting patiently."

"Okay, I'll talk to him, you being good right?"

"Yes Mom"

"Okay I love you, give Sean the phone."

"I love you too. Sean, Mama wants to talk to you." Lamar said.

13

"What took you so long to get on the phone?"

"I was trying to score a touchdown."

"Boy, don't have me slap you through this phone, anyway you need to let your brother play the game."

"I'ma let him play."

"I mean like now." I said.

"Alright, what you doing, have you seen any stars?"

"Boy, don't you know your mama is a star."

"Anyway, have you seen any real stars?"

"I'ma hurt you when I get home, but I was on the plane with Free from BET's 106 & Park and with a man from the radio name Tom Joyner , do you know who I'm talking about?"

"I don't know him, but Free was coming from Oakland?"

"No, she got on in Dallas, I had a layover."

"Did you talk to her or get her autograph?

"No"

"Aw Ma, that's cold."

"Anyway boy, I'm bout to get ready, I love you and let your brother play now. I'm gonna ask grandma too, so put her back on the phone."

"Alright Ma, I love you and have fun and tell Auntie Mya I said What up, Bye."

{He gave his grandma the phone}

"Hey Ma make sure Sean let's Tank play the game and thanks again."

"Girl, enjoy yourself and don't be calling here every hour, I told your husband the same thing when he called an hour ago, have you talked to him?"

"Not yet, but that's my next call, talk to you later, bye."

"Who you talking to?" Mya yelled from the bathroom.

"That was Mommy, I was checking on the kids. Are you finished in the bathroom?"

"Yes, for now"

"Ok, I'm gonna jump in the shower. Oh, I need to call Big Eric, oh well I'll call him when I get out. Mya can you try to call Alisha while I'm in the shower?"

"Yeah, cause it's about that time, didn't she say that nigga live outside of New Orleans, that might take at least an hour to get here."

Ring, ring, ring….

"Lisha, Lisha"

"Who is this?"

"Bitch, who you think it is, are you getting ready to leave?"

"Oh Mya you didn't sound like yourself, yeah we gone leave out in like 20 in minutes."

"Don't it take like an hour?"

"Yeah about that"

"Okay you should still be here before ten and the House of Blues is right around the corner. Alright I'll see you soon. Peace."

THE WAIT GAME

"Damn, I can't stand these damn pasties. I always waste a pack before I get my damn breast to sit up right."

"Sony, you know you are a card-carrying member of the itty bitty titty committee, so does it really matter? Don't wear any."

"I may not have much, but what I have has lost its perk. I guess breastfeeding four kids will do that."

"Whatever, just hurry up, I need you to help me tie my shirt."

"What shirt?"

"This shirt."

15

"Bitch, that is not a shirt, that is a scarf, and it's white, so what are you putting over your nipples?"

"Well this scarf is a shirt tonight and once I fold it you won't be able to see my nipples. Make sure you tie it tight. Don't want one of my puppies to fall out."

"Them boobies are full grown dogs, is that tight enough, can you breathe?"

"Okay comedian, yes it's tight and I can't breathe, but you know my motto, "beauty before pain." Mya said.

"I heard that sis, remember we used to go to the club in the winter, no coat, 'beauty before pain'." I agreed.

"Girl, the line at Geoffrey's used to be hella long, and dare a bitch to shiver. Damn Sony, them used to be the days. Remember that nigga called Alisha a bitch?"

"Do I, girl she called Taiwan and in minutes he was up at the club mopping the floor with the nigga."

"Um, God bless the dead, I miss Taiwan, he was crazy but he loved Alisha's ass." Taiwan was Alisha's high school sweetheart, her baby daddy, her man. He was killed a few years back on a fluke.

"Speaking of Alisha, shouldn't she be here. Let me call her."

{phone ringing}

"Oh, I know this girl is not playing, she ain't answering her phone."

"It ain't nothing I hate worst than getting dressed and having to sit around. Is that your phone ringing?" Mya said.

"Yeah, I don't recognize the number though. Hello---."

"Hey girl"

"Hey girl, hey girl where you at, who number is this? I know you ain't still at that nigga house?"

"No, I ain't, stop talking so loud, this is his cell phone, my battery went dead so if ya'll need to call, call this number."

"Why should I have to call, you should be here. So when you gone be here?"

16

"We'll be there in 30 minutes."

"Alright nigga, because we sitting up in here dressed and ready to go. Bye"

"Man, Sony, how we let her hold the tickets? You know how many events we been late too or missed fucking with her, that's your cousin!"

~ (Forty minutes later) ~

"Okay, I'm about ready to just come off another fifty and just go pay to get in the club, fuck them tickets."

"Man, I ain't tripping, I wish I had Eric's 'Player's Card' then we'd get VIP treatment. They need a 'Player's Wife Card'."

(Phone ringing)

"Look at my phone and see who that is." I said to Mya.

"It's a 504 number, must be Alisha, I'll answer.   Hello, where you at, we about to go."

"Don't go, I'm almost there, it was hella traffic, I'll be there in 15 minutes." Alisha pleaded.

"She says she'll be here in fifteen, what we doing?"

"Tell her we're walking down to the lobby, so don't front." I said

"Ay, Alisha, you hear that?"

"Yeah, I'll see ya'll in a minute. Alisha replied

"Now Sony, you know that bitch lying."

"Yeah, I know, but I'm tired of being in this room, so let's go downstairs and people watch. How do I look?"

"Almost as good as your big sis, it look like you got some booty in them pants. OK, I need a tittie check."

"They're cool, alright let's roll." I said

"Why do they put mirrors in these elevators, can you see my pasties?" I asked.

17

"No, you look fine. What did Keisha say when she called?"

"Oh yeah, she said they're coming after they leave the concert. She said put your phone on vibrate so you can feel it."

"I still don't understand why the lobby is on the eleventh floor, you got to take one elevator down and then get on another one." I complained.

"I know that's a little too much to think about when you're drunk."

We exited the elevator we took down from our room and walked around to get on the other elevator to go the 1st floor. As we approached the 2nd elevator a couple of guys were exiting with bags looking confused on where to go.

"Yes, this is the floor that you check-in on." I could tell that the brothas were a little confused as most people would be their first time visiting the hotel."

"Thank you, Do you work here?" One of the guys asked.

"No, I've just seen that look before."

" Oh, well thanks Ma, you all look nice in your white, what's hot tonight?"

Mya jumped in. "Thanks Pa, we're going to the Magic Johnson All White Party and we're late, So nice meeting you."

"I don't know why you're in such a rush, you know Alisha is not downstairs. They must be from New York or somewhere on the East Coast."

"Who? Oh them dudes, yeah not only from how they talk, but why do they rock Timbs with shorts, I don't get it."

"I don't know, but I like that East Coast flava, 'What up Ma, what's good'" I did my imitation of East Coast lingo. "Like I said, I knew Alisha wouldn't be down here, let's stand outside for a minute."

"Good evening ladies, can I call a taxi for you?"

"No thanks, we're just waiting on someone."

"Is this your first time at Essence?"

"No, we've been coming for the past few years. So how long have you been working here?"

"I've been working here for a couple of years, this is my part-time gig." I could hold a conversation with anyone, Mya on the other hand was looking like 'why are you talking to this minimum wage doorman.' We sat outside for about twenty minutes talking to Diondre, the doorman, but the heat/humidity was getting thick. So we decided to go sit on the bench right inside the hotel.

"Okay, on the real, how long we gon wait on this girl, because I don't have a problem leaving her." Mya said.

"Alright Mya, we gon give her 17 more minutes, I don't know why 17, it just sounds right?"

Several people walked in as we waited and we assisted them in finding where the lobby was and they all asked 'do you work here'." Some made jokes like 'Man, now I see why this hotel cost so much, two fine Black women greeting you at the door, this is the life.' Diondre came in to check on us, he then went into a door that said employees only and returned with a couple of bottles of water for us.

"Thank you," we both said.

"So what kind of car will she be in, I can let you know when she gets here."

"Thanks Diondre, but we don't know ourselves."

About 12 minutes into their 17 minutes of waiting, a group of guys walked in with one who was quite flamboyant in personality, basically he needed attention.

"Man, look like the party is right here." How are ya'll doing?" Mr. Flamboyant said.

"I'm fine." Mya stated.

"You look it." He replied (Okay how corny!) "And you?" He said to me.

"Oh, I'm good," I replied. How are you gentleman doing?" In unison, they all responded,

"Good."

"So where ya'll from?" Mya asked. Okay this is a shocker, Mya is holding a conversation and she is not drunk, she must be getting tired.

19

Mr. Flamboyant went on talking. "So are you guys going to Magic's party or are you fallen angels in all that white?"

I don't know, I usually am a talker but I was just not feeling his convo, but Mya talked.

"Yes we are angels, but we also happen to be going to Magic's party."

"Ya'll might want to get around there, the line is pretty long?"

"Are ya'll going?"

"Yeah, but we ain't worried about no line, matter of fact if you have any problems just say you with Fred City."

Okay this nigga must think he P-Diddy. I gotta say something.

"Oh! Thank you Mr. City, but we have tickets, we're just waiting on our cousin."

"Well, you know the name just in case." They got on the elevator. One of the other guys, who I assumed was mute because Mr. Flamboyant had been doing all of the talking asked,

" So where ya'll from anyway?"

Mya said Oakland and normally I would say the same because I been there for all my life. Before the last couple of years, being from Oakland can tend to be a conversation piece, so I replied Arizona. And the elevator door shut.

CHAPTER 2

"Damn Alisha, that muthafucka look hella mean. Shit, we the ones who been waiting for hours, what he mugging for?" I said.

"Girl, he just look like that, he's a big ol teddy bear."

"That's because you just got some, that dude look like a grizzly bear." Mya responded. We laughed. "So where's your luggage?" I asked.

"Oh I left them in his car since we are pressed for time. I'll get them after the party, he's gonna be in there too."

"Oh so is this is the missing Supreme? " Diondre, the doorman questioned.

"Yes, Diana Ross has arrived and now the show can begin. Nah, on the real, hey I'm Alisha and don't believe whatever my cousins told you. What's up, ya'll ready?"

"Don't ask stupid questions." Mya replied.

As we headed up the street towards the House of Blues, a couple of guys who had noticed us waiting at the hotel shouted out, "ya'll finally leaving ya'll post, we thought ya'll was one of the Hotel amenities."

"See Alisha, we gone kick your butt, be glad I don't want to mess up my white. And you know the first round is on you because as ugly as that nigga was, and as fat as his Benz was, I know he paying. Hunh, sis what you drinking?' Mya asked me.

"Man after all them hours of waiting, I think I'm feeling like a bottle of Cristal and I don't even like Champagne."

As we walked up toward the club, they could see a big crowd, men who didn't have fifty to get in so they post to get at women going in or coming out and women waiting for men they could slide in on the arm of with VIP hooks. It was the same ol scene.

A large security guard yelled, "the club is at capacity, there will be no more entrances."

"Oh hell naw, I'm gon kill you if we don't get in. Sony do you have some pull. Damn, where is that nigga we met at the hotel that said he was the man, Fred City whatever." Mya was running off at the mouth, she was pissed.

I always kept a cool head so I said, "hold up, let me go talk to him, we already have tickets so we may be able to get in." I tried to talk to the bouncer, but there were chicken heads surrounding him trying to give up anything from head to ass to get in and it was definitely not that serious. I walked over to the box office, as I approached, a lady said, "sorry we are sold out for tonight's party."

I replied, " I know ma'am but we already have tickets we bought in advance, can we get in?"

"Oh sure honey", the lady said with her southern twang, "you can enter right over here."

"Thank you, let me go get my family." I waved for the crew and you could instantly see relief on Alisha's face. She knew she was gon hear it if we didn't get in.

"Who was you over there talking to on your cell phone, Lish?" I questioned.

"I was trying to call Rock to see if he was in there, to see if he could get us in, he supposedly got VIP hooks."

"Don't trip, we in there, now let the games begin."

We walked in the jam-packed club like we owned the place. It was beautiful, a jam-packed club of Black men and women from all over the place all decked out in white. There were white pants, dresses, skirts, and shorts. Everyone looked different but together it was a Kodak moment.

"Let's find the bar so I can buy you ho's ya'll drinks, so I can hit the dance floor."

"Oh my goodness, is that Biz Markie Djing?"

"Not only is that Biz, look Sony your man is up there too." Mya said laughing. She was talking about Doug E. Fresh.

"Ooh shit was that high school, I swear he was looking at me at that concert at the Coliseum, he was singing, 'Cut that zero, get with this hero'. Girl, remember I bought the shirt from the concert and got Young Sony on the back with iron-on letters.

22

Man, those were the days. That was me, you, Alisha and Bri. Damn, I wish Bri could've come."

We laughed at the memory and sipped on their cocktails. We let Alisha off with just buying a round of Malibu's and Cranberry.

Biz Markie was bumping, playing all the current Hip Hop and R&B jams.

"Man, I'm gonna have to get him to DJ Eric's 30th Birthday party, he is jamming." We were approached by several men asking to dance but we were enjoying our space, posted at the bar, bopping to the beat, people watching, talking and laughing. Everybody was in the house, Magic Johnson himself, Jamie Foxx, Lisa Raye, some NBA players, didn't know their names, but the faces were familiar.

"Ay, ya'll hungry?" Alisha asked, "I'm starving."

"I guess all that fucking will do that, but anyway I can eat something."

"Mya, how you know I been fucking?" Mya and I laughed, Alisha had to laugh herself.

"Fuck ya'll. Come on let's eat something."

On the other side of the club was the restaurant. The music was calmer over there, more old school. There were tables and booths, dim lights with candles. There were mainly couples, older people, and people who had met on the other side of the club who came over for a quiet place to talk.

"What time is it? I hope they're still serving food."

"Ooh look at that." I gawked over a plate of shrimp being carried by a waitress. "Come on let's find a table."

Shortly after being seated, our order was taken. While we waited on our food, we bopped to Michael Jackson's PYT among other songs and talked about the club.

"Ay, did you see Jamie, man, I think he is a freak and he's packing?"

"Mya, how do you know? Alisha asked

"For one, I can sense a freak. I have radar and I know he's packing because remember when he had them leather pants on at his concert in Oakland. He grabbed his dick, I swear it was halfway down his leg."

"Oh she ain't lying about that Alisha because shit I was with Eric at the concert and believe me my husband is packing but I was like daaaaamn and the nigga Eric knew what I was damning about."

The food arrived, we had fries, buffalo wings, Cajun shrimp, and stuffed mushrooms. We ate, drank more Malibu, joked and laughed. It was almost 2am and people were still arriving at the club.

"Ay, wasn't Miko and them coming?" Alisha asked.

"Oh shit, I almost forgot, Mya call Keisha on your cell."

(Mya called)

"Hey Keish, where ya'll at?"

"Girl, we in a cab on the way there."

"Is the show just now ending?"

"Girl, it ain't ended yet. I love some Stevie Wonder, but his ass been on stage for over 2 hours and he still going. Man, we had to cut. Is the club crunk?"

"Yeah, it's off the hook, it's hella crowded, but we over here in the restaurant area where it's calm right now."

"Okay we'll be there in about 10 minutes."

"When you come in it's a courtyard and we gon stand out there and wait for ya'll."

"Aight, see you in a minute." Keisha hung up.

"Come on ya'll, let's stand outside and wait on Miko and Keisha and get some air." Mya suggested.

"Girl, it ain't no air in this humidity hell called New Orleans, but I did bring my camera, so let's take some pictures outside." I replied.

We sashayed our way through the packed restaurant dance floor, the DJ was playing Brick House and the floor instantly got packed. We all sang "36, 24, 36 oh what a winning hand" as we made our way to the courtyard. We were all in our element, full on food, fine, and a little keyed.

"Hold up, take one with me sitting down. I just ate, does my stomach look big?" I asked.

"Girl, stand up, you the only bitch I know with four kids and a washboard stomach." Alisha shouted.

"You do have a little pucker." It was so like Mya to hate, but it went in one ear and out the other.

We took turns snapping pictures and posing differently. You would have thought we were doing a Vogue spread. Alisha asked a man sitting, smoking a cigarette if he could snap a picture of us together, he said sure. We took several pictures imitating the Charlie's Angel stance and the typical kneel down jail pose, among others.

"Thank you." We sang in a sexy voice to the man. He probably thought he was Charlie himself. He was grinning ear to ear like he had just photographed a KING spread. We all laughed.

Alisha joked, "Ay Sony, go feel him up, I bet he got a hard on!"

"I'm cool!" I replied.

As we laughed a group of men walked in through the courtyard.

"Oh shit." I said under my breath.

"Hey Sony ain't that Fred City?" Mya excitingly asked. His arrogant flamboyant ass obviously didn't irritate her.

"Hey ladies, I see ya'll made it."

I just grinned, but in my head I was saying, "Muthafucka, I said we had tickets."

Mya replied, "Oh yeah, this is our cousin, Alisha, we were waiting on."

"I see beauty runs in the family, ya'll want to come up to VIP?" He asked.

"I'm sorry," I responded, "we are waiting on our other cousins." As I was finishing my statement, another guy walked up. He was obviously with them. Although I didn't focus on the group when we were at the hotel, this guy could not have been with them earlier.

25

"Hey G, who are your friends?" The man asked not taking his eyes off me.

Did he say G? Who is G? I thought his name was Fred City. Oh well, it's not important, but who is he? Oh my, I can't believe I just said that if only in my head. Mya and Alisha were being entertained by the crew, so they missed the quick intrigue that came over me, but Mr. Flamboyant, G, City, whoever, brought me back.

"Oh these are our peeps we met earlier, they're staying at our hotel."

"How are you guys doing? I'm C. Are ya'll going up to the VIP?" The mystery man asked.

"Oh no, we're waiting on some people." I replied.

"Okay hopefully we'll see you around." He spoke to all of us, but his words appeared to be directed at me. As he walked away his hand brushed my arm and my eyes followed him. What was this feeling? I know I'm not drunk, was that a tingle? This is not a feeling a married woman should be having. I was truly thrown off. Before my crew noticed, I heard Keisha's loud mouth.

"Where my girl's at?"

Mya responded, "your girls and you could have been in VIP if you got hear a few minutes earlier."

"What happened?" Miko questioned.

"Girl some nigga named Fred City we met at the hotel, he must be something because he was asking us to go to VIP."

That nigga ain't shit, I thought to myself and his name probably ain't even City. I wonder why a guy like C would hang with him. Oh my goodness, I'm tripping! His name probably ain't C. I don't know, this is some strange shit. I ended my thoughts and came back to reality. "What's up ya'll, let's get a drink."

We made our way back through the restaurant and back into the packed club. We squeezed up to the bar and ordered. I ordered five Malibu's and Cranberry and five shots of Petron Tequila.

"Come on ladies, we on vacation, let's toast." I shouted.

"Okay, let me do this," Miko cleared her throat as if she was going to say something profound, "ya'll ready." She said.

"Bitch, come on." Alisha responded. "I'm thirsty."

"Okay, to deep pockets, long tongues and fat dicks!"

And with that we took the shots back like pro's. Doug E. Fresh was on stage performing his old hits. We all danced and sang along La di dodi …………..

We drank several more drinks, taking turns with rounds. Everyone in the club appeared to be having a good time. I was finally ready to hit the dance floor. I grabbed the hand of a big Warren Sapp looking dude who had been talking and drinking with us at the bar. We broke through the crowd to the floor. As we danced I was feeling the alcohol and the music. I didn't have to think about moving to the music, the music was moving me. Just then Biz Markie put on R. Kelly's Snake.

"Oh shit," I yelled, "this is my song."

It's like the dance floor was on fire. At this point, I could have been dancing by myself. I had danced by myself so many times at home to this song. My body moved in syncopation, rolling from my head all the way to my feet. Gyrating my hips, isolating my pelvis area in and out. I knew I was working it. Besides the big kool-aid smile on my dance partner's face, I couldn't see anyone, but I had a feeling that I was being watched, so I put it on thick. I decided to make the Warren Sapp look-alike's day, so I backed up and bent over gyrating my ass on his pelvic area and like I expected, his dick was hard. We danced to the end of the song. As we walked off the floor, the Warren Sapp-a-like stuttered as if he was cumming, "damn your husband is lucky." Ugh he probably did cum on himself, just like a man. My husband's lucky because I can roll my ass. As we were walking off the floor, Alisha approached me.

"Hey Sony, let me get your key to the room."

"Why?'

"Because Rock is about to leave, so I need to get my bags and put them in the room. I'll be in the room because there's no in and outs, so if ya'll do something else come get me."

27

"Aight, don't disappear Bitch." I responded. I gave her the key although I knew this could be a mistake dealing with Alisha, but at least Mya has a key."

"Ay, Son?" Alisha jumped into my thought.

"What's up?"

"Before I go, I got to say you wrong for what you did to the big boy on the dance floor." We laughed and then Alisha made her way through the crowd to exit as I made my way back to the bar.

"What happened to Alisha?" Miko asked.

"She had to get her bags out of her friends car and then she's going up to the room."

"Does she have a key?" Mya asked.

"I gave her mine."

Mya, Miko, and Keisha all responded, "Bad move!" It was funny how everyone knew Alisha's track record.

"So what ya'll getting into tomorrow? Keisha asked.

"We are gonna try to make it over to the convention center to eat, maybe hit the casino. We're going to the concert tomorrow night. What do ya'll have planned?"

"I have some work to do, since my job did pay for this trip? Keisha replied.

"What about you Mik?"

"I don't know, maybe I'll catch up with ya'll while Keisha works."

We spent probably 30 more minutes drinking and discussing plans for the weekend before I decided I was ready to go.

"Hey Mya are you ready because Alisha is probably in the room waiting on us?"

"Yeah I'm ready, what time is it? It's almost 3:30 am. Oh yeah, I'm ready."

Keisha and Miko decided to stay longer. We said our good-byes and made our way out of the club. You could still hear the music blaring loudly. The streets were still packed. It was unbelievable that it was after 3 in the morning.

"Oh shit Mya, they playing my song, Uh oh, Uh Oh." I sang Beyonce's Crazy in Love as I walked down the middle of the street heading toward our hotel. Mya and I imitated the R&B diva's signature booty-pop dance. We continued to walk, skip, sing and dance when we were interrupted by someone saying, "Did you ladies enjoy the club?" Oh my goodness is that butterflies? It was him, the guy, the club guy. Damn, if I wasn't drunk, I could remember his name.

"Yeah it was off the hook. What's up with ya'll? Mya asked the crew of men. They all answered differently.

Mr. Flamboyant responded, "Man, I'm loving this, this is the place you come to find a wife."

Okay, I know I'm drunk because this was my response, "I'm sorry, I'm already married, but my sister would make a perfect wife." I continued to skip and dance up the street and since we were all going to the same hotel we walked and talked together.

'C' yeah that was his name. C asked me where I was from?

"Well, I'm from Oakland, but I live in Arizona."

"Arizona, why are you in Arizona?"

Believe me I wonder that myself, I thought.

He continued, "Well since you're married and I don't think I met anyone as beautiful as you, maybe we'll just talk to each other, so you don't have to worry about not having anyone to talk to out here and I can have the privilege of talking to someone so beautiful, no strings."

Okay that was hella weak, but I don't know, it was something about him. I responded, "you know if I was sober that little story you came up with wouldn't fly, but you're in luck, I'm not sober so it was kind of cute."

The couple of blocks to the hotel seemed like a mile. We walked and exchanged small talk about the food out here, being at Essence, and how off the hook Biz Markie and Doug E. Fresh were. Mya managed to keep the rest of the crew entertained. She loved to be the center of attention. We were now approaching the Wyndham.

"Sonya can I have your room number so maybe we can talk later?"

At that point I noticed Mya paying attention to our conversation.

"Sure it's 1614." I replied.

"Okay, my room is 2803. It was really nice meeting you."

"Likewise." I replied. By this time Mya was so in our mouths that I could suddenly feel my high coming down.

"Hold up, Hold up." Out of nowhere came Diondre's loud mouth. "Aren't you missing a member, where's Ms. Diana Ross?"

"Oh she's up in the room, we think." Mya and I laughed.

By this time our friends had made their way into the hotel and were getting on the elevator. Mya and I sat in front of the hotel and filled Diondre in on how the club was, all the people who were there and about the music. Diondre was hella cool, country but hella cool. I think he was digging on Mya and right now she was being nice. I'm sure the alcohol had a lot to do with that.

"Hey Mya, do you think we can exchange phone numbers?" Oh shit, I knew it. I can't wait for her response.

"Sure D, Sony do you have a pen?" She asked.

"Oh my goodness." I thought to myself

"Here this is my cell number 510-555-2563 and we're in room 1614."

D took the number and handed her a paper with all his info. He must have planned this. We said out goodnights to D and headed in. Soon as the elevator doors shut, I couldn't wait to ask Mya about giving her number out, granted D was nice, but he was in the wrong tax bracket for Mya.

" Girl, you must be drunk, you giving out your number, the real number."

"Shit I am drunk, but I'm thinking about the long run, he can probably get us his employee rate for next year."

Okay that was more like Mya.

30

"However, I ain't that drunk. What was up with you and ol boy, you giving out room numbers?" By this time we were reaching the 16th floor.

"Girl, that ain't nothing. I'm on vacation, we were just talking."

"Okay nothing." Mya said sourly. We got to our room and of course there was no Alisha.

"Maybe she got tired of waiting," I said, "oh, but I guess her luggage would be here, right?"

"Girl, you act like you surprised. She didn't have to take your key if she was rolling with dude."

"That broad could have called" I was saying as the phone rang. "Maybe that's her."

(Mya answered the phone)

"Hello, hold on. Sony it's for you." The look on Mya's face let me know who it was. It wasn't Alisha.

"Hello, where? I guess for a little while. Okay, by the elevator on the 16th floor?" I hung up the phone.

"What are you doing? Mya asked.

"Oh I'm about to go sit by the pool and talk to 'C'."

"What! Girl, you are tripping. Have you forgot you're married? All it takes is one hater to fuck your shit up."

Although I agreed with her and my going to talk to him surprised myself. I responded, "Mya, I am a big girl, I got this."

"So what if my brother-in-law calls?"

"Considering it's almost 5am where he is and he ain't called this far, I'm not worried. However, he would call my cell phone."

"Whatever, you grown." Mya said as I walked out the door.

31

Chapter 3

"Man, you must have been calling me from this floor. You out here sitting down like I had you waiting hella long."

"You know you was in the room preparing for our date." He replied.

"Anyway nigga, I wake up looking good and I hardly call sitting by the pool and talking, a date. Now push the button for the elevator." I shot back.

"Okay, 'I wake up looking good', what would you call a date? Tell me how Sonya's ideal date would go down."

Okay I know this is going to be some good conversation, I thought to myself.

"Well, I've never really dated in the since of the word 'date'. I've always been in long relationships, but a good night out or in for me can consist of different things."

"Tell me a little more about those nights in." C replied.

"You are so nasty."

"No Sonya, you are nasty because I wasn't even thinking like that." We both laughed, but strangely enough I was thinking like that, even when I answered the question. What the hell is wrong with me. The elevator coming interrupted my thoughts.

"Can you push '10', my lady?"

"Yes I can. Can I ask you a question?"

"Sure but I get to ask you a question in return."

"What is this elementary?" I replied.

"That's the deal, is that cool?"

"Yeah but my question ain't that deep. I just want to know what 'C' stands for?"

"Oh is that it, my name is Charles, however I still get to ask my question." As he was saying that we had reached the 10th floor. As we exited the elevator, he began.

"Don't worry, I'm gonna hold my question until we get by the pool."

"Okay but I get to ask another question and if I think you lie, I'm pushing you in."

"Oh I'm really scared Sony."

"How you know that name?"

"I heard your sister call you that when we were walking, I think it's cute."

That's funny, Eric never calls me Sony. "Okay well I guess you have permission to call me Sony." We got to the doors of the pool and pulled on them, not noticing the big ass sign that said the pool closed at 11:30pm.

"The pool is closed." A voice came from out of nowhere.

We both turned and froze as if we had stole something, my heart was beating fast because reality hit, what if that's the voice of someone that knows Eric.

"Hey is that one of my Supremes? What up Sony? Yeah the pool don't reopen til seven in the morning."

"Hey D, we were trying to find somewhere quiet to talk."

"Try the lobby, it should be quiet right now."

"Thanks D, we'll see."

Me and Charles headed back to the elevator, and of course I felt like shit. Diondre heard me all night turn men down telling them I have a husband and here I am trying to get Q.T with another man.

"So Sony you want to go to the lobby?"

"No I don't think that would be a good idea for me. I can't chance it. I am married."

"Well that's not fair. I still have to ask my question." He pushed for the elevator. "You want to go sit in my room and talk?"

"Is this a good idea Sony," I thought to myself. I heard about women going up to men's rooms to talk and next thing you know they were taken advantage of. And people always say, "well why did she go to the room," like that's an excuse for rape. For some reason I wasn't worried about that.

"I guess we can. That's probably the safest place for me, but don't even think about no funny shit because I will cut a nigga."

C thought to him self, "this girl is funny, nothing like I thought at first.

"Anyway Sony, you better not try nothing with me, you already exposed your dirty mind."

We both laughed as the elevator doors opened, however when we got on we acted like we didn't know each other since there were a couple of people already on. Luckily everyone got off before we reached the 28th floor. The last person got off on the 20th floor and soon as the doors shut, Charles continued talking as if there hadn't been a break.

"Are you ready for my question?" I gave a look like go ahead, but damn is it that deep that I have to get ready.

"So Sony are you married to an entertainer"? I laughed and shook my head no.

"A Big-Time Realtor? He asked.

I shook my head no

"A Drug King Pin?"

I busted out laughing. "Hell no, why would you ask that?

"Honestly," he replied.

"Yes, honestly, although I can't push you in the pool for not being honest."

"Well you have the look, the confidence, a big City girl and then you say you live in Arizona. So I say a lot of entertainers live in Arizona."

"Well a lot of regular people live in Arizona too."

"No not like you, especially not Black."

"I don't know, is that a compliment?"

"Of course"

"Okay, where did the King Pin come in?"

"Well if you're not married to an entertainer, he must have some paper, that's a je-wel on your left hand."

I held my hand out admiring my wedding ring, it was fat, but not gaudy.

"But damn Charles, a King Pin? Come on let's step out of the hood.

"So what does he do?" He asked.

34

"He works, and I thought it was a question for a question and you done asked hella questions without me asking one."

"Saved by the bell," C said as the elevators opened on the 28th floor.

"You not saved, I haven't even got started yet."

I don't know why but I felt like I knew this man all my life. I felt comfortable saying whatever. It made me feel like back in the day, in the hood, before I had to play the role of NFL wife. When he opened the door of his room I wasn't prepared for what was on the other side of the door.

"Damn, what is this, the presidential suite?"

"So is that your question?" He jokingly asked.

Damn what am I gonna ask him. I want to know what he does for a living, are you a kingpin? I'ma try to feel him out before I actually ask.

"No that's not my question, my question is uh, where are you from?"

"Oh that's easy, I'm from E.O. Jersey."

"Okay, so I'm suppose to know what E.O is, where I'm from E.O is East Oakland, so I need you to be a little more specific."

As I was finishing up my comment, I heard some laughter coming from the living room. Oh yeah, this suite was decked out, living room, formal dining room, couple of bedrooms.

"Oh yeah Twan, she is a comedian." Charles said to his friend in the living room watching T.V.

"Oh my bad, I didn't mean to disturb you." I said.

"Oh no, I was going to bed." Twan said as he was getting up off the couch.

"Don't leave on our account."

I had remembered his face from earlier when we met them in the lobby.

"Oh no, the T.V. was watching me, I'm tired." He responded.

"Well, good night."

"Aight ya'll." He said and departed to one of the rooms.

35

"So Sony would you like something to drink?" Charles asked pointing at the makeshift bar out of the coffee table.

"I'm cool, ya'll don't have what I drink."

"What do you drink? So I'll know next time."

"So, you're assuming there'll be a next time, um I'll make it interesting, Malibu and Cranberry."

This nigga was straddling the line of confident and cocky, but it was kind of sexy. He let me know that E.O. stood for East Orange. His next question was what did I do for a living, in which I answered other than being a wife, I'm a full time mother of four children. I always figured a way of throwing in the fact that I have children early in conversation. It's been times when I've held a two-hour conversation with a person and not only did they not mention that they had kids, but nothing they said led you to think so. A look of shock came over his face.

"Damn girl, you look good and you have four, I know people with one child about 10 years old and still blaming their weight on the baby. Hold on excuse me for a second." He said then he headed towards the other bedroom. What in the hell am I doing here, what is he going to get, I know he don't think I'm gonna follow him to that room. Maybe I should leave, but just as I was thinking that he returned with a picture in his hand.

"Look, these are my angels, do you have any pictures of your kids?" Okay this shit was real big for me, this nigga is really getting cool points. Half the time men don't claim their kids and they sho in the hell don't be trying to show off their pictures.

"Ooh Charles they are so cute, how old are they?" I asked as I fumbled around in my purse to find my pictures. I handed him a picture of my kids from this past Easter.

"My girls are seven and five, and look at your princess surrounded by all them boys. I know she's spoiled."

Um, seven and five, that's good because young kids bring baby momma drama. What am I thinking? He might be married himself, at least I wouldn't be the only sinner.

"So what about their mama or mama's?" I asked.

"What are you asking, Ms. Sony?"

Okay, I'm getting deeper and deeper.

"Well, do they have the same mother, are you with the mother, you know what I'm asking?"

Charles went on to tell me about his Baby Mama drama. Basically he was with the five year olds mother for some years, actually before he had the seven year old. He cheated on her and got another lady pregnant, hence came the oldest girl. However his chick stayed with him and a couple of years later she had the other girl. The break came because his chick was treating his older daughter differently than their daughter. She told him, "what do you expect, of course I'm gonna despise the child that came out of you cheating on me." He says he kind of felt that but for her to say it was the stamp to seal the deal. So he left her and it's been three years. He feels that getting into another relationship would require a woman to realize his girls always come first.

"Well I think any real women would respect that your daughters are priority but you being a man are you sure you just don't want a pass to deal with your baby's mama."

"Oh hell no, I ain't fucked. Oh excuse me Sony."

"Nigga, I ain't trippin, be real with me."

"Okay, I ain't fucked the oldest mama since she got pregnant, over seven years ago. She ain't got no interest in me as long as I keep her mortgage paid and her child support on time!"

"Okay and the younger one?" I asked.

He just laughed.

"Um hm, I know that laugh"

"Nah, on the real Sony, after we broke up I was cool on her for a minute and then Christmas came and she was like you ain't gon wake up with the baby on Christmas, and you know I wanted to wake up with my daughter, so anyway one thing led to another…"

"So ya'll still fucking?"

"Damn we're sure straight forward." He replied.

"Well, shit we just rapping, that's how you said it."

"Anyway, nah I ain't hitting that no more either. After that Christmas we would kick it, you know when I drop off or pick up the baby. So about a year and a half of doing that and just that passed. One night I was out at a restaurant with a lady friend of mine and she happened to be there with a couple of her messy ass friends. Anyway to make a long story short, she caused a big ass, embarrassing scene. The restaurant even called the police, so after that I was cool on that. She tried to keep throwing the pussy at me but I wasn't biting, so after a couple of months, one day I'm walking out of my house and she had somebody come serve me with court papers to take me to court for child support."

"Damn, but was you paying her child support?"

"Come on now Sony, I'm a man. Shit, when we broke up I bought her a house. She had a brand new car, paid in full. I give here a check every month, even though I pay the mortgage and my daughter's school tuition."

Okay what does this nigga do for a living? I'm thinking to myself, shit he paying this mortgage, that mortgage. I know this suite is hitting him a pretty penny.

"So Sony, that's my story, what's yours?"

"I'm sorry, I don't have no Baby Daddy drama to share." Although I've had my share of drama, I didn't know this nigga.

"I ain't talking about that, I'm just talking about you in general, what makes up Sonya?"

I didn't know how deep to go with the answer. Although I felt like I've known him all my life, I really didn't know this dude. So I told him the basics. I was the youngest of six. I have one sister and four brothers. I was born and raised in West Oakland by both my parents. We were far from rich but we weren't poor, especially by my hoods standards. Both of my parents worked but with six kids we went with out some things, although they struggled to give us everything. I explained when I became a teen, I thought what my parents had to offer wasn't enough, so I decided to try things my way. Charles listened attentively with a sincere look of interest across his face. I went

38

on to tell him I got pregnant with my first child at seventeen, which was the beginning of my transformation. I went to college, got a couple of degrees, had more kids and got married. "Lots of pain, sweat, tears, falling, getting up, joys, success, blessings, that's me in a nutshell." I said with a sigh, just thinking of my life in a nutshell was an emotional roller coaster.

"Wow, Sony that's amazing, you said a lot without saying a lot."

"Well that was the quick version, because normally I can talk forever."

"I don't mind, I could listen to you forever." Something really awkward was happening for me. In all my years of being with Eric I never had the opportunity to open up my soul to him and he never seemed that interested but strangely enough I felt like I could tell this man my whole life story - good and bad.

"Oh really, unfortunately we only have tonight." I said.

"Ooh don't look at me like that Sony."

"Like what?" I replied.

"Like that...I know people must tell you about your eyes."

"Un unh, what about them?"

"They are powerful, sexy, sleepy, hypnotic."

"Really, all I know is I got plenty of ass whoopings from my mama behind them, she would always say I was looking a certain way."

"So what else did you get whoopings for?" he asked. I just looked as if to say, boy if you only knew.

"Have you ever sold drugs?" he asked.

"What are you? The police or something."

"No, I'm just trying to figure you out."

"Have you ever sold drugs? Are you a kingpin?" I asked. Shit, maybe he's on some next level shit, trying to find a runner and I'm way past that shit. I don't know, he doesn't seem like that. Okay he is cracking up laughing.

"Yeah, I'm a kingpin, Nino Brown, you are crazy. Nah, but on the real, like most inner city Black kids, I tried to do that when I was growing up just to get by, but once I got to high school, I had to focus on sports."

"Well I never sold hard drugs, I just can't do it, I can't lie. I've dealt with drug dealers growing up on personal and professional levels. I've moved some stuff. I sold weed though."

"Oh so are those high eyes?"

"Nah, I ain't smoked it. So what sport did you play?"

"I played football and basketball." He replied.

"So were you any good?"

"I was alright." He went on to tell me how important sports were in his life. It was his ticket to college. We discussed the importance of Black kids using their talents to get an education. We realized that we both have our bachelor's degrees in Sociology. We talked about how things have changed so much whereas kids now believe the game (sports) owes them, when the game is the reason they are no longer in the projects, driving fat cars, having jewelry and all that. He was so deep, but so hood. He had a lot of characteristics like Eric, but he was more like me, from the hood. "Yeah, I promised my mother I would finish college and that's rare for people in my field."

Finally the door opened for me to ask what he does for a living.

"What do you do?"

"I play professional basketball."

"Stop lying! Are you serious, um most of ya'll be done said that from the onset of the conversation, Oh you must have really thought you was getting some pussy tonight."

"Oh here you go, well most of ya'll, meaning women would have known from the onset."

"Okay, you right, so who do you play for?"

"New Jersey."

"Oh duh, you did say you live in Jersey."

"No I said I'm from Jersey, E.O, but I don't live in that part anymore."

"Oh you must live in a nice area, let me see New Jersey, New Jersey, oh my goodness, Charles, Charles Knight. You don't even look like you. You actually look shorter on T.V."

" Oh really."

"So that's a blessing right, to be able to play in your home state?"

"It is now, when I was younger it was a bit much. Too much of the wrong elements."

"How old are you?"

"Thirty-one."

As the night, now morning went on we continued to talk about our childhoods. We talked about our dreams, our goals, we talked so much that I had not realized that the sun was coming up.

"Oh shit Charles, I need to go, it's morning time. I don't even have my key, let me call and wake my sister up." I called the room and she was not answering.

"Hold up, let me try her cell." I dialed her cell and no answer. "I know this girl hear the damn phone."

"You can stay here, I'll sleep on the couch." Not that I think he'll try anything but I am married, I can't stay in another man's room and ain't no telling how many bitches done been through this room.

"No that's alright, I'm just going to go down and bang on the door, I know she's in there."

"Alright, I'll walk you down there."

Knock knock bang bang

"Who is it?"

"Me." Mya cracked the door open and returned to her bed, although I know she was still ear hustling.

"Can I have your cell number to call you later, Sony?"

"Sure, it's 510-555-5353." And for about the longest five seconds, everything felt really strange.

"Ok, well, uh, I guess I'll talk to you later."

41

When I walked into the room, Mya was sitting straight up in her bed.

"So that was a long talk."

"Yes it was," I replied because I was not feeling like and was not going to let Mya kill my mood, "good night, Mya."

"You mean good morning."

"Whatever." Lying in my bed I realized that in a few hours I shared more of myself with a stranger than I've shared with my husband in 10 years. Eric would never understand the things I did growing up. Sadly, I don't even feel bad.

CHAPTER 4

"Bitch get up, you ain't bout to sleep the day away." Mya shouted loudly as she pulled the curtain open to let some sun light in.

"Dang girl, do you have to open the curtain, what time is it?"

"Yes I do, it's raining out there. Oh it's 12:20 and I've already been in the shower. So get it going so we can go to the convention center before it gets too late."

Mya pulled the CD discman out of her carry-on bag and attached the portable speakers. Her selection was the Junior Mafia CD "Conspiracy", that used to be our get ready to go out CD a few years back. I rolled out of the bed because as tired as I was, I wanted to experience all that the Essence Festival had to offer. The Convention Center had daily seminars for free during the festival, everything from money management, fitness, health and inspirational speakers. They also had food vendors from all over New Orleans, with the best food costing an average of five dollars a plate. Just the thought of the food made me put some pep in my step. Before I showered, I styled my micro-size human hair single braids.

"Mya, you think I should wear my braids down or pull them up somehow?"

"I don't know, but they look hella good. Next year I may get my hair braided. You went to 'Jallah's African Braids' right?"

"Yeah, you know I got to fool with Jenifer, anyway, let me jump in the shower."

I pulled the braids up in a ponytail and covered my hair with a shower cap. I turned the water on while I brushed my teeth. After rinsing thirty seconds with Listerine I jumped in the shower. The shower was always my place to think, having four kids, it was sometimes the only private time I got in a day. Normally, my thoughts consisted of bills, the kids play dates, writing a book, but mostly shoes. However today's masturbation under the shower water wasn't stimulated from the new Manolo

Blahniks I saw at Saks. I kept replaying my conversation from last night in my head over and over again. It was this man's essence that had me tickling my clit, with every thought my pace increased and when I thought about his flawless chocolate complexion and thick dark eyebrows and brown eyes. "Oh my goodness," I let out sounds of pleasure, then right before I was about to explode, I stuck my index finger in my pussy and did ten kegel contractions. I'm working on getting those muscles back. Four kids ain't no excuse for loose pussy, not when they have tantra exercises to get it right. After I came, I washed up and got out. After getting out the shower, I got dressed, a micro-mini jean skirt, wife beater and some prada tennis shoes, cute but comfy since we would be doing some walking in the convention center. I pain'ted my lips with Mac Explicit lip glass and extended my eyebrows with eyeliner. I thought about calling Eric, however I felt guilty due to my shower activities and decided against it. I pulled the scrungy off my ponytail and gave my braids a shake, blew myself a kiss in the mirror and was good to go.

We headed out our room downstairs to a cab.
"So you still ain't ready to talk about last night?"

"Girl, it ain't nothing, he was hella cool, we talked and realized we had a lot in common. Oh did I tell you he plays basketball?"

"Um, is that right." Mya said sarcastically. She was practically green. Envy is a mufucka. "So what about Fred City?"

"Girl, what about him, we didn't talk about that nigga. What you wanna know?"

"First of all, who is he, what does he do, the whole run down, man he acts like he big Willie!"

"Well when I talk to Charles later, I'll get the 411."

"Later, oh does that mean ya'll exchanged numbers?"

"Oh yeah, because after we come from the concert, if we go out he wants to go to the same club."

"Um hm, is that right, hold on, my phone is ringing."

Whew, saved by the phone, hopefully whoever will talk all the way until we reach the convention center because I ain't feeling this conversation. Mya was talking to one of her past best friends, Ryan, who was meeting us at the convention center. By the time she hung up her cell phone, I was paying the cab driver and I saw Ryan's big 6'4, 230 pound butt waiting for us. Ryan and Mya were high school sweethearts, but when he went away to college to play football, they broke up. However, they remained best friends.

"Ya'll sisters are way too used to nigga's waiting on you, Mya you said be here at 12:00."

"It was Sony's fault today."

"What's up Sony, how's Eric and the kids?"

"They're good. I'm sorry I had you waiting."

"Oh, it's okay."

"It's okay? If it was my fault, I'd be hearing it all day."

"Be quiet Mya, come on ya'll, I'm hungry." Ryan said.

Inside the convention center was hectic. There were local radio stations with booths set up, giving away prizes. There was celebrity meet and greets and vendors selling merchandise and passing out information about various things. We didn't go in the auditorium where the speakers and seminars were held. The most amazing thing there was the giant get well called, over 5 feet tall, for fans to sign for Luther Vandross, who had fallen ill a few months earlier. After we signed the card, we ordered food from the food vendors. Mya and I got shrimp po'boys and Ryan had red beans and rice from another place. We ate and talked and laughed until Ryan realized he needed a drink so we decided to head to Bourbon Street. People were lined up for cabs so Ryan suggested we walk. The rain had stopped, so we agreed! On the way to Bourbon Street we passed Harrah's Casino.

"You know what ya'll, I think I'm going to pass on Bourbon Street. I'ma see how my luck is running and drink for free at the Blackjack Table."

"Them drinks ain't free, not when they taking your money. You might as well come spend that money on Bourbon with me and your sister."

"You must don't gamble." I said.

"Never."

"Well to each its own, have fun. Mya I'll see you back at the room. What time are we leaving for the concert?"

"I don't know, maybe about 7, 7:30 – enough time for you to make some money and you know I want my cut off your winnings."

"Alright, girl I'll see you in a while."

Mya and Ryan kept on walking toward Bourbon and I entered Harrahs. I've been in casinos all over the world and New Orleans Harrahs Casino is the only one that cards you as soon as you walk in the door. After getting through the security check point, I did a walk through, checking out what the table action was looking like. I saw a lot of five dollar and ten dollar tables and just a few twenty-five dollar tables. Most of the tables were full and I wasn't feeling the vibe anyway. "Excuse me, can you tell me where the higher stakes pit is?" The security gave me directions to the High Roller area which was right by the door that I entered, but oh well. This was more like it. The tables weren't too full and the minimum table bet was $50 and most were $100. I surveyed the tables before I sat down, just trying to get a feel for how the other people's luck was going. I decided on a table and sat down. The dealer was in the middle of a deck, so while I waited for the shuffle, I took of my Christian Dior sunglasses and put them in my purse and pulled out ten – one hundred dollar bills from my wallet and sat it on the table. When the dealer finished with that deck he reached for my money.

"Can I have all black chips?" Which are $100 chips. The dealer counted the money across the table so that the cameras above could see it.

"Changing one thousand black out" the dealer said waiting on the approval from the pit boss. When he got the OK nod he asked, "Do you have a player's card?"

"I do, but I don't have it with me, can you get it from my I.D.?" I answered.

"Yes, that's fine, Tracking." He yelled to the pit boss. The pit boss walked over to get my I.D. and made idol small talk. They always get hella over friendly with you when you in there dropping paper.

"Oh, you're from California, my wife's sister lives in San Jose, is that near you?"

"Yeah, it's about an hour away."

"Okay, let me go pull up your number, good luck." The dealer began to deal, I was sitting at the 3rd base position. There were two other people playing, an older Black man at 1st base and a white woman with a European accent in the middle. As we were playing, I felt my cell phone vibrating. I retrieved my phone, but I didn't recognize the number. "617, 617 where is a 617 area code-?" Then I realized that must be my new friend, but you can't use your phone at the table and we were all winning, so getting up was not an option. Oh well I'll call him back when I leave out of here. I continued playing Black Jack, I noticed that at the table across from me a couple of basketball players had began playing. I didn't know their names but they looked familiar. One other person had joined in at our table. We all talked about the Essence atmosphere, the concerts we were going to, our hometowns, the dealer was really cool and he was racking in tips because we were all winning still.

"What's up C. Knight?" A voice from the other table yelled out. I looked up and across at the table where the other B-Ball players were and now stood Charles, money in hand, waiting to play. He hadn't noticed me, so I pretended as if I hadn't seen him as well.

"Changing five thousand," the dealer from his table yelled for clearance from the pit boss, whom just happened to be standing at our table asking me more questions about California.

47

At this point I knew he saw me and I couldn't fake like I didn't see him, so I gave a smile and nodded my head what's up. Lord have mercy, why did this man give me chills, I couldn't concentrate, I almost hit my 15 with the dealer having a four showing. I calculated my chips in my head and realized that I was a couple hundred dollars away from $5000, so I decided when I reach $5000, I would leave. Why is it every time you say that, you lose the next hand? Okay, this dude likes to play Black Jack too, this is getting eerie. Every time I looked over to their table, he was looking at me. Lucky for me everybody was looking at their table because they had the loudest players in the whole area. Some people just need to have attention.

"Hey Sony, 'C' wants to know how you're doing over here and asked how long you'll be here? His friend Twan, who I met last night in the room was playing messenger.

"Tell him I'm doing fine and that I'm probably about to leave in a few. Is he over there winning?"

"I think he's up and down right now."

"Tell him I said that we can split our winnings 50/50."

Twan went over to pass the message, I could tell that he was amused by my message because he laughed. I looked over at him and smiled, he nodded okay. It didn't look like I was going to reach that 5 grand mark so when the pit boss brought over some new cards, I decided to cash in. My chips totaled fifty-six hundred dollars, a forty six hundred dollar profit. The dealer yelled color up and handed me 5 thousand dollar chips, 1 five hundred chip and gave me one black chip back, which I gave him as an extra tip.

"Bye Charles, Bye Twan" I said as I waved good-bye to them, I wished the players at my table good luck and then I was off to the cashiers booth to cash in my chips. I still had enough time to take a little nap before it was time to get ready for the concert.

"Hello Charles." I said when I answered my phone.

"How did you know it was me calling?

"Uh, Caller I.D."

"Oh so you knew it was me when you didn't answer earlier when I called?"

"Actually it took a minute for me to realize, but I was at the Black Jack table and couldn't answer."

"Where are you at now?"

"I'm in my room laying down, what about you?" I asked.

"I'm walking from the casino heading to the hotel."

"How did you do over there?"

"I lost, I couldn't catch a hand for nothing, plus everybody with money can't play and that loud dude was an example of that."

"Well. I got two grand for you, I told you we would split our winnings. I won $4500 but I'm gonna give my sister five hundred, so your cut is two thousand."

"Anyway, I don't want your money, girl."

"I would've wanted my cut."

"You are crazy. Yo, I'm walking in the hotel right now, why don't you come meet me at my room."

"Ooh I would, but I am so tired and I'm going to have to start getting ready in a little while for the concert."

In the background I could hear some women who were trying their best to be heard.

"What ya'll about to have a party up there?"

"Why are you asking? You don't wanna come." He said joking.

"You are right about that, so let me continue my nap and you can get back to your women." I hung up the phone and for a really brief moment, I felt a touch of jealousy. He must truly have me mixed up, I ain't no fucking groupie. What did he think I was gonna come hang with a bunch of bitches I don't even know, shit even if I did know the broads, I wouldn't be up there kickin it. I am married and I surely don't trust no females. After the phone call, I tossed and turned in the bed, I would never admit it but I was really bothered that he was up there with some women. These athletes are all the same I thought. It didn't matter, before long Mya's loud mouth would be coming in so nap time would be over anyway. I had to ready my ears to hear

49

about all the niggas that tried to holler at her, all the people she saw, blah blah blah.

Chapter 5

"Bitch! You should have been down on Bourbon St. Girl, Razzo's was off the hook. Nigga's was buying drinks left and right but you know that nigga, Ryan was hating. Anyway it was hella people, ballers. Oh hold up did you win because you know I want my cut if you did! And girl the bitches in there were off the hook, they was on stage dancing, showing they stuff for free. Okay that was a bit much. I passed our spot too, Seaport, we definitely have to go there tomorrow. Ryan said he would treat us. So, Bitch did you win or what?"

"Well, damn seems like you had an eventful afternoon, yes I did win. Pass me my purse so I can give you your cut." Now normally Mya's ass would be like 'I ain't your servant, get your own purse' but since I'm giving her some money oh she would walk to Oakland. This was my gambling ritual, if I win, I tip my loved ones or whoever is with me at the time. However when I lose ain't nobody kickin me down, so really this ritual was a little one sided. So anyway, is Ryan going to the concert tonight?"

"He said he is but he is so drunk he'll probably go to his room and pass out."

"Ya'll are a mess, you seem a little keyed yourself." I said as I handed her the hundred dollar bills folded up."

"Thank you, ooh- this is five hundred dollars, damn how much did you win?"

"A little something, so have you talked to Alisha today?" I tried to change the subject before she continued to pry into my business about my winnings.

"Yeah she called me. She said she tried to call you but your answer service came on. She said that she'll be here by the time we come back from the concert, so come get her before we go out. Girl, she said that dude left her in his house and was gone all day. Girl, she say he on some next level shit, with hella surveillance cameras everywhere. Have you been in the shower yet?" She asked me.

51

"No, I'm about to get in so answer my phone if it rings because I left Eric a message so he'll probably call back." I got in the shower and now my thoughts had changed from this morning's shower thinking about Charles' ass. I washed my face with Neutrogena face cleaner and rinsed it. I then lathered my wash cloth with Dove soap washing from head to toe making sure to spend plenty of time on the coochie and ass. That's one thing I ain't never got to worry about, a stanky twat!

Meanwhile Mya was running her mouth on the phone to her best friend that was back in Oakland.

"Girl, you should be out here, hella ballers are at me. And girl, Sony won some money and kicked me down five hundred dollars."

"Where's Alisha?" her friend asked.

"Girl, we ain't barely saw that broad, hold up Sony's phone is ringing."

"Mya is that Eric?" I yelled from the bathroom.

"Nah, it's Bri, do you want me to answer?"

"I'll call her later, are you on the phone because you need to be getting ready?" I yelled back.

"How am I gon get ready if you in the bathroom? Shelly, let me call you back so I can start getting ready."

"Hey Mya did Eric call?"

"Nope, have you talked to him since we been here?"

"Girl no, you know how he be hating when he know I'm kickin it, I'm sure he's been calling the kids though."

I was really bothered that Eric's ass wasn't calling back. I'm with our kids year-round while he's playing and when I take a little funky trip he wants to act like a broad. Whatever, I ain't bout to let him ruin my trip. Mya got ready and we were set to go. Mya tried to call Ryan at his hotel but no answer, so he was either sleep or already left for the concert. It was now 7:30 p.m. We had originally bought tickets for tonight's show because there was going to be a Bad Boy performance including Faith, Carl Thomas, and our real reason for going New Edition. Man, that was going to be off the hook. We caught a cab to the superdome. After it dropped us off, we still had a little walk

52

which my feet were not feeling. We got to the show in time to see LL Cool J rip it. That man still has it after all these years and my god he gets finer with age. He started doing this little water thing, where he drank water and then spit it back down his body. Now normally that shit would gross me out but damn that shit looked sexy. Mya and I were screaming like some teenagers. Man, if New Edition would have been here we would have been really having an old school flashback. The Bad Boy performance was canceled because they scheduled a tribute to Luther Vandross due to his illness. At the end of his show, he asked for a moment of silence for the legendary Barry White who passed away today. It was the 4th of July. It was now intermission so we decided to head up to the Superlounges to see what was going on up there.

"Come on Sonya, my friend just called and said that Biz Markie and Doug E. Fresh are in the 'Groove Lounge' and it's crankin. He said it's crowded so let's hurry up."

One thing for sure is Mya had hella friends, guy friends. We can't go nowhere with out her knowing someone. She was looking really cute tonight, it was like she was glistening. She had on her paper denim jeans, with some strappy Manolo Blahnik sandals and a bronze shimmery tank top. She wore a hint of eye make up and some neutral lip glass. When we reached the super lounge it was thick, wall to wall people. In the back was a bar so we made our way to the back. I ordered a Madris and Mya ordered a Cosmo, they didn't have any Malibu rum so it was going to be vodka for the night.

"Hey don't you know that dude right there?" I said pointing at a guy by the bar.

"Oh yeah, that's who I was just on the phone with. Mike, what's up?"

"Hey Mya, ya'll made it up here, what are ya'll drinking?" he asked.

"Madris and Cosmo." We sang like a choir.

"This is my sister Sonya, Sonya this is Mike." I extended my hand to shake and as he shook my hand he said, "so you're the one married to Eric Jackson?"

Man, I thought being outside of Oakland, I wouldn't have to get that statement.

"Yes, I'm the one," damn a muthafucka had an identity before him. We decided to stay up in the Superlounge for a while. We danced and sang along with the songs. Alisha was blowing both of our phones up, so we decided to leave the concert. The cab ride back to the hotel was quick. During the ride I had to listen to Mya complain about me catching an attitude with her friend after he asked if I was Eric's wife. Her argument was, damn you are his wife. This broad truly didn't have a clue, if my husband worked at Target, a perfect stranger's first comment, wouldn't be are you Eric Jackson's wife. It would be one thing if he knew Eric. We were now back at the hotel and her mouth was still running.

"I mean damn Sony, you act like he called you out your name."

I knew she wasn't gon let this rest so I had to agree with her to shut her up.

"You right Mya, it wasn't about him, I'm just mad at Eric. You think I should apologize to him?"

"Girl, hell no! It ain't that serious."

Okay, but you been talking about the shit like it was that serious. I really can't win with that girl. So why try. As we reached our floor, Mya started in on Alisha.

"I swear this bitch better be in here. Why in the fuck did she come to Essence, she could have kicked it with that nigga on any other weekend. She is supposed to be kickin it."

"Why you worried about what she's doing?"

"I really ain't, she just better be in this room."

Mya's ass always had something to say about what somebody else was doing like her shit was always sweet. When we reached the room, Alisha was sitting on the bed watching T.V.

"How was the concert?"

"It was cool," I replied, "how was your day?"

"Girl, it was crazy, I told that fool I wanted to come back over here early. He gets up early and was like I'm gonna go play

54

basketball so feel free to make you something to eat and I put a towel and wash cloth in the bathroom. Okay so bust it, I think the nigga gon be gone like an hour or two tops. Man, I make me some cereal and while I was in the kitchen I noticed a little camera by the stove. Girl, then when I went back upstairs I was noticing camera's everywhere. Granted the muthafucka's house is hella fat, it looked like some MTV Cribs shit but damn, he had a bitch funny about taking a shower like somebody was watching me."

"So did you look in his drawers or medicine cabinet?" Mya asked.

"Girl, didn't you hear me say he had camera's everywhere. I acted like I didn't see them but they were definitely on. Plus the nigga had hella money on the floor like he dropped it, okay that's a set up. I just picked it up and put it on his nightstand and didn't count it or nothing."

"So how long was he gone?"

"Sonya, that fool didn't come back until 5:00pm. Shit I had breakfast, lunch, snack and dinner before he got back. I was hella pissed and then he thought he was about to fuck, come on now dude."

"So you didn't fuck him today?" Mya asked.

"I didn't say today, I did this morning but not after he came back."

"Come on ya'll, let's go, which spot are we going too?" Alisha asked.

"I don't know, where are your friends going Sonya, oh yeah Alisha, Sonya had an exciting night herself. She has a new friend."

"Whattt! My cousin out here being a player!"

"Don't listen to Mya, she got to always put the extra on it, to answer your question Mya, I don't know where they are going and really it's not a concern of mine."

"Rock said that spot at the trade center is going to be cool, well I overheard him talking to someone on the phone."

"Oh that's that 360° place, yeah I like that club's set up."

55

I was cool with that, we freshened up our lipgloss and perfume and we were out the door. We were all getting our Hollywood on with sunglasses at nighttime. When your glasses cost $400 you should be able to wear them night and day. We were able to walk to the club because it was a short distance from the hotel. I carried my flip flop sandals in my purse because by the end of the night the feet were going to be on fire, so I would definitely be taking my heels off and putting on the flipflops to walk back to the hotel. When we got to the club, the line was starting to get long. Alisha shared with us too many details of her last night and this morning sex-capade as we walked.

"I swear he had the biggest dick I ever seen. I was scared, oh and the nigga ate the shit out of my pussy and ass, well not literally the shit, but if it was any up in there, he got it. Hahaha." She laughed as she finished up her story.

"Thank goodness people are around now because that is TMI, too much info."

"Please Sony, we know you a freak, all them babies you done popped out that pussy, all natural with no medication, you probably used to a King Kong dick."

"Alrighty then, anyway I got ya'll cover charge for the club, since I did win some money today."

"All damn you won, I'm gone have to tell Rock he made me miss out on my cut."

"Girl, I still got you." When we reached the front of the line downstairs we were directed to an elevator to take up to the top floor where the club was. As we waited on the elevator my cell phone vibrated in my pocket.

"Hello, hey...oh we're at the 360°, about to go in, we left the concert a little early." Charles was the voice on the other end of the phone, however I was not all that enthused to be talking to him.

"Oh we are on our way over there, are ya'll going to wait, or are you going to wait on me to go in the club?"

"Oh, I'm already going in." I bet them other ho's will wait on you to go in is what I wanted to say but I had to remain cool because Alisha and Mya were listening word for word.

"Oh Okay, well keep your phone on, ok?"

"Alright, bye." As I hung up the phone the elevator arrived. I was receiving 'the eye' from my sister and cousin. The look continued as we got off the elevator, paid to get in and were making our way to the bar. I ordered three cosmo's with Malibu Rum instead of Vodka and I was still getting 'the eye' from them as we waited on our drinks.

"What bitches? Why are ya'll looking at me like that?"

"Like what? Mya is someone acting paranoid? Either she's high or someone is crushing!"

"Crushing! Alisha you are trippin."

"So what's his name?"

"His name is 'C', remember the guys we were talking to at the White Party, the one's that had the VIP."

"Damn Mya, I thought she was talking to me. Anyway his name is Charles, but it ain't nothing. We talked last night and that's it. He was hella cool, so we decided to exchange numbers in case either of us new of something that was happening out here. Now can we get our drinks and find a table?" I said.

Both Mya and Alisha looked as if they weren't buying my story, shit I didn't know if I was buying it myself, but oh well that was that. The club got its name 360° because it was a complete circle. It was hella nice, glass windows were the walls all the way around. There were tables, chairs and couches around the outer circle and in the center was bars and the inner circle was the dance floor. We were able to find a high table with some high bar stool seats near a window, which would be our spot for the night. The D.J. was pretty whack but we were still enjoying the atmosphere. It hadn't got too crowded yet, but since the concert just let out, it would probably get a little more thick.

"Alisha call Miko and Keisha and see what their doing tonight."

The cocktail waitress came around and we ordered more drinks. Alisha finished talking to Keisha and she said she was on her way up here. She had a few of her co-workers with her as well. In the meantime we continued to talk and clown.

"Ooh look at your sister with that blue hair, you know she wrong." I said jokingly to Alisha.

"Ooh but look at your man with that big ass leather coat on in the club and it's summer, you know he stankin."

"Okay you got me."

"But on the real Sony," Mya said, "ain't that your man right there." She said pointing in Charles' direction.

"Oh, I remember him from last night, he's cute Sonya." Alisha said.

"Anyway, ya'll stop pointing." I responded.

"Ain't like he can see with all the bitches and niggas in his face."

"Oh yeah Alisha, I didn't tell you Sony's man plays in the NBA." Mya said.

"What, oh you holding out on info, Sony?"

"Well Mya been giving up her version of the story, I don't know how she forgot that part."

"Well, it looks like he's looking for somebody. Don't look now, he's coming this way."

I saw him coming our way. I wondered if he was looking for me, but I acted like I wasn't tripping. My girls knew how to play it up. We acted like we were talking about the most interesting topic as he approached us, still not even giving him satisfaction of feeling like his presence was felt. However it was being felt, shit my coochie was all tingly.

"Hey Sony," he said.

I looked over as if I was shocked to hear someone saying my name.

"Hey Charles, you met my sister Mya and this is my cousin Alisha."

"Hey Charles," Alisha and Mya both said.

"Hey Mya, my man was asking about you."

58

"What was he asking?" Mya responded.

"Just what's up with you, he's on the other side, you want to walk over with me, I'm about to go over to the bar and get your sister a Malibu and cranberry." He looked my way and smiled as if he deserved some brownie points for remembering what I liked to drink. That didn't impress me.

"Alright, I'll walk with you," Mya replied.

"Alisha, what would you like to drink?"

"Oh, you can get me the same thing, thanks."

Mya and Charles walked off and Alisha had a big ass kool-aid smile on her face.

"Sony?"

"What?"

"No that's it, Sony, he called you Sony. Only family and close friends call you Sony. You like that nigga!"

"He heard Mya's big ass mouth calling me Sony last night, he is being funny."

"Okay, but you do like him."

I held out my ring finger to display my ring, "have you forgot I'm married?"

"Married yes, but you are still human and that muthafucka is fine and he a charming little thing too."

"He's cool, I'm just having fun! You see how bitches line up around that nigga, I am not the one."

"Okay who is he lining up around, searching the club for and now on a drink run for. Obviously he knows you ain't one of those chicken heads."

"I can only imagine what your cousin, my sister is filling his ears with over there, probably a bitches whole history, transcripts, resume, everything."

"Look at you, all you need is a baseball player and you'll have all the major sports sewed up."

"Fuck you Alisha, hold up, don't forget about Hockey though."

"Now you know ain't no niggas playing hockey."

"On the real though, you know I don't get down with athletes, but he seems different, he don't come off like an athlete."

"Just like Eric, he don't come off like that either."

"That's true, he doesn't even know that my husband plays professional football. Should I say something?"

"Why? This is just fun, so why bother?"

As we were talking Keisha, Miko and Keisha's two co-workers walked up.

"Who ya'll talking about?" Miko asked.

I gave Alisha the look, cut the conversation and she knew the look. Keisha and Miko were family but family could be a muthafucka and I sure didn't need everybody in my mix behind nothing, plus I didn't even know the other broads.

"Girl, we just talking about the people in the club," Alisha replied.

"Where's Mya?" Keisha asked.

"Oh she walked to the bar," I replied, "did ya'll go to the concert tonight?"

They responded yes and all the women shared in their lustful thoughts about LL Cool J. Alisha was pouting because she missed it. Keisha introduced us to he co-workers, they actually live in New Orleans and it was their first time coming to the Essence Festival. The club was getting even more crowded but the D.J. was still terrible. Mya, Charles, and an unidentified man walked up with our drinks. Alisha asked me was the other guy Mya's hooks. I had never seen this guy before, but he wasn't the guy she was initially interested in.

"Here's your drink, beautiful." Charles said.

I could feel all eyes on me from Keisha and Miko. He must have felt the eyes too because he instantly said the same thing to Alisha and handed her her drink. This eased the stare a bit. Alisha kept at me about Charles' friend. It was obvious he wasn't for Mya because she was now on the dance floor with somebody else.

"What's up Alisha, you want to holler, you ready to leave them thugs alone?" I asked.

"Girl, never that, I think I know him from somewhere. Ask your friend if his name is Jamal?"

Since the stares from Miko, Keisha, and their crew, Charles had kind of distanced himself, so I had to call his name out. Perfect timing though because Miko and them went to make a round of the club.

"Charles."

"Yo was them girls your husband's people?"

"Oh no those are my cousins, well two of them, but shit family can sometimes be worst than a stranger."

"You know I know, but what's up?" He replied.

I thought Alisha had said does he know Jamal, so that's what I asked Charles, "hey does your friend know someone name Jamal?"

"He may know someone name Jamal, I can ask him, however his name is Jamal."

"Alisha, his name is Jamal."

"That's what I asked, yeah I know him, well not know him, but I met him years ago."

"Oh you know my boy? Where you know him from?" Charles asked.

"I don't know him, I met him. Did he go to Clark University?"

Charles nodded his head yes, while I'm still trying to figure our where she knows him from.

"Yeah that has to be him."

"Hold up, let me get him," Charles walked away.

"Bitch, where do you know him from?"

"I kicked it with him when I was in college." Alisha said laughing.

"What do you mean kicked it, because in college I remember you being with Taiwan and your head in them books."

"I'm still in love with Taiwan but anyway remember back in 1996 I caught him fucking with that tramp that used to wash hair at Toni's hair shop." I nodded yes, waiting on her to

61

continue. "Remember I went to that debate conference in DC? He was my debate partner in a workshop."

"Ok, so ya'll hung out."

"Ha Ha Ha," Alisha laughed, "girl, you should see the look on your face."

"Don't play Alisha, you fucked him?" I asked.

Alisha just smiled.

"Ugh, you slut puppy, well was it good?" I asked.

"Like I remember, girl I got so paranoid I thought Taiwan had people in DC following me. Girl you know he was crazy, so after it happened I never talked to him again."

Charles must have already told Jamal Alisha knew him from somewhere because as he was walking up you could tell he was trying to make out her face.

"How are you ladies doing, I'm Jamal."

"Muhammad." Alisha finished his sentence.

Jamal looked at Charles, "Black man you got these beautiful sisters playing a joke on me or something?"

I whispered in Alisha's ear, "I see why you gave him the panties, 'Black Queen'."

"Yeah, he talked like that years ago," she whispered back to me.

"No, Black man ain't nobody playing jokes on you, I know you in a way that your boy doesn't, so he ain't gave me no info to play a joke on you." Alisha said.

Charles looked at me shocked. I just hunched my shoulders like I didn't know what was going on.

"Okay, I know ya'll playing now, because if you talking about that, I know I would remember that, if I'm not confused about what you're saying we did."

"Damn, was it that bad?" Alisha said. Jamal just continued to stare at her looking confused.

"Why do you think gays shouldn't be in the military?"

"Oh my god." Jamal responded and Charles and I looked even more confused, what did that shit mean.

"Alisha Brown, it can't be. I must have been that bad because you never called me and you changed your number the next day."

Alisha and Jamal hugged and laughed but I still wanted to know what gays and the military had to do with anything. Come to find out, that was there debate topic that they won and their victory celebration led to some extracurricular activities. As they finished telling the story Mya walked up. She said Keisha and Miko left. Honestly the club was weak and the D.J. was whack but I was enjoying myself anyway, I was really starting to feel this guy. Alisha introduced Mya to Jamal and began to tell her about their history while Charles and I made our way to the dance floor.

"Sony don't be mad if I embarrass you on the dance floor." Charles said.

"Anyway, you gon embarrass yourself if anything."

The D.J. was playing some reggae music, this was probably the best music he had played all night. As we danced I tripped on how much his mannerisms reminded me of Eric. I turned around and backed my butt into his pelvic area and grinded to Sean Paul's "Get Busy". Please don't get hard, that is such a turn off, you have to know how to contain yourself. After a few minutes, I decided he passed the test, "no woody" in his pants, so I turned back around and whispered in his ear.

"You know you're trouble right?"

"What do you mean?" He said with a devilish grin.

"I don't know, maybe it's me."

"So how come you couldn't come hang out with me earlier?"

"Charles, what I look like coming to hang out with some people I don't know. I am married. Any of them broads could have known him, you know how groupies are, anyway I'm sure I wasn't missed."

"Yes, you were missed, and if you would have come up we could have chilled in my room. I didn't have them chicks in my room, they were in my man 'Gs' room or Fred, whatever ya'll call him. "

"I don't call him anything, but what is his name?"

"His name is Greg."

"Why he lie about his name, he obviously has my sister mixed up. She ain't trippin off his ass. So did you fuck one of them?"

"What?"

"Did you fuck someone today?"

"Why would you ask that?" he responded looking like a kid with his hand stuck in the cookie jar.

"You giving up your answer with your body language, you can't even stay on beat to the music. You are nasty Charles."

"I don't know what you are talking about Sonya."

As much as I didn't want to like this man, I couldn't help it. Hey it's not like I'm going to fuck him, so he might as well be getting it elsewhere. We both agreed we were getting tired, so we walked off the floor and I was really tripping because he was guiding me by holding my hand and I was just like a kid in a crowded mall holding on to a parents grip. While we were on the dance floor I was in our own little world, oblivious to our surroundings, but as we walked off the floor, I realized that we might as well have been on Soul Train because we were definitely being watched! When we made it back over to our table Greg (Fred City) had made his way over and he was all in Mya's ear, I'm sure he had some drama. Jamal and Alisha must have forgot they were debate partners because they were engaged in a light-weight argument about who knows what. I was starting to feel a bit uncomfortable about how comfortable I was feeling with Charles, plus I was tired of being watched by half the women in the place. I've never figured out how some women could just smell when an athlete is in the place, they could be 5th string, it really didn't matter. I decided I was ready to go.

"Hey ya'll, are ya'll ready to go?" I asked Mya and Alisha.

"Yes, we are." Alisha answered for the both of them.

Mya put up one finger for us to hold up while she and Greg exchanged numbers. Why is she giving that loser her number, but now if I say something it's like I'm hating but if I don't, I feel like I'm allowing my sister to be part of his game. Maybe he told her his real name.

"I'm going to stay a while, can I call you when I leave?" Charles asked me.

"Oh I know you going to stay because it's work in here and right now I'm blocking. It's cool, you can call me later as long as later ain't too late."

We all said our goodbyes and we were out. On the elevator down we decided to go over to Bourbon Street. As soon as we got outside of the club, I took my flipflops out my purse and put my heels in it and I was ready to get my stroll on. Bourbon Street was hella crowded and the locals were definitely out. I had to make sure I held my purse tight for real! We made our way to Razzo's where we drank $2.00 shots of Alize out of test tubes two at a time. Time flies when you're getting drunk for cheap. By the time we made our way back down Bourbon to Krystal's to get something to eat it was already 3:40 in the morning. Oh shit, I forgot all about Charles calling and my phone was in my purse, ain't no way I coulda heard it with all the noise in the bar. As I paid for my 'chilipups'(mini chili dogs) combo from Krystals, I looked to see if I had any missed calls on my phone, um none. Oh well, fuck him and Eric too for that matter because he ain't called either. Krystals was hella thick and the lady with the bad weave calling the numbers to pick up the food had a big attitude like she didn't know how it was going to be when she saw she was scheduled to work during Essence time. Man, I have my own problems I just want to get my food so we can go.

"Order number 77," Ms. Attitude yelled.

"That's us," Mya replied.

We got our food and headed back down Canal. It had to be something about Essence because on the normal my stomach would explode if I ate some greasy shit like this at 4 in the morning. We got back to our room and sat around eating and talking about the night's events.

"Okay, how funny is that you come to Essence to run into your long lost one night stand." I said.

"Bitch, how funny, I know Tai is up in heaven cussing me out right now. How about you coming to Essence to cheat on your husband?" Alisha replied.

"Ain't nobody cheatin, this is just all in fun. I don't know why you laughing Mya, because Mr. Flamboyant sure had you grinning ear to ear over there tonight."

"Shit, I ain't feeling that nigga, his conversation was weak. My grin was probably to hold back the laugh."

Thank goodness I thought to myself, no need in me telling her he lied about his name since she wasn't feeling him anyway. I don't know how long we talked or even remember when we fell asleep but it couldn't have been that long because it was 5:15 am when my phone ringing woke me up. Now initially I thought I was dreaming, next I got nervous because I thought something might be wrong with my family or something but now I'm pissed looking at this 617 area code in my caller ID.

"Hello" I said damn near spitting fire.
"What up?"
Okay this nigga act like its 5:15 in the evening. What about don't call too late didn't he understand.
"What's up is I'm sleeping, Good night Charles."

Since I know all closed eyes ain't always sleep – I know Mya and Alisha were listening word for word, but as tired as I was I truly didn't care. He truly has me fucked up and now that my sleep is broke, I'm about to be up like a dope fiend all night thinking about why my husband hasn't called and how this guy has created a spark. Well I guess I mean all morning. Why me!

Chapter 6

"Get up." Mya's mouth was so damn big! "Come on Sony, Ryan said meet him at Seaport in an hour and I can't wait to eat some of them red beans and rice and that jambalaya, girl, Sony get up. I've already been in the shower and Alisha is in the shower now, so get your punk ass up!"

"I'm up, damn stop talking so loud."

"So what's up with your man calling at the crack of dawn, he was even late for a booty call."

"Okay, he was tripping, so what happened with Ryan last night?"

"Just like I thought he went to his room and passed out and didn't wake up until this morning, that's why he up rushing us to go eat, but since he's treating I'll rush."

"Okay, I'm going to get that seafood platter with the alligator legs and the oysters and catfish. Let me tell Alisha to hurry up in the bathroom."

I jumped up and told Alisha to hurry and then pulled my suitcase out to figure out what I was going to wear. I have a bad habit of living out of my suitcase when I'm on vacation, I don't hang stuff up. The down side of that is I don't like to iron. I really am not good at ironing. I decided on some cargo capris with a vintage Bob Marley ribbed tank top, and some black Diesel tennis shoes. Luckily, I packed a couple of hats because today was one of those days when I felt like being on the under. Alisha had finished in the bathroom, so after the steam cleared out, I went in. After showering and getting dressed we headed down stairs, as we were leaving the hotel we ran into Diondre.

"Hey ladies, where ya'll headed?"

"To get something to eat," Mya replied.

"Where ya'll going to, Mothers?"

"Nah, the lines be way to long over there, we're going to Seaport on Bourbon."

"Alright then, enjoy your luch. Oh yeag Sonya, I saw your friend a little while ago, isn't he a basketball player?"

Ok, why did I have to run into him the other night, now he thinks he is my friend. He probably seen him with another broad and looking at me like I'm the dummy.

"Yeah, he does play basketball, but he is not my friend like that. He is a patna."

"Oh I figured that, he asked if I had seen you this morning."

"Oh well, alright 'D' we'll see you later."

As we headed to Bourbon, Mya talked on her phone to God only knows, Alisha led the pack because her tall ass walked so fast with them long legs. She really needed to be on somebody's runway. She is 5'10 with no body fat, but of course she's shapely, that's a family trait.

"Sony can you call Ryan to make sure he is either there or on his way?" Mya asked while she was holding another conversation on her phone.

"What's his number?"

As Mya gave me the number, I realized that after Charles early morning call, I turned the phone off and had not turned it back on. When I powered it on, it revealed that I had three voice messages but since the phone was off, I couldn't tell from who the calls came. I decided to call Ryan before I checked the messages. Ryan was already at the restaurant waiting in the bar area. I told him we were a couple of minutes away, so go ahead and get a table for four. Of course he made a joke about Alisha being with us.

"Man Sony, all it took was a free meal to get Alisha up from under that nigga." Ryan said.

"You are stupid, anyway we'll be there in a minute. I have to check my messages, so peace." I ended the call.

I know one of these messages have to be from Eric, I thought to myself as I keyed in my password and listened, "you have three new voice messages and two saved messages, first new message sent today from an outside caller," the automated voice spoke.

"Hi Mommy, are you having fun, we saw fire works last night, E.J. was scared. Sean and Lamar went home with Uncle

68

Jr. Well I was calling to say hi, I miss you and I love you, oh call me back – Bye."

The first message was from my princess Kayla, I pressed 4 on my phone to see what time she left it, it said 10:30am, which means it was 8:30 in Oakland when she left it, I pressed 9 to save the message.

"Next Message"

"Bitch, why you ain't answering your phone, I got to tell you about my fourth of July drama. I went by your mama's house with my parents for barbecue and of course your kids and your nephews and nieces had me entertained, and reinforced my reasons for not wanting kids. Anyway, I hung out with that fool Darnell after and that's when all the drama began, oh I know I'm getting at least some diamond earrings out of this shit, okay so call me so I can tell you, are you having fun, okay call me, Bye."

Seven to erase that message, the last message was completely unexpected. That let's you know it wasn't my trifling husband.

"Hey Sony, I hoped to get you but your voicemail will have to do. I just wanted to apologize for calling you so late or so early. I really lost track of time when I was in the casino, I honestly didn't know what time it was until you hung up the phone. After talking with you the other night, I know the type of woman you are and I would never intend on disrespecting you. Anyway just in case you don't allow me to see you again, I left something for you at the hotel's concierge desk. Sorry again, peace."

I pressed nine to save that message, I can't help it, I like the sound of his voice. What could he have left for me, maybe flowers...

"Girl, what you smiling about?" Alisha broke my thought.

"Oh I was listening to a message from Kayla." Ok I lied a little but I'm sure I was smiling when I listened to Kayla's message as well. We reached the restaurant and joined Ryan at the table.

"Damn, Sony who you hiding from with that hat and sunglasses on? Hey Alisha."

"Hey Ryan," Alisha responded waiting on what Ryan was going to say next.

"I'm just saying hey because I haven't seen you, did you just get in town today?"

"Fuck you Ryan," Alisha replied.

"Hey Beautiful"

"Don't start with me Ryan," Mya said.

"Damn I can't say hey beautiful, and you ain't gon get me drunk today because I'm not missing Frankie Beverly tonight, so how was the show last night?"

"Before we talk about that does everybody know what they want because here comes the waiter and I am ready to order," I was hella hungry.

We all ordered and then filled Ryan in on last night's events. He had heard mixed reviews about the party we went to, he obviously knew someone else that was there. They said it was off the hook, which it wasn't. Alisha spent most of the time calling the crazy muthafucka that kept her locked in the house all day. I couldn't wait for the food to arrive because everyone around us food looked so good. Mya was running her mouth about something while Ryan looked on admiringly. I never understood why Mya never hooked up sexually with Ryan. He was handsome enough, he had good manners, he had money, and most importantly he could put up with her. Every time I always asked her she would reply, "ooh wee" but I never understood why!

"Hey Ryan, how come you and my big sis never hooked back up?" Fuck it, I had to ask.

"Well the one time we did," he started to say but was interrupted by Mya and the bad timing of the food coming.

"Um, the food is here, I know ya'll ready to eat." Mya said giving Ryan the shut the fuck up eye.

70

"Actually, I'm ready to hear the story." Alisha said as she put her cell phone in her purse.

Alisha and I were definitely curious but we knew we couldn't get nothing out of Ryan with Mya being here, so fuck it. We all began eating. The platters of food were so big that it could feed a couple of people but we all had one to ourselves. We all sampled stuff off each other's plates. We were all too stuffed to eat dessert, so Ryan paid the tab and tip and we headed over to Razzo's to have a few cocktails. The bar was packed so we made our way to the back patio where there was a water fountain with fire (sounds strange but you have to see it) and a couple of other bars. It was packed out there also but not as bad as inside. We all started with two shots of Hennessey, me, I had a Malibu and cranberry to chase it. Before you knew it everybody was taking turns buying rounds of shots and basically I was fucked up. I had about ten shots of Hen and about three Malibu's and cran. I was good, plus when I get loaded my emotions come out and right now Eric had me pissed off so I knew I needed to get out of there. I found Alisha in a corner on her cell phone apparently arguing with Rock.

"Lisha, you ready to go?" I asked. She nodded her head yes.

"Okay, hold up let me find Mya." When I found Mya she was still having a good time with Ryan and some of their other friends from Oakland, so she decided to stay. I went back to meet Alisha who was no longer on the phone and we made our way back through the crowded club and back onto crowded Bourbon.

"Girl, do you believe this nigga?" We both said in unison.

"Go ahead, you first." Alisha said to me.

"Okay, do you believe this nigga Eric ain't called me once since we been here, and I done left his ass all types of messages, just like what's up give me a call messages. Oh but he is about to get a message for his ass in a minute." I think I was

71

talking loud because people were looking at us but at this point, I didn't care. "What about your friend, what's up with him?" I asked her.

"Okay you know how I missed everything yesterday except the whack ass club. I missed going to the convention center, the casino, seeing LL's sexy ass at the concert."

"Yeah, and…"

"Do you believe that this nigga was in his basement the whole time on some ol' crazy surveillance, trust a bitch bullshit."

"Hold up, you mean the muthafucka was watching you to see if he could trust you."

"Girl the fool said that in his lifestyle he can't even trust some of his family, and then he gon say don't trip baby you passed, now I know you a ride or die."

"What did you say to him?"

"I basically told him to go fuck himself and trust that."

We laughed at the disgust we had at the present time for the men in our lives, but the only difference is that Alisha had been dealing with dude for only a couple of months and I am ten years deep into this shit. When we reached our hotel we were both ready to lay it down to rest up for the night. We had decided on not going to the concert we were just going to hang out. As we exited the first elevator on the 11th floor, I remembered that Charles had said he left something at the concierge desk for me. The walk plus the intrigue had somehow sobered me up instantly.

"Hold up Lish, Charles said he left something for me at the concierge desk."

"Something like what?"

"I don't know girl, he left me a message apologizing for calling so late last night, anyway he said he left something at the desk for me."

"Well girl, what you waiting on. Come on let's see what he left us."

"Okay us."

We walked over to the desk and I asked the man working there if there was a package left for a Sonya Jackson. He pulled

72

open a drawer searching for something, which let me know it wasn't flowers. After a minute of searching he pulled out a manila envelope.

"Thanks for waiting, here you go Mrs. Jackson."

"Thank you sir," I replied. What in the hell could this be, it's too heavy to be a letter unless he had a whole lot to say.

"Open it bitch," Alisha anxiously shouted.

"Hold up, I'ma wait until we get to the room."

It seemed like the elevator took forever to get up to our floor. Once we got to the room, I rushed to my bed and ripped the envelope open like a kid on Christmas morning. There was a note that read:

Dear Sony,

I'm truly sorry for calling you at such a disrespectful time in the morning. As soon as you banged on me (hung up) I wrote this note so if it doesn't make sense don't trip, as you know it's hella early in the morning. Well I hope I will get a chance to talk to you again but if not I am glad to have met you. I lost track of time in the casino and although I may never talk to you again, a deal is a deal. However, in retrospect winning at Blackjack may have cost me your friendship.

C. Knight

I folded the letter back up and looked in the envelope and there were several stacks of hundred dollar bills.

"Oh my goodness." I screamed.

"What bitch, what did the letter say, what's in the envelope?" Alisha questioned.

I poured the money out on the bed and threw Alisha the letter.

"Do you believe this, it's ten thousand dollars here."

Alisha finished reading the letter, "what kind of deal did ya'll have?"

"We said if either of us win at the casino, then we would split our winnings, but I ain't keeping this money. He probably thinking the money is going to make me cool with him but money don't move me, he probably didn't even win, this is all a game."

"Well Sony, what would he get out of running game? It's plenty of chicks that he needs no game for, plus you really overreacting. It ain't no such thing as late night calls in New Orleans. I mean why not keep the money, if this is just some weekend fun that would be a good profit."

"Alisha I am married, I can't take $10,000 from another man."

"Well your cuz can so pass it over."

Alisha sat there counting the money and I couldn't figure what I should do. I got to give this money back, I just need to figure the approach. I scrolled through my phone to find his number and pressed send. Even as I was hearing his voice say hello, I wasn't sure of what I was going to say.

"Hey Charles, I got your message, by any chance are you in your room?"

"Yeah."

"Do you have female company?"

"No." he said laughing.

"I'm on my way up there so chill for a minute, ok?"

"Alright."

I hung up the phone and snatched the money from Alisha and put it back in the envelope. I went to the bathroom to touch up my lip gloss and perfume and stuck a piece of trident in my mouth.

"I'll be right back Alisha."

"What are you going to say?"

"I'll figure it out on the elevator, you staying in here."

"Yep."

"Okay, I'll be back."

My nerves were seriously jumping as I rode up on the elevator and unlike earlier when the elevator seemed slow this

74

one was flying. As I exited on the 28th floor I took a deep breath and headed towards his room.

(Knock, Knock)

I knocked although the door was cracked.
(Knock, Knock)

I knocked again, just as I was going to turn around my phone rang.

"Hello"
"Hey Sony, I left the door open because I'm in the bathroom, so just walk in and I'll be out in a minute."
I was already in the process of walking in before I hung up the phone. I shut the door behind me and had a seat on the couch and turned the T.V. on to ESPN, it really wasn't nothing on, but I heard him coming so I tried to act really interested in what was on.
"Thanks for waiting."
"No problem, you was in that bathroom for a minute, did you wash your hands?" I asked joking.
"Yeah I did, but I didn't spray so if you have to go I suggest you use the other one, man that Cajun food ain't no joke coming out."
"That's real talk, but anyway, I came to return your package." I handed him the envelope and he pulled his hands back, not accepting it.
"A deal is a deal, regardless if you're mad at me, that money is yours." He said.
"I know a deal is a deal, but I can't take the money because I'm a married woman and that's not cool. You didn't take the money I offered you either so we're even."
"Well I don't want the money, so you have to take it."
"I'm sure it's plenty of women out here who wouldn't have a problem taking the money and you might get something in exchange."

75

"You're probably right but that's where you're different."

"So, what you been doing today?"

"I've been chilling pretty much, I walked over to the convention center but that's about it. What about you?"

"I went down on Bourbon to eat and have a few drinks at one of the bars over there, well probably more than a few but that's it. I actually just got back before I came up here." I was trying my best to avoid eye contact because I knew it would be over then.

(Knock, Knock)

"Somebody is knocking at your door, are you expecting company?" I asked.

"No, let me see who it is."

"I'm about to go anyway."

"No, hold up, let me just get this first. Who is it?"

A voice from out side of the door answered, "Jamal."

Charles opened the door and let his boy in, it was Alisha's friend from the club.

"Hey what's up ma, where your cuz at?"

"Hey Jamal, I think she's in the room."

"Why don't you call her and tell her to come up here."

"Well I'm about to go down there so I'll tell her to come up."

"Where you going, we about to kick it." Jamal replied.

"Are we really, I didn't get the memo. Charles, can I talk to you for a minute in the room, Jamal our room is 1614, you can call her."

I got up and followed Charles towards the room and closed the door.

"Don't get all excited I just need to ask you something."

"Ha ha, you don't get excited, I don't give of myself that easy."

"Yeah right, anyway I don't mind kickin it, but I need to know is that your friend, you know like your real friend, can you trust him because I have a lot to lose."

76

"I have a lot to lose as well, Sony." He replied

"Are you married?" I asked.

"No"

"Well what do you have to lose?"

"You are married, what kind of image is that for me?"

"Oh, your career, well if that's the case I have a double whammy."

"What does that mean?"

"Don't trip, nothing. So you can trust him?"

"Yes, I can."

"Okay, cool."

We both walked out of the room and Jamal was on the phone pleading with Alisha to come up. I took the phone from him and told Alisha to stop tripping over her psycho nigga and come up here. I was wondering if I should tell Charles that my husband plays professional football. That was the double whammy, he wasn't the only one who had to worry about an image, but then if I told him he played, he would wonder who he was. What if he knew him, I mean I know he didn't know him, know him, but ain't no telling, these athletes cross paths sometimes, plus a couple of Eric's friends play in the NBA.

Alisha was at the door giving me the eye, the 'what's up with this' eye. It's funny we had been around each other all our lives, the Brown girls – me, Mya, Alisha and Bri, We could communicate with our eyes, no need for words, a certain look spoke volumes.

"What's up Black man?" She said to Jamal.

"Nothing ma, you look beautiful today."

"Thank you, now what's the cause for this meeting and what do you have to drink up here because I'm having a bad day."

"Girl, well I can tell you, it ain't no Malibu." I replied.

"Excuse me Sony, I do have an unopened bottle of Malibu, remember what I told you the other night?"

I thought back to the other night and remembered him saying he would have it the next time and I said what makes you think it will be a next time. Damn, why is he so cute, cocky muthafucka.

"Boy, are we cocky." I said

"I call it confidence. Nah on the real I thought it was going to go to waste. What do ya'll want with it, cranberry juice?"

"Yes, that's cool. Are you calling room service?" I asked.

"Yes."

"Can you order me a shrimp Caesar salad too?"

"Sure, do you guys want something?" He asked Alisha and Jamal.

Alisha ordered a chicken Caesar salad and so did Charles, Jamal ordered chicken strips and my salad and a pitcher of cranberry juice. While we waited on the food we talked about everything from Beyonce and Jay Z, dancing to food and music. And then an ESPN Sports Center commercial came on with highlights of football training camps.

"Ay Charles, Miami look like they gonna be good. What's up with your J-E-T-S jets?" Jamal said to Charles.

I think Charles noticed the awkwardness as Jamal talked about the Miami, this was the team Eric played for but he answered Jamal without saying a word to me, thank goodness.

"Oh my Jets gonna be cool, what about your Eagles?" he asked.

Jamal didn't respond to him, "do you ladies watch football?" he asked us. Alisha acted like she saw a ghost, "uh, uh I watch it every now and then, I go to the Raiders Monday Night games." Alisha answered.

"What about you, Sony? " Charles asked me.

"Oh I love football. Everybody that knows me knows that on Sundays, it's wrap during football season because I watch football all day. That's the luxury of living on the West Coast, you wake up and it's on at 10am. But I really like all sports, but football is the only one I like to sit at home and watch. With baseball and basketball, I like live games."

As I was finishing my statement, room service was knocking on the door. Alisha looked at me like what a relief. The talking was minimal while we were eating until I damn near choked on my salad. I couldn't believe my eyes, a new commercial was on for the video game Madden 2004 and this nigga Eric was in it and he hadn't even told me about it. Really, I was really coughing like a cigarette smoker.

"You okay Sonya?" Charles asked. "You look like you saw a ghost."

Alisha didn't say a word but she looked at me as if she knew it was more to it than seeing a commercial with Eric on it.

"Oh I got to get that, when did they say it comes out?" Jamal asked.

"I think like August 15th," I replied just to let everyone know I was okay.

"Oh you can talk, are you okay?" Charles joked.

"Yeah, I'm good, something just when down the wrong pipes."

Charles looked as if he wasn't buying that but he just let it ride. Jamal was still talking about the Madden game.

"Ay Charles, you ain't got no plug to get that early? Man E.J. better hope he don't get hurt this year, you know they say it's a curse to be on the cover of that game, that's crazy, huh?"

That is really crazy, but I don't believe in curses so it really don't matter. Eric better hope I don't hurt his ass for not telling me. It was taking all of my energy not to call him and clown but its not like he would answer the phone anyway. Then my phone started ringing.

"Hello, hey Tank."

"Did you see my Daddy's commercial?" The voice on the other end of the phone shouted.

"Yes, I saw it, did all of you guys see it?"

"Yeah, Daddy called to tell us to watch it."

Oh did he?" I swear that nigga ain't shit I thought to myself.

"Okay, well Mommy's in the middle of something so I'll call you back okay."

"Okay Ma, peace."

"Peace." I responded and hung up.

Next thing you know my phone was ringing off the hook and all for the same reason, so I turned the muthafucka off!

"Damn, people are trying to holla at you today." Charles said.

"Anyway, ya'll want to play some cards or something?"

"You know I can't play cards girl, can we play something else?" Alisha said.

Charles suggested we play Concentration, for shots. Since it was four people, the first person out took three shots, the next person took two, then the last person would take one. The winner chose the next category. We played for several rounds and before long we were all either tipsy or flat out drunk. I was tipsy. The radio was playing and somehow we all began dancing, we started a soul train line, well it really wasn't much of a line because it was only four of us. Charles started the old school dances off, by going down the line doing the "Smurf." We all followed suit breaking out the 'wap', the 'cabbage patch', and the 'robocop'. We were having a ball. Then a slow jam came on and that killed the dancing for me. I sat on the love seat couch and Charles followed. Alisha and Jamal continued dancing.

"You think you can dance, huh." I said to Charles.

"Think, girl you know I turned you out last night on the floor."

"I don't think so. Man I'm up here dancing like I'm on solid gold." I took my hat off because it had got a little hot and wrapped my braid in a bun. Charles was watching me very attentively.

"Am I doing this correctly?"

"What, you uncomfortable with me admiring your beauty?"

"Oh is that what you're doing, okay well continue then."

80

He then touched the nape of my neck which made me jump a little. I guess since I didn't cuss him out, he felt it was ok to massage my neck. Lord knows it felt good, but I had to pump my brakes. I eased myself over enough for him to know that I felt awkward.

"Sony, why do you have braids in your hair, from the baby hair on your neck, I can tell you have a nice texture of hair."

I had to laugh at that statement. "Ha ha, ok, I know you from the hood talking about some baby hair. Nigga, I'm damn near thirty, I ain't got no baby hair left. Anyway, step out of the box, women don't get braids or weaves for that matter, just because there hair is nappy or short. It can be about style or reinventing ourselves or like my reason, it's low main'tenance. However, you are really perceptive."

"Not always, I can't help it, I think you are beautiful. Not just your looks but everything, your personality, your energy.

"I think you are cool too, it's really strange I haven't held a conversation with a man outside family for longer than five minutes in about 10 years."

"I must be special." He said with that sexy ass smile.

"Anyway, you alright." I returned the smile.

"Sony, can I ask you a question?"

"Man, I don't know you got that serious look on. Go ahead, what's up?"

"The other night when I asked you what your husband did for a living, did you lie to me?"

"Did I lie to you?" I thought back to the other night when he asked if my husband was a realtor and entertainer, or a drug dealer. "No I didn't lie. I answered no to what you asked right?"

"Yes, you said no." He said looking at me as if I lied. "So your husband doesn't play football?"

"Actually, he does." Hell I ain't gon lie, if he ask.

"So you lied." He said a little excited.

81

"No I didn't lie, he is not a realtor, a drug dealer, or an entertainer. He is an athlete, you didn't ask that."

"An athlete is an entertainer."

"That's debatable, so I did not lie. If I was gonna lie, wouldn't I have said no to you when you asked if he played football?" He just sat quiet. "Oh that's what I thought. So how could you tell, what do I look like an athlete's wife?"

"Well from the gate, your ring was blinding me plus you live in Arizona, that's why I asked you in the beginning. When I said entertainer I meant athlete as well. However when you said no, I just let the thought ride, but then tonight when we played concentration and I picked football positions as the topic, I knew you and your cousin would be taking some shots back, but to my surprise I ended up taking shots. You knew every position," I started laughing. "That tripped me out, so then I thought back to when you said you didn't want to be around no females you didn't know, you said, 'they might know my husband, you know how groupies are', it all makes sense now."

"Oh I see, well is there any other question you need answers to."

"Does he play in the NFL and who does he play for?"

"I was talking about questions about me, yes he plays in the NFL."

"Who is he, I might know him."

"I don't think so, anyway I would hate for you to see him and be like yo, I kicked it with his wife."

"Come on now Sony, I ain't that type of nigga, I don't run my mouth."

"I feel you Charles, but I ain't ready to give all that up. Sometimes we have to keep some things to ourselves."

"Okay I can respect that, so about us will this be our last time seeing and talking to each other. I can't front, I know your situation but I can't help the feeling I have when I'm around you. I've never met anyone like you and it's fucked up that you're married but I want this to continue."

"Whoa, this is all too much for me right now."

"So tell me, you don't feel something."

"I feel something, but it's really weird and I wish it would go away because I shouldn't feel this way. Charles it's not wrong for you to have a feeling, but me, I'm married. Friends that's all I can give and even that is skating on thin ice."

Meanwhile, Alisha's alcohol had got the best of her and she was stretched across the couch with her head in Jamal's lap. That was my cue that it was time to go.

"Alisha, girl you okay?" She tried to lift her head but she was over.

"Charles, I have to go, I need to get my cousin downstairs to her bed."

"She ok laying there, my man got her."

"No she's not alright because she wouldn't be laid out like that if she was sober, so since she isn't sober I have to have her back. I really enjoyed myself today."

"Do you need help getting her to ya'll room?"

"That's ok she is about to get her butt up and walk, come on Alisha."

I pulled her up and wrapped her arm around my neck and we made our way to the elevator. When the elevator came I told him I would call him later and then we got on and headed to our room. Once we got in the room, I took Alisha's clothes off and put her in the bed. I got a garbage can and put it next to the bed in case she had to throw up. It was evident that Mya had been back to the room to change. I hadn't realized we had been in Charles room for some hours. This broad didn't even call to say she was going out. Oh shit I forgot I turned my phone off earlier. I turned my phone on and I had seven messages. I skipped through the first five because they were all people calling about Eric's commercial, the sixth message was from Mya.

"Sony, where ya'll at, well you're probably at the casino. Well anyway, I'm gonna go to the concert with Ryan because he has an extra ticket. I'll call you later to let you know what we are going to do after that. Bye."

I pushed seven to erase that message, the next message was from Mya too.

"Damn bitch, you still ain't answering. Well we're going to the Sheraton after the concert so try to meet us up there, I don't want to kick it with Ryan by myself all night, alright peace."

I pushed seven to erase that as well. I looked at Alisha, it wasn't no chance of her going out. It was almost 10pm, so I decided to jump in the shower so I could meet Mya at the Sheraton, I was not about to spend my last night in New Orleans stuck in the room. In the shower, I thought about my day. How was it possible for me to have such a good time and feel so comfortable with another man. I really wanted to blame it on the fact that Eric was acting an ass, but I knew that wasn't true. During me and Eric's ten year relationship he's acted plenty of fool, cheated and everything and I have never kicked it with another man, not even before we were married. It was something about this man, or maybe it was me, maybe I was at a transformation point in my life. I really needed to call Bri. I needed my best friend/cousins advice, but if I call her I'll never make it to the club. I'll have to fill her in on the way from the airport tomorrow. I finished bathing and got out the shower. It was 10:25 pm now, I didn't realize how long I was in the shower. I lotioned up and put the clock radio on to help me get pumped up; Alisha was knocked out sleeping. I felt like showing some skin so I decided to wear some shorty shorts with a halter bikini top. I sprayed my body with Issey Miyake before putting on my shorts and top. I parted my breads down the middle and put them in two buns, one on each side of my head like Princess Lea from Star Wars. I put on my lipgloss and touched my eyebrows, I even put on some mascara tonight. I put some money, I.D., lipgloss, cell phone and my room key in my Gucci fanny pack. I put on my most comfy hooker high sandals and I was good. The clock read 11:10pm, I blew myself a kiss in the mirror and gave myself a look over and I was ready.

"Bye Alisha." I knew she couldn't hear me but oh well.

I cut through the mall entrance of the hotel to come out on Canal street. I paced myself walking because the club probably wouldn't get poppin until about midnight. I tried to call

Mya but obviously she couldn't hear it and it went to her voicemail. Then my phone rang, it was Charles, my stomach instantly started twirling. Damn, should I answer it, oh well might as well, tomorrow this will be all over.

"Hello"

"Hey Sony, how's Alisha? Are you going to get into something?"

"Alisha is sleep so I hope she's cool, I'm walking down Canal right now headed towards the Sheraton."

"Really, we just left out of the Sheraton, who are you with?"

"I'm solo. Alisha is done and my sister is at the concert."

We're about to go to the House of Blues, you want to roll with us?"

"Thanks, but no thanks, I'll try to call you later."

"Alright, peace."

I hung up the phone thinking that I would probably have a good time going to the club with him but that would definitely be doing too much. I must have been deep in my thought because I didn't even notice Charles, Twan and Jamal as I passed them on Canal Street.

"Uh un." Charles cleared his throat to get my attention. However I didn't even acknowledge it because I just assumed it was some nigga making noise. "Excuse me miss," I looked around to see if someone was talking to me, when I looked back I noticed Charles and his friends standing in front of a liquor store. I waved my hand to them and said "what's up ya'll" and was going to continue on my journey to the Sheraton until Charles called my name.

"Sonya" he yelled and threw his hands in the air signaling what's up or maybe signaling how you gonna just walk by me. Whatever the sign, it made me stop, turn around and walk back.

"What up ya'll, what ya'll doing, watching all the women who walk by, hooting and clearing your throat. Ain't no real sister going to stop for that."

"Okay Sister Souljah." Charles joked.

85

"How you doing Sonya, I didn't even know that was you, you look very nice tonight." Twan said, I could tell he was talking about the fact that I was a little exposed plus my hair was off my face, so you could really see my face. I was more covered on the other occasions we saw each other.

"How's my girl doing?" Jamal asked.

"She's loaded, but she'll be alright tomorrow. I mean, hey, that's what you come to these type of things for, right?"

"Sony, let me holler at you," Charles motioned for me to the side, "why are you doing this to me, you see you got traffic stopped on Canal."

"What are you talking about?"

"Girl, you knew what you were doing when you put on them short ass shorts and that little top. Don't let me see you talking to no other niggas, you know I get jealous and don't be doing none of that sexy dancing like you were doing at the 'All White Party' the other night. Matter of fact don't even dance on that snake song."

"Charles you are crazy, I'll talk to you later. Bye guys." I said to Twan and Jamal. As I walked away, I made sure to take long, sexy, seductive strides because I knew I was being watched. After I got maybe a few yards away, Charles yelled, "I'm serious Sonya." I just laughed and waved bye because I knew he was watching me. He also let me know that he was watching me the other night when I was dancing with the fat dude at the club. I felt bubbly inside like the quarterbacks girlfriend during homecoming time, why? I don't know! Anyway, I finally made it to the Sheraton. I realized that walking by myself with this outfit on might have been a bad idea because I was being stopped every couple of steps. However, one person who stopped me proved beneficial because he gave me a pass to bypass the line and a VIP band. The line was hella long so I was blessed with that. The club was beginning to get packed. I tried calling Mya on her cell but there was still no answer, I left her a message telling her I was here and that I would be in the VIP. I know my sister, she would find a way to get in the VIP, she has a killer mouth piece. The VIP crowd was pretty laid back at the time. I was able to find me a table to sit at. The waitress came to take my order.

"Can I get you something to drink, ma'am?"

"Yes, can I get a bottle of Cristal and a double shot of Petron with a lemon."

"Sure how many glasses do you need?"

"Just one, thanks."

Hell it was my last night so I might as well do it big. Quite a few people were starting to fall in. The regular dance floor was packed and the DJ was jamming. My table gave me a good view of the dance floor and the whole VIP area, I might be posted here all night. The waitress was making her way back to my table.

"Here you go, ma'am. Do you need salt for your tequila?" I nodded my head no. "So you chillin by yourself, I heard that, okay that will be $416, do you want to start a tab?"

"No thanks." I handed her $440, she thanked me for the tip and said she'd check back on me in a few. All of the tables were full and I could people were hating because I had a table to myself but if you ain't gon ask to sit down I ain't gon offer. The concert must have ended because I heard people talking about the show. I continued to people watch and put a dent into the champagne. A couple of people asked me to dance but I didn't want to lose my table, so I had to decline. I wanted to dance too, especially when they played 'Get Low' by Lil Jon.

"Are you good?" The waitress had returned to check on me.

"Yeah, I'm straight."

"Why aren't you dancing?"

"I didn't want to lose my table."

"Girl, is that it, hold up, I'm going to get you a reserved marker and let the security know this is your table."

She returned quickly with the marker and the security to show him my face. After that I was able to dance and walk around and return to my table with no problem. I gave Sandra, the waitress another tip for hooking me up. I didn't realize how many people were up in the spot, I don't know what happened to Mya. I checked my phone to see if she had called, but no calls. The D.J played 'Snake' and all I could do was laugh to myself but I was having a good time. After returning to my table, I ordered a Malibu and cranberry. I still had half the bottle of champagne but since I walked away from it I was not about to drink anymore. When the waitress returned she told me someone had paid for my drink. I looked around to see if it was someone I knew but she said she didn't see him anymore. I told her to thank him if she saw him again.

"So you switching drinks on me?"

"What are you doing here, I thought you were going to House of Blues!"

"I did, but it was whack, you weren't there. I did see your sister there though."

"Are you sure?"

"I'm pretty sure, she spoke to me."

No this bitch did not do me like that. Oh well I'm chilling doing my thing anyway, I thought to myself.

"So you drug your patna's back over here?"

"They are all grown, they wanted to come back over here. Now how you end up with a table to yourself. I know all these women in here are mad at you with their feet hurting and you over here chillin, drinking Cris."

"How you know what I've been drinking on?"

"I've been here for a little while, Petron and Cristal, you trying to get loaded. Nah, I wanted to buy you a drink, so I asked the waitress what you were drinking and when she told me, I asked her was she sure. I have been here long enough to see that you didn't dance off the 'Snake' song though. It took me a minute to find you, it's a lot of people in this muthafucka."

"That's so sweet you came to look for me, but you gonna have to get up from my table because before you came in I was in my own space and not that I don't like your company, but look at all bitches and niggas crowding around my table now." A crowd of men and women had closed in on the table, the women I could understand but I could never figure out groupie ass niggas. "Damn, I feel for ya'll athletes, I feel like I'm in a fish tank, muthafuckas just staring.

Twan joined us at the table.

"Man, it's some dimes up in here tonight. Charles, whose Cris?"

"It's mine, you can have it."

"Oh yeah C, Greg in them on their way up here too, he just called my cell."

"Who is and them?" Charles asked Twan.

"Them broads he was with at the House of Blues." Twan replied

"Charles let me holler at you." Charles scooted in so I could talk quietly. "Ay, I really ain't feeling this setting, well what the setting is about to be, so why don't ya'll post up somewhere else. I mean your partna said it's some cool chicks up in here and honestly I'm tired of looking up and seeing chicks licking their lips and shaking their asses to get your attention, so why don't you see what the club has to offer."

"I've found the person I want to get to know, but if you want me to leave just say that, don't come with no weak shit about some broads."

He said that with a little authority and force, I guess he still got some thug in him, but I still got some in me too.

"What, first of all, don't nobody have to come at you with nothing weak, this is the real. I ain't feeling all this attention and once your patna 'G' come it's gonna get worse because that nigga tries the hardest to get attention, so yes nigga, you just might have to cut."

Charles was laughing as if Jamie Foxx was doing his stand up routine.

"Woman, you are so damn sexy. Look at you trying to be hard. Damn you just met 'G' and you got him pegged already, that's funny. Alright baby, I respect what you saying, I'm going to be watching you though."

He tapped Twan and let him know they were going to go post up by the bar. Once he left the crowd began to disperse.

89

Once he reached the bar, he sent me another Malibu and cranberry. However everybody didn't disperse. First a bold ass bitch approached my table.

"How you doing sister?" She said hella fake.

"I'm good, what's up?" I said because I could feel some shit coming.

"Oh nothing, I just noticed the bling on your hand and I wanted to tell you that your ring was pretty."

"Thanks." Come on now bitch, you can come better than that.

"Are you married to Charles Knight?" Damn this broad was real bold.

"No, I'm not."

"Oh because I was about to say you are lucky, my girl fucked him last year during All Star weekend and she said it was all that."

Okay that ain't my man but this chick was borderline disrespecting me, that shit didn't fly. "I'm sorry, do you know me?" I asked the chick.

"No, I don't think so."

"Okay, what would make you think you could come sit at my table and share information about who your patna fucked. If it was my husband, would you have been so inclined to share that info. So how lucky is a woman that has a man who is fucking tramps they meet at All Star weekend."

She smacked her lips and walked away, which left an opening for the weak ass nigga that approached the table next. He wanted to tell me about the houses and cars he owns, but he was sipping on a glass of melted ice, nigga the drink is gone. I was trying my best not to be rude, but he was irritating me. I told him that my husband would not appreciate another man posted up with me and this dude had the nerve to flip out and say, "oh but it's cool for you to post up with C. Knight?" Okay I really feel like I'm in the twilight zone. Muthafuckas are tripping, I was about to respond but he wasn't worth it. It was after three in the morning and it was time for me to go.

"You know what, you have a blessed night." All I can do is kill the haters with the Lord. As I walked past Charles and his crew, I threw up the peace sign to let him know I was leaving and I was out. It was three in the morning and the lobby at the Sheraton was still packed. Once I got outside the humidity hit me, thank heaven for my hair being braided. The streets were still cranking. I was hella hungry but I didn't feel like the crowd at Krystals. I decided to fall into the liquor store. I bought some crunchy gator chips, a snicker and a lemonade. As I glided down the street, I thought about my day from beginning to end. Even with the groupie bitch and the hating ass nigga, I would have to say this was the best day of the whole weekend. Oh well tomorrow its back to reality and figuring out what my husbands issue is. For now I'm going to enjoy my last stroll down Canal until next year. It's funny, tonight the air didn't seem that polluted, the locals didn't seem so overbearing and feet were not sore from the high ass sandals I was wearing. It was a perfect ending to a beautiful story. When I reached our hotel room, Alisha was still sleeping and Mya had not returned. I took off my shoes and started my shower water but before I could get in, I heard my phone ringing.

"Hello."

"Hey you want to watch the sun come up with me?"

"That sounds nice but I'm about to jump in the shower, however I really enjoyed our day and I want you to know I'm glad I met you."

"I'm glad I met you as well, Mrs. Eric Jackson."

"Oh, so what you did your research?"

"Oh so that is your husband, I would have never thought that. You are down to earth, not like the typical wife of a superstar athlete. No wonder why you choked this afternoon when that Madden commercial came on."

"Yeah that was partially the reason I choked, so how did you find out?"

"Do you know Aaron Johnson?"

"The basketball player, right, I don't know him, but I know who you're talking about."

"Oh well he was in the club tonight and he was at the bar talking and he said that 'Eric Jackson's wife is posted over there by herself usually she be with a crew of fine ass women, her and her cousins' so I put it together."

"Oh I don't know him, but I've seen him at some events in Oakland when he played for the Warriors. I bet you couldn't wait to call and let me know you knew who he was."

"Nah, I was just calling to make sure you got in."

"Oh okay, well I'm in and my shower is calling."

"So this is it huh?"

"Yes this is it. I'll be watching and cheering for you this season. Like I said, it was good meeting you, have a safe trip back to Jersey alright."

"Alright you have a safe trip as well."

And then I hung up the phone, no good-bye. I really felt awkward. I jumped in the shower and for the first time in life I understood how some people have affairs. Damn, what if he knows Eric, Eric does have friends who play basketball. I can't worry about that now I hurried up bathing so I could be in the bed sleep by the time Mya got in. As soon as I was in the bed getting comfortable, I heard the door opening and so I played sleep.

"Sony...Sony wake up."

I put on my dead to the world voice, "What's up Mya."

"Girl, I was so loaded I forgot to call and tell you we were gonna go to House of Blues."

"Really, don't trip, I was good."

"It was off the hook, your boy was in there."

Then it hit me, that's exactly why she didn't call me, because Charles was in there, but she ain't even knowing that he left there to be where I was, but I ain't even about to give her the energy.

"Was he? That's cool."

"Yeah he spoke to me."

"Oh ok, but I was sleeping so fill me in tomorrow on the airplane."

"Alright, I'm gon jump in the shower, but why is that garbage can next to Alisha's bed."

"Girl, I'll fill you in tomorrow about that."

Chapter 7

The 4 1/2 hour flight back to Oakland seemed like it only took and hour and a half because of our nonstop talking. Although Alisha didn't come into New Orleans with us, she was on the same returning flight. As the pilot announced our initial descent into Oakland, we all pinky sweared that everything that happened at Essence would stay in the dirty South. We all had some dirt over the weekend. Ryan slipping up and saying him and Mya got busy before, Alisha and her drunk ass having skeletons fall out of the closet and me, I take the cake with my married ass getting all googly over another nigga. We all agreed that we would bypass those parts of the trip when we tell about our weekend. Of course I have to fill Bri in on my dirt though. I was ready to get to my mama's house and see my kids.

"Who's picking us up from the airport?" Alisha asked

"Bri is picking us up, well her and Kim are coming. You know they can't wait to hear some stories."

As soon as we landed, I turned my phone on and it was ringing. The caller ID displayed Bri's name.

"What's up Bri?"

"I take it ya'll are here since you're answering the phone.

"Yeah, we just landed. Are you here?"

"Yeah, we're circling so we'll meet ya'll curbside."

"Alright, see you in a few."

By the time we exited the plane and got down to baggage claim, the luggage from our flight was already coming out which was cool. Mya had Louis Vuitton luggage, which was easy to spot. Alisha and I had black rolling bags like everybody else on the flight. At least Alisha was smart enough to put a colorful ribbon on hers to make it stand out. Our luggage didn't take long to come out, we headed outside to wait for Alisha to come back around. It used to be a time when a woman could flirt with the security and parlay her way into parking curbside to wait on a person, but since 9/11 ain't nothing going down, they barely let you get your bags in the car before they moving you on. I could see Bri's black Escalade approaching so I waved my hand to make sure she saw us. She pulled up to park and she and Kim both jumped out to hug us like we've been away for a year. We loaded the bags and jumped in the truck.

"Damn, you bitches look good, ya'll look so stress free. I ain't playing, I'm definitely going next year." Bri said.

"I'm cool, I ain't had no desire to go back to the South since I moved from there." Kim jumped in.

"Girl, you was about 5 or 6 years old when you left the South, you was too young to know anything. I tell you this, if you go to the Essence festival one time, I bet you'll be returning again." I said.

"That's whats up" Mya and Alisha agreed.

"Okay who am I dropping off first." Bri asked.

"Me, I need you to drop me off in Maxwell Park at Tai's mama's house to pick up the girls, my car is parked over there." Alisha said.

"Alright, then I'll drop you off Mya since you're by the lake."

"Kim's house comes before mine since she lives off Redwood."

"Duh, I know where that broad live but her car is in West Oakland at her Mom's along with her children. Then I'll drive your ass way to San Ramon." She said to me.

"San Ramon is not that far, anyway don't you want to see your Godkids?"

"Girl please, don't be trying to throw the kids in this because I just saw them two days ago on the 4th of July, which reminds me, I still got to tell you about my crazy date."

We arrived at Tai's mom's house which was Alisha's kids grandmother. She lived in Maxwell Park which was a pretty nice residential area in East Oakland. I got out to let her out the middle and helped her unload her baggage.

"So what you got planned for tomorrow, Lish?" I asked.

"I'll probably take the girls to the movie or something, when are you going back to Arizona?"

"I'm going to probably leave on Wednesday, so maybe me and my kids will go with ya'll to the movies tomorrow."

We hugged and I got back in the car. Next stop was Mya's house. Mya lived in a new ritzy apartment building on the lake called Essex, we got there in about ten minutes. We unloaded her stuff, hugged and then we were off to Kim's mother's house. Kim's mom still lived on Linden Street, the street we grew up on. As we drove into West Oakland, we passed the liquor store on 12th and Market Street, where there was a crowd of nigga's hanging out. Returning to West Oakland brought back so many memories, how we used to post up at that same corner store when we were running the streets. Once we turned on Linden, I could remember how we used to run up and down that block. I remembered how we used to have our boyfriends drop us off on the corner by Lowell Park so our parents wouldn't know they had cars. Those were the days, the Brown four plus one, our crew.

Time Out

Get to know the crew

Before I get any further, I may need to break down our crew. As you may already know Mya and I are sisters and Alisha and Bri are our cousins (first cousins). All of our fathers are brothers. Mya and I are daughters of Liz and Maxwell Brown. We also have four brothers. Mya is an executive in marketing at a computer company. She never went to college, she started working for the company in the mailroom right out of high school and climbed the corporate ladder the legit way, she didn't sleep with anyone. She is making big paper but she still acts a little bit envious of me, Bri and Alisha for having degrees. I think she fears what might happen if her company was to lay her off but she's too stubborn to go to school. "Why do I need a piece of paper to do what I'm already doing," is her philosophy. Mya is single with no kids.

As for me, I am the youngest of my parent's six children. I've always been grown for my age. Growing up I spent most of my time sitting on the block with the elder women of the community. Well all that ended when I fell in love with fast cars, fast money and bad boys. I loved the streets and by the time I graduated High School I was expecting my first child. Although I was hot, I was also a brainiac. Upon graduating I was awarded a full scholarship to UC Berkeley, that fall I enrolled for my freshman year. Over the Winter break I became a mother and by the end of January I was back in school for my second semester. I never really held down a nine to five for long, that was never my thing. However I have always worked or hustled in some form or fashion. I got my B.S. in sociology and went on to get my M.S. in psychology. In between time I got married and had more children, four children all together.

Bri is my best friend and cousin. We really didn't have a choice. We were born two months apart. As mentioned before our dad's are brothers. Bri's dad is Brian Brown. This is the crazy part; Bri and I are cousins on both sides. Our dad's are brothers and our mom's are sisters, sound like incest but it's not.

Back in the day my dad was dating my mom and he hooked his brother up with my mom's sister. Who would have thought they would all stay together. Our dad's say we are carbon copies of our mothers, "double trouble." We've always been together, that's my crib mate, accept for when she went to Spelman for undergrad. She then aced the LSAT and did her postgraduate studies at Boalt Hall, UC Berkeley's Law School. She is now one of the most sought out criminal attorney's in the Bay Area. Bri dates but the lawyer in her makes it hard for her to settle down; She can't trust any one. She is the only child and has no children.

Alisha is my uncle Al's daughter. Alisha is the oldest of three kids. She has two brothers. My uncle Al used to have it going on. He was a Long Shoreman for years making big paper. Alisha's mom's name was Sarah. She died when Alisha was thirteen in a car accident. That was the summer before Alisha entered High School (she skipped a grade in elementary). Uncle Al couldn't deal with the loss of Sarah, he fell deep into a depression, alcohol and drugs soon followed. Alisha found herself at thirteen taking care of a house and her two younger brothers who were nine and seven. At first Uncle Al was a functioning addict but after being introduced to crack he soon lost his jobs and bill began to go unpaid. Soon Alisha started getting calls form bill collectors for everything from the lights to the mortgage. She couldn't go to anyone for help because she was afraid her and the boys would be split up. Our family tried to help with money but it just scraped the surface. One day after a long day of going to school, cooking dinner and preparing her brothers school clothes, she sat on her porch puffing on a chronic laced blunt contemplating her next move. She thought about selling anything from drugs to ass to make some money. That's when Taiwan a neighborhood guy we knew from elementary school rolled up in his drop '67' mustang. After asking Alisha if he could hit the weed, he joined her on the porch. He was just playing about the weed, he didn't smoke but he asked if she wanted to go to the movies. As much as she wanted a night out she told him her situation and let him know that wasn't feasible. They decided to watch a movie at her house. They didn't watch the movie instead Alisha told him of her problems and asked if he could put her on with the game. After laughing at her he assured her things would be alright. The next morning he was at her house to pick her and her brothers for school with an envelope full of money. After that Alisha and Tiawan was an item. After being a mother to her brothers for two years she gave birth to her first daughter at fifteen. She ended up having another daughter after she graduated from Cal State Hayward University. Just as she was about to start a Master's Program Taiwan was killed. Alisha is the last person to make up "The Brown 4."

The last person to make up the crew is Kimberly Johnson. Kim came to West Oakland with her mother and younger brother and sister when we were six years old. They came from Houston, Texas running from her abusive father. She moved on my street and we actually kind of took pity on her, she was so homely. We lived across the street from each other for practically our whole life; she's like a cousin too. Growing up in Oakland, she never lost her country gullibleness and became a magnet for loser men. One in particular stuck and she married him. Ray Johnson her High School sweetheart. They have two handsome sons. Ray's hang up is he likes to use Kim as a punching bag so of course we hate him and he hates us too. Kim has been working at FedEx since the beginning of time.

Life has dealt us all different cards but the one thing consistent amongst all of us, was the fact that we are all beautiful Black women and we have each other's back.

NOW BACK TO THE STORY

"Alright then Kim, thanks for coming with Bri to get us," I said as we pulled in her Mom's driveway, "is anybody in there, it looks hella dark."

"Yeah they in there, you know my mama still be complaining about the electricity."

"Alright well tell my Godson's to call me, I brought them something back from New Orleans."

"What you bring me, did you stuff a man in that suitcase."

"What for, you ain't leaving crazy alone so what you need a man for?"

"Yes I am this time for real, ask Bri, I was telling her about it on the way to the airport. I'm filing for divorce."

"Oh okay well you can fill me in later, Bri has her own drama to fill me in on tonight."

We said our goodbyes and then Bri pulled off and we headed to the freeway. Bri was taking me to my parents' house in San Ramon, which is a suburb about 40 minutes outside of Oakland. My parents moved out of West Oakland about five years ago, they rented the house out and bought a fat house in San Ramon.

"Alright Bitch, tell me about your 4th of July drama."

"Oh nigga that shit, remember the dude Dante, ok he comes to get me and the first no-no was he had his daughter with him. You know I don't like being around people's kids if we ain't like that. No-no number two was that she was probably about one, she looked younger than E.J. Now you know young babies bring 'Baby Mama Drama." We both said in unison.

"Anyway, I'm like okay let's make the best of this, so he says he was dropping her off at his mom's house. When we got to his mom's house everybody is speaking to me by name and all juiced to meet me, so now I'm thinking he done told his people that we like a couple, and you know I've only known him a month. But girl, you ain't heard nothing yet, why his baby mama show up acting a fool. She was outside screaming and cussing, talking about bitch you can't fill my shoes, girl all type of crazy shit. Then she started crying and carrying on talking about how she's lost without him. All the while, she had her patna with her. Bitch if you ever let me make a complete fool out of myself and you don't slap some sense into me. Finally his mom convinced her to leave. After all that he still thought we were going out. I told that fool to take me home. After I have him buy me some 2 carat stud earrings I'm about to be cool, but anyway fuck that drama, what's this I hear about you being a slut puppy with some basketball player?"

"What, damn where did that come from?"

"Who you think, your sister."

"Damn, when she tell you that?"

"Well I tried calling you yesterday because I saw Eric's commercial."

"Oh bitch that's a whole nother story."

"Well anyway, your phone was off so I called Mya's phone, she was on Bourbon with Ryan, anyway she told me that Alisha's psycho nigga had her locked in his house for a day, why that broad love her some thugs, and she told me that you was all goo goo over some basketball player, so bitch give me the real because I know how my cousin, your sister put the two on the ten."

"It ain't nothing."

"Bitch, it's something because you blushing like a muthafucka."

"Ooh, I can't stand you, I ain't blushing. Girl, I don't know it was something about that man. He was fine, but we both know fine nigga's come and go, it wasn't even his looks it was his essence. His life was like a good book, all the stuff he's been through, his outlook on life and family and education, and girl he is hood like us."

I continued to fill her in on how we met. I told her about our first conversation and about me going to his room. Then about the afternoon Alisha and I spent with him and his boy, I told her about the money I didn't keep and about Mya hating. I also told her how he bumped my thoughts about shoes while I masturbated, that shocked her. I then filled her in on how I haven't talked to Eric and the commercial shit and how he acting like a total ass. By the time I finished rambling on about that 6'5" pure chocolate creation, we were pulling up in front of my parents' house.

"Whoa, that's something else. First of all, I love my cousin in law but that nigga is tripping, but on another note, are you going to talk to him again?"

"Bri, I can't, I ain't been attracted to a guy since I got with Eric nine years ago, and you know my attraction to Eric wasn't even initial. This shit is scary because I really dig him, bitch I really was goo goo over him. I couldn't even really look him in the eyes. So no, I can't talk to him, I have to try to fix this crazy marriage."

"Like I always say follow your heart, but I can't believe it Ms. Monogamous done had herself an Essence affair."

"Shut up, I ain't had no affair, thank goodness it was only a weekend, if it had been a week I don't know, nah, I'm playing."

"So what's his name, who does he play for, does he know Eric?"

"His name is Charles Knight, he plays for New Jersey. No he doesn't know Eric. He knows who he is, but he doesn't know him. I didn't tell you. That nigga, Aaron Johnson, who used to play for the Warriors is how he found out that Eric was my husband. Girl, remember you went out with him?"

"Ugh, don't remind me."

"Okay you know that this shit got to stay between us. Alisha and Mya don't even know I was feeling him."

We locked pinky fingers to signify a pinky swear then we got out of the truck and unloaded my luggage. I wasn't worried about Bri telling my secrets, we have acted as each others diaries for all our lives. I actually trust her more than I trust myself. As soon as we walked in my mother's door, my kids were running to greet me and in an instant flash, it was clear to me why

102

continuing a friendship was out of the question. I could never risk my children's happiness. I carried my bags to my room, yes I've been out of my parents house for ten years and they have since moved but they keep a room for me, I'm the baby! I grabbed my carry-on bag and took it to the family room so I could pass out everyone's souvenirs. My mom had cooked my favorite meal, fried chicken, potato salad, green beans and cornbread. The kids were competing for my attention. E.J. stuck to me, Kayla wanted to snitch on everybody, Tank wanted to tell me about beating Sean at Madden and Sean wanted to tell me about all the girls that were trying to talk to him when he went to the carnival with my brother and nephews. I hadn't realized how much I missed my family while I was gone. My mom made me and Bri plates and brought them into the family room as we began to eat, she began to talk.

"So Eric sure looked handsome in his new commercial."

"Um hmm, he sure did." I replied trying not to give clue that I was pissed with him at the present time. We continued to discuss the commercial until something jumped out at me.

"Kayla, where are your earrings, you know you are not supposed to take them off."

"I know but Uncle Mykal told me he was taking them to get cleaned at the jewelry store."

All the adults in the room had a look of shock on their face, they knew I was about to flash.

"Kids go upstairs to ya'll room and start getting ready for bed. I'll be up in a minute. Sean take E.J. please."

The kids went upstairs and I waited a minute to make sure they were out of hearing reach, my mother tried to say something before I exploded but she wasn't fast enough.

"So ya'll trifling son is back on that shit, huh?"

103

"Sonya I know you are not cussing at us." My mom responded.

"Ma, you on me about cussing, but you let your crack head son come in here and steal my daughter's one carat diamond earrings."

"Maybe he really took them to get cleaned."

"Yeah right, damn he can't steal a T.V or something, how he gon' violate my baby, my fucking five year old baby, I swear I'ma have him fucked up."

"You need to calm your behind down," my mom yelled.

"No she doesn't Liz," my Daddy replied, "that boy ain't right, he come right in here and lied to our faces and say he been clean for six months. He could have asked for money, he doesn't have to steal from the baby."

All I could do was cry, it wasn't about the earrings it was the fact that he stole from my baby. He used my daughter, he played on the trust and vulnerability of a child, that shit was weak. And this nigga was my brother.

"Don't cry Sony, what he's feeling now that his high is over is probably far worst than anything you can have done to him." Bri hugged me.

That quick, a happy homecoming had been ruined. I felt bad because I knew my mom felt bad and it wasn't her fault, I didn't mean to be disrespectful.

"Ma, I'm sorry for yelling and cussing. It's not your fault that your son is a loser, five out of six is not bad." I tried to laugh although I was pissed.

"Baby, I'm so sorry, this is supposed to be a safe place for my grandbabies, that's why I moved out of West Oakland. Try not to be mad at your brother. He has a problem. I'll go to my jeweler tomorrow and get Kayla some new earrings."

"That's ok Ma, we're leaving tomorrow anyway. I need to get back home."

"I thought ya'll were staying to Wednesday," my Dad said.

"Nah, we are on the first thing smoking to Arizona, I have to be honest, I might really do something I regret if I stay out here. Matter fact I need to start getting the kids packed."

Bri decided she better get on her way back to Oakland. I promised her that I wouldn't do anything stupid. She probably remembers when we were teenagers I had my boyfriend beat him up because he called me a bitch, that nigga was probably on crack way back then. I told her I would call and let her know what time we were leaving. I had to call and try to get us a reservation. After I walked Bri out, I went upstairs to get my kids ready for bed. I told them about my weekend, minus the getting drunk and hanging with Charles. My oldest son wondered why I didn't get him any autographs. I tucked them in and told them to get some sleep because we would be leaving in the morning. They were excited, we had been in Oakland for about three weeks and they missed home, their rooms and toys. My mother retired to her bedroom. I really felt sorry for her, I wouldn't know how I would deal if one of my children grew up to be a trifling crack head. I needed to pack our clothes, but tonight's events, a weekend of partying and a long ass flight from New Orleans had taken its toll. I decided to take a shower and get my butt in bed. These clothes can stay out here until we come back, it's not like they don't have enough at home. I called America West Airlines and was able to get on a 11:20 am flight which would get into Phoenix at 1:10pm. After doing that I called to schedule a car service to pick us up from the airport. I got my toiletry bag out of my suitcase from New Orleans and headed towards the bathroom, on the way there I passed by the family room where my father was still watching T.V.

"Hey Pop, can you take us to the airport in the morning?"
"Sonya, you know we wish you guys would stay longer, but of course I'll take you."

105

My Dad was always the peace maker but he knows how I am once I make my mind up about something. This was routine, my mom and I have always butted heads. Everyone says it's because we're so much alike. When we are apart we are like best friends but up under the same roof for too long and all hell breaks loose, that's why it's time for me to go home. I went ahead and showered and then cleaned the kitchen before I laid down. My body was tired however I could not fall asleep. I thought about why I was so unhappy in my marriage, from the outside looking in it looked like I had the fairytale life, but for me it was falling apart. People always equate financial stability with happiness, and most damn sure wouldn't understand that our problems didn't stem from cheating, I think it all boils down to two people who came up different. Laying there I started daydreaming (although it was night) about Charles. I wondered how he was able to break through the wall, maybe it was my vulnerability, he probably just like the average young black man with money, off the hook! My daydreaming was broke by my cell phone ringing, the caller I.D. said Eric, oh so now this nigga wants to call. As bad as I wanted to tell him off, I really didn't have the energy. I'll deal with that tomorrow. As soon as my phone stopped ringing my Mom's house phone started. My Dad came to my room to tell me Eric was on the phone but I didn't respond, I acted like I was sleep. He told him I was sleeping, he must have asked about the kids because my Dad said they were sleeping too. When he hung up the phone he waited by my door for a moment.

"Ms. Sony, you know I know all closed eyes ain't sleep. I hope ya'll work it out." He said as he closed my door.

My Dad knew me well, I was truly a 'daddy's girl', he was the only person who wasn't blinded by thinking wealth creates a happy home because honestly in his eyes wasn't no man good enough for his daughters, no matter how much money they have. Don't get me wrong, Eric is a good dude. He is an excellent father, he is very respectful, he barely drinks, he

106

doesn't smoke and he financially provides for his family. I guess that's why people think I have Prince Charming. Hell, I thought that myself, lord knows I had to kiss a couple of toads before I found him. I didn't remember falling asleep, but I must have, because the alarm clock was waking me up. I jumped up to start getting the kids ready but to my surprise they were already up, dressed and eating breakfast. My mother had got them ready.

"Thanks Ma, so when you coming out to Arizona?"

That's how it was for mom and me, we could never be mad at each other for long. I showered and got dressed. Before we got ready to leave, I packed my carry-on bag with snacks, books, pencils and crayons to keep the kids busy for the two hour flight. I made sure E.J had enough diapers and a change of clothes and then I was ready.

"Sony, you don't have any bags to load?"
"No, daddy I'm just taking this carry-on and the diaper bag. Matter of fact, I am gonna take the suitcase I have from New Orleans so I can wash the stuff in that bag when I get home."

We gave my mom hugs and kisses and I thanked her for everything. My mom watched us as we pulled off. Every time I leave she has the same look on her face of when I was eighteen and pregnant. On my ride from San Ramon to Oakland Airport I made phone calls. The first call was to Mya.

"What's up Bit, I mean girl." I almost forgot I was in the car with my daddy. I was about to call her bitch.
"You must be with Daddy, what's up?"
"I was just calling to let you know I was on my way to go home, so I'll see you next month. I'ma try to come back out before the kids go back to school."
"Yeah, I know I just talked to Mama. So you tripping off the earrings?"

"No, I'm tripping off your tweaked out twin."

"What a five year old need some diamond earrings for anyway?"

"You know what, I was calling to tell you I'm leaving, so since you know I'll talk to you later, Bye."

That broad really knows how to rub me the wrong way. My calls to Bri, Alisha and Kim were much easier. I let them know I was on my way leaving. Bri asked was I okay and told me to call when I get in. Alisha told me to have a safe trip and asked if her girls can come out next week so she can go on a cruise with Rock (the crazy nigga). Kim didn't have much to say, I asked was her psycho husband there, she responded yep, so I knew that would be a story later on tonight for her to tell me. My dad pulled us up curbside and got out to unload the stroller and the suitcase, while I unloaded the kids. After giving our hugs and kisses to my dad or granddaddy as the kids call him, we headed into the airport. Sean pulled my luggage, Lamar carried the carry-on bag and Kayla carried the diaper bag. I pushed E.J. in the stroller. Traveling was routine for my kids, this was how we rolled, me by myself with four kids across country.

By the time we made it through the security check point and to our gate they were boarding for pre-boarders. People who are traveling with kids or need special assistance, that meant us...

We arrived in Phoenix about twenty minutes early however the driver was waiting for us in baggage claim already. It didn't take long for my bag to come out and before long we were on the 202 headed for the 101 on our way home. When we pulled up at my house, I noticed that my trees needed to be trimmed, I remembered that I forgot to turn the air conditioner on before we left three weeks. Like I expected it was hot as hell when we entered the house. The kids were complaining about the heat, E.J. who had been up the whole trip had now decided to go to sleep and my nerves were bad. There was so much going on trying to get settled that when my cell phone rang I answered it without looking at the caller I.D.

"Hello."

"Hey you, can you talk?"

"Hey, I just got back to Arizona, I'm just walking in my house, I've been gone for three weeks so I need to get my kids settled and my head right, can I call you back?"

"Sure, I hope you don't mind me calling."

"Nah, it's cool—I'll call you later."

Oh my goodness he called, well no time to trip off of him, I have too much to do. I laid E.J. down in his crib, while he slept and the other kids got reacquain'ted with their rooms, I unpacked my luggage. I sent a text message to my mom and the girls to let them know we made it, I really didn't feel like talking to anyone. I made my rounds around the house, this was my daily routine when I was home. I knew I was very blessed, however I told myself that I would never be one of those people with too much stuff that that I didn't need. So although our house was big, I made it my business to at least touch every room everyday or at least try. I tried to call Eric but I got his voicemail so I left a message. The day had creeped away and I didn't feel like cooking dinner so we ordered pizza. After we ate the older kids showered and I gave my baby a bath. We popped some popcorn and got lots of junk to eat so we could watch a movie in the theater. The kids call this 'movie night', they picked Dr. Doolittle 2. I had such a blast in New Orleans but these were the moments I lived for. After watching Dr. Doolittle and Shrek it was time for bed, Lamar and E.J. had already fell asleep. After getting everyone in bed I called Eric back, he had called while we were watching the movie.

"Hello"

"What's up," I said.

"Nothing watching sports center, what are you doing?"

109

"Just put the kids to bed about to take a bath."

"I ordered ya'll some Nike stuff out of the catalog, but the kids can probably save some of the shoes for school."

Eric had a Nike contract so we were able to get Nike stuff for free.

"I just got them some stuff at Nike Town in San Francisco, so I hope we didn't get the same stuff." I replied.

"Have you started their school shopping yet? We can probably get some stuff when ya'll come out here for family day."

"When is that again?" I asked

"In two weeks."

"Oh okay because Taisha and Taira are coming out here next week."

"Oh, what's Alisha doing?"

"Nothing, there just coming to visit." It ain't his business what she's doing. He is really acting like everything is cool, like he ain't not talked to me in the past five days. I see I have to get it started.

"So Eric, I enjoyed your new commercial, I saw it while I was in New Orleans."

"Thanks," he replied.

Oh no this nigga didn't just say thanks. No explanation, no how was your trip.

"So why didn't you tell me about that, they had to have taped it a while back."

"I must have forgot."

"So how come you didn't ask about my trip, how come you didn't return my calls from out there?"

"What you calling me for, didn't you say you need a break, that's why you go to Essence. I was giving you a break. You got to leave your kids for four days so you can have a break. What's to ask, you go every year, was something different?"

110

"Nigga don't try to bring the kids in this because they were fine, it's funny how it's ok to leave them with somebody when I need to race across the country to comfort you when you have a bad game, and for your information, yes things were different this year!"

"What I don't understand is what you need a break from, it ain't like you work."

"Oh so this ain't work taking care of your kids. Oh believe me I can go to work, but how, you don't want no nanny or babysitter. That's why you moved us out here, so I couldn't do shit, that same ol control shit."

"I moved us out there so my kids could have a better life, you just want to be out there with your friends but you can't do what they do, they ain't got no husbands."

"You think because I'm married with children that I can't do shit, well that ain't happening, I still got to live. Oh and Kim does have a husband."

"Yeah and I see she wasn't at Essence. I don't know why I'm arguing about this, you gon' do what you want anyway. I give you whatever you need for and you want to argue over me not calling and a commercial."

"Eric I didn't marry you to give me what I need, I was getting mine before I met you."

"Well, what then Sony?"

"You know what, you just don't get it Eric. I'll call you tomorrow."

This was an all too familiar argument with Eric. The topic that starts the argument varies but it usually boils down to the same things. Maybe it's just me, one thing has surely changed, at the end of these arguments I would usually be soaking my pillow with tears, but tonight the only water flowing was my bath running. Eric was a spoiled man who I had catered to for almost ten years but now with four kids and no one catering to me, it was getting hard. I sunk into my bathtub filled with Victoria Secrets apple scent bath bubbles. My candles were lit and I felt at peace. Instead of replaying my argument with

111

Eric in my head, I went to a happy place and reminisced about my Essence weekend. I remembered I was supposed to call Charles back, I thought about it for a minute and decide what the hell! I picked up the cordless phone and dialed *67 before dialing his number that's when I realized I had memorized his number. When the phone started ringing I instantly got nervous. I started to hang up because I forgot that he was three hours ahead of me, which meant it was like one in the morning there, but then he answered.

"Hello"

"Hey is it a bad time?" I asked.

"It's never a bad time for you."

"Do you know who you are talking to?" I asked.

"Yes Sonya – I know who I'm talking to."

"I'm sorry for calling so late, I wasn't thinking about the time difference. Were you sleeping?"

"No I wasn't sleeping, I was actually thinking about you. I didn't think you were going to call back. I hope I wasn't out of line for calling earlier, you have been on my mind since we met."

"On the regular, I would say you were out of line but you caught me at a strange place in my life and things are different, so it's cool."

"I can't figure out what you're talking about, but I'm glad it's cool." He said and we both laughed.

"I was thinking about you too, so did you have a good time at Essence?"

"I did, what about you? I'm sure it was a nice break from work." He said.

"I told you, I don't work."

"Being a mother of four and a wife of a professional athlete is definitely work." He said.

"You are right about that and yes it was a good break for me!"

We continued to talk about our weekend in New Orleans. We talked about some of our likes and dislikes, things we had in

112

common and did not. I was enjoying the conversation so much that my hot bath water was getting cold. I was turning into a wrinkled raisin. I wanted to tell him I would call him after I got out of the bath, but I knew it was best to end this conversation. I knew that I was in a very vulnerable place.

"Well, it's getting late here and it's been late there, so we better get off this phone." I suggested.

"Yeah, I guess you're right," he agreed although he wasn't ready to get off the phone either. "So, Sony what happens next for us, maybe it's me but I feel there's a chemistry."

"I don't know Charles, I don't want to get you mixed up in the confusion that I call my life. Shit I don't even know what I want for me right now." At this point I didn't care if he knew I was crying as I spoke because I was boo hooing.

"Don't cry Sony, I hope I didn't make you cry. Look it's no pressure, I just want to be whatever you want me to be."

At that moment I felt like exhaling....

"You know Charles, sometimes I just want someone to talk to."

Quarter 2
Chapter 8

"This is Bri."

"Bitch why are you answering the phone all professional, you know your secretary told you it was me."

"I'm sorry, I'm with a client right now."

"Why her dumb ass put me through to you then, anyway what do you have planned for lunch?"

"Um, can I get back to you in five minutes. Can I reach you on your cell?"

"Yeah."

"Ok, I'll get back to you."

As I waited on Bri to return my call, I questioned my brother Lamar on the new chick my mom told me he was seeing. Lamar was one year my senior but he was more like my little brother. He picked the kids and I up from Oakland airport and was dropping me off at my mother-in-law's house.

"I'm telling you Sony, this one might become Mrs. Brown. She is a notch, she ain't got no kids and she got a good job."

"What she doing with you then?"

"Anyway, you know I'm the man. You know mama is going to be mad that you're going to Ms. Barbara's house before you go see her."

"First of all I need to get my car from over there, and secondly I didn't get a chance to bring the kids by before we left last month thanks to your crackhead brother."

"Yeah that shit was fucked up."

"Plus who wants to drive way out to San Ramon to have to turn back around to come back to Oakland...she'll get over it."

"So, lil sis you want to switch cars. You know you wrong for having that car over there parked when I can be flossing in it while you gone."

114

"See, you answered yourself, because you would be flossing and then every time I drive my car I got to worry about your crazy ass women. We can probably switch tomorrow because I'm going to take my kids to Six Flags Marine World. I want to take Shamar (Shanae and Lamar) so ask Shanae if he can go."

"Ask Shanae, that's my son! He gone be at mama's house anyway, so it's cool."

(Ring, ring, ring)

"Hello"

"Where you at ho?"

"Oh how quick we fall out of business mode, I take it your client is gone. Anyway I'm in the car with Lamar and the kids on our way to Barbara's house.

"Tell 'Mack Mar' I said what's up, so I thought you wasn't coming out here until Saturday."

"I was but Mya said Everett and Jones in Jack London Square be going down on Fridays so I decided to come today so I could check it out."

"So what's up for lunch?"

"We pulling up at the house right now, so I'm going to get them settled and come meet you at your office. I want Le Chevals."

"Yeah that would be good, so I'll see you in a few." Bri responded.

Lamar helped me unload the kids, we didn't have any luggage because I left clothes here when we were here last month, all I had was a carry-on and a diaper bag. Lamar was in a rush to go pick up his son, so once we got in the house he was on his way. You would have thought it was Christmas because Barbara had a room full of new stuff for these kids, so it obviously didn't take them long to get settled. My mother-in-law and I were very tight. She had been my sounding board for many years when I had problems with her son. She felt partly

115

responsible for his ways, she had spoiled him to overcompensate for the fact that his dad was a deadbeat, plus he was the only child. She created a monster and I guess I get the blame for picking up where she left off. Barbara was different than what you would think of a typical athlete's mom cause you know how Black women can be about their sons. I was like the daughter she never had. It was times early in our relationship that Eric was cheating and Barbara was the one who told me that 'no money was worth compromising my self worth' and advised me to leave him and make him pay big time for child support and palimony (this was before we were married). I could honestly say that she had my back, she believes what's right is right and wrong is wrong, no matter who it is.

"I'm about to go have lunch with Bri, do you need anything for the kids?"

"No, we're fine. I'm about to make them some lunch and then go outside and play."

"Okay, I'll call you later, I'll probably stay over here tonight because I'm going to go out with my cousins."

"Do you have your keys to the house?"

I told her I had my keys and kissed my babies and told them to be good and then I was off to meet Bri. Bri's office was downtown in the City Center. I didn't feel like going into the parking garage so I called her and told her to meet me on the corner of 12th and Broadway. We were able to get a good park on the same block of the restaurant, We also missed the lunch crowd and was able to be seated as soon as we walked in.

"Damn, it took you long enough to get here, I was starving. You know I got to eat lunch by 12:30 or I can't function." Bri exaggerated her hunger.

"It's only 1:05 pm, I know you ate breakfast too."

The waitress arrived and we ordered two claypot rice, no beef, an order of fried chicken wings and some imperial rolls. I

116

ordered me a Karma Sutra and Bri ordered a Lemonade. Bri doesn't drink during work hours. As we waited on our food, she caught me up with all the latest happenings in Oakland. We talk everyday on the phone about our personal business so she filled me in on other people's business. Our gossiping was interrupted by the food coming and my cell phone ringing.

"Hello."
"What up, did ya'll make it to Oakland?"
"Yes, we're here."
"Did I catch you at a bad time?"
"I'm sitting down having lunch with my cousin Bri."

Bri's eyes and ears perked up, she mouthed, "who are you talking to that don't know me." I waved her off and continued to listen to my phone call.

"Oh Bri is the cousin you told me about, your best friend, right?"

Bri's curiosity was really peaking now.

"Did you tell her about me and you talking?" The person on the phone continued to talk.
"Nope, but can I call you after I eat….alright later."

I closed my phone and proceeded to put food on my plate without even looking at Bri, but I could tell her mouth was gaped wide open.

"Uh um, Mrs. Jackson, I'm waiting on an answer."
"An answer to what?"
"To who you were talking to or should I guess. You little hoe, you bitch, you've been holding out on me. I can't believe you still be talking to that nigga! What's his name again?"

117

"I don't know what you're talking about. That wasn't no nigga on the phone, that was my friend I met in Phoenix."

"Bitch, stop lying, you don't even roll with females and all your friends are your family, except for Kim and she might as well be. I should have known, because lately I ain't heard no stories of Eric getting on your nerves or the kids driving you crazy so somebody must be bringing you some peace and joy."

I couldn't lie, he was doing that for me but I couldn't admit it either. I just laughed and continued eating my food.

"Oh my goodness, did you fuck him at Essenee?"

"Hell no, I ain't fucked, I am married bitch, I ain't that trifling. I just talk to him on the phone. I enjoy talking to him, he's a cool person and he keeps my stress low, that's it."

"Are you sure that's it because it seemed to me from the first time you told me about him that you had a tingle for him."

"If or if not, it doesn't matter, that's all it's going to be, friends."

"So what do ya'll talk about?"

"Different things, just about us. I never discuss Eric and I. I'm sure he can tell at times that I'm going through something but he never pries, he basically is being whatever I want him to be and right now that just someone to talk to, someone I can be Sonya with and not super mom or a super wife, I can just be me."

"Bitch you sound like you on a soap opera, but I feel you. However are you sure you know what you're doing, you have a lot to lose girl."

"I know Bri and I have prayed on this so much but for some reason it feels right."

"Well you know I got your back, does anyone else know?"

"Come on now, you know you the only one person I trust and I know you gonna be real with me."

"Well this is going to the grave with us. So when do I get to meet, what's his name again?"

"His name is Charles, and I don't know when you are going to meet him. It ain't all like that."

"Well I know I'm getting tickets when they play the Warriors."

"You already have Warrior season tickets."

"So what, his tickets may be better than my seats."

We continued to eat and Bri decided she would go against her no drinking during work hours policy and have a cocktail with me. I truly felt like a ton of weight had been lifted off my shoulders. After eating, I dropped Bri back at her office and got on the highway to head to my mother's house. I was tired and I really could use a hot shower and a nap. I sure hope her son is not out there. I called Eric to leave him a message letting him know that we made it here and that the kids are at his mom's house. I knew he would be practicing; their first preseason game was next week on August 13th. It was funny that we never settled any arguments but for him as long as I wasn't arguing then everything was cool. Well I guess he could thank Charles for that because talking to him made me a whole lot less uptight. Speaking of Charles, I decided to return his call while I drove to my mom's house.

"Hey are you busy?"

"I'm at the park with my girls but we can talk, they are running around."

"No, you need to get your butt up and run around with them. You can call me back later."

"You are crazy, alright I'll hit you back."

The drive to San Ramon wasn't bad because I had beat the after work traffic. As soon as I walked in the door, my mother was on me.

"Well it's about time you made it out here, didn't your flight come in around eleven. Where are my babies? Shamar is

119

coming to spend the weekend and I told him his cousins would be here."

"I took the kids by Barbara's house because I didn't get a chance to take them by there before I left the last time, but I'm going to take Shamar with us to Marine World tomorrow so they'll be together then. Then I went to Le Chevals for lunch with Bri and now I'm here. Ma, you do live hecka far out so I had to take care of all my Oakland business before I came out here."

"Have you talked to your sister?"

"Not since I've been here, I talked to her early this morning when I was at the airport. We are supposed to go out tonight. Where's daddy?"

"He went to put some money on your brother's books."

"What? Mykal is in jail, that's what his butt get, but hold up, daddy went to put some money on his books?"

"Well he drove but Junior was going to go in and put the money on the books. I did get Kayla's earrings back though. Maybe this will help him get clean and get his life right."

"So why ya'll didn't tell me, I mean I am still mad at him but he is my brother."

"Well, we knew you were mad so we figured you would find out when you came back."

A part of me felt bad for Mykal, but another part had no sympathy at all. He had all the same opportunities as the rest of us. My mom continued to fill me in on what was happening with the rest of my siblings. My oldest brother Maxwell (Junior) and his family were thinking of moving to Fresno where the cost of living was better. His wife was from L.A. so that would be a middle point between Oakland and L.A.. My brother Kevin just got accepted into a doctoral program at Stanford. Kevin was the second to oldest and he had no trace of being from West Oakland, he was corny as hell. He would remind you of Braxton from the Jamie Foxx show. There was nothing new with Mya, my mom just wished she would find a man to settle down with. Last she told me about the new girl Lamar was dating. Although she had already told me about her, I still let her retell me. She also told me that Shanae, his baby mama has another baby on the way, by him. Lamar didn't tell me that, though. After hearing all the stories about my brothers and sister and some stories about her employees, I finally had to tell her I was tired and needed a nap. As I was headed to my room, my cell phone rang and it was Charles. Somehow my tired voice disappeared when I answered.

"So did you tell Bri about me, what did she say?"

"Man, you don't have nothing to worry about."

"Well you know I was against you telling anyone because you really can't trust people in this sort of situation, and I have a lot to lose."

"What do you have to lose, you ain't married, plus ain't nobody making you talk to me. I can trust my cousin." I was getting a little heated so I decided to tell him I was about to take a nap. Although he seemed hesitant to get off the phone he said ok and we hung up. I took off my clothes and got in my bed with just my panties and bra on. I turned the radio on 102.9 KBLX and closed my eyes but before I could drift into my sleep my phone rang again.

"Yes Charles."

"Are you sleeping yet?"

"I'm on my way, what's up?"

"Ok we both have a lot to lose."

"Whatever, Charles."

"You know you are so cute when you get mad, you gonna make me bite you."

"Really, What you gon' bite?" Oh my goodness, did I say that.

"Your peach." He replied.

"What's my peach?" I asked since I was already in to deep.

"What's fuzzy and juicy."

"Nothing is fuzzy, I Brazilian wax."

"Well what about a nectarine, I like them better anyway, what's juicy like a nectarine?"

I couldn't believe he had me a little aroused, I slid my finger into my vagina and it was juicy, I guess that might be what he was talking about, however I had to escape this conversation before I soaked my sheets. I really had to grab my hand from twirling around in my coochie, I was plunging my fingers as deep as they could go.

"So when can I?" Charles asked. I had totally lost track of what he was saying, all I heard was the sound of his east coast accent, which was the background music for my finger aerobics.

"Huh, when can you what, bite me?"

"Well that too, but that's not what I'm talking about, you didn't hear me?"

"No, what did you say?"

"What are you doing? I said, when can I see you again?" He repeated.

"Ohhh, I don't know."

"Why don't you take a trip to Atlantic City."

"Why don't you take you a gambling trip to Las Vegas." I replied.

"Ok, when should I come?"

"Oh my goodness, are you serious?"

"Yes I'm serious, I can come as early as next week, what about you?"

"Well, I can't come by myself, but Bri did ask when she could meet you. So, maybe in two weeks, my mom can come to Arizona to stay with my kids. Since Bri's birthday is coming up, it will be like a birthday trip.

"That's cool, just let me know when you make your reservation and I'll call and take care of it."

"You don't have to pay for us, I got it."

"Well since you left your money in my room in New Orleans from the casino winnings, I still owe you."

"Oh, I was hoping you found that, man that would have been a happy housekeeper."

"Well get back to me on that and I'll let you finish your nap. Hold up though, can I ask you a question without you getting mad."

"Sure, go ahead."

"Do you ever masturbate when you're away from your husband for long periods?"

First I had to laugh, before I replied. "Yes, I do even when it's not long periods of time. As a matter of fact I just, never mind."

"Are you serious?"

"Good night Charles."

"No really, tell me, I thought so!"

"Good night" I repeated and hung up the phone.

I tried to get back into my sleepy mode but that was ruined. I just stared at the ceiling thinking what am I getting myself into. My cell phone chimed letting me know I had a text message from 617-555-4353, it read, "I would kill to be your fingers." I laughed and knew that I was getting in way over my head but I was enjoying it. I laid around for about thirty more minutes and then decided to see if my mom wanted to play some cards but first I washed my hands.

"Whatchu cooking Ma?" I asked my mother as she chopped onion and watched Oprah on her 13-inch kitchen T.V.

"Spaghetti, salad and garlic bread. Why, are you hungry because it's all types of stuff in the fridge."

"Nah, I'm cool I was just asking, you want to play some Rumi?"

"Sure, I ain't beat you at cards in a while, get the cards out of that drawer and shuffle." She said pointing towards a drawer in the kitchen.

I got the cards and shuffled them and sat them on the kitchen table and waited for my mom to cut. After she cut, I dealt out eleven cards. These were the things I missed about being in Arizona. Just being able to hang out at my mama's or Eric's mama's house. I missed being able to run a quick errand by myself and not have to load all the kids up to go with me. But Eric swears up and down moving to Arizona wasn't about controlling me and I was so in love I would have moved to the moon. Now I'm out there stuck on stupid and miserable but his ass is cool. We finished the five hundred point game rather quick and like my mama proclaimed before the game she did beat me, 540 to 410.

"Let's play some blackjack, I'll be the dealer." My mother said.

"Alright, when's the last time you been to the casino?"

"Your dad and I are going to Reno next weekend, I haven't gotten used to all the Indian casinos they have now."

"Hey Ma, can you and dad come to Arizona to stay with the kids in two weeks so I can go to Vegas with Bri for her birthday."

"Well, I don't know about your dad but I'll come, I'm surprised Bri's busy butt is going to take a trip, she needs it, that should be fun."

I was thinking I hope she can take some time to go as well since I hadn't mentioned it to her, well at least I have my babysitting secure. I can't believe I'm going to meet Charles although Bri could use a vacation and it is her birthday, I was really trying to convince myself. My mama was hot today, she killed me at blackjack as well.

"So how are you and Eric doing?"

"Well Ma, you've been married for forever so you know how it goes – some good days and some that are not so good."

"Well you know you can always talk to me, about anything. We all know how you keep stuff to yourself and with you being in Arizona we would never know what's up."

"I'm cool, just a little home sick that's all."

124

"Well come back, you know I was against the move from the gate. Although I love it out there, ain't no reason for you to be out there by yourself."

"I wish it was that easy."

"It is that easy, it's not like you have a job out there, all you have to do is put the house on the market and get to packing."

"I don't know Ma, maybe I'll think that about it, I guess I better start getting ready so I can get back to Oakland."

I had been considering moving back from Phoenix since I relocated there two years ago. I knew Eric wouldn't agree I definitely needed to do something, the emptiness in my life is what probably allowed me to open up to Charles. Eric better get a clue, moving back might save his marriage. I thought about it more as I showered. If I came back to the Bay Area, the kids could grow up around their family, I could have some help during the season since he didn't believe in Nanny's or babysitters. Maybe I could get a job or at least volunteer with some organizations. What's the point of going to school for all those years if it ain't putting it to use. By the time I was getting out of the shower I had made up my mind, my kids and I were moving back and Eric would have to deal with it or not. After I finished dressing, I went to get my mom's opinion on how I looked. She, my dad, my oldest brother Junior and my nephew Shamar were in the family room eating.

"Hey Daddy, what's up Shamar, you coming with Ti-Ti to six flags tomorrow?"

"Yep, are my cousins coming here?"

"They'll be here in the morning, what's up Junior, your wife ain't cooking dinner tonight?"

"What, I can't eat at my mama's house? But anyway, she and the kids drove down to Fresno to see her sister."

"Oh you home alone, well we're going to Everett and Jones, Q's lounge, if you want to come out."

"I just might, I'm suppose to go over Fred's house and play Madden."

"Oh don't bring up Madden, I ain't whooped on you in a while."

"Nah, Sony, you can't touch me now, I'm better, I beat Lamar yesterday."

"What that mean, I ain't even played in hecka long and I'll still get with you. To bad I gotta get to Oakland but we'll play before I leave."

My mama approved of my outfit, so I grabbed my purse and headed out the door. It was 7:15pm and I was suppose to pick Bri up at 7:45, I might be a little late, I decided to call her.

"Don't you look cute, and you are only five minutes late, I'm impressed."

"I know, I'm surprised I thought I would be later but traffic was flowing."

"Okay, I'm ready, Mya and Alisha are going to meet us there. I want to run by these lofts in Jack London first so I can show them to you. I'm thinking about buying one."

"Cool, but why are you moving, this house is perfect." Bri lived in a nice two- story home in the Claremont area of North Oakland. A very quiet neighborhood."

"This house is perfect for a family not for me."

"What did your parents say?"

"I told them I was going to rent it out and when I settle down and start a family, I would probably move back."

"That's a first, you starting a family."

Bri convinced me to drive because she said she was getting drunk for her birthday although it was two weeks away.

"Speaking of birthday, how would you like to go to Vegas for your B-day?"

"That's sounds cool, I could use a break. Did you ask everybody else?"

"No, this is just a me and you trip because your boss gave you two free tickets, you feel me?"

"Oh my goodness, so I get to meet the other man!"

"Don't say that, he is not the other man. So are you down?"

"Of course, where are we staying?"

I continued to fill her in on all the details about this trip until we arrived in Jack London to see the lofts that were being built. I admit they looked nice, but $300,000 plus for some open space, I couldn't see doing it but I supported Bri in her choices. Then we headed a couple of blocks down to Q's. Mya had called to say her and Alisha already had a table for us. We were going to eat in the restaurant before we headed over to the connecting lounge. When we got in the restaurant the waiter was approaching our table to take our order, perfect timing!

Pretty soon we were feasting on barbecue chicken, beef links with greens, potato salad, yams and cornbread. The food was off the hook, I drank water with my dinner to prepare me for the alcohol that my body would take in tonight. You would have thought this was the last supper the way cleaned our plates. The restaurant was beginning to get crowded so we decided to pay for our food and go over to the lounge to make room for people dining. Alisha picked up the tab, we all alternate on who pays the tab when we all go out. We stopped in the bathroom to check ourselves and freshen up the lip gloss and then we headed over to the packed lounge area. It was no chance of us finding a table, we made our way through the crowd speaking, handshaking, and hugging all of the people we knew. Everybody was up in there, it was a hot summer night and the women were out showing skin and the men were trying to floss. Bri knew everybody from high end, like the boogie lawyers she rubbed elbows with in courthouses to low-end like the criminals she represented. Then we lucked up, I spotted my brothers in the corner and they had a table. I ordered a bottle of champagne to celebrate my brother Kevin being accepted in to his doctoral program.

"What's up Kev, how did he drag you out?" I asked as I hugged him and congratulated him on his accomplishment.

"I actually called him since I knew he was home alone, and he said ya'll were coming here. Where's Mya?"

"You know your sister, she's working the crowd."

"The Brown women back in effect." Junior shouted.

"You didn't know." Alisha and Bri responded and high-fived.

We all drank, talked and laughed the night away. Lamar came up there with Alex, one of Alisha's little brothers. Our whole generation of Brown's were there with the exception of my brother Mykal and Alisha's other brother Alonzo who both happened to be locked up. I bounced the idea of moving back out to the Bay Area and everyone agreed with it, well except for Mya, who felt I needed to be supportive of my husband's decisions, but wasn't nobody really trying to hear her.

The lounge closed at twelve and the guys were heading down the street to Kimballs Carnival, a night club located in Jack London. Mya had a date and Alisha decided to tag along with our brothers. Bri and I headed home to her house, I knew we were going to be up all night talking. When we got to her house we both got in our pajamas. Bri made us some tea and I started a fire in the fireplace.

"So Sony, are you serious about moving back?"

"I am girl, I've been miserable for a while, but did you hear my sister. I swear she is such a hater."

"Well you know Mya is going to be Mya, and you know you being out here takes away from her shine."

"What shine, I ain't even into the stuff she's into. All I know, is this summer has opened my eyes to a lot."

"Would Charles have anything to do with this move?"

"No, well maybe yes and no. I mean I've never discussed moving with him and our relationship wouldn't be any different, so no in that respect, but I will say that meeting him has opened my eyes to how much my life was lacking. All I have going on is my husband and kids. Don't get me wrong, I love being with my kids but I need something outside of that. I mean hell, if it didn't happen on Disney or Nickelodeon, I don't know about it. So yes, I think the fact that I met Charles and continue to talk to him lets me know that I'm lacking something and also that I'm not completely happy with Eric and haven't been for some time now. Maybe if I move back I can have some outside interest, I have ya'll, I can help my mom with her company, I can volunteer in West Oakland at the Boys and Girls Club. You know I ain't never been the type to just do nothing and now that the kids are getting older I need to find out what I need to do for me."

"So what if Charles is what you need, have you ever thought about being with someone other than Eric?"

"It's funny, I really like Charles, he is so easy to talk to, he's funny, he's down to earth but I don't see us in a relationship way. There would always be a trust issue. I'm not denying the chemistry, but it's all in check. As for Eric, no, I have never imagined myself being with anyone other than him, but lately I have pictured myself being by myself. Eric and my issues are not about another person they are about us and after 10 years it may be too late for him to change."

"So, Ms. Lady, we really going to Vegas?"

"Yes, when we leave Oakland, I'm going to take the kids to Florida to see Eric and go to his game next weekend and then I'll be back in AZ on that following Monday and we can leave Thursday night."

"What day is your mom coming out there again, I'll probably come on Wednesday so I can spend a night with my babies before we leave."

"I don't know, I'll ask her. Girl I'm kind of nervous, you know that nervous excitement."

"You are really crushing, so tell me more about him....

Chapter 9

It was so damn hot and humid in Miami, Eric was loading our luggage into the trunk and I got the kids situated in the truck. I was tired as hell, we had a straight through flight from San Francisco and E.J. was up for the whole five hours. The kids were excited to see their dad and I was actually happy to see him as well. I decided to drive because I knew he was probably wreck because with Eric driving and trying to look at his kids. All of my issues with him seem to disappear when I witness him with our children he was definitely a great father. The kids all competed for their dad's attention telling them about their visit to Oakland.

"So I see you're letting your beard grow in, that looks nice."

Eric pulled the visor down to look at himself in the mirror as he brushed he facial hair with his hands, he replied, "you know a nigga got to switch it up, so you like it?"

"Yes, I like it." I replied.
"You guys hungry?" He questioned the kids, and in unison they replied, "Yes."
"Daddy can we have McDonalds?" Kayla asked.
"Of course, anything for my princess, next stop McDonalds. Baby, are you hungry?" He asked me.
"Yes, but you know I ain't eating no McDonalds."
"Well once we get settled at the house, I can go back out to get us something."

We stopped at McDonalds and then arrived at our place. We bought a townhouse out here a couple of years ago when Eric signed a six year contract with Miami. I didn't want to live in Miami but the townhouse was a good investment and enough space for when we visit and not too much space for Eric when he was here by himself. When we walked in you would have thought it was somebody's birthday, Eric had bought all types of gifts for the kids.

"Don't get jelly, baby, I have something for you too. It's in our room."

"Ain't nobody getting jealous, you just spoil these kids too much and then I got to deal with they bad asses."

"I spoil you too, baby." He said and then hit me on my butt. This of course made the kids giggle and hide their faces. I set the kids up at the kitchen table to eat McDonalds. I told Kayla to help E.J with his food while I put the luggage in the rooms and got settled. Eric was sitting in the family room watching T.V.

"Sonya, when are you going to look at your gifts?"

"In a minute, let me get settled first." I said as I walked in our room. On the bed were some roses, a teddy bear and a Victoria's Secret bag.

"Thank you Eric." I yelled out. "I haven't looked in the bag yet, but I bet it's going to turn into a present for you as well."

"I don't know what you're talking about, Sonya."

Eric was the one person who never calls me Sony. I don't think he has ever called me Sony. After unpacking some stuff, I looked in Victoria's Secret bag and found probably every bra and panty in my size that the store had. On the real, he had bought me hella panties and bras and just as I thought he bought me a sexy little negligee, and I do mean little. I fell across his lap and planted a kiss on his lips to thank him again.

"Did you decide what you want to eat?"

"I ain't really tripping, what about a burrito. I just want something quick."

"That's fine, do you want me to take the kids so you can rest for a minute."

131

"Nah, when they finish eating, they are going to shower so they can get ready for bed. It has been a long day. I'm going to let them play for a few then it's lights out because I'm tired myself."

He left out to go to Chipotle's and I went to check on the kids. My babies must have been hungry because they were all finished, well except for the baby. I told them to go play with their presents or do whatever because they would be bathing and going to bed shortly. I surveyed the kitchen and was surprised. Eric had taken the liberty of going to grocery shopping. He had all of the things the kids and I like to eat. He even bought me my Malibu Rum and cranberry juice. He was definitely trying to get on my good side. I guess it was always like this when we visit for a short time, there's really no time to focus on our real problems because we want to make the little time we have together good for the kids.

"Come on E,J,, Mommy is going to give you a bath before you fall asleep." My baby was about to fall asleep in his high chair. By the time I finished bathing lil Eric, Big Eric was back with the burritos, so I waited on putting E.J. to sleep until after I ate. Eric woofed down his burrito very quick, then he made the rest of the kids take their baths and get in the bed. He even put E.J. to sleep, this nigga was definitely trying to get some pussy. I had eaten and let my food digest before Eric made it back into the family room.

"Are they sleeping?"
"Yep, Sean was the last to fall off. Are you tired?"
"Yes I am, I'm about to take a shower and lay it down."
"Are you going to model your present for me before you go to bed?"

I knew he was trying to get some, but what the hell, I'm due for some myself.

132

"I'll model for you if I can get a massage, deal?"
"Alright deal."

I took my negligee and my Bobbi Brown beach body oil in the bathroom so when I stepped out I would be all shiny and ready. When I came out of the bathroom, Eric had made me a drink and had some soft music on in our room. He was in his boxer shorts watching Sports Center but quickly turned it off, when I entered the room. I did my best Tyra Banks imitation, like I was straight off the runway of Victoria's Secret Fashion Show. I was trying to keep a serious face but I had to giggle. Eric was sitting straight up staring like a man's first trip to a strip club. I climbed on the bed and crawled seductively up to him and began to kiss him starting at his legs and then up to his thighs. At this point his Calvin Klein boxer briefs could barely contain the stiff muscle between his legs. I pulled his underwear down as I began to gather the saliva in my mouth. I got his underwear to his ankles and he kicked them off the rest of the way. I put my moistened mouth on his penis and began to bob my head up and down. The sounds of his moans excited me more, as I continued to suck and stroke his dick alternating with playing with his balls with my tongue. Eric was the one and only man that I had ever given head but it took lots of years to get to this point and now I was something like a pro. He pulled me up and lifted me atop his penis, I instantly screamed out, I was feeling him in my stomach. I put my knees down to give myself better balance to ride him. After gyrating up and down, round and round, he turned me over into the missionary position. He placed both of my legs over his shoulders.

"Yes baby, right there." I screamed. That was (is) one of my favorite positions. Ooh I forgot to call Charles and tell him I made it here. Oh my gosh! Am I thinking about Charles while making live to my husband. What the fuck is wrong with me?
"You like it like that." Eric moaned which brought me back.

"Uh huh." I moaned but now I was concentrating on trying not to think about Charles, which of course made me think of him.

"Baby, I'm about to cum." He said as he quickened the pace of his motion.

"I'm cumming too baby." But I lied. I couldn't believe this, the first time in nine years that I did not cum from having sex with Eric. Hell, I usually cum from him just messing around with me and to top it off, I was thinking about another man. Eric laid out spread eagle and I laid on his arm looking up at the ceiling deep in thought. I was trying to figure out if all this meant something. When Eric reached over to grab his boxers off the floor, I got up to go to the bathroom for my after sex pee and to wash up. By the time I made it back to the room, Eric was already snoring. The clock said 11:45 pm and when I tell you I was still watching the clock at 2:33 am, I was scared to go to sleep, I've been known to talk in my sleep. I thought I might say Charles' name in my sleep. I really don't remember going to sleep but now I was being awakened by Eric's thing up against my butt and it looked the clock said six o'clock which was about right because Eric had to go to practice. Normally I like to feel his hard dick against me in the morning but not today.

"Eric, I'm sleeping, I couldn't go to sleep last night."

"That's ok you don't even have to wake up, you can stay just like that." He said as he slid my panties down and began to try to get my juices flowing, by using his fingers to play with my clit. He entered my coochie from the rear and as hard as I tried to act sleep, it wasn't going down, he was packing way too much for me to be able to do that. In an instance I was cumming and for real this time. I tried to bury my face in the pillow to muffle the sound because I wasn't trying to wake the kids. Actually this is what I needed to wear me out and help me get a few more hours of sleep. After we finished making love, I went to the bathroom and called myself stumbling back to bed but Eric obviously had other plans.

"Baby, since you up now can you scramble me some egg whites and make me some turkey sausages while I get ready. Oh and some toast."

No this muthafucka didn't, what part of I didn't get no sleep last night did he not understand. This is the shit I am so tired of, everything revolves around his ass. What have you been eating for breakfast, I mean damn, give a bitch a day to get settled.

I looked in on my kids on the way to the kitchen, they were all still sleeping. Thank god for that. Hopefully I can cook his breakfast and get a couple of hours of sleep before they wake up. I slid back into the bed and closed my eyes tight. I guess thank you would have been too much to ask for, for waking me up out of my sleep to get a nut and a hot meal. I guess it was my own fault, I had catered to him for so long expecting nothing in return, I mean that's what we do when we're in love, right? These thoughts were the segue into my dreams, or at least I thought so until I felt ten little fingers tracing my face.

"Mommy I wan cereal" that was E.J language for letting me know he wanted some cereal. I tried putting him in the bed with me thinking maybe he would go right back to sleep, but the rest of the crew was right behind him. They all jumped in my bed fighting for the spot next to me and then it was clear why I deal with Eric's shit. It was also clear to me that I wasn't going back to sleep. I guess I'll sleep tonight.

"Hey Alisha, I'm just calling to double check that you are picking us up from the airport tomorrow."

"Girl, I didn't forget, but Bri is going to come get ya'll. Is that cool?"

"I ain't tripping as long as we get picked up, I can't wait to get back out there! Why you can't pick us up chick?"

135

"Girl, I'm about to be on my way to the airport. My man misses me."

"So you are on your way to the N-O (New Orleans), well have a safe trip and tell your crazy ass nigga I said what's up. Where are the girls staying?"

"They're staying at AuntyCarol and Uncle Brian's house. You know they love to play grandparents since Bri's ass ain't giving them no grandkids. When are you going back to Arizona?" Alisha asked me.

"In a couple of days, so I'll probably see you in a couple of months, I need to stay my ass at home for a while."

After I got off the phone with Alisha I finished packing the kids bag, they were all sleeping. Eric was in the living room watching T.V and for a hot second I thought about giving him some pussy one last time before I left but like I said that thought lasted a hot second. I couldn't wait to get back to Oakland so I could call Charles. Next week this time, I'll be in Vegas, Sin City, I guess that's a fitting nickname. I packed my suitcase and hurried to get in the bed so I could be dead sleep by the time Eric got in the bed…

Bri was waiting curbside when we walked out. The skycap loaded her trunk with all of our luggage and I put the kids in the car. Sean rode in the front seat so I could hold E.J. in the back seat because we didn't have his carseat.

"So how was ya'll trip?" Bri asked the kids took the liberty of answering.
"We had fun." They sang.
"What about you missy? She asked me.
"We'll talk later." I responded.

It didn't take long for us to arrive at my mother-in-laws house. She wasn't home but she left a note on the refrigerator saying that she had a doctor's appointment. I sent the kidss outside to play so I could talk to Bri.

"So are you ready to go to Vegas?" I asked.
"Oh so we're still going?"
"Of course, why would we not be."
"I thought seeing your husband may have changed your mind."
"Girl, seeing him made me want to go more! How come it took me so long to see how self centered he is, I swear if it wasn't for these kids!"
"Stop talking crazy girl, you ain't going no where. To answer your question, yes I am so ready to go. My case load has been so heavy, I need a break. When are you going home?"
"As soon as the jetlag wears off, probably Sunday. That will give me a few days at home before we leave. I still haven't told Eric I am going, I know I'm going to hear his mouth so I'll wait until right before I leave. I need to call Charles to make sure he made the hotel reservations."
"I can't wait to meet him, I have to see the nigga that got your nose open, this is a first."
"First of all, my nose ain't open. Second of all, I can't wait to see him too, I have to make sure it wasn't just the Essence vibe, and the mix of heat and alcohol that made me fall for him. A part of me hopes he turns out to be an asshole then I can get over him."
"I doubt that Sony, he ain't shown no asshole traits since you've been talking to him over the phone and by now it would have shown.
"Girl, I didn't tell you, why was I thinking about his ass while me and Eric was doing it. I was scared to go to sleep because I thought I might say his name."
"Oooh! You got it bad bitch!"
"I know, I couldn't wait to get back to call him."
"Well what you waiting on, I'm about to find something to eat in Barbara's kitchen."

137

Before I called him, I call to leave a message letting Eric know we made it here. Then I called my mom to let her know. She had decided that we, meaning me, her and the kids were going to drive back to Arizona instead of her flying down next week with Bri. She needed to go to some factory in Phoenix to buy some material and she didn't want to ship it back. I told her I wanted to leave on Sunday which was cool with her. I didn't have a problem driving, it would be all good for the kids, it reminded me of the trips we would take when we were kids. Being one of six children, I didn't fly until I was in high school and hustling. All of our family trips were road trips. My mom had a little bit of an attitude when I told her we were going to stay in Oakland at Barbara's house tonight, but that wasn't nothing new. We were going to have plenty of time together, hell the drive to Arizona was going to take at least eleven hours in itself. After getting her off the phone, I called Charles.

"Hello."

"Hello Charles."

"Hey Poopie." He said to me.

"Poopie? Do you know who you are talking too?"

"Yes, Sonya I know your voice, plus I have caller I.D."

"Well what's up with calling me Poopie."

"You don't like it, it's my nickname for you."

"I guess it's cool, I have to think of a nickname for you."

"What about Big Daddy." He said laughing.

"Let me think about that---Not!" I replied laughing as well.

"So how was your trip?"

"It was alright." I said in an obviously unconvincing voice."

"Well I'm sure it was good for him and the kids."

"Yeah you're right."

"I missed you, did you think about me?" He asked.

Man, if he only knew when and how I thought about him, I thought to myself.

138

"Of course I thought about you and I missed you too." I replied.

"So did you give any of my good stuff away?"

"What! I'm sure you don't want the answer to that." I laughed, "your good stuff, that's funny."

"I'm just playing with you, on the real though, what's good? Are you ready for Vegas?"

We went on to discuss the logistics of our upcoming meeting I know that I'm going coo-coo but I really liked the sound of him asking if "I gave some of his good stuff away." I don't know what this man has done to me and I have a feeling that going to Vegas is only going to intensify things.

Oh well I'm still going!

Chapter 10

The flight from Phoenix to Las Vegas was less than an hour. It seemed like less than that because Bri and I talked non-stop from take-off to landing. She updated me on all her "friend guys" and I listened and laughed because Bri is funny as hell. When we made it to baggage claim we were greeted by our driver with a sign that read, "Sonya and Bri Brown," we both laughed at Charles, putting my maiden name wouldn't change the fact that I was married.

It was hot as hell when we stepped out of the airport into the Vegas air. Our driver opened the door to the limo for us and then proceeded to put our luggage in the trunk. You would have thought that we were staying at least a week from the size of our bags. Even with all the stuff we packed it was a must that we hit the mall while we were here too. The limo was stocked with Cristal so of course we popped open a bottle, we were here to celebrate as well as see Charles.

"Okay let's make a toast." I suggested
"Alright, you go first." Bri said. I raised my glass and began.
"This toast is for my cousin, my sister, my friend. Thank you for always having my back and being down for me, even when it's some crazy shit like this. Thanks for being my sounding board and keeper of my secrets, but most of all this toast is to wish you a Happy 28th birthday! Go Bri it's your birthday." I sang as we clinked glasses and took a sip.
"Look how, how you gone have me all teary eyed and then start singing and dancing to 50 Cents 'In the Club'!"
"Girl you know how we do! We are going to have so much fun this weekend. Even if I ain't feeling Charles, we get an all expense paid for weekend of kicking it!"

"I doubt that you won't feel him but whatever. I just hope he has a cool friend to entertain me for the weekend but if not I'm sure I'll find someone."

We were approaching the Palms hotel, so we downed a couple more glasses of champagne before we got there. When we pulled up Bri remembered that she hadn't did her toast yet.

"Hold up, I have to do my toast. It ain't as deep as yours."

"Get on with it, I only have a drop left in my glass and I'm ready to get out of this car." I said.

"Alright, here's to my cousin, my sister, my friend finally loosening up and living one time, even if it took you twenty eight years!"

"Ha ha funny, alright I'll drink to that, now let's go."

We both put on our Hollywood sunglasses and then we let the driver know we were ready to exit the car. The hotel lobby was busy. It didn't matter what time of the year it was, Vegas always had an off the hook vibe but in the summer it was definitely jumping. Bri scoped out the scene while I got us checked in. Charles had already taken the liberty in leaving a credit card for our incidentals. We declined the bell hops offer to carry our bags up, we weren't that diva, we could handle it. Although it was just about three hours ago that we were getting dressed in my house in Arizona, our first task was to shower and change. I was looking cute in a Juicy Couture mini skirt, a wife beater, and flip flops, and so was Bri in her paper denim capri's and D&G baby tee but those were our travel clothes cute. We needed to change into our "Vegas Strip" cute. As I was hanging my clothes, the hotel room phone rang. I assumed it was Charles, so I answered the phone playing around.

"Yes."

"Good afternoon, Ms. Jackson. I'm calling from the hotel's hospitality desk to check and see that everything in your suite is to your liking?"

141

"Yes, it is. Thank you."

"Great well if you need anything don't hesitate to call us."

"Okay, bye."

"That was nice, I thought to myself. When I hung up the phone, I realized that the message light was lit up. Charles must have called while I was on the phone. I listened to the message and it was him. I finished unpacking before I called him back. Bri was in the bathroom so I had some time.

"Good Afternoon Ms, Jackson, how can I help you?"

"Can you connect me to Charles Knight's room."

"It would be my pleasure." The hotel operator responded.

"Hello."

"Hello my Poopie bear."

"What are you doing?"

"Waiting on you to get here. How was your flight?"

"It was fast. So have you been gambling?"

"Yeah a little bit. Where's Bri, I can't wait to meet her?"

"She's in the shower. Who did you come with?"

" I brought Greg and a buddy of mine name Dre met us out here. He's from Texas."

He just had to bring that overly flamboyant friend of his.

"Well you know I don't trust your friends like that, so we have to make it like our running into each other was pure coincidence."

"I know. So can I come to your room and give you a hug."

"When?"

"Now."

"Well, not now because Bri will be getting dressed and I need to get dressed too."

"Didn't I get ya'll a suite with two bedrooms and a living area?"

"Yes, but when we get ready, we walk all over in our under clothes and that might be a bit much for you to handle."

142

"You're right, well can't you come up here and give me a quick hug before you get dressed, please?"

"Alright, what's the room number?"

I got off the phone and told Bri that I would be right back. I gave myself a look over in the mirror, I glossed my lips up and sprayed a squirts of Issey Miyake perfume on. I don't know why I was so nervous but I was. Its not like this is my nigga, we are just patnas. I'm glad I had those four glasses of Cristal or else my nerves might really be bad. Which reminds me, let me stick some Trident in my mouth, I don't want to smell like a wine-o."

Knock, knock, knock

Charles opened the door as soon as I knocked.

"Damn nigga, you must have been waiting by the door." I said joking.

"I sure was." He replied as he swooped me up into his arms and held me for about a minute. I wasn't complaining my body melted right into his. Then he kissed me on my forehead. Now I don't know if you remember the movie the 'Best Man' when they spoke about a kiss to the forehead that was damn near erotic. Well I just experienced it. Come on Sonya get it together, I said to myself.

"Ok Charles, what are you trying to do, smother me?" I said pushing him away. He laughed as he loosened his grasp. God knows I could have stayed in his arms for hours but I had to main'tain my composure.

"You look lovely, why do you have to change?"

"This is my travel gear, I got to switch it up to my chilling fit."

"Oh I see, so what do you want to do?" He asked.

"Where are your friends?"

"I don't know, probably gambling in their rooms."

"So you in this big ass room by yourself?" I walked around admiring his suite. He was staying in the NBA suite. I had seen it on one of those VH1 specials, but it was even nicer in person.

"Yeah, I'm by myself. I wanted you to be able to come up here if you chose to and be able to be comfortable."

"Where's my key then?" I asked – just joking though, but he wasn't. He handed me a key. I was a bit taken aback but I just continued talking like I wasn't tripping.

"Okay, I figure after I get dressed Bri and I will be ready to grab a bite to eat, we'll probably go down to P.F. Chang's. Do you want to come?"

"Are you sure?" He asked.

"Yeah, I'm sure but just you, not the crew! Then we can probably stage our running into each other at a black jack table or something tonight while you are with your friends. I want you to meet Bri before everyone else is around, so she can feel you out." I said laughing.

"Oh so I'm auditioning." He replied with a slight attitude.

"I mean you want the part, right." I shot back at him.

"Yeah ok Sony." He said with more attitude.

"Oh so you don't want to the part." I said while massaging his shoulder.

"Stop playing Sony." He replied. I could tell he was trying to stay hard but he couldn't and he began to laugh. "Yeah I want the part." He said

"Look at you getting sensitive, I'm just playing with your butt. You don't have to audition, you got the part already. I know you guys won't get a chance to talk once we get around your friends and I want to be able to talk openly. I want my best friend to see who she will be sharing her spot with."

"Aah nigga don't get all mushy on me." He said, but I could tell he wanted to grin like a muthafucka.

"Shut up, I ain't getting mushy. Just meet us in the lobby in about an hour, ok."

"Ok, Poopie, I'll see you in an hour."

"Oh so I'm Poopie again, I was Sony when you had your 'tude." Alright I'll see you in a few."

144

"Ok, I see that it wasn't Essence that had me feeling him, I am digging him period. Damn, that nigga is some kind of fine to me and his personality is hella cool."

Meanwhile back in the room Bri was stretched out on the couch in the room, in her bathrobe, watching T.V.

"Girl you ain't dressed?"

"Why am I going to get dresses when you still have to shower and I didn't know how long you were going to be gone."

"I guess that makes sense. I'm about to take my shower because I told Charles we would meet him in the lobby in an hour so we can go eat."

"Well all I have to do is put on my clothes, so you the one who needs to get it going."

"You're right." I said as I headed towards my room, before I made it there Bri stopped me.

"So Sony, how was it seeing him again?"

I skipped back to the couch so I could be close enough for my cousin to really feel me.

"Oooh Bri, I like him." I said shaking my head with embarrassment.

"Nigga, you didn't have to come get all close to me to tell me that, I could tell when your ass came skipping in the room. Um, I'm scared of you, now go get dressed!"

An hour later we were dressed, looking good and smelling good. Bri asked me if I was going to call him to tell him we were headed down to the lobby. Since I told him to meet us in an hour I hadn't planned on calling, he knew the time. Honestly I was giving him an opportunity to mess up. I had to find some quirk that might make me stop feeling him.

However, I guess tardiness would not be the quirk because when we arrived in the lobby, there he was, looking sexy with his New York Yankees baseball cap pulled down low on his head.

"I'm impressed, I just knew ya'll was gonna have me waiting." He said to us.

"Oh you don't know, we were born beautiful, it don't take us long." I said before introducing him and Bri, "now smart ass this is my favorite cuz Bri Brown, Bri this is my new folks Charles Knight."

Charles extended his hand to shake Bri's hand but he was surprised.

"Boy give me a hug, this ain't no business meeting," Bri said as she gave him a hug, "thank you for the trip. I needed a break." Bri continued.

"I'm glad you could come. Thanks for giving me an opportunity to see my Poopie." He responded.

"Poopie!" Bri responded with confusion looking at me.

"Shut up, Bri," I said laughing, "ain't ya'll ready to eat?"

"Okay Poopie, how are we getting there?" Bri asked me, being funny by calling me Poopie.

"We're gonna walk, it's right up the street in the Aladdin."

"Walk!" They both said in unison.

"Okay, is it lazy or spoiled. Oh my bad, I know it both for one of ya'll."

"Shut up bitch, it's hot out there and yes I am spoiled and lazy." Bri admitted.

"Alright, let's grab a taxi then."

When we walked out, there was a little line for a cab, but Charles took the liberty of making things happen and in about a minutes time, there was a town car pulling up for us. While Charles squared the doorman up, Bri and I got in some girl talk.

"Sean John jeans, Ryan Kenny button down shirt, Prada tennis shoes and Burberry cologne. Girl, he got some taste." Bri whispered to me.

"Damn girl you can tell all that from a quick hug." I was amazed with Bri's skills.

"So what do you think of him so far?" I asked.

"Girl don't worry, I'm sure I'll like him if you do. He likes him some Poopie though, I can tell by how he looks at you."

"For real girl," I said all corny and excited. "Well we're just friends, that's it, that's all." I was trying hard to convince myself.

"Are you ladies finished talking about me?" Charles asked as he got in the car.

"Ain't nobody talking about you." I said.

"I was talking about you and yes I'm finished, for now." Bri honestly replied.

"You are crazy girl." Charles laughed.

When we arrived at PF Changs there was a lot of people waiting to be seated but Charles had called ahead and they had a private room waiting for us. I had grown accustomed to the perks of being involved with an athlete, but it was really appreciated at times like this......

We ordered enough food and drinks to feed an army. We started with Chicken lettuce wraps, calamari, and crab wontons. Then for our meal we had honey crisp chicken and shrimp, orange peel shrimp and sweet and sour chicken and chow mein, brown rice and white rice. We ordered the "great wall of chocolate" chocolate cake for dessert, but I was way too stuffed to eat that. Oh and of course Bri and I had several glasses of Malibu and cranberry juice and Charles matched us with his Belvedere and cranberry juice.

During dinner Charles' cell phone was getting lit up. Finally while we were talking after dinner, he excused himself to go to the bathroom, but I knew the real was that he had to return his calls. I wasn't tripping, I wanted some time to talk to Bri anyway.

"You know he's going to use his phone." Bri advised me.

"Girl, I know but I ain't tripping. So what do you think of him now?"

"I think I know why you are open, he is hella cool. He ain't hell on himself, he can converse about the streets and about the world. Girl, don't be mad when I say this but he got mannerisms that remind me of your husband."

"Girl, I ain't mad, that nigga reminds of me Eric too."

Charles was returning from his so-called bathroom run, so we wrapped up our conversation.

"Yes, we were talking about you." Bri said as she got up to go to the bathroom.

"So how is my audition going?" Charles asked me as he played with my hand. I just laughed. I really wanted to ask him why he had to lie about going to make his calls, but I decided to chill.

"It's tough when you know you're auditioning to be the understudy." He said after I didn't answer his question. Oh that was funny, not!

"Oh I think you got it twisted, I ain't looking for a back-up. I thought you were creating a role all on your own because it's a lock on the leading role." I shot back with big attitude.

"Damnnn, who was talking about somebody being sensitive earlier. I was just playing with you, I thought it was funny, I'm sorry."

I tried to hold my frown but I couldn't. I had to laugh, it was funny.

"You laughing now, I'm going to have to ask my cousin Bri if you are bipolar." He said.

"I ain't bipolar but I am crazy." I said.

"I believe you." He replied.

Before Bri came back, I told him that I wanted to do something really nice for Bri for her birthday tomorrow. He told me to leave it all up to him, he would take care of it. He told me that he had talked to his boys when he went to the bathroom. I'm sure that's not all who he talked to but anyway, he told them he had been sleeping and that he was going to meet them in the high rollers black jack pit in a few. I figured that Bri and I would sit at the bar in the casino for a few and then make our way over to the black jack area so we could have our chance meeting. This is a damn shame, grown people plotting and scheming a hook up. Bri returned from the bathroom and Charles requested the check from our waiter. I decided I might as well go to the bathroom to give them a chance to talk about me. I knew Bri would fill me in later.

"So you like my cousin, huh?"

"Yes, I do but I respect her situation."

"Nigga you ain't talking to her daddy, keep it real with me."

First he laughed then he went on to express his true feelings.

"I don't know, Bri I'm thirty-one years old and I've never met anyone like your cousin. I ain't never been in this type of situation, yes I really like her and I wish we could be more than friends but I would take her friendship over nothing at all. I never want her to question the life's choices she's made, she has a family and I honestly respect that. I just want to get in where I fit in, and I know that it is as a friend. So hey it is what it is, you know."

"I feel you, timing is a muthafucka, ain't it. Well Sony is grown so I let her make her own decisions and I support her. If you gon' be her friend you better be that, in good and in bad because this friendship may come with repercussions. My cousin is a good woman and she deserves happiness, if you add to that happiness then I'm good. You dig."

"That's what's up." He replied.

Around this time, I was returning from the bathroom.

"What are ya'll talking about?" I asked.

"Oh I was telling Bri I wanted to introduce her to Dre."

"So what does he do for a living?" Bri asked as if they had really been talking about that.

"He's an attorney." Charles answered her.

"Oh hell No." Bri said.

"What, you don't like lawyers?" He asked.

"Sure don't. They are know-it-alls." She replied.

"Oh, Charles I forgot to mention that Bri is one of the most sought out criminal attorneys in the Bay Area, and yes she is a know-it-all."

"For some reason I should have guessed that, but he's not a courtroom lawyer, he deals more with contracts and stuff of that nature. I guess he's like an entertainment lawyer or something. He's cool people."

"I guess I'll see when I meet him."

Charles paid the check and we headed out. As we exited you could hear some of the restaurant's patrons whispering, "Isn't that C. Knight." Luckily we were able to keep it moving without a big scene. When we got to the outside of the restaurant the town car was there waiting on us. The ride down the street to our hotel took the same amount or longer than if we had walked because of all the traffic on the strip. Bri looked like she was enjoying herself so far. I couldn't wait to split up from Charles, so I could ask her what they really talked about.

Back at the hotel, Charles gave me some money to buy our drinks while Bri and I waited to come meet them, then he headed off to the tables. We found a bar area that had a band playing and ordered a couple of shots of Petron. After shaking my head from the burn of the tequila, I asked Bri for the details of her and Charles' real conversation.

"We were talking about him hooking me up." She said.

"Yeah right Bri, when I walked up you had just asked what Dre does for a living and I know if that was the real discussion, you would have been asked that if ya'll were really talking about a hook-up."

"Anyway, let's get another shot, it's my birthday, it's my birthday!"

We downed two more shots of tequila before Bri gave up any of the real info and even then she really didn't give up all the conversation.

"All I'm saying is, I do not envy your position Sony. The man really likes you, I might be jumping the gun but I think he might even be in love with you. The jacked part about it is, he is hella cool."

"What did he say?" I asked.

"Bitch I am drunk, I can't remember. It's my birthday!" She sang.

"I know it's your birthday. Come on let's go find them."

I paid for our drinks and then we left to look for the High Rollers Pit. For it to be a Thursday night, the scene was really popping at the Palms. We found the high rollers pit which wasn't all that crowded, however security had shut off the table where Charles was playing so that new players could not join the game. I really don't understand that, he was playing at a $100 table, so if someone could afford to play even if they're just playing to be near a basketball player, so be it. Let them play. We settled on another $100 table that was across from him. I know he noticed us because every man in the area did, Black, White and Asian. Shit, the women noticed us too, most of them got right up under their men to let it be known. That shit always made me laugh. Greg (Mr. Flamboyant) tapped Charles on the shoulder and pointed in our direction. Obviously he took the bait. Charles looked in our direction and nodded his head yeah, I guess in agreement to if I was the girl from the Essence Festival, I'm assuming that's what Greg asked him. I continued to play my position until Charles acknowledged me. Bri and I were waiting on the new shuffle before we started playing, so we laughed and talked about Charles playing his role. When the dealer went to shuffle we both put down a thousand dollars to get some chips. Charles was on a good roll over at his table, so he didn't say anything to me until his dealer went to shuffle.

"Excuse me, isn't your name Sonya?" Charles asked from across the tables.

"Yes it is, isn't your name Charles?" I replied going along with the game. His buddy, Greg, was nodding his head like he did something, talking about, "I told you 'C'."

"What's up Sonya." Greg said like we were cool.

"Hey what's up?" I responded.

Charles walked over to my table and gave me a hug. I fake introduced him to Bri and then we exchanged room numbers to cap off the act. We both continued to play Black jack at our respective tables, occasionally saying something to each other or giving a wink or a smile. After about an hour and a half my alcohol had started to set in. I was playing my cards right, so I knew it was time for me to turn it in, it had been a long day. Bri had already stopped playing, she had won $1500 so she was cool. I was down about $500 but there was always tomorrow to get that back. When I got up to leave, Charles put on the puppy dog face.

"Bye guys, good seeing you." I said as I waved.

"Hold up a minute." He said. He asked Greg to play his hand so he could come talk to me.

"You want me to quit playing?" He asked me.

"Nah, you are winning. Keep playing until your luck changes, I'm tired so I'm going to go lay down. I loved your acting though."

"You did alright yourself. I guess I'll introduce you to Dre tomorrow, he must be at a crap table. So are you winning?"

"Nope, but we still have the rest of the weekend so I'm not tripping." I replied.

"Alright, I'll call you in a little bit, the birthday girl looks like she is ready to turn it in."

"Okay," I said looking at Bri, "alright call me later."

Bri and I may have been tired but we still took the scenic route up to our room. We had to take a stroll through the casino to check out the atmosphere. It was a few cool looking brothers in there but I need not look, I already had my men problems. For

Bri it was all good though. She sobered up real quick and was fully alert as we made our rounds.

"Man Sony, it's some cool one's in here. It has to get better tomorrow and Saturday. I might just find me a boyfriend."

"Yeah right." I joked to her.

It was only 11:00 pm when we got up to the room. It had seemed like it was hella late. We had to stay up for another hour for it to officially be Bri's birthday. That wasn't a problem once we started talking hours passed like minutes. For the hour leading up to her birthday we talked about the stores we planned on going to tomorrow, that was one thing that every woman in our family loved to do, shop. We didn't have to watch the clock because at midnight her phone started ringing off the hook. Before she answered any calls, I had to be the first one to say happy birthday.

"Happy Birthday little cousin, I was the baby of the family for two whole months until this day." I said as I gave her a big hug.

After that Mya called then Kim and then Alisha and her man Rock who was in Oakland visiting. Then about three or four of her hooks called who she referred all to as "baby." That girl is a fool. Then she called and woke her parents up to ask why they hadn't called her yet. My aunt answered by letting her know she wasn't born until 9:15am, so let her get her 9 hours of rest! That girl is super spoiled and she knew it. The next call surprised us, it was received on the hotel phone.

"Hello." I answered the phone assuming it was for me.

"Hello, may I speak to Bri Brown?"

"Hold on. It's for you Bri."

Bri looked surprised, wondering who could be calling her on the hotel phone.

"Hello." She sang into the phone.

"Hello Ms. Bri, this is Charles, I was calling to wish you a happy b-day and to tell ya'll to get your rest because I have big things planned for your birthday celebration."

"Alright, thanks for calling."

"You're welcome, now let me speak to my girl." Bri handed me the phone.

"Hey you." I said into the phone.

"Hey, I told Bri that ya'll need to get your rest because I have big plans for tomorrow."

"Is that right, are you still gambling?"

"Yeah, I just wanted to call and tell her happy birthday and check on you."

"That was nice. I'm straight, we are having girl talk."

"That's cool, but don't stay up too late because I have a limo picking ya'll up at eleven."

"For what?" I asked.

"It's a surprise."

"For who, it's not my birthday."

"I know but it's a surprise for you too."

"Well how should we dress?"

"Casual, knowing ya'll, you might need to wear some comfortable. So get some sleep, I won't be out too late. I'll call you when I get to my room."

"Alright, peace."

I got off the phone and filled Alisha in on what Charles told me about our plans for tomorrow. I had no clue on what we were going to do. He was really making an effort to make Bri's birthday special and of course he was trying to rack up brownie points. Bri was starting to dose off and I was tired as well, so we both decided to turn in for the night. When I laid down, I thought about the possibility of being more than friends with Charles. How come I couldn't have met him years ago, at least then we could have openly been friends. I said my bedtime prayer and asked God for forgiveness for my sins. I sure hope God doesn't get tired of me asking for that.

I must have been sleeping longer than an hour but I guess not because the clock read 1:35 am as my cell phone ringing woke me up.

"Hello." I said in my dead to the world voice.

"You sleep? I didn't call the room because I didn't want to wake your cousin."

"Well you didn't mind waking me."

"Nope! I wanted to know if I could come get a hug before I go up to bed."

"Are you serious?"

"As a heart attack."

"Alright come on, where you at?"

"About to get on the elevator, I'ma talk to you until I get to the door."

We really didn't say much before he let me know he was at the door. I rolled out the bed and thought about getting one of the hotel robes to cover up my Pj's which consisted of boy brief panties and a tank top but I said fuck it. Saturday he'll probably see me in a swimsuit which is way more revealing than this. Plus I admit, I kind of had my sexy going on in the pj's so I wanted him to see.

"Who is this crazy person coming to my room at this time of night." I said as I opened the door. "Don't think because you are paying for this room you just can stop through at any hour, plus how you gonna tell me to get some rest and then break my sleep?"

"Are you finished yet?" He asked.

"Yes, I am. You want me to come in?"

"Nah because I'll probably fall asleep." He paused as if he was going to say it was cool but even if I wanted him to I couldn't, I was sharing this room with Bri and even though it was like a mini apartment, I still couldn't get down like that."

"I feel you, well let me give you your hug so you can go get some sleep. Didn't you say we need to be ready by 11:00am?" I asked.

"Not me, you and Bri have to be ready. The early part of the plan is for you ladies. I'll catch up with ya'll in the late afternoon. Just make sure you stop by my room first because a package will be there for you."

"Are you going to be up?"

"Probably not but you have a key." He said smiling.

155

"That's right." I said smiling back. I then took the initiative to wrap him up in my arms. It felt so good hugging him. I stood on my tippy toes to wrap my arms around his neck and look him in his eyes, they weren't blue or green, they weren't hazel. They were just brown, but they told stories. His eyes were truly windows. It was really hard for me not to look away.

"Charles I really want to thank you."

"Aw poopie, this is nothing." He replied.

"Not just for this trip, but for everything. I know how it feels to be unappreciated so I do my best to let people know that they are appreciated, when they are."

"Didn't I tell you about getting all mushy on me." He said trying to conceal his embarrassment.

"Alright boy." I said releasing him from the choke-hold I had around his neck, but Charles still held on to me.

"Just give me one more minute." He said and so I did and he held me for one more minute in silence. For that minute I laid my head on his chest and lost myself in what could have been. I don't know if he was having the same thoughts but when we broke our hug we both had the same look of happy sadness across our face.

"Ok Poopie, see you tomorrow. And next time put some clothes on, what you trying to do to a nigga!"

That night I fell asleep thinking, what if I would have met Charles years ago, what if things don't work out with me and Eric. What if……..

"Wake yo punk ass up." Bri joyfully screamed as she walked through the living room area to my room. I opened one eye and saw that the clock read 9:57am. I swear I need to get some of these hotel curtains for my house because on days when you want to sleep in, they make it seem as if it's still nighttime. "I ain't playing Sony, get up. It's my birthday and I'm anxious to see what your man has planned."

"I'm up." I moaned.

"I know you're about to be." Bri said as she pulled my curtains open and let the bright ass sun in.

"Where you get all this energy from?"

"Girl you know my mama called to wake me up at 9:15 to tell me Happy Birthday. She said she was getting me back for waking her. So after I got off the phone with her, I jumped in the shower. Now you need to do the same because I already ordered us some room service and we need to eat and get dressed in an hour."

"Alright, I'm getting up for real." I had to get with it, I was tired no doubt, but I owed to Bri to match her enthusiasm, it was her birthday.

After getting dressed and eating a bagel with cream cheese and a fruit salad, it was time to meet Charles. Well actually not meet him but go get the package from his room, I was hella curious!

"So do you know what he has planned?" Bri asked me.

"No, I don't and about you calling him my man earlier, he is not, we are just friends. All he told me was to come to his room to pick up a package, I guess it will explain everything."

"So he's a part of this plan."

"He said not the early part."

"We got up to his room and I pulled out the key to access his room and Oh Boy! You would have thought Bri had to pee how she started jumping around over the shock of me having the key to his room.

"Calm down bitch, he is probably asleep."

"Alright my bad but you know I'm going to be on you later."

Yes I know! Bri was a person who wouldn't tell your secrets to others but she would replay them over and over for you to regret you told her.

It was pitch black in his room he had all of his curtains closed tight. On the coffee table in the living room surrounded by bottles of belvedere, Hennessey, and Malibu Rum was a manila envelope with Poopie written on the front.

"I take it that's the package, open it." Bri said with excitement.

I opened the envelope and there were more than a few stacks of $100 bills and a letter that read:

Good Morning Poopie and Bri,
I hope you have on comfortable shoes. Downstairs there's a limo waiting on you with instructions to take you to the best shopping in Vegas, but don't take all day because you have 4:00pm appointments for massages here at the hotel spa. After that get a little rest because Bri's birthday party will be at 'Rain' tonight. So have fun ladies!

Bri and I looked at each other in amazement, we both wanted to scream but we didn't want to wake Charles. I didn't want to wake Charles, but I had to thank him so I tiptoed into his room trying to be quiet. There he lay sleeping with the covers kicked off of him in his black Calvin Klein boxer brief underwear. I tried not to look but I couldn't help but notice the imprint of his penis through his drawers and baby was packing. As I approached him attempting to kiss his forehead, he jumped in surprise.

"Sorry for waking you." I said as I kissed his forehead.

"No problem, you walked right out of my dream."

"Thank you for the package, you have already done so much for us."

"No problem, you better get going."

"Alright."

"Thanks Charles." Bri yelled from the other room.

"You're welcome, have fun." He yelled back.

"Alright, see you later."

Down in the limo, I did the official count of the money stacks. It was $15,000. I could not believe him and this was my cousins birthday, imagine if it was mine. Although I knew this was really for me, it was still nice of him to make the effort to

158

make Bri's birthday special. I gave Bri eight thousand and I kept seven. She didn't want to accept it, but I made her, she actually started to tear up, she was enjoying her birthday so far.

"First stop, the Forum shops at Caesar's Palace." The driver announced.

He handed us his card to call him when we were about to finish so he could be waiting outside. Charles must have filled him in on the plans because he reminded us that we have 4:00 appointments.

It was 3:35pm and we were running out of the mall like O.J. Simpson in them old Hertz rental car commercials. I could not believe we had been shopping for those hours. Bri bought her a Louis Vuitton purse, some more Christian Dior sunglasses, some Kate Spade sandals, perfume and lots of other stuff. I bought a Gucci purse and sandals, then I bought Charles some shoes, a couple of outfits and some cologne. I also picked up a couple outfits for the kids and a purse for my mom. We both had plenty of money to spare.

The driver got us back to the hotel by 3:50 and we had to run up to our room to drop off all of our bags and then rush to the spa. By the time we made it there we were both in need of a massage.

"That massage was right on point and now I'm ready to eat." I said to Bri and she agreed. We decided to order room service but first I decided to call Charles so he could come eat with us, if he hadn't already eaten. I tried to reach him on his room number but there was no answer, so I called his cell phone. He was hanging in Dre's room. I told him I was ordering us dinner and requested his presence. He found that to be funny but still let me know what he wanted to eat and said he would be up in a few minutes. In about five minutes Charles was knocking on the door.

"I see you know what's up, you must have run up here." I said joking with him.

"Anyway nigga, I was just hungry."

159

Bri had been in her room on the phone but when Charles got here she came out to thank him again.

"Hey C, thank you again. Did Sony show you what she bought you?"

"No I didn't big mouth." I replied to the question.

"Oh my bad."

"What you buy me?"

"Just a little something, I'll give it to you later."

He put a sad look on his face.

"Alright I'll get it."

I returned from my room with his bags and you would have sworn he was a kid on a Christmas morning. His eyes lit up with happiness before he even looked in the bags.

"Thank you Poopie, you were supposed to be shopping for you." He said as he started pulling the items out of the bag.

"I know but I had to hook my boy up too. Do you like the stuff?"

"I love it." He replied hugging me.

"Come on now, don't be getting mushy on me." I said copying off his remark used on me.

Room service arrived and we all ate and talked. Charles told Bri that his boy Dre was looking forward to meeting her but Bri was still turned off by the fact that he was a lawyer. After dinner Bri decided to take a nap. Charles and I got up and played cards. I whooped him about twenty times in 'Speed' before he gave up. He continuously thanked me for the presents I bought him, when in actuality, he bought them for himself. I could tell he was used to giving and never getting anything in return. However, he seemed appreciative of his blessings that it didn't bother him, he sure was happy that someone thought of him. Charles had to take a dump so I sent him up to his room to blow it up. I went to try my luck at Black Jack...

Chapter 11

"Girl, I see you put on some instant tan and got all shined up for your birthday, go ahead!"

"Shut up girl, I am sparkling, huh? I got to shine for my night."

"I heard that, so are you ready?" I asked Bri.

"Yes I am, and look at you in that piece of dress. Who said you got four kids, they must be lying!"

"That's what I'm talking bout." I said as I turned in a circle to showcase the back of the dress that dropped down to the small of my back. The front of the dress dropped just as low. That toupee glue sure comes in handy when going braless.

"Alright, Charles said for us to meet him at his room so we can have a toast before we go to the club. He also wants to introduce us to his other friend." I said.

"Well let's roll cousin."

When we got to Charles' room, I started to use my key but remembered his patna's might be in his room, so I decided against it. That might really put them all in our mix. I know they are probably wondering why he's going all out for Bri's birthday but oh well. Bri laughed because she knew exactly why I didn't use the key. That was our relationship we could feel what each other was thinking without actually saying a word. That's why I know she could feel that I was feeling Charles, but did she know I was second-guessing the relationship I've been in for years.

Knock   knock   knock

"Who is it?" Charles asked from the other side of the door in a playful voice.

"It's the birthday girl." Bri announced.

Charles opened the door and greeted us both with hugs. He and his friends were listening to music and sipping on drinks. Charles introduced us to Dre, who happened to be one of the

161

guys we saw when we made our rounds through the casino the other night. He was actually good looking. Dre and Greg both wished Bri a happy birthday. Charles made us a drink so we could all toast for Bri's birthday. I tried my hardest not to fixate my eyes on Charles because it would be a dead give away then.

"You ladies look beautiful tonight." Dre said.

"Why thank you Dre, you gentlemen look nice as well." I responded.

"Well you know how we do." Greg commented popping his collar.

Actually I wasn't even talking about him, but I didn't want to clown. After we had our drinks we decided to head to the club.

In the elevator Charles whispered in my ear, "you are definitely working that dress."

"Thank you. Nice outfit." I replied in his ear. He was wearing one of the outfits I bought him accompanied by the cologne.

"You like, my girl bought this for me."

"She must have good taste." I said with a seductive grin.

"What ya'll over there whispering about?" Bri asked all in our business.

"You." I responded.

"My boy is getting his mack on." Greg replied.

"His mack on, Please!" I replied. Charles must have felt I was about to go off so he rushed to say something to calm the moment.

"Nah, Sony is just my folks, she was actually helping me out with my game, giving me some tips."

"Oh I know, I was just joking. I know that Sony is the patna. Yeah Dre, she be big kickin it. I remember from when we were at Essence."

Look at this nigga back pedaling now. It kills me how these niggas that be paid homeboys don't have a thought of their own. He changed his entire opinion because Charles said something, that's crazy.

162

On to other things, when we got to the club we were escorted in with VIP treatment of course. The hostess' all wished Bri a happy birthday. The D.J. was bumping and the club was packed. We were lead to a private room which was decorated with balloons and happy birthday banners. There were bottles of Cristal chilling. Bri looked as if she was going to cry, she gave Charles a great big hug and thanked him. He really did go all out. The D.J announced that there was a birthday girl in the house.

"I want to give a shot out to Bri, wishing her a happy birthday. She's out here from Oakland, doing it big."

He put on 50 Cents, "It's Your Birthday" and the club went crazy. Bri and I made our way to the dance floor, Charles followed me and Dre had Bri. We danced for a few songs before we tired out. Back up in the VIP room a few other guys that Charles knew and ran into out in Vegas were up there. They looked like they played basketball too. Their height and the gawking groupies trying to get their attention gave it away. It was one particular guy Bri was choosing on and he was peeping her too.

"Come on Sony, let's go to the bathroom."

"Alright, let me tell Charles."

When we walked to the bathroom, the groupie bitches were watching us just as hard as they were watching them niggas. I'm sure they were trying to figure who we were or who we were with. One of the chicks was bold enough to approach us in the bathroom.

"Excuse me." The chick said.

"What's up?" I answered with an automatic attitude.

"Which one of ya'll is the birthday girl?"

"My cousin, why?"

"I just wanted to say happy birthday. Oh and your dress is pretty." She said to me.

Yeah right that's what she wants but we played the role and thanked her and continued to reapply our lip gloss. Now that she broke the ice, she felt it was cool to continue talking to us.

"So can ya'll get other people up into VIP?"

Ok, I have to be in the twilight zone.

"Yep." I responded. What did she think, she said happy birthday and gave me a fake ass compliment and now we patnas.

"Can you get me and my girls up there?" She asked.

Oh I was about to clown, but Bri always being the professional replied first.

"I'm sorry, I don't think it would be in our best interest to do so."

The broad looked at Bri as if she was speaking Spanish.

"So what, all of them can't be ya'll men up there." She said and was serious too.

"Actually none of them are our men, they are our patnas. However we don't get in the middle of their stuff like that. I mean hey, if they feeling ya'll, I'm sure they'll get ya'll up there." Bri said.

I was laughing the whole time, which I knew was making the groupie chick mad. Bri was talking to her in a hella sincere voice, which made it even funnier.

"Come on Bri. Let's go!" I said heading towards the door.

"Ok ladies, good luck tonight." Bri said as we headed out.

Bri and I shared in a long hard laugh as we headed back up to the birthday room. When we got to the room, Greg rushed to meet us. What did this nigga want.

"Sony, Bri, are ya'll having a good time?"

"Yeah, we're chilling." I responded.

"Yo would you mind if we invited some women up in here? C said we have to ask ya'll."

"So you getting some ass tonight might fall on us, huh." Bri joked.

"Come on now, Bri."

"Alright we ain't tripping, but not hella bitches to the point where I'm uncomfortable in here." I said.

"And ya'll better let them bitches know what's up, respect our space." Bri added.

164

"Cool." Greg responded looking like a big ass kid.

They invited a few women in but unfortunately our bathroom friends didn't make the cut. It actually made the party more live. The women all seemed cool. Everybody including most of the niggas thought we were Charles' sisters so that made it fair game to try to holla at me. I could tell that Charles was hot but he played it cool. Bri fell up under the dude that she had been eyeing all night. Bri Bri looked like she might be getting some for her birthday. This morning she was complaining about breaking a 12 year tradition of fucking on her birthday. It was her 16th birthday when she lost her virginity, she was the last one of the crew. We partied until the middle of the morning. I could truly say on that night I felt the saying "Party like Rock Stars." I pulled Bri to the side to tell her that I would crash in Charles' room, I did not want to hear sex noises. She gave me a five to thank me. I let her know I was about to cut, but I was making Charles stay until she was ready to leave. She decided she was ready to leave. She gave the dude her room information with instructions to arrive in about thirty minutes. That would give me enough time to get my stuff and for her to shower and freshen up.

Charles was surrounded by some people so I signaled him to come here.

"Thank you so much for my party, you are alright with me." Bri said to Charles.

"You're welcome, are you cool?"

"I'm great but I'll be better in about thirty." She said laughing.

"Yeah Charles, you're going to have to cancel any plans you might have with any of these rats because Bri is having company so I have to crash with you." I said as if I had to stay with him when in actuality I wanted to. I'm sure he knew it to but didn't bust me out.

"Alright that's cool." He responded. "Do you want me to leave now?" He asked.

"No you don't have to, I have a key." I said smiling.

I pulled Charles to the side and asked him quietly if 'ol boy' who Bri was digging was cool. He told me he was cool and gave me his whole run down. He told me he would get in his ear and make sure everything was cool. I told him I appreciated that and then Bri and I cut.

We had to be drunk because we walked round and round before we found the elevator. Back in the room I threw some things in a bag, gave Bri a pep talk and then headed to Charles' room. I wanted to be able to take a shower before he got there. I didn't want any temptation for him or me. I even packed lounge pants to sleep in and I hate sleeping in pants.

I had made it to his room, showered and plopped down on the couch and began flipping through channels when I heard him coming through the door. I faked like I was sleeping. He did his best not to make any noise, he went to one of the closets to get a blanket to put over me.

"Thank you." I said laughing.

"Aw you got me, next time I'm going to let you be cold."

"Next time, huh?"

"Yeah next time, you hungry?"

"Yeah a little."

"Well order us some room service while I take a shower and don't be trying to sneak a peek."

"Ain't nobody thinking about you." I had already got a peek this morning, I was thinking.

We ate our food and talked about the night's events. I asked him did he get any numbers and he said no.

"So you didn't get no numbers?"

"Nah, none."

"Stop lying, I saw a chick slip her number in your pocket."

"But I didn't get her number."

"Nigga that's the same thing, you be lying."

"No I don't." He tried to convince me.

166

"So when we were at PF Changs yesterday, did you really have to go to the bathroom or did you have to return a call?"

He paused for a moment as if he was thinking if he really wanted to tell the truth.

"Alright I did have to return a call, but I did use the bathroom too."

"Oh my goodness! Charles we are friends, you can call your chick around me. I won't feel disrespected but when you lie, I'm disrespected. No questions about it, you feel me?"

"I feel you but I'm not comfortable calling her in front of you."

"I got that and that's cool, but don't lie to me. You can say I need to make a phone call. Why you gotta hide shit or lie to me, hell I'm married."

"Alright I got you." He replied.

"I don't know what our relationship will grow to, I mean I'm already your sister," I said laughing, "but no, on the real, whatever we have has to be based on honesty, deal?"

"Honesty, that's all we do." He said extending his hand for me to shake.

"Come on let's go lay down and watch TV in the room. And I honestly ain't trying to do the do with you, I just want to get comfortable!"

After we laid down, he started questioning me about the men that were trying to holler at me.

"So did you take any numbers? He asked.

"No, I'm married."

"Yeah and you took my number."

"It must have been fate because I still can't figure that out."

"Yeah, I didn't like them all in your face, but I had to play my position."

"Well what about all them chickens in your face trying to dance hella nasty and licking their lips and shit."

"Did you see that shit, that was funny?"

167

"It really was, I feel sorry for my sisters and then they get all mad when somebody call them a hoe. Oooh, let me tell you about the chicks that approached me and Bri in the bathroom."

I told him the story and then we made plans for what we were going to do tomorrow. We both started to dose off, it had to be at least five in the morning, so whatever we had planned on doing would be late. As I drifted off to sleep I decided to put the disclaimers out there before I fell deep into my sleep.

"You up?" I asked.

"Umhum." He said though I knew he was drifting.

"Alright stay on your side of the bed."

"Umhum." He replied.

"And alcohol gives me gas so excuse me in advance if I start pooting in my sleep."

"You nasty." He said in his sexy, sleepy voice.

"Whatever nigga," I said, "thank you again Charles." I was really having a good time.

"Go to sleep girl."

"Alright, good night Charles."

"Good night, Poopie."

Chapter 12

When I got back to Arizona it was business as usual. The kids had only a week left in summer vacation, so we tried to cram in all the fun stuff that Phoenix – Scottsdale areas had to offer. I had done most of their school shopping when we were in Miami visiting Eric. They were really excited about this school year because their school had adopted a no uniform policy. I was happy as well because more and more I was feeling moving back to California and so this was their uniforms wouldn't go to waste.

Now that I'm back home, I'm going to try to get Charles out of my system. I had so much fun in Vegas and he was the perfect gentleman, but I realized that I really like him and that's not good. So from this day forward no more talk of Charles. Matter of fact let me call Bri because she is the only person I can talk about Charles to anyway.

Ring   Ring

"Good morning, this is Bri."

"Hey Cuz, how's your morning going?"

"I wish we were still in Vegas, but it's going. What are you doing?"

"Getting ready to take the kids to the zoo. I called because I decided that I need to get Charles out of my system. I really like him but the timing is all wrong. So do me a favor, if you hear me talking about him, please stop me and help me focus."

"Hey I like Charles, but I feel you. However I can't stop what runs around in your head and what beats in your heart."

"I know, I wish I could, but in time."

"Alright, I got another call coming in. Have fun at the zoo."

169

(3 days later)

"Good morning this is Bri."

"Bri I can't do this. I try not to think about him but I can't and to top it off he keeps calling, but I haven't answered."

"Well did you tell him to stop calling?"

"No."

"Well what do you expect? You owe him at least that much. How else will he know not to call?"

"You're right, I'm going to call him later." I said.

"Why not right now?"

"Because I'm about to take the kids to the movies."

"Girl, ya'll been going somewhere everyday this week."

"I know, they go back to school on Monday and I can't wait! Tomorrow and Sunday we are going to rest though."

"Ok then, you really need to call him Sony."

"I know I know, bye."

After a long day of going to the movies and Chuck E. Cheese, I was drained. I couldn't wait for 9:00 pm so these kids could to bed. I was more than physically tired, I was mentally tired. I had so much on my mind. I haven't even journaled since I've been back from Vegas, that would help to relieve some of this mental load but in my journal I'm forced to be honest and I'm not sure if I'm ready to relive my weekend in Las Vegas. Granted it was fun but it was that guilty pleasure. I decided to call Alisha to pass time, at least I knew I wouldn't talk about Charles.

"Hey Alisha, what are you up to?"

"Girl, not too much, the girls and I and Rock and Rockelle are in Anaheim at Disneyland."

"Really, that sounds fun. Hold up, back up, who is Rockelle?"

"Oh that Rock's daughter, he brought her out to Oakland with him and then we decided to come down here."

"Ooh I heard that, must be lovely, one big ole happy family."

170

"Shut up girl. I was surprised myself but lately he's been on this family thing and wanting to really make it official, no more playing. Girl, he gave me a set of keys that he said were really important. They weren't house or car keys, they look like box keys or something. I can tell they must be important because he was holding my hands and looking deeply into my eyes when he gave them to me. Girl, you know that no one can replace Tai but I think he is close to it. I even went to the cemetery to talk it over with Tai, so you know this is serious."

"Oh my, that's big. I'm just glad you're happy. You deserve it. Where is he right now?"

"Oh he and the girls went to pick us up some food, so I'm just chilling. Bri told me ya'll had a ball in Vegas."

"We did. Well I'm going to let you chill."

"Are you O.K.?" Alisha asked me.

"Yeah I'm good, just tired. I'm about to put these brats in the bed and lay down. Have fun."

"Alright thanks, bye."

I was so happy for Alisha, although I didn't agree with Rock's line of business and that surveillance shit he pulled in New Orleans, but he was cool, I guess. I might as well call Charles and get it over with, hopefully I'll get his voicemail.

I was in luck, his voicemail came on the first ring.

"Hey Charles, I've been really busy that's why I haven't returned your calls. I really like you Charles, but this situation is getting deep for me. I really think it's best that we don't talk, I hope you understand. When you get this message, please don't call me, it just makes things harder for me. I'm so glad we met. Goodbye."

I couldn't believe I had a tear in my eye after leaving the message. I knew I had to do it though.

Three more days passed and the kids started school. It was kind of strange, just me and E.J. being in the house again. After he laid down for his nap, I was really bored.

"Good morning this is Bri."

"Hey Bri."

"Hey girl, how did the first morning back to school go?"

171

"It went well but now I'm bored to death. I can't do it Bri. I can't believe I miss him."

"Well call him."

"I can't, I know it's my ego but I can't help but to wonder if he's not calling because I said don't call or because he's not thinking about me."

"Ok, you are tripping. Just call the nigga. Now, I got work to do so I'll talk to you later."

I stayed strong for that day but the next day I broke down.

"Hello."

"Hi Charles."

"Hi Sonya." He replied

"Don't think I'm crazy, I know I said I wasn't going to call, but I missed talking to you."

"I don't think you're crazy, I know you're crazy." He said joking.

I don't know, some how that conversation turned into him planning to take a trip to visit one of his old teammates who lives in Phoenix. I don't know how I'm going to get a chance to see him, but I'm sure I'll figure out a way.

Dear Journal

It's been 3 1/2 months since I met Charles at the Essence Festival. My life is changing so much, my marriage is still jacked, but my outlook on life and how I feel about myself is wonderful. I'm back to the old Sony. I never realized how much of myself I lost in trying to be everything Eric needed, that's what you do when you're in love. I just wanted to be the perfect wife and mother. I talk to Charles everyday, we talk about nothing in particular but I always get off the phone with a smile. He's kind of like one of my girls, the way we talk, except my girls can't make my coochie tingle like he does. I've seen him a couple of times since Essence and every time I see him, I grow fonder and fonder. I have a confession, a couple of weeks ago when he came to visit Phoenix, I took E.J. with me to visit him. I know I'm wrong, I timed it around his nap so he would fall asleep in the car. All we did was sit in the car and talk and E.J. slept the whole time. I am glad E.J. is only one, but he's smart as a whip. He was in Phoenix for a few days but that was our only visit. It was only for thirty minutes, three weeks ago and I'm still high off of his presence.

Peace

I used to filter what I wrote in my journal. Always afraid that someone, Eric would read it, but now I'm to the point. If I can't get out all of the stuff that's heavy on my heart, soul and brain, then my journal can't serve it's purpose. Plus, if he reads it, him violating my privacy, would be much bigger than anything he reads. Eric will be home this weekend. He's excited. It's the first time since we've been living in Arizona that his team has played the Arizona Cardinals. As much as we've been funking the last couple of months, I'm excited for him to be coming home too. I haven't had sex since August, when I took the kids to visit, that was two months ago. My poor little vibrator is getting worn out. I can't help it, I can talk about the War in Iraq on the phone with Eric and my panties get wet...

Friday rolled around quick. After dropping the kids off at school. I came home to do some cleaning before I had to pick up Eric. Yesterday I found out that Charles would be in Phoenix next weekend playing the Suns for their season opener. This time I arranged for my mother to come out here. Their game is on November 1st, so my mom can be here for the kids Halloween festivities at school. They will love it.

On the way to pick up Eric I called to check in with the girls to see what they had planned for the weekend. I really missed being in Oakland with my family. Thank goodness for the long distance one rate plans for the phone or else my bill would be through the roof.

"Hello."

"Hey Alisha, what's up with it."

"Nothing just dropped some clothes for the girls off at Tai's mom's house because they're staying the weekend over there."

"What are you doing?"

"On my way to the airport so I can meet Rock in Vegas."

"Whaaat, don't be coming back married!"

"Nigga please, don't get me wrong we are planning to get married but it won't be a Vegas wedding. Oh my goodness Sony, I forgot to tell you he bought me a ring."

"A ring, like a proposal." I replied surprised.

"Yeah girl, well you know he a thug so he didn't get down on one knee or nothing. It was more like, 'you know a nigga need you in my life forever, so we gotta make it official' that's what he said. I know it wasn't romantic but it was real."

"Girl, I'm gone fuck you up, I can't believe you didn't tell me! I am happy for you."

"Thanks, so what are you doing this weekend?"

"Eric will be home, so that's about it." I replied.

"So you're gonna finally get some."

"Yes, indeed. Well let me let you go. Have fun in Vegas."

When I hung up the phone with Alisha. I was feeling a little home sick, my next call was to Mya which ended up killing two birds with one stone because she was with Bri. They were on their way to meet Kim at court. Kim's crazy husband was being sentenced today for his charges. She called the police the last time he beat her up. Bri and Mya were going for support plus his family is hella ignorant, so they were going for back up. That call let me know what Mya, Kim, and Bri were doing so that wrapped up my calls. When I got off the phone with them, I was even more homesick. I felt so left out. I realized I had one more call to make.

"Hey Sony."

"Hey Ma, can you do me a favor?"

"I am, I'm coming out there next week to help with the kids."

"That ain't a favor, you want to do that." I said laughing, but she knew it was true. She missed having her grandkids around.

"On the real Ma, can you find me a realtor out there. I'm moving back, I miss being home."

"What did Eric say?"

"He hasn't said nothing because I haven't told him yet. I've mentioned it but not sternly but I'm serious now. 'm about to pick him up and I'm gonna tell him, what can he say, he can either move or he can stay , but I'm moving." I said.

"Oh you had a big bowl of Wheaties this morning, I'll get on it today. You know I don't think you and the kids should be out there by yourself no way."

"Alright Ma, I'll talk to you later."

After picking Eric up, I decided to wait until after we made love to bring up moving. I knew it would spark an argument so I wanted to make sure we got busy first.

Just like I thought the idea of moving sparked a big ass argument. He tried to make me feel like I was a big baby and can't be away from my Mama. It didn't matter, I'll be that big baby because my kids and I were moving back and hopefully before the end of the year. That visit was sour.

My mom arrived the day before Halloween. The kids really didn't have to trick or treat because she brought them hella candy. They actually weren't going trick or treating, we were going to a party at our church. When I picked my mom up, I told her I planned on going to an open poetry event in Phoenix, so I needed her to watch the kids. She was excited, she always pushed me to pursue my writing. I was actually going to the poetry night but it was just to kill time until Charles got into town. Then I will go see him, I can't wait!

10/30/2003

Dear Journal,

I went to an open mic night tonight in Phoenix. It was off the hook, there were so many amazing poets there. It really inspired me to get back to writing. I also saw Charles tonight, ooh wee that man! I really like him. I have a confession to make, I kissed him. We kissed and it was magical, I know that sounds corny. More so, than the kiss, I just love his conversation, he is really cool.

High on his words like chronic,
And it's ironic, before him I never
Had a platonic, male friend

Things in common, old school
Kool-aid and Top Ramen, I'll admit
I'm growing quite fond, of him

We talk about being broke to

Fortune and fame
What's going on in the news, to his
Weak ass Madden game, at this
Point I knew things weren't the same

No longer platonic, a night of kissing
Turned that page
I take a deep breath, I know I'm
wrong, but I'm ready for the next stage

This is it, I think I'm ready for the relationship to change.

Peace

The next day was Halloween, Charles called me early in the morning to make sure I was ok with what happened last night. I am cool. I told him I couldn't make the game because it was Halloween, but I would try to watch it. They were leaving night after the game. We both knew as we talked on the phone that our relationship had changed, we just didn't know what that meant.

"Poopie I was wondering if you have someone that can watch your kids and if you want to, if you can come to Jersey in a few weeks. The city is honoring me with the community service of the year award. It would be a honor and I would love if you could come."

Instantly I wanted to say yes but I know it was easier said than done. "I would love to come Charles, but I have to arrange some childcare before I can say yes." I replied. "What day is that?" I asked.

"It's November 24th, it's the Sunday before Thanksgiving."

"Ok cool, I should be able to come then because we'll be in the Bay Area and I'll have a baby sitter. I won't be able to stay long though."

"Alright cool, I have to go to a meeting. I'll call you after the game."

He got off the phone sounding excited about the possibility, I was excited too.

The next couple of weeks, I secured babysitting. The kids would be with my mother–in-law and Bri and I would be away at the spa. Charles and I continued to talk daily but now our conversations had become sexual. I made up in my mind that on this trip, I would be fucking him. Hey it's 'karma baby' and Eric has done his share of dirt. I also found a house in San Ramon. I would be signing the papers around Thanksgiving and by Christmas we would be back in California. I was keeping it a secret until after I signed the papers, only Eric and my mom knew.

Everything was set up, it was Thursday, November 21st. I picked the kids up from school and we headed to the airport. Our flight to Oakland was leaving at 5:15 pm. I was ready for my weekend getaway, I even bought some sexy lingerie from Victoria's Secret. Charles has talked so much shit over the phone, that I was ready for the proof. I wasn't gonna let him forget that he said he was gonna bite my peach a couple of months ago.

Once we got through security at the airport, I was ready for a seat. It was work traveling with four kids. My cell phone rang, it was Eric.

"What's up?"

"Ya'll make it to the airport?" He asked.

"Yeah we're here, I'm still trying to catch my breath right now."

"I feel you. Anyway, I got you a ticket to come out here tomorrow. I'm sure the kids can stay at my mom's house." He said.

"What? The kids are already going to your mom's, but I told you I'm going to Calistoga to the spa with Bri."

"Yeah, yeah I know but it looks like I'm going to get 10,000 career rushing yards on Sunday. I only need eighty seven yards."

"I'm sure you didn't just realize this." I said with a slight attitude. Don't get me wrong, I was happy for him, but the timing was fucked.

"Well you used to be up on my numbers but I guess the new you doesn't care."

"Whatever Eric, I'll see you tomorrow. I'll call you when I get to Oakland to get the details."

I hung up the phone feeling like shit. He was right. I used to keep up with his stats but I honestly didn't know how many touchdowns he had this year. I really felt bad because now I had to call and tell Charles that I couldn't make it.

Calling Charles was a hard call to make. I explained the situation to him, he said he understood but I could hear in his voice that he was hurt. The next day before I left for Miami, I tried calling Charles but there was no answer, so I left a message. Saturday, I tried to call again but I got no return call. Sunday, when Eric left for the football field, I decided to try to call Charles again but still no answer.

"Hey Charles, I guess you've been busy because I haven't heard from you. I was just calling to say I hope tonight goes well. I really wish I could be there. I'm really proud of you. Call me when you get a chance. Bye."

Almost a week had passed and I still hadn't heard from Charles. I still called him daily leaving messages but no call back. I actually felt sick. I wasn't eating. I was depressed and I was ready to get home so I could be depressed without people in my face questioning me. On another note, I closed on my house. It was ready for us to move in too, but I decided to wait until Christmas break. I even got the kids pre-registered in their new school. I needed to call Alisha to see what time she was gonna pick us up tomorrow to go to the airport in the morning. We headed back to Arizona.

"Hello." Alisha answered the phone frantic, but I didn't notice at first.

"Hey Lish, what time you getting us in the morning?"

"Oh Sony, I might not be able to do it, I may be getting on a plane."

"What's wrong Alisha." I asked because now I heard the distraught in her voice.

"Girl it's Rock," she said crying, "he just called sounding really strange. He said some people had been following him. He didn't know if it was some niggas after him or the Feds. Either way it wasn't good." Alisha tried to stop crying in order to finish the story. "It had been rumored that both were after him. Anyway he was telling me he loved me and if I don't hear from him to use the keys he gave me there would be instructions. He tried to get off the phone with me, but I wouldn't let him. Then I heard a lot of noise and some gunshots and the phone went dead. Sony, I've been calling back and there's no answer. I've been calling his friends, but no answer. Sony, I'm going crazy."

"Don't cry Alisha, it will be Ok. Rock is smart. I'm sure he got away, he'll call you. Where are the girls?"

"With their granny."

"Ok, I'll be right over, don't worry."

I got off the phone and prayed for the best but in my heart I knew it was bad. By the time I made it to Alisha's house, it had been confirmed. Rock's friend called Alisha and told her that her man, her fiancé had been killed. Alisha was a wreck. She felt that God was punishing her, first her mom, then Tai, and now Rock. Everything she loved was taken from her. Her dad was living but he was cracked out and crazy, so he was good as dead to her. So in the wake of this event, I didn't make the flight back to Arizona. Well actually I never made it back to Arizona, well at least not to live. The kids remained in the Bay Area and I only went back to pack up. That was after I came back from New Orleans with Alisha. We all went with Alisha for support. The keys that Alisha had uncovered all the deeds to his properties in her name, bank accounts in her name and instructions on what to distribute to his mom and kids, but the bulk was for her. Alisha got a chance to meet a lot of his family, they all knew of her. Rock had spoken so highly of her. I still continued to call Charles, but still no return calls. Due to the events, Rocks death and my moving, I now called every couple of days instead of everyday.

Christmas was approaching quick. Alisha was doing better day by day. I was settled in my house and loved it. I loved being back with my family, they helped me get through my issue...Charles. One day I was on my way to the mall to do some Christmas shopping and a song came on that reminded me of Charles. Instead of getting that fuzzy feeling inside that I usually got, I got mad, I decided to call Charles and this would be the last call I would ever make to him. Of course he didn't answer.

"Hey Charles, I figured you wouldn't answer. That's alright, this will be my last time calling you. Nigga, you knew what was up from the gate, you knew I was married. Instead of being a man and telling me you were upset, you chose to act like a broad. I can't believe I wasted all them calls, all of those apologies but most important, I can't believe I wasted my feelings on you. I wish you a nice life."

181

Leaving that message was the best thing I could have done. I felt a load lifted. Normally the voicemail would have cut me off, but I was able to get everything out today. I felt good for the first time in a long time. After that call, I still continued to check on him through his team's website daily. I had to crawl before I walked, it would happen in time.

The whole family spent Christmas at my house, this is what I missed being in Arizona. The next week the crew all got together to go out for New Year's Eve. This was the first time since Eric and I got together, that we didn't bring the New Year in together. At the stroke of midnight, we raised our glasses, hugged and kissed each other and I made my resolution...

"I will remove Charles Knight from my system. No more calls or website visits. I will focus on making me a better me for me and my kids!"

Quarter 3
Chapter 13

Okay Ma, so Mya is going to pick the kids up from school but she's going to drop the boys off with you and Kayla is going to stay with her." I said to my mother going over babysitting arrangements.

"I know, Sony."

"Alright and E.J. just ate breakfast about an hour ago so he'll probably want to eat lunch about noon." I continued.

"Girl, stop acting like you ain't never been out of town before, the kids will be fine. What time do you get back on Monday?"

"I get back around two, so I'll pick the kids up from school."

"Is there any other parent from the school going with you?"

"Yeah another mother around my age and a father, he's the P.T.A. president."

"Well have fun, I don't know how much fun you can have at a National Parent/Teacher Association (PTA) conference but hey you never know, it is Chicago. Are you sure you don't want me to drive you to the airport?"

"I'm good, it's only the weekend so it won't be that expensive to park at the airport. Matter of fact, I better get going."

I hugged and kissed my baby and told him to be good and hugged my mom and thanked her again for keeping the kids.

"Alright Ma, I'll call you when I get there."

I left my mom's house and raced to get to the airport on time. I had my music so loud that by the time I got to the airport I had several missed calls and several messages. I figured I'd check them once I got checked in to the airport. The line at United Airlines was relatively short and I breezed through the security check point. I realized that I didn't have to break speed limits to get here because I still had an hour before my flight took off. My mom had called and so had Eric, Bri, and Mya. I had four missed calls and only three messages, so somebody didn't leave a message. I dialed my voicemail to retrieve my messages.

First message; "Hey Sony, this is mom, don't worry nothing is wrong, I just called to let you know that I'm so happy that you guys moved back out here. I know its been over a month but I just wanted to tell you that. Be safe, I love you." (End of message)

Next message: "What you got a cell phone for, if you don't answer it" (end of message).

"Okay he is tripping but what's new."

Last message: "What's up cuz, I was trying to catch you before you left, got to tell you something, oh well its not that big, call me later, Bye."

Okay I have to call Bri back to see what's up with her but first I have to call my Mama to tell her I love her.

"Hey Mommy, what's E.J. doing?"

"He's watching Disney with his Papa."

"Okay well I was just calling to tell you that I love you too and to let you know that I am so happy we moved back as well. I'll talk to you later. Bye."

Just as I decided to call Bri back, Allison was approaching me, so I decided to wait.

"Hey there Ms. Allison," I said to the twenty-something white lady approaching me. Allison was full blown white but her swagger let you know that she had been around black people, she didn't use lots of slang but you could tell and although I have never seen her daughter Ashley's father, I could tell from Ashley that he was definitely a brother.

"Hey Sonya, are you ready to get out there in Chicago and freeze our tails off?"

"Not really." I said laughing.

"I'm so glad you are going, your kids just started at the school and you are more active than most of the parents there. Last year the conference was in Tennessee and it was just me and Paul and he liked to drive me crazy."

Paul is the president of the PTA, a very corny, Black man who had made lots of money in dot.com investments and now he is a very wealthy stay at home dad.

"That's because its nothing to do in Tennessee but in Chicago there is plenty of distractions so we can ditch Paul."

"Girl, we are on the same page. I have a friend from college out there so we can call and find out where to go." Allison replied.

As we were talking Paul joined us and we began to discuss the conference itinerary. Before long they were announcing that they were beginning boarding for first class passengers, I stood up to tell them I would talk to them in Chicago because I upgraded my ticket the school purchased to first class. But when I stood up, I realized Allison had obviously done the same thing, so we both told Paul we would see him in Chicago. After we got to our seats, which happened to be next to each other, I tried calling Bri back, but I got her voicemail, so I left her a message, I then called Eric.

"Hey I'm about to take off, so I'll call you when I get to Chicago."

"Why didn't you answer your phone?"

"I didn't hear it, I had my music up loud. So what are you going to do since you guys have a bye this weekend?"

"I'm going to rest since my wife had to go to a PTA conference, you know you just want a break from the kids."

"Anyway, not true and you ain't said nothing about coming out there. I'll call you later. Bye." I powered my phone off and stuck it in my purse.

"So your husband plays football, right? You know everybody's business circulates at the school."

That was true because that was how I knew about Paul but I hadn't heard much about Allison though, I thought to myself.

"Yeah he plays for Miami, do you like sports?"

She answered yes which began a conversation that didn't end until we were landing at Chicago O'Hare airport. During our talk she told me about Ashley's father because she assumed that I knew her story as well. Like I assumed, he was a Black man in the recording industry, not a singer but like a producer. They broke up when she was pregnant. We compared stories of being involved with high profile men and how to keep our spoiled rich kids in check. She was cool and if I closed my eyes I would have sworn I was with a sister but I guess that proves that sisterhood extends beyond color lines. I really never 'chopped it up' with females outside of my circle. Most of the

185

women I meet are fake ass wives of players and the real ones are few and far between. Everything was running smoothly, we got our luggage from baggage claim and headed to the hotel. We arrived at the Marriott and checked-in. We then went to sign in at the conference registration table and pick up our packets. The seminars started tomorrow, but tonight they were having a 'meet and greet' that I would be passing on. I exchanged room numbers with Allison and Paul and told them I would see them later. Once I got up to my room I took my clothes off, turned on the T.V and before long the TV was watching me. I don't know when I fell asleep but I was awakened by the hotel phone ringing and the clock read 9:15p.m.

"Hello"

"Hey Sonya, you sleep?" It was Allison.

"No not really, what's up?"

"I was calling to see if you want to step out to get a bite to eat and some drinks with me and my girl Tamara."

"Sure are you guys ready now."

"She said she'll be here in thirty minutes."

"Cool, I'll get ready. Did you go to the 'Meet and Greet'?"

"No, but hopefully I can meet and greet somebody tonight."

"You are crazy, I'll come down to your room in about twenty-five minutes."

I hung up the phone and jumped in the shower. After I showered I called my mom and the kids and then Eric to let him know I made it in since I forgot to when I got in. I can't believe I slept so many hours. I talked to my mom but got Eric's voicemail, he always had a problem when my life is not revolving around his. It was cold outside, so trying to look cute was not priority, I was trying to be warm, although I did look cute in my paper denim jeans and UGK boots. I had on a vintage t-shirt that said 'overstyled' with a thermal top under it. No joke, I was trying to keep warm. I had on a big coat, a scarf and gloves. When I got to Allison's room, her friend Tamara had just arrived and they were bundled as well. Tamara took us on a quick tour of the area we were in. She asked did we want to go to a quiet place or a place where it cranks. We both agreed on something that cranks so she suggested Michael Jordan's restaurant. When we pulled up we could see that there might be a wait. Tamara said that lots of athletes hang there so it's always crowded on the weekend. When we walked in Tamara noticed a friend of hers was working as the hostess and so magically our 10:30 reservation appeared in the book. Man ain't nothing like having some hook-up. Her friend told us we had a couple of options, she could seat us in an area that had some football players or another area that had some basketball players in it. They looked at me for a decision but I would choose neither. I definitely don't want to be around no football players or anybody that knows Eric and I made a New Years resolution to stop thinking about that nigga Charles, so I really didn't want to be around and basketball players either, but why spoil their night.

"I really don't care either way." I replied.

They both answered in unison, "Basketball."

And so the hostess led us to our seats. I had been doing good lately, after I stopped talking to Charles in November, I still thought of him daily. I would hear a song and think of him, I would go on-line everyday and follow how he was playing but not since my New Year's resolution. Just think I broke my vows for our friendship. I became an adulterous. Although we never had sex, the bible said lustful thoughts of someone outside of your marriage is just as bad as the act and lord knows I had plenty of lustful thoughts and a few kisses. Well that resolution didn't last long, it's only January 9th, and I'm thinking about him. I need a drink.

"Sonya, what do you do in Oakland beside being a mom, although that's a full time gig?" Tamara asked me.

"That's pretty much it. I'm a stay-at-home mom and wife."

"Girl, you are lucky." She replied.

"Oh yeah, Tam, her husband plays football for Miami." Allison replied.

"Stop lying, girl you ain't hooked Allsion up with nobody, well you can hook me up."

Tamara was definitely all 'sista'. She said whatever came to her head. I just laughed at the comment.

"Well no wonder you don't care where we sit. Now I see that fat rock blinding me, shit you don't need to sit around no athletes. I'm going to the bathroom, can you guys order me a lemon drop when the waitress comes. I'm going to case out the place too."

"I'm sorry Sonya, she just says whatever." Allison said to me.

"Girl she is fine. She is hella funny though, I like that in people."

The waitress came and we ordered our drinks. After she brought our drinks Tamara had returned, so we ordered our food. Tamara met some guy on the way to the bathroom and she was trying to convince Allison to go out with him and his friends. I could tell Allison wanted to go but she felt awkward about leaving me, but I was not tripping, I was a big girl and could get back to the hotel.

"You should go Allison, it will probably be fun." I insisted.

"But we came together, we leave together, that's how I roll."

"I feel you Allison, but I'm cool."

"Yeah, she can take my car." Tamara jumped in.

"Oh no, that's what I'm not going to do. I'm going to call a cab, plus you guys don't know them like that. You should probably take your car and follow them."

"That's true." Tamara replied.

When our food arrived Allison and I began to eat, but Tamara was too anxious to eat. She kept going back and forth to the bar to make sure the guys hadn't left.

Do you think this is a good idea, Sonya?"

"I don't know but your friend seems determined to go and you don't want her to be by herself with some men she doesn't know."

188

The waitress came back to check on us and I ordered another Malibu and cranberry and asked her to bring me the check and call me a cab. We continued to pick at our food and talk about music and clothes.

"Let me go to the bathroom before my cab gets here, excuse me."

I went to the bathroom and peed and freshened up my lipgloss. I took a peek into the bar to see if I recognized the football players they were leaving with but I didn't. When I got back to the table my drink was there and the bill. I went to look at the tab but Allison said that the waitress said somebody paid for us.

"I asked the waitress was it the guys with Tamara but she said no." Allison said.

I looked around to see if I saw anyone looking at us, but I didn't.

"That's crazy, but oh well Thank you." I said

"It was a guy looking at you when you went to the bathroom, I mean staring but he left, I think."

"Where was he sitting?" I asked.

"I think over there with them basketball players at that table."

I looked at the table, but no one looked familiar. I finished my drink just in time, the waitress walked over and told me my cab was outside.

"Alright Allison, have fun and call me if you need me." I said and handed her a paper with my cell phone number on it.

I bundled back up in my coat, scarf, gloves and hat and headed back out into the cold. When I got outside there was a taxi but in the distance I saw a familiar tall frame, draped in a fur.

"Yo ass better not had left with them nigga's, you was going to hear it from me."

"Is that right, that's a change since I haven't heard from you in months. Thank you for dinner Charles, Good night!" I got in the cab and gave instructions to take me to the Marriott and tried to pick my heart up from out my shoes. I was breathing so heavy that I barely heard my phone ringing, it was Charles so I let it go to voicemail. It seemed like the driver flew to the hotel because we were already there.

"How much do I owe you sir?" I asked.

"It was already taken care of by the gentleman at the restaurant."

"How did he know where I was going and how much?"

"He didn't, he just paid me handsomely to make sure you got to where you were going safely. For what he gave me I can carry you to your room if need be." The driver said laughing. He actually made me laugh too.

"That won't be necessary but thank you."

I jumped out and looked around to see if there was any sign of Charles but he wasn't there. I don't know if I was happy or unhappy about that. When I got to my room I look around before I opened the door, I really felt like I was in the middle of the twilight zone. Once in the room I plopped down in the middle of my bed and buried my face in the pillows. I wanted to cry and laugh and pout and smile. I was having an emotional overload and all I could do was scream.

"Aaahhh! Why me, why the fuck me?"

That quick seeing him for that brief moment brought up so many feelings that I was trying so hard to get rid of. I remembered the last time I talked to him and all the messages I left him, that he never returned. I remember the sexy Victoria Secret set I bought for the last weekend we were suppose to spend together that didn't happen. He had no way of knowing he was going to get some pussy on that trip considering the fact that we had slept together and nothing happened. Oh well I guess it wasn't meant. Charles continued to call and I continued to ignore his calls and messages until it dawned on me that I was doing the same thing his punk ass was doing when I was trying to call him back then. I can't believe it's been almost two months since we've talked. The phone continued to ring.

"Hello."

"Hey Poopie, why you not answering the phone?"

"I don't know Charles, may be the same reason you didn't answer yours for two weeks. What's up, are you calling me because we both happen to be out here and you don't have no Chicago hoes to talk to?"

"Oh I could be out with somebody if I wanted."

"Cool, do that, please don't let me be the reason."

I was in the process of hanging up the phone when he caught me.

"Hold up, please don't hang up Sonya."

He paused for my response.

"I'm still here."

"Sonya, I have thought of you everyday for the past couple of months. Can we please talk – please."

"Talk, I'm listening."

"Where are you staying?"

"Why?"

"Come on Poopie, don't be like that, can I come talk to you?"

"Sonya." I responded.

"What do you mean?"

"My name is Sonya."

"Okay Sonya, can I come by to talk to you?"

I knew I wanted to say yes but I was so, so scared. My stomach was doing somersaults and my heart was trying to jump out of my chest but somehow through all of that I was able to respond.

"Alright, I'm staying at the Marriott Hotel. Where are you?"

"I'm still in the parking lot at the restaurant."

"Can you stop at the store and get me some Malibu and cranberry juice before you come?"

"Of course."

"Thanks, I'm in room 519, see you soon."

We hung up the phone. Having him go to the store would buy me some time to freshen up and get comfortable. It was so much I wanted to say to him. I wanted to ask him why he didn't take my calls, I wanted to explain to him in person why I had to cancel our meeting. I wanted to cuss him out for opening me up and then leaving me hanging. At the same time I was excited to see him, I longed to feel his secure embrace, I missed his singing and the way he laughed when I clowned him. I took off my clothes and put on my loungewear, I brushed my teeth and washed my face. I laid on the bed and tried to gather my thoughts until I heard the knock on the door. I turned on the T.V. as I went to the door.

"Who is it?"

"Room Service."

Its funny, all the ill feelings I had towards him, all the anger that was built up all went out the door when I opened it. When I saw him standing in the doorway with his bashful smile, I couldn't help but smile and it was confirmed—he was definitely my weakness and he was more than 'just a friend' to me.

"So can I come in?"

"Do you have my drink?"

"You been going to your meetings?"

"What meetings?"

"Alcohol Anonymous"

"Ha ha funny, come in! Yeah you damn near drove a sister to being an alcoholic with your stunts."

"Man, I just got in the door and you already on me. I guess I deserve it though. Alright I'm ready to hear it."

"Hear what? I ain't got nothing to say."

"Come on now, Poopie, I mean Sonya, you always have something to say."

"I don't have nothing to say about that old shit, its old now."

"If it's old, why did you leave me out in the cold at the restaurant?"

"You should have made yourself known while we was in the restaurant instead of waiting until I was leaving."

"I didn't know who you were with so I wasn't sure if it was cool. What are you doing out here anyway?"

"I'm out here for a PTA conference, I guess it was better because I really don't know the people I was with, so did ya'll play the Bulls tonight?"

"We play them tomorrow, you're coming right?"

"Maybe." I said smiling.

I couldn't even stay mad at this man, I watched him as he fixed me a drink. He was so comfortable in his own skin. After making my drink he plopped down in the chair and started flipping through the channels.

"Okay Sonya, you better yell at me, cuss me out, question me or whatever because after tonight we are not going to revisit this incident."

"What makes you think there'll be an after tonight?" I replied.

"I think I've heard that from you before."

"Don't be cocky, nigga! What do you have to say – turn the TV off so you ain't distracted. I'ma turn on the radio. I'm listening." I said.

I flipped through the stations of the clock radio until I found a quiet storm slow jam station.

"Alright, first of all I want to apologize to you Sonya. I wasn't ready for this. I didn't plan on falling for you, but I did. I know the situation but that didn't change how I felt. I wanted you, I needed you to be there for me and I didn't want to understand why you couldn't. I have to be honest, I'm used to having things my way and it really fucked with my ego. All I know is that I've missed you like crazy, and you've been nothing but honest with me, so basically I had to get over myself. In the beginning I didn't take your calls because I wanted to try to hurt you like I was hurt but then after you stopped calling I wanted you to call, I wanted to call you but I thought everything may have gotten better with you and your peoples so I thought it was best to leave well enough alone. I told myself that I fucked up my chance. Tonight I swear when I heard your voice at the restaurant, I thought I was tripping. Then when I saw you walk to the bathroom, I knew it was fate. So, now that I got that out, I'm ready to hear it from you."

193

"I accept your apology Charles, I really don't have anything else to say, I mean hell I left yo ass about a million messages." I said laughing.

"Is that your phone ringing?" He asked.

"I think so." I got up to get my phone from my purse and answer it.

"Hey Bri, what's up?"

"Girl, I was trying to catch you before you got to Chicago. Are you enjoying yourself?"

"Yes, it's cool so far, but what's up?"

"Ok Bitch, I know you believe in fate right?"

"Yeah. Why?"

"Ok, I was looking online to see if anything was happening in the 'Chi' to let you know since you was going to be out there, and bitch guess what?"

"What?"

"Girl, Charles will be out there, they are playing the bulls tomorrow."

"I know."

"You know – you talked to him?"

"Yes."

"You saw him?"

"Yes."

"Bitch, is he there?"

"Yep!"

"Stop lying! How did that happen? Well I guess you can't answer right now but soon as he leaves call me. No matter what time it is."

"Alright Bri."

"Hey Sony, are you OK?"

"Yes, I'm cool."

"Bitch you are more than cool – you are hella happy! On the real girl, that's fate. Call me back."

"Alright, thanks cuz."

"Tell Bri I said hi." Charles said in the background.

"Bri, Charles says Hi."

"Tell him I said what's up – Alright girl." We both hung up.

"So what is Bri talking about?"

"Boy, we sure are nosey aren't we! She ain't talking about nothing. Alright back to your apology, I have to soak this up because it's rare that you admit to being wrong."

"I don't know what else to say, I see your husband had a good season, they'll probably go to the Superbowl."

"Yeah, that would be good for him, you are having a pretty good season too, I voted for you online for the Allstar game!"

"How are you and him doing Sonya? Are things better?"

"I told you Charles, my situation existed before I met you, so me not talking to you didn't make things better. It is what it is, but hey I have a family to think about."

"What about you, what about how you feel?"

"I'm going to be alright, I'ma big girl. Plus, the last time I depended on a person to look out for my feelings, they left me hanging."

"Ouch, I guess I deserve that."

"So what about you, how are you and your chick doing?"

"You know how that is, I ain't ready for all the things she's ready for – you know marriage and a family."

"I thought ya'll might be engaged, I saw on your team website that you said you were doing jewelry shopping for Christmas. Yeah, I was keeping up with you online but my New Year's resolution was to get over you so I stopped going to that site. So did you buy her a ring?"

"Do you want the truth?"

"I thought that was all we do."

"Yeah, I bought her a ring, but…"

I really didn't hear anything after the 'but' because my heart dropped, I know I had no right but I was hurt, I almost dropped a tear.

"So when's the wedding?" I asked trying to act like I wasn't tripping.

"Who said anything about a wedding?"

"So it wasn't an engagement ring, what, it was a friendship ring? You don't have to lie to me Charles."

"Ok, after you didn't come to New Jersey I was upset. I told myself that trying to be with you was a battle I would lose, you have a husband and a family. I was acting like an asshole towards everybody and she hung in there. So then I figured I might as well try and settle down myself. At least to take my focus off you."

"So what are you saying Charles?" You are getting married? I mean we are just friends right. She just might be the one."

"You don't get it Sony, I can't stop thinking about you. I can't marry her, if my heart isn't all the way there."

"You are not being fair to her though, you can't lead her on. Anyway, this could never go anywhere."

"She knows Sonya, she doesn't know for sure, but she knows. She's always telling me that my heart is somewhere else. She says she can be patient though. So, you saw on the website what I did for Christmas, did you go on to see my New Year's resolution?"

"No, I told you I wasn't checking for you no more."

"Yeah, Ok—anyway my New Years resolution was to mend a friendship that was broken. I was talking about us."

"Well it's mended, we are cool. I'm cool. Am I going to get an invite to the wedding?"

"Yeah, are you coming alone or with Eric?"

"Ha ha, you are such a comedian."

"Well you are being funny, so I'm being funny, I'm being like you. I told you, woman how am I going to get married when I'm in love with you!"

At that moment it got really quiet. I was at a lost for words. Did he really mean to say that, did it just slip out and was he serious. The scary part was the fact that I felt the same way. The butterflies I got whenever he was around, how the mention of his name brought a kool-aid smile to my face, how I hadn't talked to him in months but I still thought of him daily. How I was pissed with him earlier tonight and now my coochie was throbbing and soaking wet. How could this be possible, I am married but I am in love with another man.

"What did you say Charles Edwin Knight?"

"Nigga you heard me, now move over and turn the TV back on. Don't nobody want to hear that love-making music."

He took his shoes off and propped the pillows up so he could stretch out on the bed with me and grabbed the remote control to see what type of movie selection they had on "On Demand" Pay-per-view.

"You want to watch a movie?" He asked me.

"Do you love me, Charles?"

"What does that have to do with watching a movie?"

"Nothing. I ain't tripping you can pick a movie." I said with an attitude.

"You are such a big baby, you already know the answer." He said pulling me into his long eagle span arms wrapping me up like a newborn baby in a receiving blanket.

"I am not a big baby, I wasn't sure if I heard you correctly."

"Sonya Renee' Brown Jackson, damn that's a lot of names! I love you and I am so in love with you as well, you know there's a difference."

"Yes, Charles I know there's a difference – and I love you and I am in love with you back." I broke his embrace and turned around to face him and look him in the eyes. "You know this is some deep shit Charles and I have to admit, I'm scared. This is a whole new ballgame and a lot of lives are involved and people may get hurt. I don't know, if I could change how I feel about you, I would, but I can't Charles. This is all too much." I couldn't help but cry like the big baby he said I was. I mean no holds bar, snot running down the face crying!

"Baby don't cry, we'll figure this thing out. It will be hard but it will work out."

197

Charles wiped my tears and snot with his hands, this nigga must really love me because that was nasty shit. Then he kissed my forehead.

"You're even sexy when you cry, baby."

"Thanks." I said laughing.

I laid in his arms and tried not to stress on what the future might hold. I closed my eyes took a deep breath and tried to enjoy the moment. I had to accept it, I was in love with this man. As fucked up as the timing could be, it was happening. I was prepared for the friendship, but not for this. What about Eric, should I leave him, should I tell him. What about my kids? And what about ol girl he's supposed to be marrying. "Come on now Sony, stay in the moment." I said in my head. "All those things will work themselves out." I thought to myself. I wonder if his thoughts are being interrupted with all of the stuff we will have to face. I looked at him and then cut my eyes away when I realized he was looking at me.

"Don't look at me like that?" He said kissing my neck.

"Like what?" I responded.

"You know you have them bedroom eyes."

"Do I?" I replied while reaching over him to grab the remote to turn off the TV.

"Why you do that…"

I turned the radio back on.

"Sonya, I thought we were finished talking about…"

I put my finger over his mouth to shut him up.

"We are finished talking, so be quiet," I said, "You hear the music?" He nodded yes. "You said it was love-making music right?" I whispered in his ear while I straddled over him and began to softly kiss his neck. I struggled to lift his shirt over his head. I was having some trouble so he helped me out by taking it off. I continued kissing his chest, his nipples were like chocolate kisses that melted in my mouth, I caressed his muscular biceps. I could feel his manhood expanding through his pants between my legs, I knew already that he was hung and right now I wanted him bad. I laid beside him so I could

198

comfortably stick my right hand down his pants to massage his testicles and stroke his magic stick. I was on the verge of cumming just from giving him a hand job. Then he grabbed my hand.

"Sony, are you sure you're ready to do this, you know there is no rush."

"I know, I'm sure. I want you, I wanted this back in November and I am not letting it pass this time."

"Alright baby, lay on your back." He ordered me in a sweet voice. I layed on my back and he began to undress me. He started by taking off my shirt, I didn't have on bra, so my breast were fully exposed and fully erect. He kissed each nipple softly and ran his tongue down my stomach to my belly button. He slid my pajama pants off, I don't sleep in panties so now I was completely naked.

"I thought you didn't have hair down there." He said as he licked around my perfectly lined pubic hair, luckily I just got waxed yesterday.

"I'm letting it grow back, another new year's resolution." I responded.

He rose up from the bed to remove the rest of his clothing, this man was definitely packing, his thing was long and thick and I was scared to death. After removing his clothes he continued to suck my titties, twirling his tongue around the nipple sucking hard to that point of pleasurable pain and then kissing gently. He paid each breast the same amount of attention, my coochie was soaking wet. I tried to reach for his dick because my nerves were jumping so much I needed something to grab hold of, but he held my hands.

"You sure you ready." He said as he scooted down and blew on my coochie. I tried to say yes but I was at a lost for words, all I could do was nod my head. As soon as he stuck his tongue inside of my walls I couldn't contain myself. My body began to have convulsions and I exploded.

"I'm cumming, I'm cumming." The juices covering his face did not stop or slow him down. He continued to plunge his tongue in and out of my vagina, while I held the sheets for dear life, and then he tickled my clit with his wet tongue. I couldn't take it anymore, I had him in a headlock, my legs were wrapped around his neck so tight.

"I'm cumming again, I can't take it, please stop, I can't take it. I want you to put it in. Do you have protection?" He got up fumbled around in his wallet while I hoped he found some because I would hate to have to pass up on this due to a technicality! Oh my goodness, what am I thinking, I am married and I'm making love to another man and enjoying it. I am going to hell! I'm glad he found a condom because if I had any more time to think I probably would have had second thoughts. He rolled the condom down his long shaft, nervousness must have been written all over my face because he kissed me and asked if I was sure repeatedly.

"I'm sure Charles, I love you."

"I love you more." He said as he gently inserted his penis inside of me. My body tensed up and I took deep breaths trying to withstand his big stick. As wet as my vagina was, I could still feel every inch, the length and width was overwhelming.

"Are you okay, baby." He whispered to me, I wish my voice could have responded as soft and sweet but it wasn't possible.

"Yes baby, I'm good. I slightly screamed.

"Baby you feel so good, I've missed you so much." He panted as he continued to stroke in and out with long strides.

"I'm cumming again, Charles."

"I got you baby, I'm trying to get you to cum at least five times. Put your leg up here." He moved my leg over his shoulder to get more leverage. Damn this nigga might get five plus orgasms. This first time was all for me because I was so overwhelmed, I couldn't even move, he was doing all the work. He speeded up his pace. I swear his thing was in my stomach.

"Oh baby right there, keep it right there." There went number four. I just knew he was about to cum until he said, "turn over baby." I don't know, it was something about those three words that just made me go wild, doggy style was definitely my favorite position. I turned over and positioned myself near the edge of the bed so he could stand and I extended my arms down to arch my back.

"Oh, I see my baby like it like this, you getting ready huh."

"Shut up nigga!"

He grabbed me by the hips and thrusted in and out pounding hard.

"Oooh Charles, smack my ass baby!"

My head rolled back and I know I was screaming like crazy.

"My baby is a little freak, huh?" He said as he smacked my ass. In twenty-eight years of living, I had never felt ecstasy like this, he was hitting every spot. I had now came five times and he was still going.

"Lay down flat, Sony."

He was still hitting it from the back but he put his finger under me and started tickling my clit with his fingers. It felt like a tongue on my clit and at the same of getting the dick. Although my body jerked he kept it up at a steady pace. This was the best shit I had ever felt in my life. He plunged his fingers in and out of my coochie, his dick in and out. He was going so fast that the headboard was banging and the bed was jumping. He was cumming and I was cumming with him.

"Oh my goodness Charles, you are too much for me!"

He laid out, after all that work I knew he was probably too tired to talk. He pulled me close to lie in his arms. He was covered with sweat but it didn't matter. There was no going back now.

"You must love me, because you don't even have your scarf on and I know you don't lay down without that rag on your head."

"You just caught me off guard but believe me this will be the first and last time that happens, I love you but I got to wrap the hair."

201

" Hey Baby, are you my Poopie again?"
"Yeah, I'm your Poopie." I replied.

Chapter 14

"Oh shit is it really 8:15?" I looked at the clock with one eye open and one closed. When Charles left at 6:30, I planned on laying around for thirty more minutes, and then getting up. I didn't even really wake up when he left, when he kissed me goodbye I just remember looking at the clock. I guess I better get myself up and dressed. I turned on the TV to help me wake up and rolled out the bed.

"Damn!" I said aloud when I began to walk to the bathroom. It confirmed that it was not a dream. My coochie was super sore, I had really made love to Charles and not only that, I had also confessed my feelings to him. Although it felt like paradise last night when we were together, today I felt like shit. All I could do was cry. I cried as I brushed my teeth, I cried in the shower and I prayed.

"Lord, thank you for this day. Thank you for all my blessings because I know I'm not worthy. Father please forgive me for my sins. Father please guide me because right now I am so confused. In Jesus name I pray Amen."

"Come on Sonya get together." I tried to give myself pep talks as I got dressed. "Ok this is not that bad Sonya, you love him, I mean it's not the worst thing a person could do. I mean hell Eric had slept with other women during our relationship." I tried to make myself feel better but it wasn't working. I had always been faithful. Ten years of sleeping with the same man – out the window. And I initiated it, and I enjoyed it, I'm a bad person, I know I fucked stuff up now! I'm going to have to tell Eric, I can't sleep with him now that I've slept with Charles. I don't know how people do this shit especially people who date three and four people. Oh well no time to stress about it now I have seven minutes before I have to get downstairs for the first session at 9:00 am. I checked the mirror one last time to make sure I didn't look like I got beat up or something. I guess I looked okay. Right before I was about to walk out the hotel room phone rang. "It's probably Allison or Paul." I thought.

"Hello."

"Good morning beautiful."

I really didn't expect for it to be Charles, I wasn't ready to talk to him.

"Hey Charles."

"I was just calling to check on you, and make sure you got up."

"Yeah I'm up, I was about to walk out when you called."

"Alright I don't want to keep you. Sonya, I know we were both not prepared for what happened last night but I don't regret it, I'm actually happy as hell. I know it's probably awkward right now for you but I hope in the end you'll have no regrets as well."

"Alright, I got to go though."

"Ok Poopie, I love you."

"I love you too."

I ran into Allison on the elevator on the way down to the lobby. I looked like a beauty queen compared to how she looked this morning.

"I see somebody had a long night." I joked with her.

"Girl, I ain't went to sleep yet, what did you do last night."

"I didn't do a thing, I watched a movie and went to sleep."

"Well that's what I'll be doing tonight, catching up on some rest."

"I feel you." I responded. I didn't even want to ask her what she did last night, shit who am I to judge. I just threw a skeleton in my own closet last night.

I turned my phone on silent and got a bagel and coffee from the breakfast area. Allison and I decided to go to the same sessions just in case they were boring we could talk to each other. I really couldn't focus on the session anyway, I had my own problems to worry about. I never thought it could be possible to have feelings for two different men at the same time but it was happening. The morning session was a blur to me, luckily they had hand-outs that bullet-pointed everything that was discussed, so I could review it when my head was in a better place. I decided to take my box lunch they provided and take it up to my room. In my room I called Mya to check on Kayla, they were in the mall shopping. I called my mom to check on the boys and they were fine and then I called Eric, of course he was acting like an asshole. I told him I went out to eat with one of the parents and his response was, "Oh so you went out there to kick it?" I wanted to say, no I came out here to get fucked really good, but I decided not. We sat on the phone for a few moments more in silence until I told him I had to get back to the sessions, I was lying, but whatever. One thing for sure, I fell in love with Charles because of Charles, but Eric was sure helping Charles out, if he only knew! I ate my sandwich and tried to sort through my situation but I could not figure it out. What would make me happy would hurt so many other people but if I continue this way with Eric, I'm no good my childrenor myself. I wanted to call Bri but I was not even ready to tell her what happened and I tell Bri everything. Charles was calling on my cell phone but I ignored it, I didn't feel like talking to him either.

The afternoon session ended around four o'clock. I wasn't hungry yet so I didn't go eat with Allison and Paul. Instead I went upstairs and used the hotel note pad to begin to journal everything that had happened in my life in the last six months since I met Charles. So much had happened that getting it all out on paper was therapeutic for me. Hell, who knows maybe one day I'll write a book about this shit because it's definitely soap opera worthy! Charles called again and this time

I took the call. He was on his way to the arena so he calling to see if I was coming to the game, I wasn't sure but I told him to leave me a ticket just in case. I decided to order room service and continued to journal.

I made a list of the pros and cons of Charles' and my relationship. I made a list of pros and cons of Eric's and my relationship. I wrote down why I love Eric and why I love Charles. I continued to write and put a dent in my bottle of Malibu Rum Charles brought me last night. The last list was a list of all the happy times I had over the last past year and who was responsible. This is when it became clear. My children, Charles, and my girls were the only people on the list for being responsible for bringing me joy. I realized I loved Eric because of the history we shared. I love him for being a good father and provider. I love him for showing me that all the guys from Oakland weren't drug dealers and hustlers, but I was no longer in love with him and all those things that I love him for were not enough to compensate for what I needed as a woman. I needed the same love that I had put out for ten years and he may be was not capable of that.

I had lost track of time. I wrote so much that it was already 7:15pm and Charles' game started at 7:30pm. I decided on watching it on TV. I called Bri to tell her the story of running into Charles last night at the restaurant. I told her of all of the night's events minus the part of me giving up the pussy. Of course she asked though, I lied but if I know Bri, she really ain't buying it. Charles was killing in the game. I really wished I would have went, ain't know telling when we will see each other again. I read over the hand-outs from the seminar while I watched the game. New Jersey ended up beating the Bulls 106 – 82. Charles scored 43 points and he sat out most of the fourth quarter. I knew my phone would be ringing soon, and like I thought Charles was calling. I was more excited to answer his call tonight, earlier I was uncertain and I'm sure he could sense that.

"Hey Baby." I answered.

"What's up, where are you?"

"I'm at my hotel, I couldn't make it to the game. How was it?"

"Nigga, don't act like you didn't watch it. Even if you ain't feeling me, you love sports so I know you watched it."

"Yeah, I watched it, but only because I'm feeling you. I know you were showing off because you thought I was there."

"You're right, you seem like you're in a better mood than earlier."

"I was tired, somebody had me up all night. So are ya'll about to leave?"

"No we're staying over another night, then we'll practice tomorrow and leave for Memphis after that."

"Are you on your way to your hotel?"

"Yes ma'am."

"Ok, I'm on my way. Hook up the PS2, I ain't whooped you in Madden in a couple of months. I hope you've been practicing!"

"You know I let you win before, that's when I was trying to hook you – I got you now, so be prepared."

"Whatever, I'll see you in a few."

"Alright, I'm in Rm. 730." He said before hanging up.

I didn't have a mirror in front of me but I could feel the biggest smile spread across my face. Just talking to him made me feel so good. It was such a good feeling to really like a person. Aside from loving or needing someone, to like someone and be around them because you choose to, not because you feel obligated. Man if only this feeling didn't have so many repercussions.

Let me get up and get cute because if I think too much, my happiness might turn back into depression. After a quick shower and getting dressed I emptied my carry-on bag out and threw a few items in it in case I decided to stay over. I phoned down to the concierge to make sure a taxi was available and then I headed out.

I slid off my wedding ring while I was in the taxi and put it in my purse. I wasn't sure of what to expect when I walked into the lobby of the hotel so just in case he happened to be down there I didn't want to look like the adulteress that I am to other people who might be around. When I walked in, there were a few people in the bar area. I did my best to avoid eye contact with anyone especially since Charles had told me that his irritating friend Greg had traveled with him on this trip. Charles told me that no one knew of our relationship not even his closest friend. Him seeing me here would definitely let the cat out of the bag. He probably is the last person I would want to know.

In the elevator I checked my lipgloss and hair in the mirrored doors. I always tripped on how they always have mirrors in elevators, well they definitely come in handy in these types of situations. I prayed that no one would be walking in the hallways of the 7th floor.

Thank the lord the 7th floor was empty. I rushed to room 730 before anyone came out of their room. Damn this man is handsome, I thought when he opened the door. I really don't know if it's his physical presence that makes him so attractive. He's not one of them talked about athletes like you see on the top most attractive sports figure shows or nothing. But in comparison to the men you see on them shows like Michael Jordan or Derek Jeter, I would choose Charles any day, but maybe that's because I know hiss inner beauty as well.

"I'm about to order some food, do you want something?" He asked.

"Yeah, order me a Caesar salad. So man, I need to give you some every night if you gon' go out there and ball like that." I said jokingly.

"I wish you could, well not necessarily give me some but be around me every night."

"No you don't. I'm sure I would start to drive you crazy, well I know you would drive me crazy. I'm used to having some me time."

"I feel you, alright who you playing with?" He said as he turned on the video game.

"Ain't nothing changed, I'm playing with the Colts."

"So what did you tell Bri, because I know you've talked to her. What did she say?"

"You know what, I talked to but I filtered the conversation, about you know. I feel bad though because I usually tell her everyrthing."

"Well call her, you don't have to tell her what happened, it's probably not the best thing to tell over the phone. Try to feel out if she seems suspicious "

"What, are you trying to get out of this Madden beat down?"

"Oh are you still talking mess about a beat down?"

We played our game of Madden and it was brutal. When we finished our room service arrived. Of course I got my usual queezy feeling that I get whenever someone knocks on the door when I'm with Charles. I always imagine it will be someone that knows Eric and I working at the hotel. After we ate our food, we played Madden again and Charles whooped my ass again!

"You know I'm under a lot of emotional stress, that's how you beat me!"

"I told you, I let you win before. Lay down on the bed so I can give you a massage. Hopefully it will relieve some or all of your stress."

Oh my goodness, a massage without having to ask fifty billion times and still getting a half ass job, I must be dreaming. I fell asleep about four minutes into the massage. It felt so good, plus I still hadn't caught up from all my missed rest from last night. I slept for about forty-five minutes. When I woke up, Charles was sitting in the chair without any music or TV on, just watching me.

"Ooh I'm sorry for falling asleep, are you mad at me?"

"Never, I'm enjoying watching you sleep. You are so beautiful to me, inside and out. So Poopie, what's next?"

"I don't know, usually I have it all together but this time I really don't know. But to respond to what you said earlier, you know about regrets, I don't have any regrets. However, you have to be patient with me. I may not be that sure of us everyday. Not because of you but because of my kids, I am definitely sure about how I feel about you. I just have so much to lose."

"I know baby, but I have so much to lose as well."

"I hate when you say that, what do you have to lose? A girlfriend that you're not even sure of."

"So, it doesn't have any reflection on me? I am in love and involved with a known married woman."

"So what do you have to lose, your image, is that it? You know what, this was probably a big mistake, I'm about to go." I said as I jumped up to find my shoes.

"What are you doing Sonya?" He asked grabbing me in a bear hug.

"Let go of me Charles."

"You don't want me to let you go. I know I don't want to let you go. Baby we know this is going to be hard and we both have a lot to lose. Baby we're here now and I don't want to go back."

He turned me around to look into my puppy dog pouting face, and kissed my forehead softly. He didn't say a word he just looked into my eyes. I tried to put my head down because the eyes tell it all, but he lifted my head up. He knew that I was scared. He knew that I had fallen so in love with him but I didn't want to cause any pain. He didn't have to say a word to comfort me because looking into his eyes, I could tell how he felt. He was ready, ready for whatever was going to come our way, he was ready to do this on my terms and he loved me. I could tell this man loved me unconditionally. So that night we slept together, our bodies fit into each other like a jigsaw puzzle. We made love without having intercourse, without saying a word we just slept and sealed the bond of friendship and our love.

In the morning I got up and took a long hot shower. I was feeling good. I'm ok with this, starting today I'm going to take care of Sonya, sometimes you have to be a little selfish. I did my new personal affirmation as I bathed. When I got out the shower, Charles had taken the liberty of ordering us breakfast.

He must have woken up before me to order because it was already here.

"My mama always told me that 'all closed eyes ain't sleep', you was acting like you were knocked out when I got up to go to the shower. See you done missed out on getting some this morning."

"Well I don't have to eat my breakfast if you have an alternative for me."

"Ugh you are so nasty, Charles."

"You know you like that, baby."

"Yeah, you right," I laughed, "but nope because I'm not going to want to stop at that and we don't have time for the whole package, you know I'm on a schedule."

"I know, alright hurry up and get dressed so you can eat before you go."

My breakfast was great. We watched the repeat of Sports Center from last night while we ate. After I finished I laid around for a minute. I knew I had to go but I wanted so badly to prolong this moment.

"Alright baby I'm about to go." I said pulling Charles up from the bed to hug me. "I'll call you to let you know I made it back to the hotel. Are you going back to sleep?"

"Yep."

"Alright then turn your phone off, so I can just leave you a message, okay."

"Alright."

I gave him a kiss and was on my way. In the cab I tripped on how he had some qualities of Eric but he was so different. Even in the beginning of Eric's and my relationship, he would have slept all the way up until it was time for me to go and still want to squeeze in a moment for some pussy and would have made me feel bad over choosing to be on time over fucking him. Charles caters to me; I've never had that. It feels good when someone wants to take care of your needs not just your pockets. Eric feels that it is an exchange. You know, Charles hasn't even asked me what I plan on doing about Eric. I guess

211

that's good because I'm not sure myself. I have to tell him, I'm not the type to have an affair.

When I got to the hotel, thankfully no one I knew was in the lobby area. I rushed up to my room to drop off my bag and call Charles to leave a message.

"Hey Baby, I made it here. I'm about to go to the meetings. Have a good practice and call me before ya'll fly out. Oh yeah, I love you, bye."

Chapter 15

"Hey Charles, we keep playing phone tag. You are probably on the airplane, so I hope you arrive in Memphis safely. The conference is finally over, other than running into you, this weekend would have been a waste. I got nothing out of the conference. Anyway I decided not to go to the banquet and instead was able to get on a flight leaving tonight. You know what, with everything that has happened this weekend, I forgot to tell you that I moved back to Oakland, well to the Bay Area. I'll call you when I make it home. Bye." I turned my phone off after I left him the message.

I was so glad to be on my way home. I missed my babies and I missed my bed. I didn't bother telling anyone I was on my way home, I figured I'll surprise them. Mya had taken Kayla to our mom's house so all of the kids would be there. I fell asleep thinking about arriving back in Oakland at 5:15pm and when I woke up from the captain announcing that we were beginning our initial descent, I realized that we would actually be landing a little early. I was so anxious to get home, when we landed I turned my phone on, surprisingly I had no messages. I called Eric but I got his tired voice mail. I left him a message letting him know that I had returned home so he can stop tripping. I wonder who won the AFC game today, the winner would be who Eric's team would face next week in the playoff game. They did well this year so they clinched home field throughout the entire playoffs. After getting my luggage, I called Bri as I walked through the parking lot to my car.

"What's up Bri-Bri?"
"Getting dressed, what are you doing?"
"Getting in my car."
"You're back!"
"Yeah, I came back early. So anyway I know your curiosity is killing you so when are you coming over because you know I ain't talking about this shit over the phone."

213

"Girl, you act like the feds are after you, girl just tell me a little bit, did you go to his game?"

"No I didn't, why you can't come over?" I asked.

"I'm going on a date tonight, girl you know I can't pass up Crustaceans, not even for your juicy story."

"I feel you."

"Plus, I have to get in early, I have a really big case I'm working on and I go to court on Tuesday."

"Girl, it will hold. You coming over on Wednesday for Soulfood night, right?" I asked.

"Of course, I can't wait. Does everyone know what they're cooking? I might as well cancel my Showtime since I always watch the show at your house."

"Anyway, we can have it at your house."

"Nah."

"I thought so! I'm going to call everybody tomorrow and remind them. Have fun tonight, and eat some garlic noodles for me."

I drove to my mom's house and listened to Musiq's Soulstar CD. I've had this CD in rotation for about a week but tonight was the first time I listened closely to track six, "Who Knows." This song was the story of Charles' and my relationship. The chorus says, "Who knows what may happen if we act on our attraction and lose ourself inside a world made for us, and no one else...." I put the song on repeat and played it over and over until I reached my mom's house.

When I got there, the kids almost tackled me as I walked through the door. You would have thought I had been gone for a month or even a week. But I admit, I loved the love I got from my kids. Even my boys didn't mind giving their mom hugs and kisses in public.

"What are you doing back?" My mom asked me.

"You know I can't stay away from my babies. Nah, really it was cold as heck and I was so bored that as soon as the last session ended I was on the next think smoking! Did ya'll miss me?" I asked my kids.

"Yes." They all sang like a choir.

214

"Ma, are we going to Miami for Daddy's game next Sunday? Sean asked me.

"No, but if they win we will go down there for the AFC championship."

"You mean when they win." Kayla corrected me.

"That's right baby girl, when they win we'll go down for the next game."

I swear my children cracked me up. I see so much of myself in my daughter, that's why I wanted all boys! They were good kids though, I thank god and pray that we will always be in a position that they will never have to want for anything, but also that I stay grounded enough so that I can teach them the value of money and so that they will always appreciate their blessings.

"So Ma, when did Mya drop Kayla off?"

"Oh she just left here with an attitude."

"Hold on Ma, ya'll go start getting your stuff together so I can talk to Nana." I said to the kids and they ran off to their rooms. "Okay, what she tripping about?"

She told me that my brother Mykal, Mya's twin had rode out here with Mya and that she thought she was going to leave him to stay overnight out here because she had plans. She got mad at my mom because my mom told her that he could not stay over here when she was keeping the kids so my sister's response was, "Oh somebody else's kids can stay but your own child can't!" This broad said, "somebody else's kids" like I'm a fucking stranger. And yes my kids can stay because they aren't crackhead thieves.

"Oh well Ma, don't trip! You know she is a hater but you see she wasn't trying to let him stay at her house while she went on her date."

"I would have let him stay but I didn't want to hear your mouth instead I had to hear your sisters!"

"My mouth! Ma, this is your house you could have let him stay. All I know is if he steals from my kids again, I'ma forget he's my brother and take it to the streets."

215

"Girl, shut your happy homemaker butt up, talking about the streets." My mama responded laughing.

"Don't be clowning me, Ma. So she left with an attitude, huh. I guess I'll call her later, she's gonna be really mad when she see that I'm back."

As we finished talking, the kids were making their way back down into the family room. My dad was with them. He filled me in with all the pointers that the men at the barbershop told him to tell Eric for his coming up game. It's funny how the men in black barbershops are experts on everything. My mom told me that she and Barbara (Eric's mom) had decided that we were having a game party at my house on Sunday. My mom and Barbara had become very close in the early years of our relationship. They were doing all the cooking, which was fine with me. Especially since I had to cook for our "Soulfood" gathering on Wednesday.

"Hey Ma, you want to cook something for our 'Soulfood' party on Wednesday?"

"Can I cook something? Am I invited?"

"Yeah."

"I don't want to be around you cackling hens, but I can probably throw something together."

"What about some greens?"

"Yeah, ok. You know you ask for a lot of favors. I may have to send ya'll back to Arizona."

"Why, so you can cry every night?" My dad jumped in and responded.

I gave my mom a big hug and kiss. "Thank you mommy." I said like the spoiled baby girl she made me.

The kids and I said our good byes and thank-you's and left to go home. In the car I gave orders of what to do when we got home. Put your clothes away, get your backpacks ready for school and then take ya'll showers. Then we can chill. Everybody was cool about the program. It was such a blessing that we lived so close to my mom now. As much as Eric wanted us to stay in Arizona he even admitted that I seemed more stress free now that we were back in California. Well he actually said that I was more stress free now that I was back under my mama and my friends but I know it's hard for him to not be a hater. As we pulled up to the house I realized that ii didn't have my gun. Although we have an attached garage and a gated entrance, I normally don't go out at night without my 38 pearl handle. Our house was in an upscale community but truth betold, I feel safer when I'm in the hood, well at least I know what to expect.

Once we were in the house, everything ran smoothly. E.J. and I played grocery store with Kayla while the older boys took turns showering. After they finished Kayla got in the shower and the boys asked me to play them in Madden. I agreed to play each of them one quarter. That reminded me that I needed to call Charles. After I whooped both of them at Madden we all ate some ice cream and then it was bedtime. I put E.J. in the shower with me and then we put on our Pj's and got in the bed too. I decided to call Mya. As soon as she answered the phone she was filling me in with her version of what happened at my mom's house.

"What you doing at home?" Mya asked.

"Oh, I got an earlier flight."

"That's cool, but let me tell you about your mama."

"What happened?" I responded like I didn't know. I just wanted to hear if she would include the "somebody else's kids" comment.

"Girl, when I called to say I was bringing Kayla out there, I told her that Mykal was at my house. So she told me to bring him out there. When we got out there, Mykal wanted to stay but Ma was like, 'oh no he can't stay', like she didn't tell me to bring him. I knew Mykal felt awkward so I just told him lets go, but girl do you believe her!"

All I could say was, "whaaatt." It was funny how she tailored her story to look like my mama was wrong. She ain't mentioned that she had plans and that's why she was mad nor what she said about my kids staying. I can't believe she said Mykal felt awkward, when has a crackhead ever felt embarrassed or awkward. I tried to get on another subject.

"So what you cooking for Wednesday?"

217

"I'm going to bake macaroni."

"Alright cool. Have you talked to Alisha or Kim?"

"I talked to Kim today, her boys are selling popcorn for school so you'll be hearing from her. As for Alisha her ass must be out of mourning because she's been in the streets. I can't catch up with her for nothing. So how was your trip? Oh and your daughter, she is a nut, my friend took us out to dinner and he was amazed by how much she knew how to order like she was grown."

"What friend? Didn't I tell you don't have her around no niggas unless you plan on making him your man, except for Ryan. My daughter doesn't need to be meeting them boogie ass guys you hang out with."

"Look a free meal is a free meal, I'm schooling her young."

"Ooh that scares me, but ya'll had fun?"

"Of course, matter fact she left a shirt I bought her over here. I'll bring it on Wednesday. Oh I got some work calling my other line, so I'll talk to you tomorrow."

E.J. had fallen asleep while I was talking to Mya. I flipped through the channels, I hated television on Sunday because nothing was on BET. I didn't like to watch ESPN on Sundays because it was highly likely that I would hear something about Eric. So a long time ago I stopped watching on Sunday during the football season. I hated how analysts would tell the world why a player did this or that like they could speak for a person, analyze the game, not a person. Then people who watch TV take what these people say to be god's word. I used to want to fight every person that said something bad about Eric but I got over that. We are entitled to our opinions and lord knows I talk about people so I can't expect for him to be exempt. I decided to pop in the Kings of Comedy DVD, I wasn't all that tired and I felt like laughing. I called and talked to Eric, our conversation was actually very mellow. I'm sure he was happy I decided to come home early. I think he was getting tired of me laughing from the DVD and not talking to him so he said he was going to

218

sleep. I couldn't help it, that movie was so damn funny to me. Then I called Charles. When he answered I could tell he was sleeping but he said he wasn't. They had made it to Memphis, he said some of his teammates wanted him to go out but he decided to chill. I know his butt was sleeping, but we all lie when the relationshipm is new, we don't want to miss out on any conversation time. I would have said the same thing if I was sleeping and he called me. He told me he wanted to call but he figured I was enjoying being back home with my children, which was true. I continued to laugh at Kings of Comedy while I talked to him as well.

"What are you watching?" He asked.

"Oh I'm sorry, I'm watching Kings of Comedy."

"Don't be sorry that shit is super funny. Who is performing right now?"

"It's the intermission when Steve Harvey has the dudes coat, this is hella funny."

"That part is funny. Hey Sonya, I just wanted to let you know that I'm sorry that I was so immature and we missed out on quality time in developing our relationship. I'm sorry if you had days that you needed someone to talk to and I wasn't there. I've been thinking about you so much today and I realize that you are probably the best friend I've ever had. So even if a relationship becomes too much for you, I hope we will always remain friends. Now that I got that out, woman I had so much fun with you this weekend."

"Me too, if I knew you could put it down like that I would have let you hit a long time ago! Nah, I'm playing."

"Oh so I didn't handle my business."

"Oh yes baby you did handle your business!"

"You know the first time is always the worst time."

"Really, you mean it gets better."

"You are crazy, Poopie."

After we finished reminiscing about our first sexual encounter I told him that I was about to go to sleep, but really Bernie Mac was about to do his routine and I can't contain my laughter on his part. It was best that I get off the phone. When I was about to hang up he caught me and told me that he loved me, I told him I loved him too and we hung up.

Every time I talk to Charles I realize so much that my marriage and my husband is lacking. Charles has never said a word to down Eric, even in times when I bashed him myself, but the man that Charles is disses Eric on its own. I truthfully can't remember the last time I said "I love you too," to Eric, because I'm the one always telling him I love him and then he replies, "I love you too." It's actually been a while since I've told him I loved him when we get off the phone. I used to not be able to go to sleep without telling him I loved him or if I was mad at him – that has changed. Then I trip off how Eric has to feel like he monopolizes my attention instead of asking what I was watching that made me laugh he felt that it was his competition so he wanted to get off the phone. I really don't remember when our relationship got this way, maybe it's always been like this and I have changed, I don't know. I easily was sidetracked from my thoughts because of the movie. At the end of that I went to sleep.

Monday, back to the routine! Up at 6:30 am so I could shower and make the kids lunches before I wake them up at 7:00am. Once I wake them up they eat their breakfast and then get dressed. We are out of the house by 7:55 am. Sean, Lamar, and Kayla all go to the same school so its one easy drop-off and then E.J. and I begin our day, which usually consists of some sort of shopping or helping my Mom with some work. My first call of the morning is always to or from Alisha because she's dropping her kids at school as well. Since she doesn't work as well, we usually bounce what we are or are not going to do off of each other. Her luxury of being a stay at home mom is a little better than mine because both of her kids are in school so she has the day all to herself! I'm surprised she hasn't called. I guess I'll call her.

"Good morning!" She answered her phone full of cheer.

"What's up chick, what you doing today?"

"You're back already?" She asked me.

"Yeah I came back yesterday, I was wondering why you hadn't called this morning."

"Yeah, I thought you were still in Chicago. So we still on for Wednesday?"

"Yeah, but we all voted for you to bring a dessert."

"Look I'm tired of you hoes saying I can't cook! My new friend likes my cooking!"

"New friend? Who is this new friend because Mya did tell me that you've been incognito? Where is he from?"

"He's from here but you ain't going to believe what business he's in."

"What, not the normal? What happened to 'all I talk to is thugs'?"

"Girl, I know but he has a little thug in him, minus the life. I can't do it no more!"

"That's good girl, so what business is he in?"

"Fast food."

"Stop lying, like Popeye's Chicken fast food?"

"More like McDonalds but yes, fast food. Alright go ahead get your clown in."

"I ain't clowning, although I wish it was Popeyes so I could get some hook up but on the real if you like him and he likes you, I'm happy. I'll take him over them hustlers you usually like any day. So anyway, you want to have lunch today?"

"Girl, I have some errands to run. I have to take care of something I'm going to tell you about on Wednesday."

"Ok, well enjoy your day, if I don't talk to you tonight, I'll talk to you in the morning."

When I hung up the phone I looked back at E.J. and asked him if he would rather go home of help Nana. Although he didn't reply, I decided to go help my Mama since I wanted her to make me some greens for Wednesday. As we drove to my Mom's house I called to check on Kim. She was running late for

221

work but confirmed that we were still having our soulfood gathering. She too had some news she wanted to share. While I was talking to her Eric's friend Mike called my other line.

"Kim, I'm gonna call you back. Mike is calling me." I clicked to the other line.

"What's up, Money Mike?" That was my nickname for him. Mike and Eric had been friends since grade school. I called him Money Mike because he must have a secret fortune that we don't know about. He gets and quits jobs more than any person I know. Eric used to try to get him to work for him, basically he would have been getting paid to just kick it and he never accepted. He is a very hardworking man but I think he gets bored really quick – but anyway he responded by saying, "What's up Bony Sony," that was my nickname from him. He gave me that name one time when we were in Louisiana; he said I wasn't thick compared to the women out there so he started calling me Bony Sony.

"What are you calling so early for?"

"I'm on my way to work." He replied. I couldn't help but laugh.

"You not working at the bar no more?"

"Nah, I quit that, I'm working in the Sales department for the Oakland A's."

"Oh so are you calling to see if I want to buy some season tickets?"

"Ha ha nigga, no I'm calling to see if you need me to bring something over on Sunday for the football party."

"Oh you not going out there with the rest of ya'll crew?" Eric's friends had all grown up together from either elementary or junior high school and they remained close. They were all supposed to be going to Miami for the game on Sunday.

"I was going, but I have to work on Monday."

"Oh, well my Mama and Mama-in-law told me not to worry about food but you can bring whatever you drinking on although it will probably be more than enough alcohol there. You really don't need to bring a thing."

"Well call me if you think of something."

I had been sitting at my Mom's house for the last portion of the conversation. When we hung up, I unloaded Eric from his car seat and grabbed his bag. We sang 'Old McDonald' as we walked in the house. I loved to hear him imitate the animals when we sing that song. My mom was glad I came today because she was designing dresses for a wedding party of 10 bridesmaids, a matron & maid of honor and three flower girls and they were coming to get measured today. I really enjoyed seeing my Mom work and more so I loved how supportive my father was of her. The day flew by, actually the next day flew by too. I think because I was so looking forward to hanging with my girls, eating some good food and having some drinks. I was also anxious to hear what news my girls had to share. The kids were excited because they had Thursday and Friday off of school for a Teacher's Planning day, so today was the beginning of their weekend. They have a minimum day every Wednesday so they got out at noon, after I picked them up and got home, I decided to call Mya.

"Hey Mya, are you still planning on bringing Macaroni and cheese over tonight?" I asked.

"Why you wait until today, on the day of the function to remind me?"

"Why do I have to remind you we do this every other week. We get together, we eat, drink, watch soulfood, cry and laugh and then you bitches go home."

"Well can I buy one of them frozen Stouffer one's and throw it in the oven?"

"See I knew you forgot, so I made one, but you can go pick up a couple of bottles of Malibu and some cranberry juice."

"Okay that's cool, what is Bri bringing? Oh please tell me you ain't letting Alisha experiment with cooking again, I don't know how a woman with kids can't cook a lick. Please tell me she's picking up some dessert. Alright sis, let me get off this phone and finish working. I'll be over around six. Is your Mama coming over?" Mya asked, I guess her and my mom was still upset with each other.

"No your mother is not coming over and Alisha is picking up a cake from It's All Good Bakery in Oakland. She ain't going to be doing no cooking at all now that her new dude work for McDonalds." I said laughing. "Nah keep that on the low until she tell you herself, we'll talk about it tonight." I said.

"We can talk from 6:30pm until 8:25 pm but at 8:30pm American Idol comes on and you hoes got to shut up. So I'll see you later." Mya ended our conversation.

"Bye Chick." I said before hanging up.

I swear that girl got issues. I yelled for my son Sean to go in my room and look in my phone book to get Bri's work number. It's sad how I was so dependent on dialing people from my cell phone otherwise I couldn't remember a number. I continued to chop onion for my potato salad and I popped in Beyonce's CD to hear my girls anthem. I cranked my Sony sound system and did the booty dance as I sang along 'got me lookin so crazy right now'. I was ready for a night with my girls. Sean yelled Bri's work number as he was coming downstairs.

"Sean why are you yelling the number if you are coming in here anyway?"

"Oh my bad Mom, so we having a party tonight?"

"No, we are having dinner like we do every night and then you guys are going upstairs to play after that."

"We don't have school tomorrow, so why do we have to go upstairs after dinner?"

"Let me see,------- uh because I said so! I didn't say you had to go to bed but that can happen too."

"No thanks. Can I have a piece of that chicken though?"

"Go ahead boy, talking to you got me missing my song."

'Uh oh uh oh' was chiming loudly from my stereo, as the phone rang.

"Damn girl, I thought I was calling a club." Bri said as I answered, not giving me a chance to say hello.

"Hello to you too Bri, hold so I can turn the music down -------- alright, you know that Beyonce is my shit! I was just about to call you at work, why are you on your cell, no work today?"

224

"Girl what time is dinner?" She asked.

"Why? You gonna be late?"

"Come on now this is me, your sister cousin, not your real sister! Nah, I'm on my way to your house now. I got to stop by my house and get the cabbage and yams. I was up hella early cooking."

"Why are you off so early?"

"I took a half day, and I'm anxious for tonight. I've been waiting since Monday to share some good news with ya'll and you know I can hold other people's business but I can't hold my own!"

"Bitch, you're pregnant." I responded trying to figure her news.

"Girl, you know it's way too many Manolo's out there for me to buy to be trying to have kids. Plus, you know I get my allergy shot faithfully."

"Allergy shot?" I questioned.

"Yes, Depoprovera every three months, you know I'm allergic to kids!"

"You are hella stupid, I swear comic view is calling you! I'll see you in a few."

While the potatoes for my potato salad are cooling, I can take a quick shower before Bri gets here. I told Kayla to listen to E.J. while I'm in the shower. He was taking a nap.

"Mommy, can I call Aunty Mya and remind her to bring the shirt she bought me while I was over her house. It shows my stomach!"

"Kayla, you know your Daddy ain't having you wear no shirt with your stomach out, but go ahead and call her. Listen for your brother and answer the phone if it rings."

After I showered, I took my scarf off and unwrapped my hair. I kept it wrapped up all morning with hopes of keeping my hair from smelling like the chicken I was frying. I threw on some around the house "daisy duke" shorts and a wife beater. Even in my kick around clothes I was looking as if I could have walked off of Top Model, just more booty. The women in my family were truly blessed in that way. As I was finishing getting ready I heard the doorbell ring. I looked myself over in my full-length mirror in my closet. Alright let the kickin it begin!

"Who is it?" I yelled through the door

"You know who it is, open the door!" Bri yelled back through the door.

"Yeah I know it's you and I know you have a key to my house, so why are you ringing the doorbell?" I replied after I opened the door.

"I know I have a key, but the football season is almost over so I'm trying to break the habit of just coming in unannounced before your husband comes home. I don't want to come in and see your ass in the air one time, ughh!"

"Anyway fuck him, this is my house and you can come up in here when you want, and it ain't like you ain't never seen some ass before."

"Oh you talking big shit, next month you'll be a poodle again! So do you think they're going to make it to the Super Bowl?"

"I hope so, for him. He works so hard and that's the true reward."

"Don't they get some type of bonus for going to the bowl, CHING-CHING we going shopping! Oh, and I know I'm going with you if they make it. It's in Chicago and I got a new Chinchilla coat from my friend guy that I've been waiting to break out. You know I can't rock it in Cali. Speaking of Chicago, we still ain't talked about your visit to the Chi, so what's up with that?"

"Girl this shit is getting deep, I'm still trying to digest it myself. We're going to have to sit down just the two of us on that one. I can't believe that Eric's season is almost over either. I'm really not ready for him to be home but the kids miss him. He better get a clue this off-season because it is really becoming hard. Girl, I be ready to throw the towel in."

"Cousin, you know your husband is spoiled, he's the only child. His mama created a monster and you picked up where she left off. Girl, I remember your ass would be cooking meals, cooler packing them and next daying them to his ass. As if he didn't have enough money to buy some meals where he was at. So don't complain, now that that spoiled shit is getting on your nerves."

I agreed with Bri but explained that shit was easier before I had four kids.

"Sonya, you know I'm going to tell you the real. Yeah, Eric does some foul shit and I support all your decisions but you ain't no quitter and he ain't stupid. You are the best thing that ever happened to him. Ya'll are going to work it out."

Bri gave me her heartfelt opinion and I needed it. I thanked her for having my back and decided it was a perfect time to call Eric before everyone else got here.

Chapter 16

I slammed my Sony cordless phone so hard that the battery flew across the kitchen floor. I screamed so loud that I imagine steam was coming from my ears.

"See Bri, this is the shit I be talking about."

"What's wrong, I begged yo ass for that phone and now you gonna throw it and break it."

"Don't make me laugh, I am pissed. After our little endearing talk, I call Eric all juiced to talk to him. So we're talking and I remind him that tonight is our soulfood night and this arrogant muthafucka got the nerve to say 'oh so you mean it's your night to sit up and talk about me to your friends...'"

"No he didn't." Bri replied.

"Yes, he did and that ain't the half. Then he said 'where are my kids going to be,' when I told him here he said, 'my kids don't need to be around that gossip shit.' He's talking about he's gonna call his mama to come get them. Now normally, I would be like cool, let your mama come get them, but yesterday when I went by there she seemed hella tired or sick. I told him that and his selfish ass said 'I'm sure she's alright, she'll be on her way, so get them ready.' That selfish ass nigga is so inconsiderate. He thinks everything and everyone revolves around him, but not tonight, my kids aren't going anywhere. He act like we having some strippers over here!"

Bri tried to calm me down. She reminded me that this is our day and to not let him ruin it. She put back on our anthem "Crazy in Love" but I told her I was feeling track seven, "Me, Myself and I" that was exactly where I was heading , me, myself, and my kids. As I vented the phone rang. I told Bri to look at the caller ID.

"It says Barbara Jackson, your mother-in-law." She announced.

Eric don't realize how tight me and his mother are. She ain't gonna come out here without talking to me. Shit I'm tighter with her than he is. Meanwhile the phone was still ringing.

"Hello." I eventually answered the phone.

"What's going on Sony, you need me to come get the kids? My son called here like your house was on fire over there. I know how he is but I can come if you need me to."

"Nah Ma, you know you made that man rotten and he is driving me crazy. He's just upset that I'm going to enjoy my evening and he's not a part of it."

"So he's acting up, are you okay?" My mother-in-law questioned me.

"I'm ok, I'll be better once I crack open my bottle of Malibu Rum."

"Oh yeah it's Soulfood night, well don't let that boy ruin your night, and have a drink for me. I could sure use one."

"Are you ok Mom, you've been looking zapped lately. Are you getting enough rest?"

"That's all I do is rest. I'm going to the Farmer's Market on Saturday morning with Millie, then you can bring the kids by and they can spend the night and I'll bring them out on Sunday for the football party."

"Okay thanks Mom, so what are you going to tell your son when he calls?"

"I'm the Mama, you just have some fun. You know how he is during the season, he can't stand being away from ya'll."

"I guess. Well I'll talk to you later or if not I'll see you on Saturday."

As we were hanging up, I could hear Mya's loud mouth complaining about the music I was playing. She and Alisha walked in together. Alisha brought Tink and Tiara too.

"Girl Beyonce got it going on, and I just love her and Jay Z but I am tired of this CD. Do you have Musiq's new CD? He got a cut on there, number six, it is the beat. I think it's called "Who Knows". Mya was flipping through my Sony disc changer and complaining. Alisha agreed with Mya.

"Yeah, #6 is the beat and the intro, Soul Star is bumping. Girl, it be making the Beamer seem like I got 15's in the trunk!"

Of course I knew of the song Mya and Alisha were referring to on Musiq's CD. I had been playing everyday all day since I saw Charles in Chicago. It was the story of our relationship but right now was not the time or place to slip into lala land over Charles. He would be a breath of fresh air after Eric's stunts. The entrance of Kim was the perfect interruption.

"I'm here, let the party begin." Kim danced into the house.

"Mya can you call the kids so we can eat and then get to the real business. Some people have some announcements to make and I'm anxious to hear them." I said.

Mya decided to go upstairs to get the kids so she could give Kayla the "Hoochie Mama" shirt she bought her.

When they came down we all loaded food on our plates. Of course I yelled at the kids about not putting vegetables on their plates. Lamar and Sean put too much food on their plates that they would not eat and Kayla put too little on hers. EJ just sat patiently waiting for his chicken and macaroni that he routinely ate with his hands. Everything was silent accept for the sounds of smacking lips. You know how Black folks are about food, we shut up when it's time to eat! Lamar was the first to break the silence.

"Mom, my Dad said all you and my aunties do is sit up and complain about men."

"Really Lamar, is that what your Dad told you? Well it sounds like he was complaining about women when he said that, right?"

I did my best to never let the kids see me pissed off especially when their Dad was the cause. It was definitely hard at times. I couldn't wait for the kids to finish eating, so I could talk about his ass alright. I tried to change the conversation.

"Kim, why you didn't bring the boys tonight?"

"They are spending the night over my mom's house. I had drama today but I'll tell ya'll about that later." She replied.

It got quiet again for awhile because we were going to work on the spread. We had chicken, catfish, greens, cabbage, yams, potato salad, macaroni and cheese, black eye peas, rice and green beans. And of course we had cornbread – it was going down.

"Damn, EJ got an appetite like his Daddy," Alisha said laughing, "look how cleaning them chicken bones. Are you sure you're only one?" She questioned him.

"Girl he be throwing down, look at him, he know we talking about him." I admired my handsome toddler.

"Cake, cake." EJ asked for cake in his baby language although he meant cornbread.

I asked Bri to get him another piece of cornbread and chicken while she ws up. Kayla asked could she be finished after eating her chicken and spreading everything else around to make it appear that she ate something. Now of course I knew this was the oldest trick in the book, but I let hr slide because I didn't feel like the battle tonight. Although I did let her know,

"You can be finished, but when you get hungry tonight you ain't getting no junk."

"Mom, can I eat her food?" Lamar asked.

"Now this is going to be the little football player. Did ya'll see all that food he ate? I have to buy his clothes in the husky department, or hella big and then get them hemmed."

"Sony you remember Mama had to do that for Mykal when we were little and he slimmed off when we got older." Mya commented.

"Well crack will do that." I sarcastically replied.

"That ain't right Sonya." Mya retaliated.

Mya hated for me to talk about her twin brother, our brother. He had recently fallen off his recovery wagon again! I don't have much compassion for his situation and it's not like everyone didn't know, even the kids knew. Sean jumped in the conversation.

"Yeah, uncle Mykal was at Grandma's house trying to sell her a DVD player with a DVD already in it. Grandma said no, but I would have bought it, he only wanted thirty bucks for it. It was one of them portable ones. Mom can we buy it?'

"Sean get out of grown folk talk, matter of fact ya'll finished eating so go wash your hands and go upstairs." I asked Tink to wash EJ's hands and change his diaper when they go upstairs. The fact that Alisha had Tink when we were so young

231

was truly paying off for me now. That little lady was my super helper. The kids all went upstairs and we began to clear the table. We were all pretty silent until Bri the comedian of the crew broke the silence.

"So Sonya, you think my cousin still got that DVD player for sell? You know I love some hot shit. I sure miss them Nordstrom gift cards he used to get. He ain't boosting no more?" Bri was serious as a heart attack.

"Girl you know I don't fool with him, since he stole my baby's earrings, but I can find out for you. Okay ladies thanks for helping clean up, let's take the dessert into the family room, the drink is already in there." I suggested.

Mya's face was still tight from the crackhead comment. She hadn't said much but I knew before the end of the night her nasty side would rain on all of us. I opened the discussion by basically sharing that nothing new was happening for me, of course my husband was still getting on my nerves but that's nothing new. We all couldn't believe that shit he told Lamar. They all said that they could tell that I wanted to flash but I main'tained.

"I know how you feel Sony, you are better than me. Ray be doing the same shit and I'm constantly telling the boys that dogging women is what landed him in jail so don't listen to him." Kim stated.

"Girl Kim, it takes a lot of patience. You know their daddy is the best thing since sliced bread. He's spoiling them like his ass is spoiled. I got to nip that shit in the bud. Ya'll see how Sean trying to talk like he's grown. He don't know nothing about a crackhead or about hardships except for what he see on TV and hear in music."

"I know what you mean." Kim agreed.

"I'm sorry Kim," Mya interrupted ready to start some mess, "dogging women didn't land Ray in prison, beating on women did."

This was Mya's way of trying to hurt Kim but Kim was such a free spirit that it didn't even bother her. She laughed and responded...

232

"You ain't never lied, but hell, that's dogging them right!"

We all laughed.

"Sonya you don't have no Belvedere? When ya'll hoes get so hooked on Malibu Rum, you even had me drinking that shit at Essence. And what happened to that bar that used to be in here?"

"Well Alisha, answer #1, we hoes realized we can get loaded and wake up in the morning and not have a hangover. I got to be able to drink and then deal with my kids in the morning. Answer #2, the hater felt like it was not appropriate to have it in the family room. I suggested putting it in the 'Game Room' but that's his room and he is a hater so that didn't happen. So, anyway it's in the garage but there's some vodka in one of them cabinets under the island in the kitchen."

"Ooh that nigga be tripping." Alisha replied and of course Mya had to say something.

"I guess he tripping because he got you breaded out living like a queen and you mad over a bar."

We all ignored Mya because we knew she wanted to spark an argument. Instead we focused on the T.V. A commercial came on advertising the movie *Out of Time,* starring Denzel Washington and Sanaa Lathan would be released on DVD next Tuesday. I asked if they had seen the movie. Bri responded yes, she saw it a while ago in the theater. Alisha said she saw it on a bootleg because she only spends money to go see kid movies and they have to be matinees. "I was asking because I saw it when I went to that NFL wives against drunk driving conference and I fell asleep and missed the end, so I'm going to buy it." I was really just trying to change the subject before Mya pissed me off.

It was now 8:30pm, but American Idol was a special, showing the bloopers from the tryouts so we decided to watch Ruben Studdard's Access Granted on BET for his new video.

"Well since I don't have anything to share, who's up next?" I said.

233

"Okay I'll go." Bri said excitedly. "You guys know I've been at Whitley, Jackson, Whitley Esquire since I was interning after undergrad. And you know I'm the most sought after criminal attorney in the 'Town' (native term for Oakland). You can't beat the combination of my West Oakland upbringing and graduating top of the class from Boalt Hall (UC Berkeley)." Bri was taking a moment to reflect on her journey.

"Yeah, yeah Bitch, get on with it." Kim pushed her. She looked like a kid on Christmas morning. Kim was one person who was always genuinely happy for other people.

"Ok anyway as I was saying, I Bria Lynette Brown has been offered a junior partnership in the firm! The youngest ever at my ripe age of twenty-eight and the first Black woman ever in the firms history."

Everyone screamed with happiness – of course I took credit for staying up late with her studying for the LSAT, Kim took credit for keeping her game sharp due to all her husband's legal problems. Everyone was so happy. Mya looked as if she wanted to say something negative but she knew she couldn't say nothing, Bri had it going on and she couldn't hate that. So of course she headed in on Alisha.

"Alisha this cake is hella good." Mya commented out the blue.

"I know, I got it from 'It's All Good Bakery'." Alisha replied.

"Um, I thought you would have brought some McDonaldland cookies since you fucking Mr. McDonald."

I cut Mya the most evil look because I told her ass that that was on the low this afternoon. I swear this bitch is always trying to kill someone's joy. However Alisha has just as much attitude as Mya so she came right back at her.

"First of all, I ain't fucking no one. Secondly, he is not a fucking employee, he is the employer. He owns three McDonalds in the Bay Area. Oh, and third of all I could give a flying fuck if he was flipping burgers, I ain't got to worry about burying another man because he was caught up in the game; I've had my share of that. Taiwan left the girls and I enough money,

234

and Rock left me enough money that I would fool with a minimum wage worker forever if it will keep me away from a funeral! After Taiwan died, I was lost, but I continued to fool with and be drawn to hustlers. I was hooked into the life. I thought I would never love again and then I found Rock, and his crazy ass had to go and get killed on me. I can't do it, Tink is a teenager now and I can't have her around that street shit. So yes Bitch, my man is Mr. McDonalds and next time if you would like I will bring you a Big Mac, an apple pie, McNuggets or whatever else you want!"

Everybody was teary eyed with the exception of Mya who just sat there looking stupid. I swear I didn't know what was wrong with her. Alisha continued talking.

"So anyway now that we got that out of the way, my real announcement is that I got accepted to the Master's program in Computer Science at UC Berkeley. In the fall I will be going back to school."

Again everyone was excited with the exception of Mya. Poor Kim was so happy that she was still crying. Alisha tried to convince me to go back to school to work on my PhD. She joked with me by saying that she was on my back so I better step up my game. I let her know that I have no desire in going back to school. Bri let us know that it was almost time for Soulfood to come on. Time sure flies when you add some drama to the night. I decided to go upstairs and check on E.J. It was almost ten so he should be asleep. Kim told me to hurry up because she had some news to share before the show comes on. I ran upstairs to check on the kids meanwhile downstairs remained silent in my absence. However Bri, Alisha and Kim were all thinking that Mya was in desperate need of some counseling or a good ass whooping!

"Alright all the kids are sleep except Tink. She's in my room on the phone. Ok Kim you got the floor."

"I'm gonna make it quick because it's not that big. A few months ago I started the process of getting divorced again, but I didn't say anything because ya'll know I've tried before and Ray didn't cooperate. Well, I heard that if they are in jail when you file, they can't dispute it. So I did it and this past Friday I got the word that it's final, I am FREE! However ya'll know that the drama ain't over. I guess Ray just got word because he's been having his mama call my house. I have the collect calls blocked. Then I walk out of my job today and I had four flat tires, so I know his ghetto ass sister did that. That's why I took the kids over my Mom's house because ain't no telling what his crazy family will do. I am damn there 30, I'm too old to be fighting, plus I've whooped on all the women in his family except for his mama. Anyway, amidst all the drama, ain't ya'll happy for me?"

"I know I'm happy for you, you better be careful though. Ray is a crazy muthafucka." Bri replied.

"You ain't never lied, that nigga is crazy but we know crazy too! You know you can borrow my baby 'Pearl'." Pearl is my name for my pearl-handled thirty-eight pistol that my dad bought me for my 21st birthday.

"Thanks, but no thanks. I thought Eric didn't like you having a gun in the house."

"Kim, I am from the hood girl. Fuck an alarm system, I'm off in the middle of nowhere. I got to protect mine." I replied to her.

"Ok Rambo." Bri said to me. "Kim we are so happy for you and you know we got your back, now turn on the show."

We all laughed at Bri as we focused on the intro to Soulfood. We watched the show in pretty much silence with the exception of a few high fives, laughs, and tears.

"Damn, I can't wait until next week. They keep it real on this show, I can't believe this is the last season." Bri said.

"Me either, them Joseph sisters be funking though. Ooh, but I love me some Lem and Bird they shit is straight hood. I really love me some Lem, I can do some big things with him." Kim stated.

"Who Mr. Bye Bye Bye." I said mocking the commercial for Daren Dewitt's dance video tape. Everyone laughed because they new exactly the commercial I was talking

236

about. "Girl, you can't do nothing for him, he's probably gay!" I continued.

"Bitch stop lying." Kim said in shock as if he was her baby daddy.

"Kim don't listen to Sony, she is the same person that told me that the girl from the group Blaque that had the baby by Korupt was Left Eye's sister when they first came out. Here I am telling everybody and come to find out, this broad made the shit up." Alisha said.

Mya spoke after being silent for the whole night after Alisha checked her, "that's right Alisha, remember she told me that Tony Dungy and that other Black football coach was brothers. What's his name?"

"Herman Edwards." I replied laughing at myself.

"Yeah she told me they were half brothers, same mama different daddy's. Of course I believed her because her man plays football." Mya said.

"Ok, I made it up, but you got to admit they do look alike, just like Lem ass looks gay, he's probably on the down low."

"See on that note it's time for me to go. I can't listen to you talk about my man." Kim said.

"Alright Kim be careful. You sure you don't want 'Pearl'."

"Nah, I'm cool. I'm going to my mom's house anyway."

I got ready to walk Kim to the door and told her to call when she made it home but then everybody decided to walk out. I told Alisha to not worry about getting the girls. It wasn't any point in waking them and they didn't have school tomorrow anyway.

"Oh shit, I ain't got no kids. So what do women with no kids do on a Wednesday night?' Alisha asked Bri and Mya.

"Well women like Bri and myself who have jobs, go to bed." Mya responded and Bri high-fived her in agreement. It was amazing how our night always went from one extreme to another when we got together. But at the end of the night, it was all love, we were family. One thing for sure, I will be calling my dear 'ol' big sister in the morning and checking her for always trying to fuck up the night.

"You want me to come get them in the morning before I go to my business meeting?" Alisha asked.

"Hell No! They both have clothes here so you can come in the afternoon or whenever but not in the morning."

We all hugged and said our good byes and then they left. I picked up around the house before I went upstairs. Like I thought Tink had fallen asleep on my chaise lounge chair in my room with the phone attached to her ear. I sure remember those days from my teenage years. I hung up the phone and covered her up with a blanket. I turned the TV on to ESPN and decided to watch Sports Center to keep me up until everyone called to say they made it in. I thought about calling Eric but I really wasn't feeling his shit tonight. I want to call Charles but I don't want to get too in the habit of that yet, so fuck it, I guess Stuart Scott will have to do it for me tonight! As soon as I turned to ESPN, I saw the highlights from New Jersey's and the Spurs game. The commentator was talking about the explosive game Charles Knight had in their win over the Spurs.

That's what's up, my boo had a triple double – 42 points, 11 rebounds and 10 assists. I wasn't going to call him but a game like that deserves a call. I dialed *67 to block my house number and then proceeded to dial his number.

"Hello."

"Hey you had a good game tonight. I done gave you some and you been balling ever since." I said to him.

"I know that's right baby you got the hit. It's been five days, does the affect wear off?" He asked me.

"Don't worry, I'll break you off before that happens." I joked back, but I was so serious.

"I'ma hold you to that! I was hoping you'd call. How was Soulfood night?"

"Oh baby, let me tell you about that…"

238

Chapter 17

"Aunty Sony, does E.J. eat eggs?" I was awaken by Tink questioning me about food.

"Am I dreaming? Did you cook breakfast little girl?"

"Yes and if this house wasn't so big you would be able to smell it."

"Taisha Tinker Stone, I'm going to steal you from your mama! What you cook?"

She cooked eggs, smothered potatoes, grits, biscuits to go with the left over chicken and fish. She definitely got that from her grandmamma because Alisha can't cook a lick!

"Are all the kids awake?" I asked her.

"Yeah, we been up, it's going on 10:30am."

"Did I drink that much last night?" I thought to myself. "I didn't even hear E.J. wake up." I said.

"That's because he didn't make any noise. I was up and I saw him stand up in his crib so I got him before he woke you up. You and uncle Eric was on the phone hecka late."

"Well I see closed eyes ain't always sleep. You was over there ear hustling last night?"

"Nah, I heard when you went to the bathroom because the light woke me up. I just heard you say 'baby I'm about to go to sleep and the clock said 2:42am."

"Oh, I see...I'll be downstairs in a minute so ya'll wait for me to eat and yes E.J. eats eggs." I said.

I rolled out of the bed and brushed my teeth and washed my face. I sat on the toilet to pee. Damn was I on the phone that long last night. I'm glad Tink thought it was Eric, but that nigga ain't called yet. He probably thinks the kids are at his mama's house, Oh well.

Oh my goodness, Tink got down on breakfast. After we ate, the kids all dispersed to do their own thing around the house. Kayla was just so happy that Tiara was there, she didn't know what to do with herself. She was so used to being the only girl in

239

the house. The older boys were in the room playing Playstation and EJ was in the family room with Tink watching videos. I asked them if they wanted to go to the movies, but these crazy kids wanted to stay in the house. I cleaned the kitchen and started ironing the kids clothes and that's when I received my morning call from Eric.

"Hello"

"What are you doing?" Eric asked.

"Ironing, are you on your way to practice?"

"Yeah, what time are you going to get the kids?"

"The kids are here Eric, they didn't go to your mom's house."

"Why is that?"

"Anyway Eric, what's up?"

"Well what are they doing?"

I told him what the kids were doing and then he asked why I had Alisha's kids. Uh, because they are my little cousins, oh my, he drives me crazy. That conversation ended quick, he really didn't want anything, he was used to calling out of routine. I wasn't mad at him because I had to program myself to call him lately as well.

My day went by pretty smoothly, the kids were so happy to be out of school that they were just chilling. When Alisha came to pick up the kids she brought her new guy friend over for me to meet. He was cool and the girls seemed to like him. His name is Jason Miller, he's thirty-four and he has one fifteen year old son that lives in Texas. You know I got the whole run down. Alisha explained to him that I'm the mama of the crew so don't trip off all the questions because I'm looking out for her. He wasn't tripping, he even joked with me and offered his driver's license and social security number if I needed that.

"That's alright I got pull, if I need that info I can get it." I replied but he knew I was joking. I checked with Alisha to see if it was ok to invite Jason over on Sunday for the football party. I almost slipped up and broke the code and invited him without checking with her, but I caught myself. She said it was cool so I extended the invite. If he could make it through a day with our whole family then he had to be a keeper or just as crazy as we are. After they left I thought about Alisha for a minute, she was one of the strongest women I know. She has been through so much and she definitely deserves some happiness. It was only 6:00pm, I decided to take the kids to the movies because tomorrow I would be cleaning my house for Sunday's party.

Ooh my lord! Now I see why I take the kids to matinee movies, for the admission and snacks I spent $85. I was surprised they all stayed up through the movies and they didn't even have naps today. By the time we made it home, E.J. and Lamar had fallen asleep in the car. I woke Lamar up and carried E.J. in and put his pajamas on while he remained sleep. I didn't have to tell the others it was bedtime, they must have been tired too because they went right up to their rooms and went to bed. I got in the bed myself after I brushed my teeth, washed my face, and wrapped up my hair. I guess I'll write in my journal before I go to sleep.

Dear Journal   1/ /2004
I haven't written in a couple of days. The whole Chicago moment was overwhelming. I'm trying to follow my heart but it's not that easy when you have four little ones who love their Mommy & Daddy. All I know is, I think of Charles all the time. When things happen in my day I can't wait to share them with him. I used to feel that way about Eric until I realized that he was never really that excited for anything that I accomplished. The things that were important for me really weren't that important to him, so I stopped sharing my news with him. I know this is wrong, I was raised to be a good Christian, I strayed from the Lord before while growing up

but I'm grown now and I know I'm wrong. I
pray for forgiveness because right now this is
what I need..

My journaling was interrupted by the sound of my phone ringing. I instantly got excited because I realized it was my cell phone which meant it had to be Charles, anyone else would have called the house phone.

"Hi Baby." I said happy to receive his call.

"Hey Poopie, how was your day?"

"It was cool, I met Alisha's new boyfriend, he seems nice. I took the kids to the movies. How was your game? You sound tired."

"Well we lost, but it was a good game. I am tired; it went into double overtime. I don't know, the good luck serum you gave me might be wearing off."

"Is that right, why did you play bad tonight?"

"I mean we lost, so I'm sure I could have done something better, but I played cool."

"Where are you now?"

"I'm on the plane, we are about to take off in a few. I'm glad it's a short flight to Houston and then we have an off day tomorrow. This road trip has been something but we go home Saturday after the game, I can't wait."

"What, you miss your chick?" I asked like I didn't care but knowing I did.

"Yeah I miss my chick..." My heart fell to the floor "...but she is in Cali not Jersey."

"That's what's up, so where do you guys stay in Houston?"

"We stay at the Four Seasons, it's really not that nice, but it's cool."

"I tell you about ya'll spoiled athletes."

"Alright Poopie, we are about to take off, are you going to sleep?"

242

"Yeah but call me still, so I know you made it."

"Okay, I love you."

"I love you too, bye."

I said a little prayer for Charles, I hope that's not sacrilegious.

> *Thank you for my blessings*
> *I know that I am not worthy*
> *Lord I just want to ask that you watch over Charles and*
> *his team so that they make it to their destination safely*
> *In Jesus name I pray. Amen*

I really was about to go to sleep, but talking to Charles gave me the idea to do something spontaneous. First I had to make some calls.

"Hello"

"Hey Bri."

"What's up chick?"

"I need you on some G4 classified down low shit."

"What's up?"

"I want to fly to Houston to surprise Charles and I need you to watch the kids tomorrow and drop them off at their grandma's house on Saturday."

"Bitch you are lying."

"No I am not, can you do it?"

"Okay now I know you've been holding out, you fucked him in Chicago!"

"No I didn't, but I might in Houston." I kept up my lie.

"Shut the fuck up." Bri responded.

"So can you?"

"Of course I'll do it, but you are crazy. What about the party on Sunday?"

"I'm coming back on Saturday, it will be like I never left. I'm going to tell Eric you wanted them to come spend the night and it ain't like we don't go all day without talking to each other anyway."

"Alright, well I guess I'll get up in the morning and get some groceries. What time does your flight leave?"

"I don't know, that's my next call. I'll call you back. Thank you cousin."

After hanging up with her, I called the airlines and booked a straight through flight that leaves out at 12 noon and arrives in Houston at 6pm. My return flight leaves out of Houston on Saturday at 12 noon as well and I get home at 2 pm. I am going to be in Houston for 18 hours, not even a full day, but I bet it will be worth it. I called to give Bri my schedule and to thank her again. Next I had to call my beautician to see if I could come in early tomorrow. I originally had a 12:30 pm appointment but that wouldn't work.

"Hello"

"Hey Gee Gee, this is Sonya."

"Hey Sonya."

"Gee Gee I need a big favor. If I wash my hair myself, can you squeeze me in, in the morning at like 9:30am?"

"What you got going on, girl?"

"I just forgot that I had another appointment at 11:30am." Boy I see that this affair shit was truly going to make a liar out of me.

"You know it's cool for you Sony, my first client is at 9:30am so after I wash and put her under the dryer, I can flat iron you."

"Thank you Gigi."

Everything was falling into place. Now I have to pack the kids clothes so I can drop them off by 9:15am and still make it to 'Discover Your Illusions' hair salon by 9:30.

After about an hour I had packed the kids clothes and ironed their clothes for tomorrow. I packed my Gucci duffel bag with everything you need for an 18-hour trip and then I laid my head down to finally rest. It took a while for me to go to sleep because I was going over every detail of my plan to assure no mess-ups. Of course as soon as I fall asleep my phone rings.

Charles let me know he had made it to the hotel, he gave me the hotel number and his room number because his cell phone was going dead. Things sure happen for a reason, I was wondering how to ask for his room number without him getting suspicious. We were both tired so we got off the phone pretty quick.

Now that I lay me down to sleep
I pray the Lord my soul to keep
If I should die before I wake
I pray the Lord my soul to take
Father please watch over all my loved ones
I thank you for all my blessings and pray that you
continue to guide me.
Father please for give me for my sins, Amen.

I can't believe that I am in Houston Intercontinental Airport bathroom taking my clothes off down to my Victoria Secrets panty and bra and wrapping up in a trench coat. Luckily it's not that cold in Houston. On my cab ride to the hotel I called to check in on the kids, I called Eric and luckily got his voicemail, so I ran some game. Next I called Charles he had left a message after his afternoon meeting but unbeknownst to him I was on the airplane. I was really just calling to check if he was in his room, when I found out he was, I told him I would call back.

Arriving at the hotel I started getting nervous. What if he had another woman up there or what if he had plans to go out with someone and I show up there damn near naked. Why did I come here? I guess it's too late for nerves. I paid the cabbie and exited the cab. Entering the hotel I noticed a couple of Charles' teammates and I noticed them checking me out. I tried not to look them in the face, you never know who knows who. As the elevator rose so did my confidence, by the time I reached his floor I was ready. Alright, Sony you are looking good, smelling good and you are about to surprise your man. Hell, if he did

245

have plans on seeing someone else tonight that plan just got cancelled!

Knock, knock, knock

"Room service." I sang in a sweet voice as I knocked on the door.

Charles opened the door and you would have thought he saw a ghost.

"Surprise." I said.

He didn't reply, well at least not verbally. He grabbed me in the air and kissed me passionately. When he put me down he had the biggest kool-aid smile on his face.

"I take it you are happy to see me." I said laughing.

"I sure am, when did you plan this?"

"Last night after we got off the phone. I figured you needed some refueling so I had to come break you off."

"Give me your coat, you are going to stay a while right?" He asked joking.

When I dropped my coat it became clear that all parts of him were happy to see me. His sweat pants could not hide his instantaneous erection, but hell I couldn't front, my panties had been wet from the time he opened the door. He picked me up to carry me to the bed.

"My baby traveled a couple thousand miles, damn near naked to hook me up, must be love." He said as he pulled down my panties and began to serenade my coochie and believe me the music was beautiful. After about twenty minutes of him giving me head and me cumming, I remembered that I came here to serve him. I wasn't pleased with my performance our first go round. Good thing some good pussy can stand on its own; my nerves were so bad, I basically just laid there.

I pulled him up and kissed him, his hard penis laid on top of me and teased my insides. Somehow I was able to flip him over so that I could straddle him. His dick was so big that it was all up in my stomach but I took a deep breath and took control like a champ. I gyrated round and round, my hips moved like I was a dancer from a Sean Paul video, Charles held on for leverage. While still riding I turned around so that my back was to him, I held his ankles while I bounced up and down. This position was an easy transition into doing it doggy style and somehow in a swift motion he had me on all four, he was hitting it from behind and I was cumming like crazy. I couldn't hold myself up any longer, I fell flat to the bed, but Charles adjusted and kept serving me, I couldn't take no more I had to make his ass cum. I reached my hands under me and started playing with his balls with one hand and tickling my coochie with the other while he continued to plunge into me. Just as I thought his pace began to quicken and we both came. However, I was the only person shaken from the extreme orgasm, Charles was shaken for another reason that I had not even thought about.

"I'm sorry Poopie." Charles said kissing my face.

"About what you killed it." I said joking with him, but I was for real!

"So you are ok with this." He said looking at me seriously. That's when I realized we were talking about different things.

"What's up Charles?" I said matching his seriousness.

"Baby I didn't ask you, I didn't mean too, it just was feeling so good..."

Still not tripping on what he was talking about, I started getting a nervous feeling inside of me. "Just say it Charles!"

"Baby I came in you."

I knew that but I really hadn't tripped until he said it. I was so used to sleeping with Eric and we hadn't used protection in about hella years. I don't believe I had unprotected sex with him. I can't be mad at him; I was slipping. Okay I can deal with this.

"Charles it's not your fault, it's our fault. I love you and I trust you, but we both know that it is what it is. I know that you are sleeping with at least one other person for sure. I admit that shit was feeling good to me too, I was slipping, you should have had on a rubber. I have the five-year implant, so I ain't worried about getting pregnant. I just want you to know that, although I love you I will kill you if I so much as get an itch down there, my pee better not even look funny or I'm looking for you."

Charles was cracking up laughing.

"Nigga this shit ain't funny."

"You, are funny though, girl you ain't gone bust a grape."

"Don't fuck with me Charles!"

"Baby, I don't get down like that, I ain't went raw in nobody since I made my daughter so you ain't got nothing to worry about."

"So you don't be going up in your girl raw and ya'll supposed to be engaged?"

"I ain't trying to have no babies right now and she says she's on the pill, but you know how ya'll be so I got to be safe."

"What you mean how we be."

"Not you but some women, I know she can't wait to get pregnant but I ain't ready for that."

"But you went in me raw, you didn't know that I had a form of birth control. So what you trying to get me pregnant?"

"You the one that caught a nigga off guard with your sexy ass. Come on lets take a shower." He said getting up and heading to the bathroom.

"Here I come." I said as I watched his fine ass walk to the bathroom. He was like a masterpiece sculpture walking. I layed there for a moment thinking about what just happened. Call me crazy but I was flattered by the fact that I was the one he went raw dog with. I trust him, but I'll go see Dr. Richmond when I get home, just in case, it's time for my yearly anyway.

"You can't hog the water if you want me in there with you." I said as I stepped in the shower.

He must have figured I wasn't getting in because he had already washed up.

"I have perfect timing, now you can wash me." I said handing him the soap and a wash cloth. He was very happy to hook me up. After washing me thoroughly from head to toe, his patna was standing at attention. I tried to ignore it but that shit had my full attention. I knew he was aroused so I messed with him more. As I rinsed off, I played with my nipples erotically.

"Don't do that baby." He said holding his thang.

"What?" I said. "I'm rinsing off." As I continued rinsing I inserted my finger into my vagina then I spread the lips to make sure all the soap was rinsed off, yeah right. He grabbed me close and hugged me tight.

"Don't do this to me baby." He pleaded.

"I don't know what you're talking about, I'm rinsing off. You didn't rinse off good your self, let me get that soap off of you. " I said as I kneeled down to give him some killer head. He was so caught off guard and I knew he was loving it because he was holding on to the shower rod for dear life. Oh well so much for GeeGee's super flat iron, I wasted my money because my hair was now soaking wet. Charles picked me up in the air and put me on his penis and bounced me as if I was a little baby. This dude was strong!

"I'm cumming baby." I screamed out in ecstasy.

"Let me feel it baby." He moaned back.

"Oh baby." I screamed

"Ooh Sony, I'm about to cum too."

"Cum in me baby." I moaned back.

"Are you sure? " He asked panting as he propped me against the shower wall and drilled the shit out of my pussy.

"Yes, I'm cumming with you."

"You hungry?" Charles asked. We were both laid out butt naked across the bed, with the exception of a towel wrapped around my hair.

"I can eat." I said mocking the Antoine Fisher movie. Charles called to order us some room service and I turned the TV on an ordered a movie.

"Sony, I'm so happy you came to be with me, I thought you were having a party at your house on Sunday."

"I am, I leave out tomorrow at noon."

"You're not coming to the game?"

"I can't, but I'll be home in time to watch it on TV though."

I could tell he was a little bothered, but hey, it is what it is and I know he understands. Our room service arrived and we both ate in silence. I wonder if he is thinking about the same stuff I'm thinking about. I guess the only way to figure out is to have "the talk."

"So you ready to get home, huh?" I asked him.

"Yeah, I am. When I was younger I liked going on the road, but it gets old quick now."

"So what are you going to tell ol girl?"

"What do you want me to tell her Sonya?"

"Whatever you want to, I'm not in the position to tell you about that, but I just want to be clear. I mean I don't want you to tell me one thing and then I hear something different elsewhere, it has to be honesty or nothing at all with us. So if you still want to be with her I have to be cool with that."

"So you cool with me being with her? He asked me with a non-believing smirk on his face.

"I have to be, I'm married." I replied.

"You don't have to be cool with it, hell I'm not cool with you being married but that's the situation."

"Do you want me to get a divorce?"

"I want you to do what's best for you. I understand it's complicated because you have a family." He replied.

"Ok, I'm going to keep it real, I don't like you being with her but I know that's selfish. However if you decide to get married, I'm through. I chose to disregard my vows but I don't want to be a part of ruining someone else's marriage. Also, let me find out you fucking somebody other than her, shit I ain't thrilled about you fucking her. And nigga you better put on a rubber if you even think about getting some pussy, and that goes for you and her since she is the only person you will be fucking."

"You are crazy, Poopie."

"Charles, I ain't playing, call me crazy if you want to. So what do you request of me?" I asked.

250

"Let me think, well I know you ain't going to be sleeping around, you ain't that crazy." He said laughing. "On the real Sony, I just need for you to be you, don't change and of course to be straight with me no matter what. As for the rest, I'm a big boy I can handle whatever comes our way."

"So you ain't going to pull a missing in action again, if things don't go your way, right?"

"Nah, I'm cool."

"Charles, I just need for you to be there for me. This shit is serious and we both have a lot to lose, so I need to know if it all crumbles that you are going to be there. And I promise that I will be there if you need me, I am sorry for the last time."

"I know baby, we're straight." He said wrapping me up in a bear hug.

"As I laid there drifting off into my sleep, I felt bad for Charles' chick. I wondered if she ever cheated on someone. Then it might not feel that bad. I guess no one ever gave a fuck about me when they were fucking my man, but I'm not like that. I really wish he would break it off with her but I could never ask him. I know I'm being selfish.

Unbeknownst to me, Charles laid there thanking God for giving him another chance with me. He also contemplated ways of breaking up with his girl without hurting her to badly. He knew there wasn't an easy way but decided it needed to be done.

The next afternoon on my flight home I came to a point of realization and acceptance. I was having an affair, somehow out of nowhere this thing happened and I was ok with it. I found myself daydreaming about Charles and I. Thinking about our next visit, thinking about funny things he did or said. My body quivered as I thought about the way he could make my body tingle from the slightest touch. I hadn't daydreamed about Eric in a couple of years. I used to daydream about Eric all the time, about how our life would be. I always thought we would be the one's to make it. I saw his shortcomings from the beginning but they didn't matter. It was my joy to love him but I guess after a while it takes more than love. So now here I am doing things I told myself I would never do but what else are my options. Of course I love Eric but my loving him is compromising my love for myself and Charles, he loves me and I love how he makes me feel about myself.

"So that's it, I guess I'm an adultress." I thought to myself laughing out loud, but no, that's really sad!

"Bri, I just landed in Oakland, it's 2:30pm. I'm trying to see if you dropped the kids over Barbara's house yet. Call me when you get this message, Bye."

I'm going to kill that girl for not answering her phone. I can't call Barbara to check, because I don't know where Bri told her I was.

Ring   Ring   Ring   (cell phone ringing)

"So you screening your calls or something." I said to Bri as I answered my phone.

"No, I left my phone in the car while I ran into Starbucks. Where are you?"

"Walking to the parking lot at the airport. I take it you dropped off the kids."

"Yep, so give up the goods, what happened?"

"What happened was," I paused thinking if I should tell, "well just come to my house and I'll fill you in."

"Why I got to come to your house, you're in Oakland you can come to my house."

"Alright are you on your way home?"

"Yes, just tell me this, did you do it?" Bri asked too anxious to wait until I got to her house.

"Anyway, no I didn't." I lied.

"Stop lying ho, I'll see you in a minute. Bye!"

When I reached my car I called to let Charles know I made it home and I was going to Bri's house.

"Okay Sony, you're gonna get enough of telling people your business. I know we can trust Bri, but you got to keep your mouth tight with others, while we're in this situation."

"I know Eric." I said irritated, I hated when people told me shit that was obvious. Although I know he was looking out for me, the problem was I was talking to Charles not Eric.

"I'm not Eric, I'm Charles."

"What, I said Charles."

"No, you didn't, but it's cool. Just don't make a habit of it." Now he had an attitude.

"I'm sorry baby, but I know not to run my mouth. I have a lot to lose and I know it."

"Alright, well I'll call you after the game, before we leave Houston."

I can't believe I called him Eric. Well I guess it was better me calling him Eric and not vice versa, calling Eric, Charles. At any rate, I can't slip up like that again. Next, I called to check on the kids. They didn't have much to say because they were playing. I told them that I would see them tomorrow. They were excited about the play-off game party we were having at the house. When I pulled up at Bri's house, she was outside talking to the elderly couple that lived next door to her. The sight of my car made her wrap up that conversation real quick. Before I got out of the car, my cell phone rang. It was Charles.

"Hello"

"Are you busy?"

"No, were you thinking about me." I said.

"Yes, I called back to ask do you have a P.O. Box?

"No, why?"

"Monday, I want you to go open one so I can send you stuff in the mail."

"Ok, have a good game." I agreed and said, "thanks. Bye."

"Who you talking to on the phone that got you grinning, or should I guess?" Bri said as I got out the car. "My neighbors want to know if Eric can come to their church fundraiser. I told them I would ask you. Just think, you could have Charles come too and raise a lot of money." She said laughing.

"Why did I tell you about Charles again?" I said being sarcastic.

"So I could clown, now how was your night?"

"Anyway! Bri, girl it was amazing."

"I see." She said touching my hair, which was pulled back into a ponytail. "Didn't you get your hair done yesterday?"

"Yes I did and I know it's a mess now."

"So you did it huh?" Bri said with excitement.

I didn't say yes but I laughed in a way that gave away that I did and it was good.

"Tell me Sony, you can't hold out now, was it good, did he eat it? Tell me Sony."

"Okay, don't kill me when I tell you this."

"What?"

"This wasn't the first time."

"You fucked him in Vegas, I knew it!"

"No, I didn't! I did in Chicago though."

"I'm going to kill you, but after you tell me about both times. I can't believe you holding out."

"I'm sorry but it's awkward to talk about, I got a problem though, if Eric and them win their game tomorrow the kids and I have to go out there for the AFC championship game."

"Yeah, Ok, what's the problem?"

"The problem is you know Eric is going to want to fuck. How am I going to sleep with him when I slept with Charles this morning?"

"Nigga, you tripping. That's a whole week away. You'll damn there be a virgin again by then. Girl, once you douche and take a vinegar bath, you'll be back."

I laughed and shook my head at Bri's "get back" remedy. It was obvious she had been in the situation before.

"He wore a condom, right?"

"Hell yeah." I lied putting the extra on it. I didn't want to expose everything about Charles and my sexual experience.

254

"Well that's even better, no sharing of bodily fluid, you can deny that one for life."

"Okay Bri, you really have a problem. I'm getting concerned about you." I said joking.

"Alright give me the goods."

"Bri, cousin, that is the best love making I have experienced in my twenty-nine years of loving. First of all the nigga is hung!"

"Tell me more."

"Alright, what happened in Chicago was......"

Chapter 18

April

2004

Dear Journal,

April couldn't get here soon enough, this nigga Eric is getting on my last nerves. Good thing he'll be leaving for training camp soon. That time had flown by but I guess considering he walked around with an attitude for a month after they lost the AFC championship game. The kids are doing well, I just potty trained EJ. Right now the kids are the only thing Eric and I have in common but we even argue when it comes to them. He's trying to spoil them like his mom spoiled him and that's not going to work. I'll be damn if my son grows up to be a man like him. I told him that his mom spoiled him because his father was absent and he does things to try to compensate for his Dad not being around. He tells me to sve that psychology shit. Well at least my education isn't going to complete waste!

On a good note, I've been writing lately. I told Charles about my love for poetry and he sent me a book called "Ain't I a Woman," which is a compilation of poetry, it inspired me to start writing again. I've written some poems and a couple of short stories. I'm thinking about writing a novel but that's just a thought. Well speaking of Charles, I'm excited because I'm going to see him tonight. They are playing the Kings tomorrow, but they get to Sacramento tonight. I haven't did it to Eric in weeks, so it might be on tonight. I will write tomorrow, well I'll try!

"Eric, don't forget I'm going with Bri to a Pleasure party tonight."

"Pleasure Party? You ain't been trying to give me none so why you want to spend some money on some lingerie that you ain't gone wear."

"Actually, I'm hoping to find a new vibrator, my favorite one is getting worn out." I replied. Hell we can both be funny, but while he joking I will be doing my thang tonight for real.

"That's fine the kids and I are staying at my mom's house tonight."

"Whatever." I replied.

The off-season had done nothing to make my marriage better. The only thing that kept my spirits up was my daily calls from Charles even when I'm in the house with Eric. I know it sounds crazy, but a part of me wants him to ask if I'm cheating. I wouldn't lie but on the other hand I don't want it to go down in the books, like I'm to blame. The problems were before Charles. Anyway, that works, they're spending the night at his mom's house. I'm still not going to spend the night out, but I can come home smiling and not have to worry about Eric killing my joy. Um, Um, Um, how did it get to this point.

I got up and showered and threw on some sweats while Eric took the kids to school. Thank god it was Friday, I had been looking forward to this weekend for weeks. I had taken some chicken out last night so I could prepare a good meal for my family before I went out. Charles was playing the LA Clippers tonight so they wouldn't make it to Sacramento until kind of late but I'm gonna still leave out early enough to hook up with Bri and go by the Pleasure Party, I wasn't lying. "the Bullet' my vibrator was wearing out!

When Eric and EJ got back to the house I did my best to be cordial.

"So you not going to the gym this morning?" I said to Eric.

257

"Nah, I'ma chill with my man." He said play punching EJ and EJ play boxed him back. It was no denying what kept me around, although he over spoiled our kids, he was a great father and our kids adored their dad.

"You want some breakfast?" I asked.

"If it's not too much trouble, I know you have to get ready to go out tonight?"

"It's nine o'clock in the morning, what does breakfast have to do with me going out. I wouldn't have asked if it was too much trouble."

I swear he knows how to fuck up a nice gesture. Like his ass really cares if it's too much trouble for me. That's what he specializes in, asking me to do hella extra ass shit. Now I don't even fucking feel like making breakfast!

The rest of the day was pretty much the same. I would try to make conversation with him and he would say something salty. Maybe he was cheating on me, it's not like it would be the first time. However it would be the first time that I could care less. It didn't matter, I walked through the house singing and dancing all day, which seemed to annoy Eric. It's not that he knew why I was happy but the fact that I was happy seemed to bother him.

When Eric Jr., woke up from his nap it was about time to go pick the kids up.

"Eric watch that cornbread in the oven while I go pick up the kids."

"I'll go get them. Come on EJ, let's go get your brothers and sister."

"Alright cool." I replied.

I continued to finish up dinner. The chicken and macaroni salad was ready and I was waiting on the string beans and cornbread to finish. Thirty minutes passed and dinner was ready but they had not made it home. I figured they must have stopped at the store. When thirty more minutes passed I decided to call Eric's cell phone.

"What's up?" He answered.

"Where ya'll at?"

"About to pull up at my mom's house."

"I know you are joking."

"No I'm not, I told you we were staying over here tonight."

"Eric, why would you let me cook dinner if ya'll wasn't going to be here to eat. Why didn't you say that you were going straight there."

"I thought you knew."

"Why would I have been planning to pick them up from school? When you said you were picking them up you could have said that you wasn't coming back. This is the shit I be talking about, why do you do shit like this?"

"I don't know what you're talking about but I know I don't feel like arguing with you." He said.

"I can't do this, I'm not happy Eric."

"Well do what you have to, I'm not going no where. Obviously unlike you, my family is the most important thing in my life."

"Nigga what's that suppose to mean?"

"I'm not about to argue, matter-of-fact I'm putting you on speaker so the kids can talk to you."

Oh his ass is playing games. What does he think, I'm supposed to question the importance of my family to me. I put the kids and him before everything.

"Hi Mom." My kids sang.

"Hi babies, how was school?"

"Good." They all replied.

"Except for Lamar had to sit on the bench at recess." Kayla tattled.

"Lamar what happened?"

"I was playing in the line in the morning."

"Alright we'll talk about it tomorrow. Have fun at granny's house, Bye."

"Bye Mom." They replied

"I'll call you later Eric." I said.

259

"Alright." He replied.

I finally got up the nerve to say that I was tired and unhappy and then he lays a guilt trip on me about my family. Although I didn't want to admit it, it was true, I would probably be with Eric until my kids were grown. Here I go again putting everyone else's happiness before mine. It wasn't about Eric, honestly it was all about my children. Eric wasn't going to change, he had me just where he wanted me. He knew me well enough to know that I wanted what was best for my kids at any cost so he would continue to hold that over my head. The only way he would leave me was if I was cheating, which I was, but he was too blind to see. The signs were all there but he obviously didn't notice. I figured he must be cheating too but if he was he had figured a way to tighten his game. He used to be a sloppy cheater like most men, but I haven't found out nothing lately. Sadly, I wish he was, that would give me an out. Charles said that Eric not being suspicious was a sign of his trust in me, but I know that Charles has to say the things that don't make him appear to be hating. I know that Eric isn't suspicious because of his arrogance. Eric thinks that I would never cheat because he feels I'm privileged to have him. Yeah, he needs to get over himself. Here I am stuck, married to an asshole and I have a good man that chooses to play second fiddle. That's alright, from this day forward, I am married to Eric solely for the purpose of my children. If I feel like talking to Charles, I will. If I feel like seeing him, I will. I'm not going to go out of my way to put it in his face but if he finds out, oh well. I just can't do this anymore. I decided to call Eric back.

{Phone ringing}

"What Sonya?"
"You don't have to answer the phone like that."
"I thought you were going out, why are you calling me?"
He was making things so much easier for me.

"Eric, I'm so tired of this back and forth with you, you know that my children are the most important thing in this world . I will do anything for them, even dealing with you. Don't get it twisted, I'm not going no where either but it has nothing to do with you, it's all about my kids."

"You act like you got it so bad, it's plenty of people who would love to be in your shoes."

"You don't get it, there's more to life than money. The sad thing is you may never get it. I ain't never had to be here, I was doing fine before you came along. I always wanted to be with you but now that has changed and sadly, now I have to be here."

"You don't have to do shit! I told you I ain't leaving my family so if you want to cut, whatever."

"Fuck you Eric!" I said as I hung up the phone.

This is the life, the life that people wish and dream for. The life that groupies flock to hotels and VIP parties to get a shot at. I always said I wouldn't be one of those athlete's wives who stayed when things got bad, but here I was staying. I always assumed those women stayed for the money but now I see. Good thing he will be leaving next week. I'm strong I can deal with him for that long. Watch his crazy ass come home tomorrow like nothing has happened. I wonder if he noticed I wasn't crying. I used to cry all the time over our problems. Eric would hate for me to cry and I would tell him, "don't worry when I'm crying that means I care, now when I stop crying, worry because I have lost the ability to care." It's been a while since I've cried over him.

What I need to do now is eat some of my good dinner I cooked, and get myself prepared for a good night with my man!

The last couple of months had been wonderful. Charles' season had ended so we were able to spend some stolen moments together. Eric was in the midst of his training camp, so he had little time to get on my nerves. Charles had been out here every

261

other weekend since the end of April. Although we couldn't go out in public, we enjoyed each other's company. The better I got to know him; the more I loved him. We got along well but we still had our little arguments, which I usually started. It was hard for me to believe that he was being faithful to me when he knew my situation. It was so hard keeping him a secret because he did so many things that I wanted to share with my loved ones. Just like I wanted him to meet the people that meant the most to me, like my parents. I knew in my heart that he was truly my soul mate. I remember once when I was growing up and I had gotten my heart broken and I cried my eyes out on my mother's shoulder, I must have been fifteen years old at the time. I asked my mom if she believed that every person has a soul mate. I remember my mom telling me that "everyone has a soul mate but unfortunately we don't always end up with that person. Everything in life depends on timing." That wisdom was given to me so many years ago didn't mean a thing until now. Here I was living out that prophecy.

The kids are out of school for summer vacation and anxious to go visit Eric but right now that is not top priority for me. I am excited about my upcoming annual trip to the Essence Festival. The whole crew is going this time, even Kim. The atmosphere of Essence was so laid back that you don't have to get "G'd up" but that didn't stop us from shopping. I don't know why, half the stuff I buy for Essence I don't even wear while I'm out there. This year we bought concert tickets hella early. When we found out Prince was performing on the first night, it was a done deal. Then we heard New Edition would be performing on the last night, now you know all Black girls who grew up in the eighties, loved New Edition. When we were growing up it was five of us in our crew and five of them. We each had a person; my person was Michael Bivins. I had to laugh out loud just thinking about it. Charles said he probably won't make it to Essence this year. I'm kind of upset because that's the anniversary of our meeting each other but I didn't tell him. It's hard to believe it's only been a year, it seems like I've known him for a lifetime. Just then, my thoughts were interrupted by the phone ringing.

"Hello."

"What up chick." Alisha said.

"Nothing, thinking about Essence. What are you doing?"

"Just came from San Francisco and I bought some cute D&G Capri jeans."

"Girl, your model figure ass is the only one that can wear that D&G shit, you know I got too much booty." I said.

"Whatever girl, I'm thick." Alisha replied.

"Why didn't you call me, I would have went with you."

"I had met Jason out there for lunch but Kim wants somebody to go out shopping with her when she gets off work."

"Are you crazy? You know don't nobody like shopping with her indecisive ass, I'm cool."

"Come on Sony, I can't go by myself, she'll drive me crazy." Alisha pleaded.

"I'll think about it, Eric's calling on the other line, so I'll call you back, Bye."

"Hello."

"What's up, what are the kids doing?"

"They are out in the back playing, how's your day going?"

"Cool, well I found out I got nominated for an ESPY award for Football player of the year."

"Really, Congratulations! That sounds exciting!" I said although he sounded dry.

"Yeah, so I'll have to leave training to go. It's in mid-July, so I guess your mom can figure out what we should wear."

"Alright, I'll ask her."

"Well have the kids call me later."

I was excited for him but I wasn't excited about having to play the role of happy homemaker for the ceremony. However this would be exciting for my mother to pick out a designer for us to wear, she loves fashion. It's more than just a business to her. I guess I better call her so she can start thinking, that's only a little over a month away.

Ring, ring

"Hello."

"Hey Daddy, is Ma there?"

"Yeah, hold on."

"Hello"

"Hey Ma, I need a favor."

"I know it's not babysitting, when you have Essence coming up and the kids will be staying here for five days."

"No it's not babysitting." I said. My Mama was always complaining about babysitting but if I take them elsewhere she gets jealous.

"Eric is nominated for an ESPY Award so we need the best stylist in the world." I said buttering her up.

"Oh my goodness, tell him congratulations. He deserves it for the season he had last year. Of course I'll do it; I would be honored. When is it?"

"Mid-July, I'll get the exact date to you. Ma, I'll call you back because my cell phone is ringing."

It had to be Charles, because anyone else would call me at home.

"Hello." I said answering my cell phone.

"Hey Poopie, are you busy?" Charles said sounding excited.

"No, what's going on." I replied.

"Guess what, I got nominated for an ESPY for basketball player."

"Oh my! Congratulations!" I said.

"Thank you. What's wrong you sound strange. Aren't you excited?" He asked.

"I am very excited but I have to tell you something. I hope you are prepared for our first awkward moment."

"What?" He asked confused.

"Eric just called and told me that he was nominated for an ESPY as well, so of course I have to be there on his arm for the ceremony. Are you ok with that?"

"Well he is your husband." He replied in a sour tone.

"I know what he is, but are you cool?"

"If I wasn't would it change things?" He asked.

I just sat quietly on the phone. Sometimes saying nothing is the best thing.

"That's what I thought." He said.

Well at least I would be there for him as well, I thought to myself but decided to keep it to myself. That might not sound so good coming out.

"Charles, I know this is a hard situation to be in and that's why I tell you all the time, I understand if you can't do it. You know how it is, it's all about image. You know the real, I'm in love with you." I did my best to comfort him but I could tell my words fell on deaf ears.

"Alright Sonya, I'm going to call and tell my Mom the news. I'll call you later." He said then he hung up. I knew he was bothered because he called me Sonya. Hopefully it would pass. Man, my husband and my boyfriend both nominated for an ESPY. If this isn't some Hollywood Jerry Springer shit. I had to call and tell Bri.

Chapter 19

I don't know why I let Mya convince me into taking a 8:00 am flight to New Orleans. I didn't get to bed until 3:00 am, up packing and talking on the phone to Charles. I was still a little bothered that he wasn't going this year. He is so crazy, why did he come out here last weekend and have me bring all of the outfits I bought up to his hotel to show them to him. I modeled every single outfit for him to get his approval. He joked about my clothes saying, "you already have a husband and a boyfriend, what you got to look sexy for!" He is so crazy but I love it. So now my alarm is going off, it's 5:00 am and I have to get ready so I can be out of my house by six to make it to the airport by seven. Do the math, that was two hours of sleep. I knew I shouldn't have waited to the last minute to pack. I talked to Eric last night to tell him I was dropping the kids at my mom's house. Mark my word, that will be the last time we talk until I get back. Oh well, New flash, I am so not tripping this year!

When I was pulling up at the airport, Alisha was being dropped off by Jason. I had picked up my brother Lamar so he could drop me off, he didn't mind getting up as long as he could drive my car. Alisha and I were the last to arrive at the airport. Bri, Kim and Mya were waiting for us at our gate. We were set for a weekend of fun. No matter how much we loved each other, with five bitches together for that many days, it was sure to be some drama too!

Kim talked the whole way to New Orleans. She was so excited, she hadn't been anywhere in, forever! I was so proud of her, she had really taken a new lease on life since her divorce from the fool. Actually everyone in the crew was doing well. Alisha was kind of quiet this morning though, this was her first time returning to Louisiana since Rock's death.

"We have begun our initial descent into New Orleans. We should be on the ground in fifteen minutes. Flight attendants please prepare for landing." The captain announced.

"The first thing I plan on doing once we reach the hotel is taking a nap, I am tired as hell." I said aloud.

"Not me, I'm about to eat." Mya responded.

"Yeah, I can eat something." I said.

"I'm ready to hit Bourbon." Kim said excited.

"Girl, slow down. You will get enough of Bourbon, trust." Alisha said to Kim.

When we got to baggage claim, our limo driver was waiting with a sign with all our names on it. This year I took the liberty of reserving a limo ahead of time. I had to make sure the sign had everybody's name on it or somebody's feeling would be hurt. Pulling up in front of the Wyndham Hotel brought back memories of last year. In retrospect, Alisha taking hella long that night was a blessing in disguise. My life has changed so much since meeting Charles. I got back to being me. I'm writing again, I'm secure and I'm happy.

"So what are we going to do tonight?" Bri asked.

"Well since the festival doesn't officially start until tomorrow, we can just play it by ear." Mya responded.

We had gotten checked into our rooms, we had two adjoining rooms. I unpacked and ordered me some room service. Bri, Mya and Kim decided to go out to eat and see the sights. One of Rock's friends had come to pick Alisha up to take her to his grave visit.

Since I was by myself I decided to call Charles, I missed him already.

"Hey Baby, are you there?" He said when he answered.

"Yes I am, what are you doing?" I asked because it was somewhat loud in the background.

"Nothing, thinking about you."

"Well that's something, what are you doing?" I replied.

"I'm laying down waiting on room service, everybody else went out. Somebody had me on the phone all night so I'm tired."

"You had me up all night, ay baby, I got to go, I'll call you back, ok."

"Damn! You rushing me off, it must be important."

"I'm sorry, it is important though baby."

"Ok, I love you." I replied.

"I love you too."

That was odd, if Charles was any other man, I would be skeptical but I truly loved and trusted him. After I ate, I fell asleep and didn't wake up until my phone rang, it was 9:30 pm.

"Damn, I must have been tired." I said aloud before answering my phone. "Hello." I said in a sleepy voice.

"Are you sleeping?"

"Sort of, what's up?"

"Well I was calling you back like I said."

"Charles, that was hours ago."

"I know. I got caught up. Are you mad?"

"Yeah, nah I'm playing. I fell asleep after we talked and I'm just waking up anyway. I wish you were here."

"I'm sorry, but we're still taking a trip in August, right?"

"Yep, somewhere on another continent. Somewhere we can walk down the street together. I can't wait." I replied. It was hard for Charles and I. When you're in love, you want to hold hands and kick cans but we weren't able to do that.

"You're not going out tonight?" He asked me.

"Nope, I'm going to do some writing and then rest up so I can be ready to see my man Prince in concert tomorrow night."

"Alright baby, I'll call you tomorrow." He said before hanging up.

When I got off the phone, I got up to use the bathroom. In looking around the room, I noticed they had been back and left again.

"Them bitches ain't shit, they could have woke me up." I said aloud. I really wasn't tripping; I needed the rest. I knew that this would probably be the last rest I got all weekend. Tomorrow we were going to get up and go eat at Seaport on Bourbon Street, we will probably hang on Bourbon Street until it was time to come back to the room to get ready for the Prince concert. I most definitely wouldn't be late for that.

I brushed my teeth and washed my face and got back in the bed. I'll see them tomorrow!

I didn't know what time it was but I knew it was too early to be getting up or so I thought.

"Get up." Kim said in an overly loud voice as she pulled the curtains back.

"Look, your country butt is used to waking up with the roosters, what time is it?" I asked.

"It's 10:30am." She replied.

"Is it?" Bri said popping her head from the bed across from me. Kim had slept in the bed with me and Bri had a bed to herself. I don't know how that happened considering I paid for the room, but whatever.

"Yes it is, so get up." Kim replied.

"Alright, go over there and wake up Alisha and Mya." I said.

"Oh them drunk bitches may sleep until the concert tonight." Bri said

"What! What happened?" I asked.

Bri started filling me in on last night's events. She said they were hella loud when they came in, she was surprised I slept through it. Kim's attempt to get Mya and Alisha up failed so she decided to get in the shower. She was excited to get out in the streets. Bri and I talked a little longer and then about 11:00 am we decided to fall out of the bed to get ready. I couldn't wait to get to Seaport, I fell asleep thinking about that restaurant and their good food.

Kim was the slowest person to get ready. She took a shower before me and Bri, but by the time we were ready she was still curling her hair. Kim curls her hair everyday, she just can't wrap it and comb it down.

We attempted one last time to wake up Mya and Alisha before we went out but all they woke up for was to say Bye! That was cool though, that's how we rolled during Essence. We didn't have problems separating to do our own individual things or kicking it as a group.

This was Kim's first time in New Orleans, hence her first time going to Seaport. Bri and I warned her not to let her eyes get bigger than her stomach because believe me everything on the menu was good and reasonably priced. I ordered my regular, the seafood platter. After eating we fell into a little bar that had a live band and had a few shots. The band was jamming and the sister that was singing could blow too. We convinced Kim to go on stage and dance. That was hilarious! After her performance we decided to head back towards the hotel. We decided, well Bri decided we should walk through the mall since it was downstairs from our hotel. As we walked, we talked to people on the street. Some people trying to holler, some asking for directions or giving out flyers, and some people just being friendly, saying hello!

"The people are hella nice out here." Kim said.

"Yeah they are." I replied.

"I need to add a country nigga to my team." Bri joked.

"You are crazy." I replied.

"Hell, I need a country one, a city one, any kind right about now. I ain't dated since Ray." Kim said.

"Girl, stop lying. You went out with that guy last week." I said.

"No, I mean a date, date. You know a physical date."

"You mean fucking! Bri said bluntly.

"Yeah." Kim replied.

"Damn!" Bri and I replied simultaneously.

"Shut up ya'll." Kim said laughing at herself. "It's only been like nine months."

"Only, do you know you can have a baby in nine months, that's three seasons." Bri said.

"That's alright, I'm gonna find me some hooks out here, and what goes on in New Orleans, stays in New Orleans!" Kim said.

"Shit, it's been that long, you might want to take an ad out in the newspaper if you get some saying, 'the drought is over!'" Bri replied.

We laughed our way back to the Wyndham. When we entered the mall I saw a guy that looked like Charles' friend Twan that came to Essence with him last year. I had to remind myself to ask Charles if Twan came when I talk to him later.

I don't know why I let Bri do this to me all the time. I had no intentions on buying anything but here I was lugging bags up to our room. It wasn't just me; she had Kim shopping too. I was so happy Kim was having a ball, she had saved her tax refund for this trip and she was spending it.

Back up in the room, Mya and Alisha had finally come to life. They actually had made it downstairs to do some shopping themselves. We all agreed that we were going to get ready early because we didn't want to miss any of Prince's show. I had heard that Chaka Khan might perform with him as well as Morris Day, Sheila E., and Larry Graham. Rumors had been circulated that Prince had cancelled but I wasn't believing it. Essence would have a riot on their hands.

Once we got dressed, we all posed in front of the hotel room door to snap pictures. We have so many pictures in front of hotel room doors, it's become a routine whenever we go out of town to take pictures before we go out. I looked at my friends, it was amazing they were all beautiful and I'm not being biased because they are my girls. We had some of everything a man might look for in our crew. You know that's rare because it's usually at least one ugly one in every crew. No lying just look at all the female singing groups, at least one ugly one, well except for TLC. I ended up wearing a little skirt I bought today and I do emphasize little! Mya had flirted with the limo driver yesterday and hooked it up for him to pick us up for the concerts. He was calling to let us know he was downstairs. Oh and did I forget to mention that Mya did keep in touch with the doorman from last year, Diondre, so we got the rooms for a killer discount. She told him she would fit him in for a lunch date, I felt bad for him. He had actually taken the whole weekend off to hang with her. You know that wasn't going down.

"Can ya'll hurry up, he's waiting." Mya yelled.

"I'm ready." Kim said.

"I'm not, but he'll wait. Give me five minutes." Alisha said.

Bri was ready too. So her, Mya and Kim went downstairs. I waited For Alisha, which gave me a chance to call Charles. I'm not even going to bother calling Eric because he ain't going to answer anyway.

"Hello, may I speak with my baby." I said joking with Charles. I knew it was him.

"This is him, what's up?"

"Getting ready to go to the concert, what are you doing?"

"Chilling. Have fun and don't let me find out you messing around on me."

"Oh shut up nigga. I'll call you later. Bye." I replied.

Alisha and I had to rush down to the limo before them hoes thought about leaving us, just playing! Then we were off to the concert. The limo dropped us off as close as he could but we still had a little hike to get to the entrance of the Superdome. It didn't matter we were anxious to see Prince.

Once we got down to our seats we decided to get some food and drinks. I was drnking Smirnoff Ice because they didn't have any Malibu Rum. We sang along with Larry Graham and did the "Bird" with Morris Day and then it was time for Prince.

Prince came on jamming. We all jumped up dancing and singing along. He sang most of his songs except for the really raunchy ones. They say he stopped performing them because of his religious faith. Next thing I knew, I heard the music to "Adore". That was one of Charles' and my songs. I tried to find a quiet place to call Charles, but before I could call him, my phone was vibrating.

"Hi Baby, I was just about to call you." I said when I answered. It was so loud that I could barely hear his background.

"Hey Poopie, are you having a good time?"

"Yes, Prince is jamming and he's singing our song right now."

"Until the end of time I'll be there for you." Charles sang.

"Yeah but he sounds a little better than you baby, but you sound good too." I said laughing.

"Poopie, tell me this."

"What's up?"

"I don't remember seeing that little short skirt when you modeled your clothes for me."

"What." I replied sounding confused while looking around.

"I mean it's cute, short, but cute. I just don't remember it." He said as he walked toward me in the open walkway area where I stood. I ran and jumped into his arms. I didn't care who saw us.

"Baby, I can't believe you are here. You liar." I said as I passionately hit him in the chest. "I thought you weren't coming."

"I wasn't but since you wanted me here I had to make it happen. Man, it cost me a pretty penny too."

"I'm worth it." I said smiling.

"There's that smile that hooked me. You know I would be here, it's our anniversary."

He remembered, I knew that was Twan I saw earlier. I knew my cousins would be looking for me before long so we agreed to hook-up after the concert. I was so excited. I probably smiled the rest of the concert.

The rest of the weekend flew by. I spent a lot of time in Charles' room. He was staying at the Wyndham too. Everybody except Bri thought I was at the casino when I was with him. I still hung out with the crew, we did our thing on Bourbon and of course we did the electric-slide at the Frankie Beverly and Maze concert on the last night. However the highlight of my weekend was my time with Charles.

On the flight home, we replayed all the weekend's events. Of course my stories were tailored to protect my secret. However one person's weekend was a little more eventful than others.

"So Kim how's the coochie feeling, it's been a while." I asked

"Girl, I'm cool, real cool." She replied smiling.

We all laughed and cracked on her damn there the whole flight back home. The drought was over.

Chapter 20

It had only been a week since I returned from Essence and now I was off to L.A. to meet Eric for the ESPY awards. Bri, Mya and Eric's mom were coming as well to support Eric. Well his mom was coming to support, Bri and Mya were coming for the eligible men. My mom had packed a suit by Gucci for Eric and we went with a Gucci dress for me. She dressed Charles in Armani. Of course she didn't know it was for Charles, I told her it was for a friend of Bri's who played basketball. His measurements gave away the fact that he played basketball. Anyway, I admit I was slightly nervous about this trip. I'm not good at putting on a 'game face' so seeing him might blow everything up. Honestly I wasn't even looking forward to having to put on my fake ass wife personality. The flight to L.A. was a quick 55 minutes. We were flying in for the ceremony today and leaving out tomorrow. Eric had sent a limo to pick us up from the airport. He would be busy doing press stuff all morning. My mother-in-law and I had spa appointments scheduled for when we arrived at the hotel.

Everything was running smoothly. We got to the Kodak Theater early enough to do the whole "Red Carpet" thing and still get to our seats well before the show began. I admit, that was kind of exciting, I felt like a Hollywood star. All kids growing up in the ghetto have dreamed of being stars, so that was my moment and I worked it! I was anxious for the show to start. Jamie Foxx is the host and that dude is funny as hell. I just pray to God that Charles' seat isn't close to ours.

Just like I thought Jamie Foxx came out being funny, the show was progressing well. I found myself looking around to try to spot Charles, but I couldn't find him. During what would be a commercial break for people watching at home, they announced that next award would be for basketball when they went back on air. As they counted down to going back live, my palms began to sweat. I really didn't hear much after that until they said the winner is Charles Knight from the New Jersey Nets. I want to scream with excitement but all I can do is a conservative clap, I hate this feeling!

The first thing he did when he got to the podium was rub his chin, this was a ritual he created to let me know he was thinking of me. He does it at the beginning of every game before Jump ball. Of course, I'm crying on the inside with happiness. After his award, they gave out a few other awards. Then it was time for Eric's category.

"And the winner is, Eric Jackson." The presenter announced.

Eric kissed his mom and I before he went up to accept his award.

"First I would like to thank God for the countless blessings. Next I would like to thank my mom, whose here with me tonight for working so hard for me to have everything. I want to thank my children for giving me so much joy and inspiration and last but not least my beautiful wife Sonya, who has been my backbone for 11 years. You were my tutor in college, my shrink, my accountant, my friend. I would have never made it here without you, I love you."

Wasn't that special. Here I am having to wear this fake ass look of 'Aaaw'. I knew the camera was probably on me, so I had to play the role of loving wife. The truth is, I have been all those things and more for the past 11 years but he honestly doesn't see that, he can't, or he wouldn't treat me as if I owe him. I am ready for this show to be over!

After the show, he had to do some more press stuff, I couldn't escape it this time. There were reporters from everywhere asking pretty much the same questions.

"Oh my God." I said to myself

Right next to us was Charles. Next thing I know, the reporter interviewing Eric brings Charles into the conversation. So now here we are, the reporter, T.V. cameras, my boyfriend and my husband. Charles and Eric congratulated each other and shook hands, I just stood there feeling like the freak of the week.

How did I get myself into this? It even got to the point where the reporter complimented all of us on our attire.

"Thank you, I have to give credit to my wife's mom. She is a stylist and designer." Charles responded to the reporter.

"Who are you guys wearing? The reporter asked.

"Oh, we're both wearing Gucci." I replied.

"And what about you, Mr. Knight?" The reporter asked Charles.

"Oh, this is Armani, actually a friend of mine's mom picked it out for me as well."

I couldn't believe he said that. I could tell from his whole disposition he was a little bothered. I knew it was best that I end this interview quick.

"Come on Eric, we have to go meet your mom." I said.

"Oh that's right, nice meeting you man." He said to Charles.

"Likewise." Charles responded.

As we walked away from the press area Eric was pulled away by an old teammate. Charles had to be watching because instantly my cell phone rang. I couldn't say hello, soon as I picked it up, he was talking.

"I need to talk to you as soon as you get back to the hotel."

"How am I going to do that?"

"I need to talk to you." He repeated.

"Alright, I'll figure it out." I replied before hanging up. I could tell he was upset. I know he knows my situation but this is a lot to deal with, I would be upset too.

Eric took us all out to dinner at Crustaceans when we left the show. In the car I told Bri about the run-in and the phone call from Charles. On the way back to the hotel, Bri asked me to come help her choose what to wear to the club tonight, hence giving me some time away from Eric so I could really go talk to Charles.

Back at the hotel everyone headed to their rooms, I told Eric I would be up in a little while because I was going to help Bri.

"Whatever." He replied. Boy how quick we change when we ain't in front of a camera.

I did actually go to Bri's room to call Charles to find out what room he was in. I was so nervous going to his room, I thought there might be paparazzi hiding, taking photos or anything. It didn't matter, Charles didn't sound right so I had to see him. As soon as I walked through the door he started going off.

"Don't lie to me Sonya."

"What, what are you talking about?"

"I thought ya'll wasn't fucking."

"We haven't."

"I thought things were bad."

"They are."

"What happened to honesty, that's all we do." He said.

"What do you mean what happened to it, I've been honest. I haven't slept with him and things are bad."

"Sonya, did you forget, I was at the award show too. I heard him."

"That's bullshit Charles, and you know it. You know how that image shit is. He wasn't lying, I have been his backbone but what does that mean. It doesn't change that our relationship is fucked."

"I don't know Sonya. It sounds all good to me."

"So now, I'm a liar! I ain't never lied to you. Where am I right now? That alone should let you know I'm here with you."

He just sat there quietly, probably thinking about the fact that I was here with him.

"You want to start this conversation over." I said to him as I pulled my dress up some so I could straddle him sitting on the chair. "Hey baby, congratulations on your award." I said to him before kissing him on his lips.

"Thank you, did you see my shot out to you?" He replied in a more calmed down voice.

278

"You know I did and you know I was thinking about you too, baby. This is some crazy stuff we done got ourself into. I felt so fucking awkward tonight. And you, 'my friend's mom picked this out'. You just trying to be messy." I said as I kissed him again. "How long do you think it would take?" I asked him in a seductive tone and within a few seconds the dress was on the floor and we were fucking like animals, with my heels still on! This was the closest to 'break-up to make-up' sex that we had ever had and believe me it was exceptional. After thirty minutes of pleasure, all doubt was erased from his mind and now I had to get myself back together to go be cordial with Eric. I didn't want to leave Charles but I had to. Sometimes I wish I had the courage to just leave Eric, I'm just worried about the kids.

When I got to the room, Eric was already in bed. I had already planted tampon wrappers in the bathroom trash to make him think I was on my period, just in case he thought he was getting some. I just wanted to go to sleep so I could wake up and go home. I had a trip to plan. Charles and I had decided to go to Anguilla in August and that was just a month away. As I finished saying my prayers and just as I was about to close my eyes, Eric tapped me on my leg.
"Sonya, can I get some head?"
This nigga must be stupid, I acted like I didn't hear his ass and went to sleep.

The next month Charles and I went on a week vacation to Anguilla. Of course everyone thought Bri and I went to Hawaii. Bri really did go to Hawaii, but she was with her secretary. We planned it so our trips would be at the same time. Anguilla was one of the most beautiful places I had ever visited. We had our own private villa, which we stayed in for the most part. However, we did go out too. We walked around and shopped and layed out on the beach. For the first time ever, we were able to hold hands and kick cans in public. It was a real turning point for our relationship. After that trip, I definitely was married to

279

Eric on paper only. Where we use to talk a couple of times a day on the phone that had been reduced to one call a day if that. That was if he called because I sure wasn't calling unless I had something to report about the kids.

The football season began and I wasn't there for his first game, or second, or third. I hadn't been to any games, however when October rolled around I made sure to secure babysitters in advance to make Charles' first game of the season. I had a new lease on life and Eric didn't even notice. Well I'm sure he noticed but figured I was going through a phase. My mom noticed a change, knowing my mom she probably had it figured out, but she never questioned me. She always told me 'don't ask questions that you don't want the answer to'. On another note, I began writing short stories, Charles and my girls say they are good. Maybe I'll try to get some of them published one day. I really want to write a novel. With all my drama, I have a book already. I'll see Eric this week, the Miami are playing the Raiders, so he'll be home. I haven't seen him since July and it's November, it's been four months. That's definitely a first. I'm glad he'll be here though, the kids really miss him, usually I would have been taken them out to see him.

The days flew by, and now the day had arrived for Eric to come home. Bri was calling me bright and early.

"Hey Chick, what are you doing?"

"Nothing, just dropped the kids off at school, now E.J. and I are going to the grocery store."

"So you can cook a meal for your husband." Bri said.

"I'm gonna cook a meal because my kids gotta eat." I replied.

"Bri you are tripping, I told you I ain't fucking him, plus I'm on my period for real."

"You are tripping, that is still your husband. You better get on the mic or something."

"What, I definitely ain't sucking his dick!"

"Alright Sony, I hope you know what you are doing, he's gonna figure something out if you keep holding out on the pussy."

"Yeah I know, I just keep praying on it. It will come to me, hopefully sooner than later." I said.

"Well call me when he gets in. Did you get a luxury suite for the game?"

"Yeah I did."

"Cool, is everybody going?"

"Yeah, but you know Lamar and Kevin have Raider Season tickets so they'll probably sit in there seats. I'll call you later, I'm about to walk in the store."

After the grocery store, E.J. and I ran a few more errands. By the time we got home it was time for E.J. to lay down for his nap. I started thinking about what Bri said, it was true he was still my husband. I decided to make a conscious effort to be cool for the next couple of days.

When the kids got home from school they were so antsy. They new their dad would be home tonight. Eric made it home just in time for dinner. I made his favorite meal. I did what I had to, to make my children's home happy. Making a good meal for Eric wouldn't kill me. It was Friday, so after dinner we all stayed up watching movies. One by one the kids all fell asleep so Eric moved them to their beds. Now the big test, could we have civilized conversation, now that the kids were sleep.

"So what's up with you." He said when he returned.

"Nothing, just chilling, being a mom. I've been doing a lot of writing."

"That's good, what are you writing for?"

"Mostly for therapy, but I may try to get some of my work published."

"Really, so you still mad at me." He said as he started rubbing my leg. It was crazy, his touch used to soak my panties, but now it did nothing for me.

"I'm not mad at you."

"Is that right." He replied as he tried to reach his hands further up my legs and he began to kiss my neck. All I could hear in my head was Bri's voice saying, "He's still your husband." So as much as I didn't want to give in, I felt like I had no other no other choice. I really was on my period so I figured I'd give him a hand job, so at least he could get a nut. I reached my hand in his pants and started stroking his fully erect penis. He continued to kiss my neck and then he raised my shirt and began to twirl my nipples with his tongue. Before he thought he was going to get any further I had to let him know about the flow.

"Eric, I'm on my cycle."

"Are you?" He said sounding disappointed.

"Go get some baby oil, baby."

See, now I got to get up, he ain't knowing he barely got this dry hand job. I went ahead and got the oil and stroked his thing until it exploded. I truly hope it felt good to him because I felt so crappy for doing it. This is the first time that I participated in unwanted sexual activity. It wasn't like I was forced but I did it because I felt obligated. This is one thing that I would have to lie to Charles about and this will be a first. I kind of think that Charles thinks that I've been fucking Eric all along anyway. I went to sleep feeling cheap.

Sunday came and went quick. Eric's team beat the Raiders and he was back off to Miami. We actually got along well although it was only a couple of days. That's the relationship I wish we could have all the time. Even though it didn't change the way I felt about us, I wanted to be able to get along with him at least for our kids. Now that Eric was gone I could call and tell Charles to breathe again. It didn't matter how much I assured him that he was the man I was in love with, I could tell his whole disposition changed when Eric was home. . I guess I didn't blame him, I would probably be the same way. I still ask him about his ex fiancé although I know that he broke it off, we all get unsecure every now and then.

November flew by and Thanksgiving came and went. Now Christmas was coming quick. I already struggle with what to get Eric every year and now I had Charles to buy for too. What do you buy men who have everything. Charles and I decided to celebrate Christmas early. They were going to be home for a week and they had a few days with no games. It seemed like I was in the stores everyday of December. Every year I told myself I'm only buying gifts for kids and my parents and Eric's mom and every year, I make a liar out of myself.

I was excited about my trip to Jersey. I was actually going to experience a white Christmas for the first time, even if it was a week early.

When I arrived in New Jersey, Charles had sent a driver to pick me up from the airport. I got in around 8:30 pm, he had a game tonight so he left his key in the hiding place for me. I felt really awkward being at his house by myself. I decided to take a shower and get in my pajama's, after that I still had a while before he got in, so I decided to call Bri to distract my urge to snoop through his stuff.

"Hello."

"Hey Bri, I made it here."

"How was your flight? Is it snowing?"

"My flight was cool, it's not snowing, but it's snow on the ground."

"Oh, tell Charles I said hello."

"He's not here, he had a game tonight."

"Are you by yourself?"

"Yes."

"Have you gone through his drawers?"

"No I haven't and I'm not."

"Girl please, they expect us to do that."

"Well I'm not, so what are you doing?"

"I'm about to go to Le Cheval's with your sister and Alisha. On another note, you better start thinking about a new story because the writing seminar lie is getting old."

"Really, are people saying stuff?"

"No not yet, but it's only a matter of time."

"Alright good looking out. Enjoy your dinner, I think I hear Charles coming in, Bye."

"Bye. Have fun." Bri said before hanging up.

I layed down in the bed and played sleep.

"I could come home to this every night." He said talking aloud to himself.

"Hey baby, how was the game?"

"We won, did I wake you?" He asked.

"No I wasn't sleeping, I was waiting on you." I said as I got out of the bed to hug him.

His embrace was still heavenly. Hugging him made me feel as if I was a part of his being, that's how powerful it was.

"Come on, let's go downstairs, I got us some food."

Thank goodness because I was hungry.

After we ate, we talked and laughed and even sang Christmas carols. He gave me an ad about a short story competition for Essence magazine and encouraged me to enter. It was so nice to have someone who thought about me, who believed in my gift and who wanted to see me make my mark in the world. That night we fell asleep in each other's arms.

The next morning I got up and made us breakfast, then he had to go to practice. We decided we were going to exchange our gifts when he returned. I felt uncomfortable being in his home alone, so I sat in his room and began to write a short story to consider submitting to the contest. I started with the title, The Essence of An Affair. Before I knew it, he was back and I had completed an entire notebook.

"I want you to open my gifts first, but we have to open them in a room where you have a VCR." I said.

He began to open the presents. The first one was a big box filled with several bottles of cologne. The next box was a custom made Jacob diamond watch. He was excited about the gifts but to me these were things he could get for himself. The last gift was the most important one. He opened the box and it was a video tape.

284

"Put it in." I said to him.

He put the tape in the VCR.

"What is it a dirty video?" He asked.

"Anyway, hold on, don't push play yet. You know you mean the world to me, and there's so much in my life that I want to share with you that I can't because of our circumstances so this is my gift to you. Press play."

When the tape came on, I could see Charles' emotions all over his face.

"That's Kayla, and the little one with the chicken in his hands is E.J., in a minute you'll see Lamar and Sean."

I videotaped my kids on a typical day and then I taped my parents and my nephews and nieces. I wanted Charles to get to know my family even if it was just through the video.

"Baby, your family is beautiful, this is the best gift that I could get."

"You like."

"I love it."

"I brought gifts for your girls too. I didn't put that they were from me because, well you know. I remembered you saying the oldest was into the Bratz and the youngest liked Dora the Explorer, so I picked them up a little something."

"You are so special Poopie."

"Anyway." I said embarrassed by the compliment.

He bought me Jimmy Choo boots, with matching purse, and some two-carat each diamond studs. I loved all my gifts.

It was so sad that we were in such a complex situation. I tried to enjoy my day but I knew I would be on a flight home soon and that lingered in my mind. A few stolen moments, that's all we share.

Chapter 21

Dear Journal,
I can't believe that the football season is over already, time to prepare myself for the day to day drama. The first day Eric was home we argued. E.J. was turning three at the end of February and Eric wanted to have a big party, I suggested that we do something small. That's when he told me that he already told his mom we were having it at her house. Okay am I tripping, don't I have some say so but I'm always the one causing our problems.
The same inconsiderate shit continued over the next months. Some stuff would cause little arguments while others would cause big blow ups. I constantly told him that our relationship wasn't working and his reply would always be, "leave then." That was his game, he knew I wasn't leaving my kids. I once tried to make him leave but he wouldn't go. What was I to do; I was stuck. I wouldn't call the police, it wasn't like he ever hit me or anything. I just wanted him to leave but I refused on contributing to another Black athletes face being spread across the news for some negative shit. Our kids are getting older and they are smart. I know that they know that things aren't good between their parents. I thought our staying together was for their benefit but this is no good for them. The problem is we're both to bullheaded to leave. Good thing I have my writing. I went ahead and submitted a story for that contest. I got the first call that I was in the top ten. They told me I would be notified within 10 days if I was in the top three and or if I'm the grand prize winner. I am so excited. Hopefully I'll have time to write later.

Peace

Two weeks had passed and I hadn't heard anything from the contest, I guess I wasn't chosen. I tried not to sweat it but I was bothered. Charles did his best to cheer me up over the phone.

"Poopie, that was just one contest, there will be others."

"I know but I really thought I had a shot. I thought my story was good."

"It was good, that's their loss. You are a wonderful writer, just keep at it."

"It's easier said than done baby." I replied.

"Why don't you start your own company, publish your own work."

"I don't know, maybe my writing isn't as good as I thought."

"Stop talking crazy, look I'm bout to go into the locker room. I call you right after the game. I hope you feel better, I love you."

"Alright, I love you too."

What Charles was saying sounded good but it didn't help. I felt like a failure. Maybe all I was good at was being a football wife.

"I feel like shit." I said aloud to myself.

The day passed by in slow motion. Nothing anyone did or said could break me from my blue funk. I was so happy when 9:00 pm came so I could put the kids in the bed and put my head under the covers and go to bed. I had already talked to Charles after his game and the kids were in the bed, so sleep was calling. Maybe I could dream a better ending to the contest. When I came out of the bathroom from brushing my teeth Eric was in the room, I didn't expect that.

"Sonya what's wrong, you've been moping around all day?"

"Nothing Eric."

"It's something, what's up?" He asked.

Oh what the hell, I might as well tell him I figured.

"I'm just a little upset because I was feeling confident that I could win this short story contest I entered or at least be in

287

the top three but two weeks have passed and they said they would call within 10 days so I guess I wasn't selected."

"Short story contest, was it for a magazine?"

"Yeah, why?" I replied.

"I think they called last week. Matter of fact they said you were the unanimous choice and that they needed to talk to you before they could run the story in the magazine. So you can stop tripping."

"What! You are fucking lying, last week!"

"Yeah, why are you yelling?"

"So when were you gonna tell me?"

"I'm telling you now." He replied.

"A week later and you wouldn't have said nothing if I didn't mention it. You are so damn inconsiderate. That was important, now it might be too late."

"Oh well, how much was the grand prize, I'll give you the money. You act like this writing shit is your bread and butter!"

"Writing shit! Fuck you Eric, you don't get it. Every thing is about money to your ass. I swear I don't know why I've stayed with your ass this long."

"Because you got it better than most. You know why you ain't left and it ain't all about the kids. Keep it real, you don't want to be like your patnas. Bri's ass is too hard core to get a man, she might be border line lesbian. Alisha buries a nigga every year, or do you want a nigga to whoop your ass like Kim?"

"You know what Eric, I cannot do this shit anymore. You disrespecting my friend and family. You have a problem, you don't want me to have my shine because it makes you feel like less of a man, but tonight was the last draw."

"What you gonna do, leave," he yelled. And I very calmly answered.

"Yes, I'm leaving."

I got my Gucci duffel bag and began to pack all that I could fit in it. As I packed, Eric continued to cuss and yell.

"You ain't taking my kids nowhere."

288

I knew this, and as much as I loved my kids, I knew that I had to leave them for now. Training camp would begin in a couple of weeks, so he would be leaving anyway. He continued to yell and I continued to ignore him, which only made him more mad. After I finished packing I went in my kids room and kissed them before leaving. I hoped they would understand that this is for them. I had to break the chain of control that Eric had over me. As I left my home with tears in my eyes all I could visualize was when 'Sister' in the movie Sparkle moved out. That was one of the saddest scenes in the movie, and this was saddest scene of my life. I loaded my stuff in the car, got in and just sat there. I contemplated going back in the house. I didn't want to be viewed as a quitter.

"Dear Lord, I need you Father. I pray for forgiveness Father, I know I have sinned and I continue to, so maybe my circumstance is my punishment. I just pray that you give me strength to get through this and that you guide me. I pray that you watch over my babies while I'm away. I know I'm not worthy Lord, so I thank you, Amen."

With that I was strong enough to start the car up and drive off. I drove for about an hour with no distraction with Destiny Child's song "Free" on repeat. Then I drove to UC Berkeley campus where I met Eric. Next I drove to West Oakland and parked on the street where I grew up. I had come so far from that life, but sometimes I missed it. Those were good times back in the day. I remember sitting outside eating pickles with candy sticks in the middle, we would all fantasize about the fairytale lives we would have, and here it is. Sitting in my car crying I decided to call Charles.

"Hello." He answered sleepily.

"Hey Charles, I was just calling to let you know I left tonight."

"You left? What do you mean, why are you crying baby?"

"I mean I left, I left Eric, I left my house, I left my kids. I had to, am I a bad mother? I know I am a bad mother. I won the contest, they called, he didn't tell me, I left, I left." I cried as I talked so he probably couldn't make out what I was saying.

"Where are you now?"

"I'm in my car, parked in West Oakland, in front of my old house."

"Baby, it might not be safe down there, it's late. Why don't you go to Bri's house?"

"I'm alright, I'm about to go downtown and check into a hotel."

"You shouldn't be alone baby."

"I really don't feel like talking right now. I just wanted to let you know, I'll call tomorrow." I said and hung up.

I headed downtown to check in to the Marriott hotel. I called Bri because I knew Charles was gonna call her.

"Hello Sony."

"Hey Bri, are you on the phone with Charles?"

"Yeah on the other line."

"Did he tell you I left?"

"Yeah, he's worried about you, we're worried about you. Come to my house."

"Tell him I'm fine, I need to be alone. I'm pulling up at the hotel right now. You can tell the crew, but tell them not to call me tonight. I don't feel like talking."

"Are you sure you're ok?" Bri asked.

"No, but I'll get there. Bri, do you think I'm a bad mother?"

"Of course not, I think you are a wonderful mother. I also think you're a strong woman. It took a lot of courage to do what you did. You'll be alright and the kids are strong too, they take after their mom, they'll be alright."

"Thanks cuz, I love you and tell Charles I love him too. I'll talk to ya'll tomorrow."

By the time I got in my hotel room, my cell phone was blowing up. I know Bri told them hoes not to call me tonight. Oh well, they'll get the picture since I ain't answering.

Quarter 4
Chapter 22

"Who in the fuck has enough nerve to be calling me at 3:15 in the morning!" I said out loud as I knocked stuff off the hotel nightstand trying to locate my cell phone. The only light in the room was that of the clock. "Hello," I said in an angry tone not even looking at the caller I.D.

"I'm sorry for waking you Sony, I've been calling your house phone and Eric's cell phone and I couldn't get an answer." The person on the phone replied.

"Ms. Millie?"

"Yes baby, this is me." she said trying to hold back her crying."

"What's wrong Ms. Millie, is mom OK?" Ms. Millie was my mother-in-law's best friend.

"I wish I didn't have to make this call Sony, is Eric there with you?"

"No he's not, what is it!" I said in a hysterical voice. I'm now up out of the bed pacing the floor.

"She's gone Sony, my best friend, my sister. She passed away tonight."

All I could do is drop the phone and cry. How could this be, what happened? Was she sick? All of these questions I guess I needed to ask Millie. This had truly turned into the worst day of my life. I knew I had to pull myself together for Eric and the kids and for Millie. I wiped my nose on my T-shirt and picked the phone back up. Ms. Millie was still crying so hard that she probably didn't realize that I had dropped the phone.

"Ms. Millie" I said trying to get her attention

"Yes baby"

"What happened, where did it happen?" I asked confused.

"It's such a long story Sonya. She has been sick for a while, she was here at home when she passed."

"Are you at the house now?" I asked.

"Yes, I'm here, she's still here too. We have to wait on the funeral home to pick up the body and lord knows how long

291

that will take. Do you have a way to get in touch with Eric? Is he in town?" She asked me.

"Yeah, he's at the house. I'm at a hotel in Oakland. We had a big argument. I'll call him."

"I don't think he needs to be alone when you tell him." Millie replied.

"I know, you know my mom doesn't live to far from us. I'm going to call her to go over and then I'll tell him. She has a key to our house. Who's there with you?"

"Well, one of the police was kind enough to wait with me. He said he went to college with Eric."

"That was nice of him, I'll be there in about 20 minutes."

"Are you going to be OK to drive?" She asked me.

"Yes, I'll see you in a minute." Now, I have to get myself prepared to make this call, I guess I better talk to "the man" first.

"Father god, I know I've been talking to you all night, I hope you're not tired of me. I know I complain about Eric, but he doesn't deserve this. I know not to question you lord so forgive me because I can't help but to wonder why Barbara? I pray that she had a beautiful journey home and that she is at peace now. I also pray that you give me the strength of David to get through this and to be the support that Eric will need. Even in this time of sorrow lord, I thank you for our many blessings, Amen."

I knew my cell phone battery was getting low, so I decided to call my mother from the hotel phone to save my little bit of battery life.

Ring-ring-ring-ring

"Come on Ma, answer the phone." I said aloud. It was now 3:30
in the morning.

"Hello"

"Ma"

"Sony"

292

"Yes it's me, Ma I want to let you know I love you. I may not say it often enough but I want you to know that I love you and I appreciate everything you do for me." I said crying.

"What's wrong baby? Why are you calling from the Marriott Hotel in Oakland, it's 3:30 in the morning Sony."

"Me and Eric had a big fight and I left. I had to, it was that or lose my self respect."

"Are the kids with you?" she asked

"No, I left them but that's not why I'm calling. I just got a call from Ms. Millie, you know Barbara's friend."

"yeah"

"Ma, Barbara is dead!" I said crying

"What! What happened?"

"I don't have all the details, she was apparently sick. I'm on my way over there in a minute though"

"How's Eric doing?"

" That's why I'm calling you too, he doesn't know yet. I need you to go over my house because he's not answering the phone. Can you take dad with you so he can stay with kids and you can drive Eric out here. I'm sure he won't be in a state to drive."

"Do you want me to tell him?" my mother asked

"No I'll tell him. Call me when you get there. Thanks Ma, I love you." I said

"I love you to baby, are you Ok?"

"I gotta be." I said as I hung up the phone.

My mother filled my dad in on what happened and jumped up and threw on some sweats to go to my house. I was doing the same thing at the hotel, throwing on my sweats to head to Barbara's house. As I drove, I thought about all the times that she looked tired and sick. I wondered what was wrong with her. I wondered how long she knew and how come she didn't tell us. In between crying, I laughed at all the good times we had together, all of the advice she would give me. I thought about all of the times I cried on her shoulder over her son and times she would tell me to leave him, because it would teach him something. "I finally did it mom, but you were not suppose to leave him too." I said out loud talking to my mother-in-law's spirit. As I was pulling up to the house my cell phone began to ring.

"Hello, Ma"

"Yes, we're walking in your house now" my mother said over the phone. She said it seemed like he was awake in the family room because the T.V. was on.

"Eric" my mom called out his name so she wouldn't startle him coming in so late.

"Hey Ma and Pops" he said to my parents, looking surprised to see them there. "What's going on?' he asked them.

"I have Sony on the phone and she needs to talk to you." My mom said

"I don't mean any disrespect but I don't have nothing to say to her. She left us, her family so that's that! I'm sorry she got ya'll up in the middle of night for this" he said to my mom

"She, she- I have a name!" I was screaming through the phone. I have to take a deep breath before I forget why I'm calling.

"Eric this is not about you and Sony. You really need to get on the phone son." My dad said sternly.

My mom handed him her cell phone.

"Hello." he said and the lord instantly kicked in with that strength I prayed for.

"Eric."

"What Sonya!' he said with attitude but I remained calm.

"This is really hard fro me, and there's no easy way to say it......." I prolonged the story more by giving him the long version of Ms. Millie calling to wake me up before I dropped the bombshell. ".....Eric, baby" I paused to draw up all of the strength in my body. "Mom, died tonight"

A moment passed without him saying a word, I called his name to make sure he was still there.

"Mom who?" He asked, "not my mom." He said in a voice of denial.

"I'm sorry Eric, I'm so sorry" I said and then the next thing I heard was the phone dropping and the wails of a man who was on top of the world less than twenty-four hours ago and in a matter of one night, everything had come crashing down. I heard my mom comforting him in the background. My dad picked up the phone and let me know that they were taking care of him and that my mom and Eric would be on their way as soon as possible.

When I entered the house Millie and the officer was sitting in the family room. I thanked the officer for staying with her before he left. I hugged Ms. Millie for about five minutes, I knew this was going to be a long morning but I had to get the whole story before Eric got here.

"So, tell me from the beginning" I said to Ms. Millie. I could tell it was hard for her to tell me but after a few minutes she began. She told me that mom had, congested heart failure (CHF). She was diagnosed over a year ago but in the last couple of months it had gotten worse and her doctor declared her diagnosis End Stage Congested Heart Failure, which meant it became terminal. At this point I cut in on the story...

"I don't understand, if it was terminal, that means she knew she was dying. How come she didn't tell us?"

"Well in the beginning, she didn't want ya'll to worry and then Eric was having such a good season that she didn't want to ruin that. You know Barbara, she never wanted to be anybody's charity case and she said she was not about to start now. I wanted to tell you all but she made me promise. She felt it was the right thing and so I respected her wishes. I hope you understand."

I understood, but Eric would be a different story.

" I understand Millie. I'm so sorry that you had to carry that burden. I just want you to know that Eric might not understand and he may say some things that you know he really doesn't mean. His mother was his everything." I said.

"I'm not worried about Eric saying things, I've known that boy before he knew himself. If he gets to out of line, I'ma let him know. I'm not Barbara." She said.

"So, is she in the room?" I asked

"Yes, you want to go see her?"

I didn't know if I was ready to see her but I knew they would be picking her up soon. I nodded my head 'yes' and headed towards the room. Millie asked if I needed her to come with me but I was straight.

There she lay in her bed with the most peaceful look on her face. I kissed her forehead and sat next to her.

"Hey Mom, you know I'm mad at you. You know I've always kept your secrets, I still haven't told Eric you were dating that man from down the hill. No but really, I'm so sorry that you had to keep this to yourself. All because of that spoiled son of yours. I guess this is one way of making me stay with him, you know you ain't right." I said laughing. " I'm just playing, I know you will always be here with us and I will do my best to take care of your baby. I love you."

Just as I was finishing talking to her I heard Eric busting in the house screaming.

"Mama. Mama. Where are you, mama!" his cry was getting closer to the room. When he made it to the room he ran to her bedside and wrapped her up in his arms. "Wake up Mama, Please wake up. I need you Mama."

This was the hardest day of my life. I knew I had to do something to comfort him but what? What do you say to a person in this situation?

"Baby, come on let's walk out and get some air."

He didn't respond, he laid down next to his mother's body and held her. Then he asked if I could give him some time alone with her. I left the room and rejoined Ms. Millie and my mother in the family room. She was telling my mother how Barbara had called about 1:30 a.m. and said she wasn't feeling right. She said that she complained of her chest hurting and being really short of breath, at that point Millie said she told her to stay put and then she called 911 and rushed over.

296

Unfortunately by the time she and the ambulance arrived it was too late.

"I hate to admit, I had a bad feeling this time. That's why I tried calling your house on the way over here but there was no answer. It wasn't until I got here, that I was able to find you and Eric's cell numbers." She said to me

The funeral home arrived to pick up the body and of course all hell broke loose. Eric did not want to let go of his mother. He had gotten all the way in the bed with her and was holding on to her for dear life. The funeral home attendants were elderly men, so they were no match to Eric's weight. My mom, Millie and I tried to pull him away but he can bench press all of us put together, so that didn't work. Physical force was not going to work. I had to work on his mental. I asked the workers and my mom and Millie to give me a minute.

"Eric, baby you have to let these people do their job. Your mom is not right there, that is just a shell of a body, she is already with the lord. Baby, she went home, your mom raised you to be a Christian so you no better than others. She was tired and sick but now she's in a place were she can be at peace. Please let go baby, it's going to be alright. I promise."

Slowly he released her and got out of the bed. He sat down on the recliner chair in the corner of the room. It was obvious that he did not have the strength to move any further. I stood in front of him and hugged him and he buried his face in my stomach and cried. My mom looked in on us and I gave her the signal that it was OK for them to come get her body. Eric held up as they removed her from the house and drove off. As he watched the herse drive away the tears began to roll down his face although he tried to hold it together. Now he was looking for answers!

"So what happened Millie, how long had she been sick, how come I didn't know?" He fired off questions with attitude.

"Eric, your mom had End Stage Congested Heart Failure. She's been sick for over a year. At first she was just feeling tired all of the time. Soon after she start experiencing chest pains and shortness of breath. She went to the doctor and was diagnosed with Congested Heart Failure. A couple of months ago she was given a month to live but she continued to fight, you know your mom." Millie said with a sad laugh.

"Yeah, I do know my mom but what I don't know is why in the hell didn't I know that she was sick. Who gave you the right to keep this from me!" He yelled with rage at Millie.

"Calm down Eric" I said

"Oh no Sony, let his ass yell, because if you paid attention to your mama you would have known something" Millie replied

"What! I gave my mom attention, you know I took care of my mom. If you were any type of friend you would have told me so I could of done something."

"If I was a friend? Oh you could have done something. Boy you are a football player, not God. That's your problem but I'm not your mama or Sony. No disrespect Sony," she said to me. "You are questioning my friendship, well let me tell you that I am the same friend that cried with your mom when your daddy left her when she found out she was pregnant when we were only sixteen. I'm the same friend that scheduled my work schedule around hers so she had someone to watch you while she went to work because she couldn't afford childcare. See, I'm that friend, maybe you don't remember me and your mama selling everything short of pussy so that your spoiled ass could play Pop Warner football and go to every football camp in California. I may not be a lot of things but I have been a friend to your mother since we met in third grade. Friends are loyal even if we don't agree with it, that's why I didn't tell you because my friend asked me not to. You need to be thinking about why she didn't want you to know. My friend gave so much of her heart to so many people that her heart just couldn't take it anymore. You can be mad at me if you want Eric, I am sorry it happened this way but I'm going to be real with you. Your mom said that everybody from Sony and the kids to the mailman asked her about her health because they noticed something, but never you. Just a little advice, paying bills and giving money ain't always taking care of a person." She looked at me and back at Eric as if to give him a clue to get with it or he might be losing me, then she continued. "Alright, she entrusted her arrangements to Fuller Funeral Home. I told them we would be there at 1:00 pm. I'm going home to take a shower so I'll see you in a little while. Your mom wrote a letter for you when they told her she was dying, it's in her top dresser drawer."

Eric just sat in silence. Millie had read him good and sadly it was all true. That's how Millie is a straight shooter, no sugar coat, but it's always all love. She hugged us all, even Eric and then she left. I told Eric that we needed to get home and tell the kids. I'm sure they were wondering why they were home from school today. We both needed to shower and get back to Oakland before 1:00. He agreed but he wanted to get the letter that Millie had mentioned first. I didn't want for him to have to go back into his mother's room and break down again so I told him I would get it while him and my mom made small talk. I got the letter and then we all left.

We rode home in silence; the radio wasn't even on. I wondered if he was thinking about the things that Millie said. When we pulled up at the house he turned to me and said...

"Sonya, I don't know if I can do this. I need you to tell the kids."

I NEED YOU, rang in my ears. How can I leave him, he's going to need me more than ever now.

"Don't worry Eric, I got it." I replied
"Sonya, about last night" Eric started to talk before I cut him off.
"You know what, it's not important right now" I said.

My mom pulled up behind us, she was picking my dad and the kids up to take them back to their house after we told them the bad news. My dad had gotten the kids dressed and they were sitting in the family room watching the Disney channel. When we walked in, my dad got up and walked out the room.

"Daddy, what's wrong? Have you been crying?" Kayla asked Eric.

"Yes, Princess I have. Mommy has something she needs to tell you"

I took a deep breath and cleared my throat.

"You guys know that everything that lives must die someday, right"

They all nodded their heads yes, even E.J. I went on...

" Well when we die, we get to go to heaven and be with God"

" Like Auntie Alisha's boyfriend?" Kayla asked

"Yes, like Alisha's boyfriend. In the beginning it's really sad because we can't see and touch that person but we still always have that person with us in our heart. This is hard for Mommy to tell you......

Chapter 23

The funeral was beautiful. It always sounds strange for people to say that about a funeral but it really was. You know how sometimes you go to a funeral and the person in the casket doesn't look like the person you knew, well Barbara looked like herself and she looked beautiful. Eric had really been holding up over the past week. This morning before the funeral he apologized to Millie for how he acted on the day his mom died. He then asked her if she would move into his mother's house that way he would still have a mom there. Millie said she would be honored. Eric learned so much about his mother at her funeral. Everyone spoke about all of her good deeds and all of the people that she has helped. Most of the stories and events Eric had never heard about. Then a man walked up to the podium who for some reason looked very familiar, but I couldn't figure from where. He was trying very hard to hold back his tears as he began to talk.

"Me and B, that's what I called her, grew up together. We met in Junior High."

As he spoke, I could feel Eric's grip tighten on my hand.

"She is probably one of the strongest people I know. I just came here to say sorry that you had to struggle when I wasn't man enough to do my part. You raised a wonderful son without me and I know he'll be alright."

My mouth dropped wide open. That was Eric's daddy. No wonder why he looked so familiar. Eric had no expression on his face; to him, his father didn't exist. I on the other hand was different, I believed in change and forgiveness. I'm gonna Millie get his number for me. I had never met him in all my years of being with Eric but I had heard stories from Barbara, good and bad. Meeting him would probably answer a lot of questions of why Eric acts the way he does, because it sure isn't from his mom.

Kim sang "Amazing Grace" and "Precious Lord" and of course that made everyone cry. By request everyone exited before the family had their final viewing of the body. It was hard

301

for Eric when they closed the casket but he kept it together for the children. She was buried at Rolling Hills cemetery in Richmond. After the burial everyone went to Barbara's house, her church had prepared a ton of food. All of my family was there, over the years my family had become Eric's and Barbara's family because most of their family was on the East coast. It had been a week since Barbara's death and Eric had still not read the letter she wrote him. Alisha did not do well at the funeral, although she was happy with Jason, Barbara was buried at the same cemetery as Taiwan and that brought back memories, she also was still mourning Rock, her second chance at love. Speaking of love, I had only talked to Charles about three times in the past week. I told him what happened so I know he understands but I also know his emotions are a wreck. The last time I talked to him before this happened was to tell him that I was leaving Eric. Now this changes everything, no doubt I'm in love with Charles but I still love Eric and he needs me. How could I leave him at a time like this, when I'm all he has. I am so consumed with everything that's going on, I haven't had good sleep in weeks. I have to be strong for everyone. The sad part is, Charles is the only person that has mastered relieving my stress but I feel to guilty to lean on him in this situation. I know that time will pass and Eric and I will have to deal with our problems. I just don't know how I will handle them. Will I have to suck it up and just grin and bare it for the rest of my life or will I stick with my plans and leave. Maybe everything that has happened will make Eric change but will it be too late. Right now I feel love and sympathy for him but by no means am I back in love with him.

Everyone had left except Eric's best friends and my crew. The men were all in the family room watching basketball and Alisha, Bri, Kim and Mya were helping me clean up. My parents took the kid's home with them. I went to ask the guys if they wanted more food before we put it away and I walked in on the craziest shit. Due to everything going on I had lost track of Charles' game schedule but I found out they were playing tonight. When I walked in the family room I heard Eric's voice saying,

"Hit that shit C. Knight, that's money! That nigga is playing good this year."
I damn there choked, here Eric was rooting for the man that was in love with his wife. Shit, damn some love he was rooting for the man that was fucking his wife. I tried my best not to focus on the game but I was concerned with how his game was going.

"Hey do you guys want anything else to eat or drink?" I asked.

"We're cool" they all replied.

I definitely wasn't cool, I needed a drink, a stiff one! Of course now I was thinking about Charles. I knew he was playing so I decided to call and leave him a message. I told Bri to cover for me so I could duck in the bathroom to make the call.

"Hey baby, this is me. I was just calling to tell you I'm thinking about you and to thank you for being you. Thanks for being patient; I love you. Bye."

Everyone started to disperse because they had to work tomorrow. Bri hung with me because Mike was still there hanging with Eric watching the game. Mike had a new job that he had started but he didn't have to work tomorrow.

"Sony, ya'll come in here and watch the game with us." Eric yelled from the family room.

Bri and I just looked at each other. What could I do, say I didn't want to watch the game. Eric new better than anyone how much I loved sports, so that would not work. I really didn't have a choice, I had avoided watching basketball with him for all this time but I knew this day would come. Give thanks that Bri was here with me. A win tonight for Charles' team would mean that they would be heading to the Eastern Conference Finals. I was so excited for him but I had to sit here and watch the game as if I could care less.

After the game we all got ready to leave. I thanked Bri and Mike for being here and gave them hugs. When I hugged Bri, I whispered in her ear,

"Bri, I need you to call Charles and tell him congratulations on the win. Tell him I miss him and I love him. Tell him I'll call him tomorrow. Can you do that, Bri?"

"No problem cuz." She replied.

The ride home was long and awkward. Now that the funeral was over, that would alleviate all of the distractions we've had over the past week and now we would have time to focus on our problems. We both knew we had said things that could never be taken back but we didn't know what our next step would be. When we pulled up at the house Eric looked at me and said..

"Sonya, I'm sorry for everything. I just want to thank you for always looking out for my moms."

"It's nothing." I said smiling."

I was so tired, I just wanted to take a shower and fall right to sleep. When I walked out of the bathroom in my towel, Eric had gotten undressed and was sitting on our bed.

"I'm ready Sonya."

You ready, ready for what? I thought to myself. I know he doesn't think that he is about to get some because that is not going down. My thoughts must have been displayed across my face because he started cracking up laughing.

"What?" I asked.

"I ain't talking about that! I'm ready to read the letter from my mom but I want you to read it to me."

"Are you sure?"

"Yeah I'm sure," he said as he handed me the letter.

I put the letter on the bed while I put on my nightclothes and then I sat next to Eric and opened the envelope. The letter read......

Dearest Eric,

Son, I got some bad news today. My doctor told me I have less than month to live. If you are reading this letter it must mean that I have passed on, I'm giving Millie instructions to give it to you after I pass. Now that I'm gone, please don't be mad at Millie. That woman has kept my secrets all of our life and I knew this one wouldn't be any different. Right now you are getting ready for the playoffs, so I am going to fight this thing with all my might because I would hate you to have to deal with my dying during the season. Eric, I want you to know that I did my best raising you but I am all woman and there are some things I couldn't give you, things you needed to learn from a man. Now that I am gone, there are a few things that I should have told you in life but now I'll tell you in death.

Eric there are a couple of reasons that I was OK with knowing I was dying, #1 is because I am a child of God, so I know that I am going home. #2, is a woman by the name of Sonya Brown Jackson. I know that you will be OK because of her, but it it's time for you to make some changes. Sonya is your blessing and you have not treated her that way. That girl has loved and supported you from day one and you have taking her for granted. I'm sure she's tired and don't get it twisted, she will leave you. Try to think about her and her dreams. She is such a beautiful and talented woman, I keep telling her she needs to write a book. Have you read any of her writing? Well anyway, the next thing is stop spoiling them kids. I know first hand about spoiled kids, I spoiled you. I'm not saying don't reward them for doing well but don't give them more than they need. Teach them the value of money and hard work. Now, don't think this letter is all about getting on you. I also want to tell you that you are a wonderful son. You made my life so full of excitement, good times and definitely love. You made it possible for me to help so many people. I remember when you didn't make the Varsity football team and you worked your butt off to prove them coach's wrong and I guess you did. I have always admired your will and work ethic. So, now that I'm gone you are going to have to draw on that same will to keep it going, to take care of Sonya and the kids and to take care of Millie. Know that I will be with you always. If all goes as I plan this letter won't reach you until after the Super Bowl, which I'm hoping you will win. I will have the best seat in the house next season. I might even be able to call in a favor from the big man if ya'll get in a tight game, that's a joke! OK, I'm getting tired and I have to take my meds. I'm

305

sorry for not telling you. Kiss my babies and Sonya, but if I know my son like I think I do, you probably have Sonya reading the letter anyway. So Sonya, kiss my son for me. Keep Jesus first and I will see you again.

Love,
Mom

p.s. Think about calling your dad, Millie has his information. We have all made mistakes, I made the mistake of passing my bitterness onto you. It's not to late for you guys.

When I finished reading the letter I kissed Eric on his forehead like the letter instructed me to do. Eric had tears rolling down his face as he looked off into space. I wish I could take away his hurt but I couldn't so I had to do the only thing that I knew would bring him pleasure if only for a while. Although I told myself that I would never sleep with him again, I really didn't know any other way to comfort him. He needed me.
Eric made love to my body like he knew it might be the last time. He didn't miss a spot, he kissed and carressed every part of my being before he entered my zone. On the normal, I probably would have been climbing the walls but tonight I was in another place. After twenty minutes of making love to a numb body, he finally came. He must could tell that I wasn't there because he continuously whispered, "I'm sorry" as his body made convulsions and his semen entered my body, he promised to be a better person. I didn't respond but I cried silently. I can't believe this mess I've gotten myself into. Here I am feeling guilty for making love to my husband. I promised Charles and myself and I broke it. Now Eric is going to try to make this relationship work, when I've finally gotten to the point where I was strong enough to leave. I am so confused…..

Dear Journal,

It's been a while. Eric is picking up the kids do I decided to write. I finally got the courage to leave him, but then my mother-in-law passed away. So that let's you know how I'm doing. On top of all that, I made love to Eric when I said I would not do that anymore. I lied to 'C' and I don't know what's going to happen between me and him now. I have to tell him, I can't lie to him. Is everything that's happening a sign or something? Am I supposed to stay with Eric? I am so confused, I haven't been eating, I've lost ten pounds. I am stressed out and I need help!

After I journaled, I got up and got dressed. I called Eric on his cell phone and told him I was going to run some errands. I first went to the post office to check my P.O. Box. There was a card there from Charles that read, "take all the time you need, I'll be here. Love, Charles." He is such a caring man, even amidst his hectic schedule, he was still thinking of me. After leaving the post office I went to Starbucks to get me a Caramel Machiato and sat in the car to call Charles.

"Hello"

"Hey Charles"

"Hey Poopie, how are you doing?"

"I'm surviving. Did Bri call you last night?"

"Yes, she did. I was happy to know you were thinking of me. I got your message too"

"That's good" I said very dry.

We both just sat on the phone in silence. I was quiet because I felt bad about what I did last night. I was contemplating if I should tell him. I'm sure he was quiet because he was wondering how Eric's mom passing would affect us.

"So when do the Finals start? I asked.

"They start on Friday"

"I'm so happy for you Charles"

307

"Thanks Poopie." he replied
"Oh, I got your card, thank you."
"No problem"
"I guess I'll talk to you later" I said
"Alright Sony, I love you"
"I love you too." I said crying, "Bye."

Charles heard me crying, he wanted to ask what was wrong but he was scared. He had the feeling that I was caught between him and Eric and he knew that due to what happened Eric had a slight edge. He knew it, but he didn't want to hear it, so he decided to let it play out.

The next few days were the same. I was dry with Eric at home and dry with Charles over the phone. I had finally had an emotional melt down. No matter what my friends would do, it could not pick my spirits up. I tried my best to act in front of my kids but they even knew that something was wrong. I decided that I had to tell Charles about sleeping with Eric. At least it might ease some of my guilt. First thing in the morning I would call.

The next day came and Eric got up to take the kids to school. As soon as he left, I popped up to call Charles. I wasn't thinking at time that it was Friday, the first day of the Eastern Conference Finals. I was just thinking about getting this heavy load off of my chest. Charles answered his phone on the first ring...

"Hey Poopie, are you coming from taking the kids to school?"

"No, Eric took them this morning. Charles this is really hard so I guess I just have to say it, we promised to always be honest, so this has been killing me for the past couple of days." I breathed heavily into the phone and then continued on. "I had sex with Eric."

"On the night of the funeral?" He calmly asked in response.

"Yeah, how did you know?"

308

"I could tell when you started crying the day after when we talked on the phone. Didn't you wonder why I didn't ask why you were crying. I knew, I just didn't want to know. I'm not going to act like I'm not hurt but given the situation, I understand. Sony, regardless of how I feel for you, he is still your husband."

"I can't do this Charles."

"What do you mean Sony?"

"I'm confused. I was set to leave him and then this happened. I know that I love you but this is not fair to you. I have become a person that I don't like. I have to lie and sneak, I can't do it any more. I'm sorry." I said before I hung up the phone.

I turned my phone off and decided to keep it off for the next few days. I knew Charles couldn't pop up out here because of the Finals. I felt bad about dropping this bomb on him today when he has a game to play but it will be better for him in the long run.

After a couple of days, Charles tried calling Bri to pass a message but I wasn't fooling with my girls either. Don't think that cutting it off with Charles meant it was cool with Eric because we were in the same house and I bareley talked to him. For the first time in my life I gave up. I just didn't have it in me anymore. I couldn't get the kids ready for school, I couldn't cook, I couldn't do anything. The only thing I did was shower and get back in the bed.

It seemed like I was in this dead state forever but in actuality it had only been a few days. I broke it off with Charles on Friday and it was Tuesday when my mom came to attempt to bring me back to life. Eric had taken the kids to school and my mom instructed him to stay out of the house for longer than usual.

"Sonya Brown" my mother yelled as she approached my room.

Oh lord, I'm really not trying to argue with my mama but I know it's gonna happen.

"Sonya, what is your problem child?" She said as she entered the room.

"Good morning to you too, Ma" I said sarcastically.

"Well it doesn't look so good from where I'm standing!" My mother is a woman that says whatever she feels, no sugar coat. You have to respect her honesty even if she was clowning you.

"What's wrong with you baby?" she asked as she sat next to me on my bed. At that moment I felt like a five year old that had fallen off of her bike and needed her mama to kiss her boo-boo to make it better. Off course I started crying.

"Mommy, I'm tired." I said crying. "I always have to be the strong one but I'm weak, I can't do it anymore. This is the life that I prayed for. I prayed to God to get me out of the street life. I prayed for a hard working legitimate man and a family. I have that but I'm not happy. I don't even know what would make me happy."

"Stop crying Sony. Yes, you are the strong one. You've always been that way even as a child but even strong people have weak moments. You can and will get through this."

"I can't Ma"

"Let me read something to you, it's a letter I got on July 2nd, 1981,

> *Dear Mom,*
>
> *Why do you cry all of the time? Did I do something, I'm sorry if I did. I promise I will keep my room clean and eat my green peas. I won't argue with my brothers and sister too. You are so pretty, I hate when you're sad, so please be happy.*
>
> *Love*
> *Sony*

You wrote this letter when you were six years old. You have a seven year old, and an eleven year old a nine year old and a three year old, and they know that something ain't right with

310

their mama. When I got this letter, it felt far worst than the pain I was feeling because your father had cheated on me. It also made me get strong because you kids were my everything, and you still are, that's why it hurts me to death to see you hurting. You have to get up and get back in the swing of things for my grandbabies. You don't want to get one of these letters."

I knew my mother was right

"Ma, why do you hang on to them old letters?" I asked laughing.

"Get up, take a shower and unwrap that hair!" She demanded.

"I took a shower!"

"Well get dressed then. Your children would love to see you pick them up from school today. Your dad and I are gonna take them to Fresno to see your brothers new house this weekend, Eric planned a weekend getaway for ya'll to Monterey."

"No, I don't want to.." I started to say before my mom interupted me.

"Look Sony, I know about your friend on the side." She said.

"What are you talking about?" I replied acting dumb founded.

"Look girl, you are my child. I know the game, I wrote the book. It ain't that many conferences, and getaways with just you and Bri. I've been there, plus he looked good in that Armani suit I picked out, at the ESPY's. That night I realized that my daughter was a real player!" She said laughing.

"Hey, have you been creeping on my daddy, talking about you wrote the book." I said joining her in laughter.

"Girl, shut up!" She replied.

It felt so good to be laughing.

"Ma, I love him, he's a good guy. His name is Charles Knight. I wish you could meet him."

"Honey, I know his name, he plays in the NBA. You couldn't find a man in a different profession."

"That's why I don't want to go away with Eric. Eric and I haven't been together like that, in I don't know how long. He has done too many things that I can't forgive and surely won't forget."

"I understand that but you've probably given up on trying. He's trying to change, I think he gets it now. Just go away for the weekend, you and him in a different environment. Then if you still feel the same way, you need to leave. You aren't doing any good to yourself or him or the kids if you stay out of pity and your heart isn't in it."

"Thanks Ma, I guess your right."

"You guess, I know!" She replied.

After my mother left, I decided to get up and take another shower. I had to call my girls and let them know I was back, I knew I had plenty of gossip to catch up on. I was scared to walk out of my room, I knew the house would be a wreck. To my surprise, the house was spotless, maybe he was trying to change. There was ground turkey in the refrigerator so I whipped up a batch of spaghetti for dinner. Eric and E.J. returned. They had been to Stoneridge Mall. The sight of me when he walked through the door brought an instant smile to his face. That afternoon I picked my kids up from school and I could tell they were overjoyed. They all competed to share the details of their school day. They overtalked each other, which on a normal would drive me crazy but today I was loving every minute of it. That night I enjoyed the dinner I prepared with my family, I helped my children with their homework, I bathed E.J. and then at 9:00pm I tucked them all in to bed.

I talked to my girls and they all treated me like I was fragile. It was funny to me but I let it ride out. I wasn't ready to be burdened with all of their problems yet anyway so if they thought I was stressed out it was better for me. Mya invited me over to her house for dinner tomorrow, so I accepted.

The next morning I rode with Eric to take the kids to school. He told me about the trip to Monterey and I acted surprised. Eric was going to get the kids fast food for the night since I told him I was going to Mya's for dinner. I got to Mya's house around 5:30pm. When I walked in, she was watching the basketball game. New Jersey was playing and getting their ass wooped! I hadn't talked to Charles, I figured I wait until after the weekend. I hadn't even been keeping up with the finals but now I was seeing that this was a must win game for them or they would be eliminated. It wasn't looking good for them. Mya brought our food out to the living room and we watched TV as we ate. She cooked fish, french fries and salad.

"Girl, New Jersey is getting wooped" Mya said.

"Yeah, they are." I replied.

"Look at that nigga Charles Knight, they hype him up and he ain't doing nothing."

OK, you know I was immediately on the defense but I had to keep my cool.

"Girl, remember he was trying to holler at you at Essence, his ass seemed shady to me. He made it to the Finals and now he is choking, and to think people compared him to Jordan. He is hella weak!" She said.

I had heard enough; I couldn't take it anymore.

"Why you always hating on somebody. Damn, maybe he's going through something!" I exploded.

"Damn nigga, you act like he's your man!" She replied.

"Maybe he is, or at least was." I said. Fuck it, I didn't care anymore. I couldn't let her dog him out. I was probably the reason his game was off anyway.

"What did you say?"

"You heard me." I said calming down some. "We remained friends after we met at Essence and we have been together for over a year." I replied

"Together, what do you mean together? You are married."

"Really, me and Eric ain't been together for a while. Did you forget I left him and if it wasn't for Barbara passing I would still be gone."

"Well now that she is dead, what are you gonna do? You know Eric needs you."

"I know, I don't know yet." I replied.

"So who else knows, Bri?"

"Nobody knows." I lied because I would never hear the end of it if I told her the truth.

"I am so mad at you, I can't believe you kept this from me. What kind of sister are you?"

"I'm sorry, I couldn't risk telling anyone. This has to stay between us." I said.

"Come on now Sony, I'm your big sister. I have your back, I'm just sorry you had to carry this for so long by yourself. So what's going on with ya'll now?"

I went on to tell her about our relationship from beginning to end of course leaving out parts that Bri was involved in. When I finished talking it was 8:30pm. I called my house to tell the kids good night and to tell Eric I would be on my way. Normally, I would catch attitude from him but he was way cool. During Mya and my conversation, I witnessed Charles' team get eliminated from the Finals. I wanted so bad to call him but I felt it was best to wait until after the weekend.

The next couple of days flew by and Friday had arrived. My mom picked the kids up last night because they were heading out early this morning. Eric was so anxious. He continued to remind me that we were heading out at 2:30pm. He didn't want anything to ruin this weekend, not even traffic so he was stern about our departure time. I knew he was excited about the possibility of getting some this weekend. I had a few errands to run but I finished up by 2:00pm. I was all packed and ready to go but Eric had to take a dump before we hit the road. I sat downstairs in the family room and watched General Hospital while I waited on him. My cell phone rang; it was an unfamiliar number.

"Hello"

"Hello Sonya"

It sounded like Charles, but it was a Bay Area phone number.

"Hello" I repeated.

"Poopie, I need you to come meet me at the Claremont Hotel, I'm in room 610."

"Charles, I can't. I'm about to go out of town."

"I came all the way out here to talk to you. If you ever loved me, just give me ten minutes."

"I do love you but…"

"Ten minutes Poopie, please." He interupted me.

"Ok give me twenty minutes to get there."

I had to think of a story quick. I ran upstairs to tell Eric some drama.

"Eric, we have to push our take off time back to 3:30"

"Why?" He replied.

"I just talked to Mya, something happened to her at work, I have to go meet her. It won't be long, I promise."

"Alright Sonya, 3:30pm, no later." He replied.

"OK I'll be back, and you need to burn some candles. You are blowing it up in there." I said referring to the damage he was doing in the bathroom.

I called Mya to tell her the deal and to ask her to cover for me. I got to Berkeley in fifteen minutes. I was flying on the freeway. When I got to Charles' room, the door was open and he was on the phone ordering room service. I thought I looked bad the other day, but he looked like hell! When he hung up the phone he hugged me and held me like he knew the end was coming. For a few minutes we didn't say a word, we both just looked at each other with tears in our eyes. Our silence spoke volumes. Charles eventually broke the silence.

"I haven't slept in days, I can barely eat."

"I'm sorry Charles, I'm sorry for the Finals and for everything."

"That's nothing Sonya, I need answers. Is it over for us?" I knew I didn't want it to be but I didn't have a choice. I was doing him no good. I tried my best to explain to him how his life would be better without me.

Meanwhile Eric was bored at home so he decided to call Mike.

"What up Mike, you want to get in a game of Madden?" Eric asked

"I can't I'm at work" Mike replied.

"I thought you quit your job."

"I got a new one, it's cool too." He replied.

"So what are you doing now?" Eric asked.

"I work the Concierge desk at the Claremont Hotel in Berkeley."

"Nigga, you'll probably quit that job next week. You might as well come play Madden with your patna."

"Nah, this one is cool. All type of people fall through here. I had only been up here to got to the 'Paragon Lounge', but the hotel is plush. Charles Knight just checked in here today, looking rough. He must be taking that loss bad. Matter of fact, I just saw Sony walk through the lobby but I couldn't catch her, she seemed to be in a rush."

"Sony who?"

"Your Sony, Bony Sony"

"Really, did you see Mya?"

"No, maybe she was rushing to meet her." Mike responded.

"Alright then nigga, I'll let you get back to work. Peace."

In the midst of Charles and my conversation, my phone rang. It was Eric, so I let it go to voicemail. He called back three times and I did the same.

"Why ain't she answering her phone! Let me try Mya's phone." Eric said out loud to himself.

"Hello" Mya answered her phone.

"Mya, is Sonya with you?" Eric asked.

"Eric?" Mya replied.

"Yeah!"

"What are you talking about?" Mya said.

"Don't fucking play with me Mya, is Sonya with you are not?"

"Don't cuss at me, I ain't in ya'll drama!"

"What does that mean? Is my wife with you?"

"NO!" was the last thing Mya said before Eric hung up on her.

"Charles you know I love you but we can't do it this way. I have to close the door with Eric first, if we want for us to work. I don't know how easy that will be, so much has changed." I said.

"What do you mean, has your love for me changed?" He replied.

"No, but it's more to it. It's hard for me to explain but I know we can't be together right now." I said.

"Nigga what you doing up here?" Mike said to Eric.

"I need Charles Knight's room number."

On the drive to the Claremont Hotel, Eric replayed all of the signs that he missed over the past year. That's why she stopped fucking me, that's why she was awkward at the ESPY's and he was hella short with me when we met. All of the little trips here and there it all made since now.

"What do you need his room number for? Mike asked.

"You know that we are patna's, we met at the ESPY's." Eric tried to convince Mike but Mike wasn't buying it.

"Then why don't you call him and get his room number." Mike replied.

"Nigga just give me the room number!"

"Damn, I should have just came to play Madden with you. He's in room 610, I hope you ain't about to do nothing stupid." Mike said.

I knew I had to get up and leave. The longer I stayed the harder it would be to go. I looked at the clock, it was 3:15 and I told Eric we would leave at 3:30.

"I'm sorry Charles, I have to go."

>KNOCK, KNOCK, KNOCK, KNOCK<

"Hold up for a minute Sonya, let me get this room service. I just want one more hug, one more kiss before you leave."

I guess I owed him that. Oddly, I didn't get that normal nervous feeling I get whenever room service arrived today. Charles opened the door and turned to walk back into the room without even looking at who was entering. In a split second I thought to myself, damn I should have got rid of that gun when Eric asked me to. As I saw the pearl handle of my gun, I heard...

>POP POP POP <

I tried opening my eyes but the bright light made it hard. "Am I dead? Is it to late to ask for forgiveness Lord?" My eyes were slowly getting adjusted to the light in the room. I began to be able to make some things out. I was in an unfamiliar place. I scanned the room for a sign or something. I raised my arm and read the hospital wristband that I was wearing.

"Sonya Jackson, Alameda County Medical Center. Oh Shit! I might not be dead but I'm definitely shot!" I said aloud.

I was at Highland Hospital, the county hospital. The place you don't go if you have a common cold because you'll be waiting all day but if you get shot, that's the place to be. They had the best Trauma Center in the Bay Area. My eyes began to blur again, not from the light but from the tears. All I remembered was seeing the pearl handle thirty-eight caliber hand gun that my dad bought me for my 21st birthday, and then came the gun shots.

"Lord forgive me, I know I have sinned. Even in my predicament I thank you for my many blessings. I may be shot but I'm alive. I just pray that no one else is hurt. Amen."

As I finished praying, I heard noises in the room. I looked around and noticed a nurse in the room.

"Hello Mrs. Jackson, I'm Carol your nurse. I hate to invade your prayers, I heard you say that you were shot but baby you weren't shot."

For a second, I got excited. Then I realized if I wasn't the recipient of the bullets then Charles was. I started to hyperventilate. The nurse tried to calm me down, she warned me that I might slip back into the shock coma that I had been in for the past eight days.

"You weren't shot, but you were involved in a high profile shooting. The police will want to talk to you now that your awake but I'll give you some time. Your family and friends have been alternating shifts. I believe someone named Kim is out there now. Would you like to see her?"

"Yes, please." I replied. I wanted to ask her about Charles but I was scared to hear the answer. I knew I was the

319

cause of him being shot or even worse, killed. I felt bad that I was OK. Then I realized that Eric must be on the run or in jail, either way, my kids had to be going through hell. I had to get out of here!

"Good morning sunshine" Kim said as she entered the room.

"Hey Kim, thanks for being here" I said in a froggy voice.

"No problem, how do you feel?"

"Like shit mentally, physically, I guess I'm alright. Who has my children?"

"There still in Fresno with your brother."

"Where's Eric?"

"He's in jail, they wouldn't let him bail out."

" I need to get out of here."

"They'll probably let you go home tomorrow." Kim responded.

"No, I need to get out of here now. Is there any police out there?"

"Not right now." Kim replied

"Good, do I have clothes here?"

"Yeah, but you are tripping!"

"Give me your keys. Where did you park?"

"On the street by Emergency, I'm in a blue rental."

"Alright distract the nurse for a few minutes while I get dressed, and then meet me at your car."

"You are crazy Sony! God please forgive me for taking part in this." Kim said as she exited the room.

"Bitch, this fucking car can't go any faster! Where's your car?"

"Well when I rented it, I didn't plan on using it as a getaway car. I got the $9.99 Enterprise special. Ray's crazy sister put sugar in my tank because she saw me on a date."

"You went on a date? Well anyway, bitch I need to get to Alameda County Jail-Santa Rita quick. Can you turn that damn music down, I'm trying to figure some shit out."

"Firstly, call me one more bitch and I'm taking you back to the Highland hospital. Matter of fact, I'll take you right to the police station. Secondly, visiting days are on Thursday and Sunday, so we are wasting our time. And, last of all, this is my theme music so, no I can't turn it down. Mary J. Blige be trying to school you sisters, so figure that shit out!"

"Nigga, is 'firstly' a word?"

"Oh, now the sinning, hospital fugitive want to be educated."

"Why is it so much traffic on 580 on a Saturday"

"I think the A's have a game, something called the Bay Battle."

"It's called the 'Battle of the Bay,' it's when the A's play the Giants. I completely forgot due to fact I've been sleep for a week."

"I knew you would know about that sports shit, it seems like that's what got you into trouble. Do you have a baseball player too?"

"That's fucked up Kim." I responded.

"Well since we're stuck in traffic, how in the hell did you get yourself into this mess?"

"Kim, it's a long story but it all started at the Essence Festival………..

Epilogue – "Overtime"

    I sat in the car for twenty minutes trying to build up the courage to go in. A hour earlier I received a call from Shanae, Shanae was a C.N.A. (certified nursing assistant) in the Spinal Rehab department at Eden Medical Center. Bri introduced us, since Bri was handling Shanae's husbands case "pro bono" Shanae kept me up on Charles' condition. When she called this morning she let me know that he would be leaving the hospital tomorrow and would be trasnsferred to a facility in New Jersey near his home. His mom and sister left today to get things set up for him out there. She said that the only person that was still out here was his big mouth friend, I knew she had to be talking about Greg. I really wasn't feeling seeing him right now but this might be my last chance to see Charles. I needed to at least apologize. My thoughts were interrupted by my cell phone ringing.

    "Hello"

    "Hey Sony, this is Shanae. I was just calling to let you know that if you're coming up here, now would be a good time. His friend is about to go run some errands."

    "Really, thanks girl, I'm actually in the hospital parking lot right now." I responded

    "Sony, there might be one problem. He has a visitation list and due to the fact of his fame, the employees don't even have access to it. They have private security that handles the visitation"

    "OK Shanae, I guess I'll see when I get in there. Thanks again."

    I hung up the phone, took a deep breath, and said silent prayer. "Father forgive me, please forgive me for my sins and forgive me for all the people who have been hurt from them. Thank you for having mercy on me and continuing to bless me, I know I am not worthy. Amen"

    OK Sony let's do this!

"Excuse me ma'am, can you tell me where to find the spinal rehab department?" I asked the elderly lady working the information desk.

"Go to the left, down the hall and take the elevator up to the 4th floor. When you exit the elevator you will see signs you can follow, it will be to your right. Oh, but if you're trying to get a peak at that basketball player he's under security."

See now this old ass lady is giving me information that I didn't ask for, what do I look like a groupie? "Thank you for your help," I replied to her.

Entering the elevator I started getting butterflies like the first day of a new job. Just when I considered getting off the elevator and going back home, a group of people got on and pressed the 4th floor. Now I was stuck in the back of the elevator and there was no turning back. For all I know I might not be on the visitors list and then at least I feel like I made the attempt. The ride to the 4th floor was quick! As the lady stated the rehab center was to the right. I stopped at the nurse's station....

"Hi, I'm here to visit Charles Knight" I said. Without saying a word the nurse pointed to a security post, where there stood a D-Bo Tiny Lister look alike. From the way he looked, I knew if my name wasn't on the list, I definitely wasn't getting in to visit.

"Good afternoon, I'm here ..." that's all I got out before D-Bo replied with attitude.

"Is your name on the list?"

Although I wasn't sure, I had to act like I belonged because the toy cop was really annoying me. Why do security guards always have big attitude? I'm sorry you didn't make it through the Police Academy. I reached in my purse and just handed him my I.D. He looked at my name, then he looked at the papers in front of him, the look of defeat on his face let me know my name was on the list. So now he was fucking with me, he studied my picture and then looked at me and said,

"So Ms. Jackson, you let your hair grow out, it looks good."

"I'm sorry what is it," I said looking at his nametag, "Mr. Fort, I would love to share my beauty tips with you but right now I would like to see my friend. By the way it's Mrs. Jackson, now which room did you say?"

He responded, "422." They had a whole wing of the 4th floor shut down for one room being occupied. I flashed back to when we met and the suite he occupied at the Wyndham at the Essence Festival, a whole bunch of space just for him. The butterflies that had disappeared during the conversation with security guard were back as I prepared myself to enter the room. I hadn't seen or talked to Charles since that day. Months had passed and I still wake up daily hoping that it was all a terrible nightmare. When I walked in the room it appeared as if he was sleeping. I realized that I had left the flowers and stuffed animal I bought him in the car. I guess by the time I go back to the car and then comeback and deal with the asshole security, he may be up by then. Maybe I'll find Shanae and see if she wants to walk with me. As I opened the door to exit I heard the East Coast twang that melted my heart the first time I heard it.

"Yo, you leaving already, without even giving a nigga a hug or nothing"

I felt so awkward, here he is in a hospital because of me and he still sounds like it is just any ol' day. "Hey you" I said trying to match his enthusiasm. "I wasn't leaving, I thought you were sleep and I left your present in the car."

"Wasn't it you that told me that 'all closed eyes ain't sleep,' I thought that was you"

" Oh be quiet Charles"

"What up, where's the real Sony, where's my Poopie?" he said

I couldn't hold back the tears that began to fall down my face, the even sadder part was looking at Charles, who looked like he was hurting because he couldn't get up and comfort me. All the months of lies, and cover-ups finally took its toll!

"I'm so sorry Charles," I cried. "Why not me, I'm the bad person. I am the person who was married, God I'm the sinner. Why did you lie to the police? Why did you say you and Eric

324

was playing with the gun when it went off? Why protect him, he did this to you, I did this to you. You'll never play ball again, they say. They say you may never walk again, WHY ARE YOU FUCKING PROTECTING HIM!" I cried hysterically

"Poopie, don't cry- come sit next to me and listen. Remember we would always argue over who had more to lose by having our relationship...

"I guess you won that argument" I interjected

"....that's not what I'm saying, the point is I knew the risk involved with our relationship. I'm a grown man and I made a grown man decision, now I'm dealing with a grown man consequence."

"But what about the consequence for his decision?"

"Believe me, I'm sure he is going through it. He is not an animal, and his guilt is probably worse than any jail sentence. Besides, I did it for you, your children need there father and I know you would be going crazy with him behind bars."

"Why are you still looking out for me Charles?" I asked

"Sony I love you. If I had to do it all over again, I would. I probably wouldn't come out here unannounced though!" he said laughing

"Don't make me laugh Charles"

"So what's up with you and him?" Charles asked me

"Well he wants to file for a divorce and get joint custody with 50/50 visitation with the kids. His lawyers advised him that it wouldn't be a good thing to do right now because of all of the attention our case got. He's at camp so I guess will deal with it in the off season."

"What about you though, how are you feeling?"

"Honestly, I feel fucked up! My marriage is over, but that was already in the making. I ruined my kid's home life and on top of that my best friend, my soul mate is laying in a hospital bed paralyzed. I really fucked up this time."

"Stop taking ownership of everything that goes wrong, Sony" he said

"On another note, I'm gonna miss you so much. I know you're ready to get back to Jersey."

"Yeah I'm ready. I was beginning to think you weren't going to come up here. So who is the nurse name Shanae? I've never heard you mention her." He said

"Why you ask me that?" I replied

"Because she took good care of me and she didn't try to slide me her number or ask for an autograph or nothing."

"Well some people are just good at their job, but yeah I know her. I told her to look out for you and keep me posted on your condition. So you been in here getting phone numbers, you know I'm jealous!" I said laughing

Talking to Charles it felt like old times but it wasn't. I realized that I loved Charles more than Eric but my loyalty was to Eric and my kids. The funny thing is, Charles never asked me to choose. Now I wonder if he would have, would I have chosen love or loyalty? I guess it's too late now.

"What are you thinking about? You look tired." He said to me

"It's not important, but I am tired. I haven't had a full night of sleep since I got out of the hospital."

"Yeah I heard you broke out of the hospital, that was funny." he said laughing

"I'm happy to humor you, anyway, I need a vacation so bad."

"Well I know you and your sister are headed to 'Essence' in a couple of weeks. That will be a vacation, right."

I couldn't bring myself to let him know that my sister's envy and hate may be the reason that he may never walk again, if she would have just covered for me. "Nah, not this year, I think I'm giving 'Essence' a break for a while."

"Really, well let's make a deal." He said to me.

"Alright, whatever it is I'm cool" I replied

"If, no not if, when I walk again, you will meet me at the Essence Festival. I won't call you and you don't call me until that time. I am using you as my will to walk again. If God sees fit, then you and I will party in the 'Big Easy' before long but if not I wish you a wonderful life."

326

This was hard to agree with but I knew it was necessary. "OK Charles, that's a deal" I said extending my hand for Charles to shake. "I guess this is good-bye" I said

"Good-bye is forever, more like see you later" he said to me

I kissed him on the forehead and replied, " Good-bye is not forever, I'm simply saying god be with you, but I will see you later." Looking in his beautiful brown eyes one last time before I left, I got the feeling that my hiatus from "Essence" wouldn't last long.... At least I hoped so....

The End